Sarah Hogle is a mom of three who enjoys trashy TV and provoking her husband for attention. Her dream is to live in a falling-apart castle in a forest that is probably cursed. She is also the author of *You Deserve Each Other*, *Twice Shy*, and *Just Like Magic*.

 Sarah_Hogle

Also by Sarah Hogle

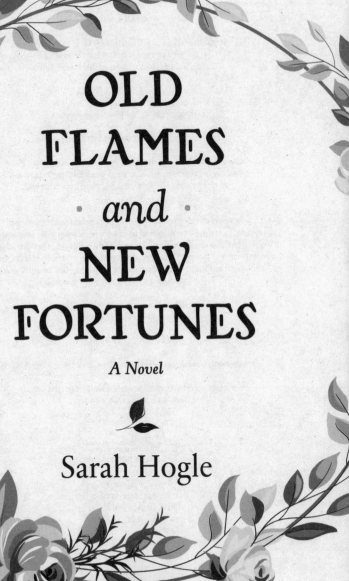

OLD FLAMES

· and ·

NEW FORTUNES

A Novel

Sarah Hogle

PIATKUS

PIATKUS

First published in the US in 2024 by G. P. Putnam's Sons,
An imprint of Penguin Random House LLC
Published in Great Britain in 2024 by Piatkus

1 3 5 7 9 10 8 6 4 2

A CIP catalogue record for this book
is available from the British Library.

ISBN 978-0-349-44243-3

Printed and bound in Great Britain by Clays Ltd, Elcograf S.p.A.

Papers used by Piatkus are from well-managed forests
and other responsible sources.

Piatkus
An imprint of
Little, Brown Book Group
Carmelite House
50 Victoria Embankment
London EC4Y 0DZ

An Hachette UK Company
www.hachette.co.uk

www.littlebrown.co.uk

For Marcus, my purple larkspur. You're the blueprint.

What's past is prologue.

—Shakespeare, *The Tempest*

OLD
FLAMES
and
NEW
FORTUNES

PART ONE

Chapter One

BLACKTHORN:
Our path is beset with difficulties.

Twin purple roses, one bud closed. *Love at first sight.*

A two-leafed red carnation. *I must see you soon.*

Eight-and-a-quarter inches of grape ivy. *I desire you above all else.* The magic hums to let me know I'm on the right track, and I smile, busily fulfilling a pickup order at my luckiest time of day.

It is late April, when flowers have begun to swallow up the stone walls, when it's just warm enough that I can take my coffee in the courtyard at dawn and watch blue chase pink from the sky, stars popping like soap bubbles. My world is alive with the fragrance of freshly turned soil and shivering mist, chickens clucking around my ankles and eating the bugs on the brick pavers before the bugs can eat my crocuses.

To my back is the carriage house I've lived in for the past three years, built in the French country style, with sandy stone and white shutters decorated with moss and ivy. Rows of elevated flower beds burst with riots of hellebores, bleeding hearts, forget-me-nots, bluebells. This courtyard, with its five-foot-tall perimeter and the witch hazel tree that's even older than the neighborhood, flowering quince with peach blooms, the shock of yellow sunrise forsythia—is all my kingdom.

My heart tap-dances to a song in my soul, inherited from my grandmother, who inherited it from hers, and yes, I can believe it. Curious tourists in my family's shop ask me frequently: *Do you believe it, truly?*

I reach for buttercups—*What golden radiance is yours!*—but catch my hand drifting, landing inexplicably on blackthorn: *Our path is beset with difficulties.* My hand jumps back.

"No, it is *not*," I tell the flowers sternly, plucking a buttercup instead. "Your path is simple and happy, and ends in a September wedding, just like Cecelia dreams." Cecelia, one of my regulars, is determined to turn her boyfriend into a husband. Of course, my flowers won't *force* him to propose. They'll merely spark an idea in his mind, if magic agrees with the pairing. The spell is informed by the flowers' traditional symbolism and how each flower reacts to the others. The twin purple roses are representative of how they met, the carnation expresses urgency, and the ivy symbolizes how Cecelia feels. They tell a special story, one imbued with magic to help spur on Cecelia's wishes: *Once upon a time soon to come, Gustav will happen to be ten minutes early for work, so he'll decide to walk the long way around, passing a jewelry shop. He'll glance in the window, and right there in the front, he'll notice a gem that'll remind him of his beloved Cecelia.* Now, magic can tempt Gustav to the shop, but whether he chooses to walk inside is his own business.

I'm pretty sure I invented flora fortunes. I call myself a *flora fortunist* since "creating floral arrangements using the language of flowers to magically bring a person's romantic hopes to fruition" is a mouthful. Much like tarot or palm readings, I can't cast my own will over a person's destiny. I can only intuit what a person's love life needs and try to attract what they desire—to get the object of their affections to notice them, to get over an ex, or to encourage their ex to get over *them*. My spells never force love, only open up possibilities.

With the buttercup added to the mix, I'm overcome by a tingly slide of wrongness; whenever I make a misstep, I get a sensation like I've put one foot through a rabbit hole in a field, I've sat in something sticky, or there's dust in my eye. Itching and muck and bad tidings, the dread of having missed an appointment, a phantom popcorn kernel I can't get out of my teeth.

Tossing out the buttercup, I use my pruning shears to snip off six inches of blackthorn (which does *not* align with Cecelia's hopes for an imminent wedding).

Just like that, the wrongness clears away.

I hear an internal *click* of a door unlocking: In my mind's eye, light glitters through a keyhole, and with it, a rush of air scented with greenery. The sensation of getting a flora fortune right is different every time—all I know to expect is something wonderful. I close my eyes, bracing—

And taste pumpkin, chocolate chips, brown sugar, and cinnamon on my tongue. The image of my grandmother's beige apron with the red stars stitched on the front pocket, which she wore when I was little, comes rushing back. Licking the icing off my hand while leafing through an *American Girl* catalogue. Standing on a stool, mixing batter. Traveler's talismans! All in a moment, I've gained access to every lost memory of the little triangular cakes my grandmother used to bake for the autumn equinox, and it's almost as if she's here again.

Every time I weave together a flora fortune the way magic wishes me to, it rewards me with a uniquely pleasant sensation, a ray of happiness that can light up the rest of the day, sometimes a long-forgotten memory unburied. There is no physical, provable indication that a spell has occurred. It all takes place in the heart. And this is why, even though I feel magic's effects as surely as I feel the brush of clothing against my skin, most folks don't believe witchcraft is real.

Ironically, I have trouble explaining my particular magical skill set to other witches, too, since as far as I know, nobody else has this ability. I know a witch who can influence the weather with their emotions, another who has lucky bakes. But magic took note of my keen interest in garden spells and floriography and combined them into a whole new branch just for me.

The symbolic language of flowers is greatly varied: There is Victorian floriography, which is the most well-known. In the Victorian days, you couldn't go around flirting openly with someone you had the hots for because everybody had to conform to oppressive decorum, so you'd wear an apple blossom if you hoped a certain suitor would try a little harder, and that sort of thing. There's also Hanakotoba, Japanese floriography, which, just like Victorian floriography, assigns symbolism to popular plants and flowers. Sometimes, a plant has different meanings across cultures, and sometimes it's more or less universal.

I go with whichever meaning feels right, favoring the more descriptive, poetic ones I've cobbled together from books and websites. Some of the symbolism I even make up myself, if I feel no existing meaning fits.

I stare at the arrangement in my hands. The composition of this magic doesn't strike me as being meant for Cecelia anymore, but I don't get the vibe that it matches any of my other customers' unfulfilled orders, either, so I'm not sure who it might belong to. Whoever it is, the poor thing's love story looks convoluted, with an undercurrent of imminence, of reunion. Cogs whirring, destiny underway.

Clutching the strange bouquet, I step through the back door of the main building, into the wraparound sunroom where more of my flowers grow, accidentally knocking over a planter and spilling soil across the floor. As I sweep it up, I elbow my toadflax, which topples into the arbutus, two plants whose symbolism are total opposites (*Be more gentle in your wooing* and *Be mine, I beg of you*). These plants don't like touching each other, clashing energies like an angry cat's bottlebrush tail.

"You all right?" Luna calls out.

I need more room in here goes without saying. "Yeah," I grumble, finishing up the job and heading into The Magick Happens. Built in 1850, the shop predates the town's establishment. A great brick square with glossy black shutters, gas lantern sconces, and a gold, purple, and green medieval banner with a gold cauldron on it that reads THE MAGICK HAPPENS by the front door, it began its life as a stagecoach inn. In the 1970s, Dottie Tempest purchased what was, at the time, a music store, and abracadabra'd it into a boutique for candles that set your love fate in motion. Luna, my oldest sister, learned candle-making at Dottie's knee and has carried on the tradition, filling the main shop floor from top to bottom with candles.

The floors are rustic maple, walls papered with a misty forest pattern of pale grays, greens, and blues the color of dusty miller in early morning frost. A bright, polished staircase that leads to Luna's apartment above is roped off from customers, shelving beneath it occupied by crystals, velvet drawstring bags filled with stones or dried herbs, and talismans. Everything smells like old wood, a long history, and wax in every scent imaginable.

The room splits off to the right into a low passageway lit by electric torches, making a 180-degree turn before ramping steeply down, directly below the shop into three small rooms devoted to fantasy and paranormal fiction as well as witchy how-to books, which we call the Cavern of Paperback Gems. Signed copies of Zelda's cozy paranormal mystery series have a table all to themselves.

Even though Zelda, the middle Tempest sister, is eight hours away in Treasure Cove, Virginia, she runs the Cavern remotely. She sends us handwritten descriptions on note cards, monitors inventory, and purchases titles to have delivered to our doorstep. A playlist called *Ren Faire* sends trills of fiddle and cittern throughout my and Luna's domains, but not down in the Cavern, where Zelda plays either the *dark and stormy night* playlist or *Bram Stoker's Dracula: Original Motion Picture Soundtrack*, depending on her mood. A special old-fashioned phone rests on the wall beside an embroidery hoop that reads *Dial 3 for Recommendations*, which connects directly to Zelda's phone.

Do I believe in magic, truly?

In a place like this, it's impossible not to.

But lately, the magic's been changing. What once was a fluttery zing is a dense churning, manic and confused thanks to the chaos of plants I've got crammed in the sunroom, all the different energies mingling at too-close range. The state of our atmosphere is downright unpleasant. Ordinary customers don't notice, but to my eyes, nettle and lady's slipper three feet from each other spells palpable disaster. I've got dried flowers suspended from the ceiling, vines swallowing up every inch of wall space, live shrubbery overwhelming my workbench. As demand for flora fortunes has grown, I've had to keep more varieties on hand, and I've run out of room. Every day, the air between Luna and me is charged with *what if*.

What if we aren't able to climb out of the sinkhole we've crumbled into? Three months ago, the vacant lot next door went up for sale, and we figured it was the answer to our prayers. Not only does the property come with a greenhouse (albeit a pretty old one), but the lot is paved, so why not use that space for a magical night market? It was a competitive sale, so our landlord and business partner, Trevor, decided to waive the inspection, and we poured *all* of our savings into a property that has turned out to be a dumpster fire.

I still cringe, remembering how we'd celebrated when the other bidders stepped back, unwilling to match our offer. I imagine they are all laughing at us now.

Without glancing up from the computer behind the front desk, Luna tells me, "It'll happen." Even though witches only get one main specialty and Luna's is candles, she's uncannily perceptive. I think this is more of a Luna thing than a witch thing.

"Mm." I tie on my apron—green, purple, and gold, like the banner out front, our shop name emblazoned in a medieval font—and turn the hand-painted wheel of fortune until it clicks to Monday. On Mondays, our deluxe subscription box brings you eight grams of dried verbena, a bottle of honeysuckle oil, a Love Awakens candle (rose, amber, and cardamom), and a historical fantasy novel of our choice. For in-store purchases only, a fresh posy good luck charm can be added to the box for $2.99.

"Your aura has an interesting little dash of happy surprise in it." Luna tilts her head and smiles. "Which ones bloomed?"

I jiggle one of the ancient leaded windows unstuck, raising it as high as it will go. A cool breeze sails in, along with a whistling *eee-ee-ere, eee-ee-ere.* I glance sharply upward, where a lark watches me from a tree branch, head cocked as if he knows a secret. "The windflowers."

"Fantastic. Dry some out when you get a chance so I can throw them into a batch, will you?" She finally looks up at me, dark circles rimming her big blue eyes, chin-length corkscrew curls tugged into a tiny blond bun. Our eyes are the only feature that the three of us sisters share. Luna's taller than I am, more willowy. Zelda's shorter and curvier, with long ginger waves; my hair's naturally pin-straight brunette, but these days I keep it in a bleached bob—and usually under a hat. Straw boaters with silk ribbons are my favorite for spring.

"Do you think I should start making lotions and bath oils?" she asks.

I blink at her. "My darling Luna, you cannot be serious. You're stretched so thin."

Snapdragon is on her lap, rubbing his gingery face along her wrists. She bends her head to kiss him.

"I'm looking at a witchcraft store run by this lady in Little Rock, and you should see all the stuff on here. She does *all* of it by herself, too. Creating, shipping, processing orders, promotion, all of it. I feel so inadequate."

"Look around you. You've made this business *thrive*."

While she and I technically don't own this place, we're undeniably the ones in charge. Grandma handed the reins over to her son (our dad) when I was twenty-two. My sisters and I once looked forward to inheriting it from him someday, but he lost the shop to our mother a year later in a tumultuous divorce, after which she sold it for a pittance out of spite. The dream is to buy it back someday. As the store's success grows, though, so does its monetary value, and our dream of family ownership recedes that much further from grasp. I can hardly blame Trevor for not wanting to sell. He fell into the witchy business entirely by chance and has seen only profit since then.

Her expression is grim. "I don't know about thriving. Not anymore. If we can't put up the night market, I don't know how we'll recoup the price of the lot."

"It's too early to start worrying."

"Can't start worrying when you never stop."

I thrust my coffee mug under her nose, which she accepts, growling at the screen. Blue light slants across her freckled face, many of which are actual freckles and several of which are tiny rainbow dots tattooed across the bridge of her nose and cheeks. I grab the mouse, closing her browser.

"Hey! I was doing reconnaissance."

"Go back to bed." The shop is open from ten to five on weekdays, noon till four on weekends, but she rises at five to get an early jump on preparing the online orders.

She hand-waves.

I pass the giant fireplace with the emerald tiles, patting Grandma's crystal ball on its mantel for good luck. My niece, Aisling, says she frequently glimpses Grandma's reflection in its curved surface; says she sometimes hears her voice curlicuing down the chimney like the notes of a song, or hears her snoring while a ghostly Dottie dozes in a rocking chair facing the hearth.

I open the front door wide to let in more fresh air and wander barefoot onto the cracked wet sidewalk, mentally scrolling through my lunar calendar to recall which moon phase we're in—waxing crescent—which means it's time for aboveground planting of annual flowers and fruits. There isn't room for anything new. I turn to go back inside, head full of strawflowers, but just as I do so, a red Nissan Cube with yellow rims whips into the empty space in front of the store, bass so loud that the boulevard vibrates.

Trevor jumps out, attempts to slide across the hood, but only makes it a quarter of the way. "What's up, beautiful!"

"I'm covered in dirt." I show him my palms as proof. "My clothes smell like chickens."

He rolls his eyes. "Stop flipping over compliments before they've baked on one side."

"I don't know what that means."

"Have it your way. What's up, ugly! Where the hell are your shoes? The sidewalk is where all the bugs live. What's wrong with you?"

"The better question is, why're you here this early?" Trevor never drops in until well after opening. Punctuality, for him, means "an hour or two late."

He slips into the shop. "Go wash up, gross-o, then tie every lucky flower you've got to a crown, because it's happening. *To-day*." He raises his voice to shout past me. "Luna! Where you at?"

I frown. "What's happening? What is *it*?"

Knowing Trevor Yoon, this could be anything. One time, he showed up with an ear piercer, and he and I spent the day piercing each other's ears. Another day, he brought in a go-kart he said was "rigged with fireworks," as a birthday gift for Morgan. (Morgan wisely has not ridden it.) He makes Luna come unglued, always accidentally knocking stuff over or forgetting to file taxes or sticking candles with polarizing energies next to each other. He's a rocket ship with no navigation system barreling through the galaxy: the tall, lanky, Sagittarius brother we never had.

He's wearing a fancy suit and has paired it with a novelty tee (Cersei and Jaime Lannister with their arms around each other: *Bros 'n Hoes*). I can tell immediately that he's feeling himself. He's gotten a root touch-up on his white-peach hair, styled in an undercut with a forward sweep. He's wearing neon green sneakers, which he only busts out for special occasions.

"We're not getting a burrito bar," Luna calls out warningly. Snapdragon is traipsing across the slope of her shoulders, paws kneading her back, forcing her to hunch with her nose an inch from the computer keys. "Trevor, we've discussed this. It makes no sense to put a burrito bar in here, and we don't have the room, anyway."

He twirls dramatically, showing off the purple satin lining of his blazer. "We're tabling that discussion for later because you're so wrong that it's ridiculous, but that's not what I'm talking about. My dad just called. He's here, in Moonville, and he wants me to meet him for lunch at eleven o'clock."

Luna stands up; Snapdragon tumbles down her back and hits the floor with an annoyed *meow*. "Because of . . . ? To talk to us? To hear our pitch?"

Trevor nods, dark eyes aglitter. "What else could it be? He *never* visits."

"I didn't think he'd come through," I say in wonderment. "I thought he was gonna leave us hanging."

"So did I!"

The air is sucked from the room. Luna and I stare at each other, dumbfounded, which Trevor relishes with a shit-eating grin, before saying: "We might actually pull this off. Today. We could get the rest of the money *today*."

We all start jumping up and down. "It's happening! It's happening!"

Chapter Two

FORGET-ME-NOT:
Think of me during my absence.

"What's happening?" Morgan Angelopoulos wants to know, trundling in with his laptop and coffee, dark eyes wild with confusion, his silky black hair windswept. "Are we finally getting a burrito bar?"

He works at Zelda's old desk, positioned in front of a window that he claims holds the most inspirational view in town, maybe the world. Two years ago, he was dragged into The Magick Happens by a girlfriend. While she browsed, he loitered by the window and stared out at the scenery: the intersection of Foxglove Creek and Twinstar Fork, banks swarmed with love-in-a-mist and flowering trees. A rounded red bridge. A bronze telephone booth in a neighbor's front garden. He sat down at Zelda's long-neglected writing desk and began taking notes. Then, he wrote an entire chapter of a book in a single hour while his girlfriend tapped her foot impatiently by the door. When we asked him what he was doing, he said he was a writer, that he'd been struggling with writer's block for eons, unable to scrape a single word out. He asked if he could rent that desk as a workspace for fifty dollars a month. He's since abandoned both the girlfriend and manuscript-writing (although he still writes for the local newspaper), but The Magick Happens remains a tried-and-true muse. His current love is the paranormal. He's utterly devoted to his podcast that nobody listens to, in which he talks to himself about Moonville's lore and ghost stories.

"Trevor's dad's in town," I tell him. "He wants Trevor to meet him for lunch."

He nearly drops his coffee. "For real? He'll give us a loan?" I smile at his *us* since he doesn't actually work here.

Trevor's glow could light a fuse. "Probably!"

"Ahhhhh!" Morgan exclaims, shaking Trevor's shoulders.

Trevor shakes him back, the glee contagious. "Ahhhhh!"

"Ahhhhh!" Luna and I pitch in, shaking each other. And then Aisling, her eleven-year-old daughter, emerges downstairs and we have to explain what we're ahhhhh-ing about. Ash tries to muster the jazz for us, but gives up. Adult ventures such as asking our landlord's rich father to give us money can't compete with the allure of Morgan's unattended macchiato.

Morgan dashes outside. "I'll be right back! I need to grab celebratory donuts." The man will seize upon any excuse to procrastinate. Often, he stretches out in his chair and naps, Snapdragon curled up on his lap, or lends unsolicited advice concerning which scents we should use for a particular new product. He keeps giving the wrong recommendations to customers and thinks he's an expert now.

"Eleven," Luna's repeating under her breath. "Okay, everybody, where are the papers? Trevor, I think you were looking at them on Friday."

We sweep the store from top to bottom. No sign of the twenty-page business proposal that we typed up a couple weeks ago in the hopes that Mr. Yoon would help us. From what I've heard about him, simply asking for money isn't going to cut it. Regardless of his love for his son, when it comes to business, he thinks in numbers only.

"I'll go reprint!" Luna makes for the printer so fast that she knocks over a row of white orchid candles molded into pumpkins, and Trevor slams his index finger through the air.

"Ah-*ha*!"

"Okay, but you do it *all* the time," she shouts over her shoulder. "I did it *once*."

He grins at me, triumphant. "I love it when she messes up."

"Why's it saying the printer's offline?" Luna calls after a minute, close to tears. "We're doomed."

Aisling grabs a donut from Morgan's box as he returns, then tries to help her mom figure out how to make the printer cooperate. None of us are able to get a hold of Zelda, a night owl who doesn't get out of bed until nine. She's going to be apoplectic when she hears she missed this news. "Can I come with you guys?" Aisling asks.

"Nice try." I tousle her hair. "Go to school so you can learn something."

She keels over and dies, emotionally. "I hate school. They force us to do labor all day, which we don't even get paid for. It should be illegal. If I come watch you negotiate a business deal, isn't that valuable real-world experience? Someday I'll inherit this store and run it into the ground because I won't have practice talking about loans."

"You've already missed seven days this year," her mom says. "If you get braces, you'll probably miss chunks of school all the time for orthodontist appointments. Can't let you take fun days anymore."

Aisling growls. Luna let her play hooky once in fourth grade to go to the movies, then once again in fifth grade to attend a *Tributales* convention. Luna cited them as "fun days" that were necessary for the well-being of preadolescent youths, and Aisling asks every single morning for another one.

Aisling sighs. "Guess I'll be sad forever."

"Go be sad while you brush your hair," Luna replies indifferently. "I shouldn't have to remind you to do that."

Aisling makes her dismay known by clamping her donut between her teeth and walking on her hands and knees toward the stairs, as slowly as possible.

"I'll take you to dance in a fairy ring under a full moon this summer, if you're good for the rest of the month," I tell her as she drags by.

She tosses her head. "Mrffmrfppph mphhhhhhff."

I remove the donut. "No talking with your mouth full. You could accidentally set a curse on someone."

"Don't tell Mom." She licks her lips to get the chocolate icing off. "But I just remembered I have homework due today. Can I still dance in a fairy ring under the full moon? Oh please oh please oh please?"

I spear my fingers through my hair. "Ash! You didn't tell me that. I didn't hear it."

"Can I finish your coffee?"

She has a lot of nerve to ask for my coffee when she's wearing my shirt, again, without permission, and it's stained from the last time she snuck my coffee and spilled it on herself. "You had all weekend! Did you really forget, or did you just put it off?"

She doesn't respond for a full five seconds. "I forgot that I put it off."

Luna's head pokes around the stairway. "What did I hear?"

Aisling bolts to the top of the steps with a shriek.

"You're helping your aunt weed her garden tonight!" Luna yells up. "From now on, you're doing your homework as soon as you get home from school. No more waiting until after you've *wound down*."

Aisling emits horse noises.

I turn to Luna. "How dare you suggest that my garden has weeds." Then I laugh at her frenzied expression. "What's it like to raise a little me?" Aisling certainly does not take after Luna, who has Oldest Child embedded in her DNA and spent her youth pleasing adults by anticipating and diffusing conflict. When she was *little* little, our parents found this behavior a nuisance. They'd yell at her for inserting herself in other people's squabbles, so she'd hide in her room crying, not knowing what to do. But by the time I was around ten, she'd gotten so masterful at concealing her fear and anxiety that my parents began to depend on her to be the peacemaker between them, between Zelda and me if we were spatting, between a neighbor dog and our own— whoever.

Luna paces. "She's such a smart kid! She reads about ten books a week! If she'd just pay attention in school, she might find that she actually enjoys learning."

"Luna, haven't you learned anything from television? Cool kids don't pay attention."

She snatches a rubber band off a stack of to-be-mailed parcels, then snaps it at me.

"Ha-ha. You missed."

She doesn't miss the next time, and my arm's still smarting when Aisling leaves for school. I weave together crowns of silver dollar eucalyptus, bay laurel, and heather for us—then a couple peonies for good measure. We need all the luck we can get. "You think I should change my clothes?" Luna muses, pulling at her cropped tank. Luna likes to wear shirts that display the stretch marks on her hips, which she says are self-grown tattoos that chose their own pattern. Hers resemble palm leaves, symbolizing victory.

"You look like a goddess."

"Correct, but that doesn't answer my question."

Luna's hands are shaking as we staple four copies of the proposal. I wrench her down into a tight hug, our optimism switching bodies. "We're going to do great. What's ten thousand dollars, to a rich person? Crumbs."

Nobody wants to think about what will happen if Mr. Yoon says no, like all the banks in town already have.

After purchasing the lot and snatching up the keys to the greenhouse, we eagerly opened the door to discover a wood floor covered in sewage. So, right away, the floor needed replacing. Not so bad! We needed to replace a few missing windows, anyway. The budget would be a bit snug, but no big deal.

But then.

We discovered black water gurgling in the sink, and *bam*, now we've got to replace the entire sewer line. Old clay pipes plus tree roots equals extensive damage. The quote we were given to fix it was about seven grand, not including the cost of demolition and repair of the asphalt. On top of what we need to spend for a new greenhouse floor, windows, booths for the night market, additional gardening materials. Trevor rented a jackhammer in a woefully misguided attempt to do some of the job himself, trimming costs, and now the pavement is riddled with holes. Even if we wanted to ignore the sewer line and set up the market, anyway, we can't because the pavement's all messed up.

Luna worries her bottom lip with her teeth, springy blond hair a cloud around her face. She's sweating like a glass of iced tea. "The

GoFundMe hasn't moved in a week." There was an explosion of donations right when we announced our fundraiser in March, but it's since petered out. If it weren't for the fact that (1) The Magick Happens is Trevor's only successful business endeavor, after tanking the three other businesses he bought when he first set out to be an investor like his dad, and (2) the banks gave us side-eye for not doing our due diligence before buying the property, we might have been able to secure a proper loan. Trevor, who has a somewhat tense relationship with his dad, didn't want to ask him for the money, so it was a last-ditch effort when he called him up at the beginning of this month to ask if he'd help us. Mr. Yoon gave him a vague brush-off, said they'd "talk soon," but hadn't reached out until now.

Our building accommodates Luna's candles and Zelda's books, but the porch and back garden simply aren't cutting it when it comes to my part of the business—every festival, I sell out within an hour of setting up. Imagine if I could grow more product and came prepared with enough flora (that I've grown and tended myself, which is crucial—magic doesn't seem to respond as well to flowers I've purchased or picked in areas outside of my garden) to last the whole day? I could afford a real vacation. Not to mention, Trevor's idea to create a night market has morphed into a full-on obsession. He's always saying to Luna and me: "*You both already have your thing!*" He's itching to put his own creative stamp on The Magick Happens.

At last, we're ready. "Don't let anyone in till after we get back," we instruct Morgan. And to Snapdragon: "No parties."

"I won't tell them if you won't," Morgan whispers to the cat as he scratches behind his ears. Snapdragon gets so into it that he flips backward into a cord, unplugging a lamp.

And then Luna's phone rings.

She stares at the screen. "It's the school."

Morgan rolls his computer chair away slowly.

Luna turns, heel of her hand pushing hard against the space between her eyes. "Hello? Uh, yes. I'm her mom." A few beats elapse. My sister is turning raspberry. "You've got to be joking."

My stomach sinks.

I know that look. It's the one she wore when I told her what happened with my ex-boyfriend, Spencer. When she found out our mother sold the store. When Ash's dad promised he'd take her to Cedar Point for her tenth birthday and then never showed up.

Trevor and I squeeze each other's hands. A second later, Luna stuffs her phone in her pocket and screams.

Loud.

"What's wrong? What happened?"

"I have to get down to the school. Do you think we can put off the meeting for a couple hours?"

Trevor grimaces. "If I ask him to wait, he might get offended and decide to take off. He's *super* big on punctuality. Last time he was in town was . . . four years ago, I think. He was in and out in twenty minutes. Not too fond of Moonville."

She kicks a file cabinet, then hops around in pain. "Damn it."

"What's wrong with Aisling?" I ask again. "What'd they say?"

Luna grips her purse so hard that her knuckles whiten, pointing at us as she backs out the door. "You've got this. I trust you."

"I don't! We can't do this without you, it's a team effort. Trevor's got the charisma and I've got the big Disney eyes that make people feel sorry for me, but we need your backbone to pull this off. You always know how to get your way."

"I have utmost faith in you. I have to go meet with the principal. We'll celebrate when I get back." Before she runs out, she adds, "They said she put drugs in her teacher's tea."

Chapter Three

LUPIN:
Who goes softly goes far.

"W*HAT?*"

Trevor, Morgan, and I take a minute to screech incoherently. Then we have to press pause on that because we're running out of time, so I climb into Trevor's car, internally screeching instead. I don't do much driving these days unless it's an absolute emergency because I've always hated driving, so Trevor's my ride today.

Trevor bought this store, along with three others, with the money he was supposed to spend on college tuition, in an ill-advised act of showing his father (a successful property developer and the CEO of his company, Twin Trestle Group) that he could be a property developer, too. At the time, Trevor was barely twenty years old. He'd asked his father for a job, expecting a senior partnership, then was insulted when Mr. Yoon told him he'd have to start from the bottom and work his way up. So, Trevor gathered up all of the local businesses that were for sale, anything with a good price, and went all in. He figured, why go to college to learn about business when he could jump-start his mogul days as early as possible? Mr. Yoon, who researches all of his potential investments exhaustively before making any leaps, was shocked and angry. The two have had a strained relationship since then. While Trevor's three other businesses went bust in spectacular fashion, The Magick Happens miraculously only got better and better. It's why he's grown to be so attached to our shop, loving it just as much as we Tempests do. In his own words, it's the one thing he's done right.

Trevor is impulsive, easily distracted, constantly devising terrible get-rich-quick schemes only to quit them at the first sign of a challenge. But to his extraordinary credit, he hasn't quit the shop. He knew nothing about candles when he started, or owning a business, or managing employees. Luna, Zelda, and I were horrified that our mother sold our store outside of the family—Luna especially, as she's been dreaming of taking over it since she was five. I wasn't around much during the changeover, as I was going through relationship problems, and Zelda's been bouncing around from city to city. It fell to Luna, who was manager at the time of the sale, to train Trevor for his job, all the while bitterly resenting him for usurping her birthright.

They got on like cats and dogs until eventually my relationship imploded and I wound up here. Trevor took to me immediately, probably a little bit because he felt sorry for me and wanted to try to cheer me up, but also because I was an excellent buffer who distracted my mother-hen sister, keeping her fussing over me rather than snapping at him. Since Trevor doesn't have witchy inclinations, the way he contributes to the shop is through social media genius—over the past six years, he's grown our online presence a hundredfold. I'll forever be grateful that he didn't kick Luna and Aisling out of the apartment above the shop, and that he allowed me to reclaim the carriage house out back. In an ideal world, my sisters and I would be the legal owners, but I'm at peace with how it all worked out. Plus, Trevor's a ball.

"What are you doing later?" I ask him. Trevor and I spend a lot of time together because most of our other friends have migrated to bigger towns. My childhood best friend, Yasmin, left for Cincinnati two years ago, and we promised the distance wouldn't change our friendship. She still hasn't responded to the last text I sent her in November. "Wanna hang out?"

"Sure. But you're not gonna sit on my couch and play your Disney Dreamlight Valley game for twelve hours. Tonight, we're hitting up a bar."

"I don't do bars."

"Too bad. It's my turn to pick what we do, and I'm tired of watching you run around with the dude from *Frozen*, pretending he's your husband. You can be my wingman."

I sigh, wistful. "I'm never gonna meet a guy like Kristoff in a bar."

I turn my mind away from the prospect of cruising for disappointing dates at Moonshine, focusing instead on this meeting, trying to remember that I'm an idealist. *Mr. Yoon might say yes. He'll probably say yes. Except, he will probably find us irresponsible for waiving the inspection, and say no. Then we'll be left with all these problems, and no night market, and no room for expansion, and stop spiraling! Spiraling is not helpful!*

I reach into my pocket for my charm bag. It's a small drawstring pouch containing malachite, a peach pit, one teaspoon of dried mistletoe, seeds, moss agate, a long-spined star shell, and the tiny plastic ballerina from a jewelry box Grandma Dottie gave me when I was a little girl. Handling the contents of my charm bag always helps to calm and center me.

Our meeting place, Half Moon Mill, used to be a gristmill before it was converted into a restaurant and inn. The lady who runs it, Ms. Vaughn, cooks round waffles that break down the middle to become half-moons. She likes to give half to one customer and half to another (always to people eating alone, whom she presumes are single), and the deal is that if the couple decides to sit together to eat their waffles, they get them for free. Moonville is rife with meddlers and matchmakers, which I suppose is charming if you're partnered. When you're lonely and yearning for someone to do life with, all this talk of true love loses its shine.

Grandma Dottie had prophetic dreams. When I was a teenager, she told my sisters and I that she dreamed someday we would all fall for our one true loves within the same year. We'll know it's our year when we see a silver luna moth. At that time, she said, one of us will be waiting for love, one will be running from it, and the other will already be in over her head. Zelda thinks it's a fanciful lie (she loved our grandmother dearly but does not believe she was psychic); Luna has absorbed it into her identity and refuses to seriously date anyone until she's seen the moth; and as for me, I waffle between wanting the prophecy to come true as soon as possible and being scared to death of ever falling in love again.

"Showtime," Trevor announces, dissolving my thoughts.

I hop out of the car onto crunchy gravel. "Sheesh, it's busy."

"Stupid busy," he agrees. "It's eleven o'clock on a Monday. What are the . . . Oh, no."

"Trevor," a young woman with a long black braid greets him sardonically, exiting the car beside his. She's wearing a blue-and-white-striped romper and hemp wedge sandals. "I heard about you and Haley."

Trevor glowers. "How?"

"I am omniscient, my dear cousin," she replies with rosy smugness. "See, this is exactly what I warned Teyonna about. You plow through girlfriends like a worm through dirt and can never hold on to them for long."

His eye twitches. "You're annoying. What are you doing here?"

"Don't see how that's any of your concern."

This must be Cousin Allison, eternal thorn in Trevor's side and half of the reason why he was dumped years ago by her best friend, Teyonna, who remains close with his entire family. I sling an arm around his shoulders. "I don't think he has any problem holding on to girlfriends, actually."

Allison's gaze flits to me, widening. "Who're you?"

Trevor smushes his cheek against mine. "My other half."

"You were *just* with Haley!" she cries. "Good grief. That's exactly like you, Trevor. Date somebody for five minutes and you start calling them your other half."

"Special circumstances," he replies airily, lacing our hands together. "She and I"—he nods in my direction—"have been friends for ages, but we secretly had feelings for each other and shit. We only admitted it after my last breakup. We've been wanting to boink this whole time, though."

I elbow him.

"And now we boink every day," he continues proudly. "Twice a day! On my leopard print protective car mats." He squeezes me close to stop me from digging my elbow in deeper. "She has me on a Quaker Oats regimen, for stamina."

She closes her mouth, with effort. I tug Trevor away, into the restaurant, which is uncharacteristically crowded. "Overkill, Trevor."

"What do you know? Your judgment's clouded from all the stamina." He abruptly comes to a standstill in the entryway, pointing at a woman. "That's my aunt." Then points at a little boy running around with spoons in his fists. "That's my cousin."

I study his confused expression. "Do they come here often?"

"I don't think so? Some of them don't even live in Moonville—like that old guy over there, he's from Akron. It's like a goddamn family reunion. What's going on?"

I'm starting to sweat. "Did your dad invite everybody he knows to this lunch? Are we going to be pitching in front of an audience?" Even as I say it, it doesn't make any sense.

"Trevor! Isn't this crazy?" a teenage girl squeals, embracing him.

"Holy shit. Ashlee!" He dazedly hugs her back. "I haven't seen you since your eighth-grade graduation. What's everybody doing here?"

She begins speaking before he's finished, words flying a mile a minute. "Isn't it exciting? Uncle Daniel asked Mom if we could drive down to Moonville on Sunday, but then Aunt Susan found out Daniel was actually going to arrive here *today*, so she told Mom she was coming early. And then Mom told Uncle Daniel she was coming early, too, to spend more time with him since I'm homeschooled and we can just pick up and go. Then I guess he invited other people to show up but didn't even tell them what it was for. I couldn't believe it when Mom told me!"

I'm still deciphering the gibberish when Trevor interrupts, "Believe what? Why did he want all of us here?"

She barrels off, leaving us at a loss. I'm developing a sinking feeling that this lunch with Mr. Yoon might not have anything to do with our request for a loan.

We make our way through the room; ahead, a woman turns and our gazes catch. My brain feels dipped in freezing water, so shocked that it takes a few moments to connect what she looks like to who she is.

She gapes, too, lowering her drink. She has ruffled bangs and shorter hair. Her glasses have been updated, too, the ginormous eighties style swapped for smaller rectangular frames. The rest of her remains exactly the same. I recognize that windbreaker, green and periwinkle with the white zipper, how she'd zip it up halfway. The ultra-blue jeans. Funny how an old windbreaker and a specific shade of denim have the power to rush me through the space-time continuum at the speed of light, forcing tears to my eyes. It's like slipping into a warm, comfortable sweater, when you run into a figure from your past and they're still the way you left them. "Oh, my goodness," she breathes.

Her arms are around me before I can put myself back together enough to recall her name. Kristin. "Mrs. King." The mother of my high school boyfriend. "Holy cow, what are you doing here?" She moved away from Moonville while Alex was at college, and he never returned to his hometown, either.

"Not Mrs. King for long!" she exclaims. "I'm getting married this coming Sunday. What are *you* doing here?" She pulls back to give me a once-over. "You're so different! Your hair!"

Married? I can't imagine Kristin remarrying. "Congratulations," I sputter. "Who's the lucky guy?"

"Right over here!" She leads us through a pack of Trevor's relatives. "Daniel," she calls. "Daniel, I want you to meet somebody."

Trevor's face blanches. "Dad?"

We're face-to-face with a gentleman in his late fifties or early sixties, with wire-rimmed glasses and a plain blue cotton button-down, khakis, and penny loafers. He gives me a kind nod hello.

"I believe I recognize you. From the dance picture in the up-stairs hallway, right?" He checks with Kristin, who ducks her head in mild embarrassment.

"It's just that the prom photo is such a good one of both of you," she begins to explain, but before I can digest the bomb—*Mrs. King still has my prom picture hanging in her house???*—she's cut off by Trevor:

"You said you're getting *married*?"

Daniel's smile is understated, but warm with feeling. "Surprise." Then his gaze returns to me, registering our hands, which are still fastened together—at this point, more so we don't lose each other in the mob than to make our white lie to Allison convincing. "Trevor, won't you introduce me to . . . ?" He lets the question linger, but a different voice responds.

"Romina."

Every atom in my body sits up straight at the sound I've unconsciously both feared and desired from the moment Kristin turned her head toward me—the way it shapes my vowels into a smooth, rich spell—and it's as if nobody else has spoken my name in the eleven years since I last heard it fall from his lips.

Chapter Four

SWEET PEA:
Your memory is a lingering presence.

THEN

It's Alex King. Again.

"Hey, Romina."

"You buy stuff from here a lot," I reply wonderingly, passing a Milky Way across the checkout scanner and tossing it into a bag.

"Oh, that's all right, I don't need a bag," he says quickly.

I size up his other purchases: a bottle of Windex, three cans of Red Bull, a bag of chips, a tub of potato salad from the deli, and a pack of double-A batteries. "Why not? You want to hold it all?"

"Uh." He flushes as red as his plaid overshirt, which probably wouldn't button up all the way if I were to try it on. He's skinny as a needle, and I spent my summer losing my best shirts to puberty. All of my friends who are boys don't know how to act around me anymore; I'll walk by and they'll start punching each other's ribs or try to show me how they can staple their socks to their pants.

"Suit yourself." I pluck his candy bar out of the white plastic bag and start piling his stuff up on top of the bagging carousel. He doesn't look at me, twisting to survey the busy store, the other two registers beeping nonstop as my coworkers and I rush each shopper through the line. His hands fidget with his pockets, in and out and in again.

"Thirty-eight seventy-two," I say. Then say it again, louder, because he still doesn't turn back toward me.

"Oh, right." He fumbles with a credit card, sliding it the wrong way at first. I raise my eyebrows. My parents would never trust me with a credit card. I'm sixteen, so the only money I ever get is crumpled green bills that I end up spending on bowls of baked mac and cheese at Our Little Secret.

Alex wears his hair like a privacy curtain, golden brown ringlets hanging in his eyes. He sits near me in world history but doesn't talk much. All I know is that teachers adore him because he makes straight As and doesn't give them any trouble. (Like I do.) My friend Yasmin and I got paired with him for a group project freshman year and he did all the work while Yasmin and I sprawled on my bed, trading magazine quizzes. All he said during the two hours he was in my house was "Do you have any markers?" and "I've never been in a girl's room before."

"Thanks, bye," he tells me, ducking his head as he grabs all his stuff and holds it to his chest. One of the Red Bulls slips out, lip denting when it hits the floor. A slow dribble of reddish liquid seeps out onto the linoleum tile.

"You want to grab a new one real quick?"

His reply is barely audible. "Nah, it's fine." He picks up the drink, which begins leaking down his arm. I'm both fascinated and disturbed by his weird behavior, just standing there with his wounded drink, pretending he doesn't notice it's getting all over him.

"I think you need a bag."

I can tell he agrees, but that he's going to double down on the poor decision out of embarrassment. He glances at the line of people behind him, carts full, attention magnified. He blushes again, throws the Milky Way at me. I watch horror spread through his wide eyes when the candy bar catches me on the chin.

"Oh god! Oh, shit. I'm sorry. I didn't mean for it to hit your face."

"Why did you throw your candy at me?" I try to hand it back to him, but he swerves it for some reason. Confused, I place it on the ledge next to the credit card machine.

"I'm so sorry." He drops the Windex. "Crap. Sorry." I don't know why he's apologizing to me for dropping the Windex. Maybe he's apologizing to the Windex.

"Do you need some help?" the lady in line behind him asks.

"See you," Alex murmurs, then runs off without the Windex.

"Probably tomorrow" is my reply, since he comes by the store just about every day after school and sometimes multiple times a day on weekends, but he's too far away to hear me. He must have plenty of money to burn on snacks. When he reaches the automatic doors, he dashes through the ENTER ONLY side, another one of his items tumbling from his grip right as somebody walks in with a cart, wheels crunching this poor kid's jalapeño chips. The expression on his face is pure misery as he casts a hasty glimpse at me over my shoulder, apologizes to whoever ran over his food, and is gone.

Chapter Five

FERN:
You have deprived me of your heart
and left mine a wilderness.

A lex King is here.

Because of course he is. Alex King's mom is getting married to Trevor's dad. This coming Sunday. If I am given any more surprise information today, I will fade into the wind like a leaf.

His voice has aged like deep, oaky mead, with a laugh that rumbles just beneath. In my memory, Alex's timbre is frozen at eighteen years old. Still cracking when he got nervous, then a rough scrape when it was just us alone, hands on skin. It was amusing then, to see how quick I could spin him from bright-eyed boy to feverish, flushed, raspy, pupils devouring all light.

He is preternaturally still, absorbing every speck of me in so thorough a visual inspection that it's astonishing I don't start voluntarily stripping my clothes off to make it easier for him. Wonder flashes through me, hot and luminous. But when it burns away, all that is left behind is pain. No matter how bad it hurts, though, I can't rip my eyes from that gaze, just as striking as I remember—beautiful blue with sun flares of green-yellow around the pupil. A million brilliant thoughts spinning behind them like a many-colored pinwheel.

His power to reach into my throat and halt its functions is still fully operational. "You have to stop staring at me like that," I finally say, unnerved.

He looks faint. "You have flowers in your hair."

I pat it gingerly. "Yes."

"Your hair is white."

"It is."

He indicates, swallowing. "You have tattoos."

"I do."

Three on my left upper arm: a pink carnation, a fern frond, and lily of the valley. The outfit is likely throwing him, as well. I used to not give much thought to my wardrobe, wearing whatever hand-me-downs were at the top of the drawer. I'm dressed in an olive prairie dress with burgundy tights and soft faux leather ankle boots, and four or five beaded necklaces of varying length. My brown ponytail is gone. I'm more comfortable in my skin than I've ever been, but he wasn't around to witness the evolution, so this version of me is a total stranger to him. I'm floored that he recognized me straightaway.

"You have flowers in your hair," he repeats.

"For luck." I bite my lip, unbearably shy all of a sudden. Distantly, I'm aware that people are watching and listening but can't bring myself to care. "Your hair's different, too."

He touches the top of his shorn head, blunt fingernails teasing along the bristles where silken rings used to hug my fingers; oh, how I'd loved it. The zing of electricity as I realized my influence over him, how my movement could accelerate his heart, pulling his chest out and pushing it back down in irregular breathing affected by my mouth, my exploring fingers. How my hands became defibrillators wherever they pressed.

It's disorienting to see Alex this close again. The truth that years have passed in which I have no idea (designedly so) where he's been, what he's done, who he has become, is glaring. Every change is fascinating. Every similarity is an ache.

He rounds a table and moves toward me, expression unreadable while I'm positive mine is bleeding alarm, and before I know what's happening he's wrapping his arms around me. My soul knocks backward out of my body, through the floor—we are sixteen and he's giving me my first kiss, his hands a little shaky and unsure; we're seventeen, lying on the trampoline in his backyard with my head on his stomach, gazing at the stars; we're eighteen, and he's in my rearview mirror, watching me back out of my driveway with my car packed full of cardboard boxes, his eyes stricken with heartbreak so naked and ruinous that I felt it following me for days, months, years. But he broke us, too. No other relationship will ever come close to destroying me like ours did, which is saying a lot.

Alex lets me go.

Everything around him is vaporous, colors of the wall swirling into colors of the light fixtures, people watching curiously smearing into diagonal streaks. I have never been slammed so far beyond my own control with such quickness, grappling to school my features, project calm normalcy. The hug was brief. Friendly. It's been eleven years. I should not be this affected.

I'm not, I'm not, I lie to myself.

We can't stop staring at each other. The biggest distraction in my mind is how *substantial* he's gotten. He takes up more room, he's taller and harder, filled out in ways that make me feel strangely weak. My peripheral vision has constricted to black circles, narrowing and widening to the beat of a fluttering in my chest.

"You are," he manages. "So—"

"You're so *tan*," I interrupt, a blush staining my ears, my neck, and wish I hadn't. How was he going to finish that sentence? *You are so different*, probably. Or *you are so awful. You are so unwanted here.* "You get a lot of sun for a doctor."

A tiny frown develops between his eyebrows, then disappears.

"Are you seriously marrying this lady?" Trevor asks Mr. Yoon, gesturing at Kristin. "For real?"

Mr. Yoon nods. His expression is solemn, but there's a quiet happiness about him. Unlike Trevor, Mr. Yoon doesn't seem like the type who'd ever jump up and down enthusiastically. "Yes. I'm glad for you to finally meet."

Trevor stares at Kristin, agog. "Well, damn! Bring it in!" He dives forward and embraces her. She gasps as she's lifted off the ground, but then starts laughing. "When did y'all get engaged? You said you had a girlfriend, but you never told me anything about a *fiancée*. You should've brought her around."

"Oh, it's not his fault," Kristin rushes to say. "It's been a real whirlwind—we only met for the first time in person four months ago! Online dating. He's in Philadelphia, I'm in Sandusky, and neither of us could believe that we'd both lived in Moonville years before, at the same time, but never crossed paths. We decided last week that we want to get married. I thought it'd be fun to just do a wedding right away and not draw it out long enough that I'd go into stress mode. Surprising everybody was my idea."

Pragmatic, even-keeled Kristin King, throwing a surprise spontaneous wedding? Unfathomable.

"I know," Alex says, and I glance up to see him watching me. "I found out about half an hour ago." His focus switches to Trevor. "I think I remember you. Did you go to school here?"

"From eighth grade onward. Moved around before that."

"He's a few years younger," I tell Alex. We didn't have any classes with Trevor, and he ran in different circles. Hanging out with the golden boy senior and his girlfriend (who wasn't so golden, but was trying to be) wouldn't have held his interest.

Alex's frown deepens. "Didn't you spray-paint dicks through all the letter Os in the stop signs?"

Trevor brightens. "Yes! It's nice to know my work is remembered."

Mr. Yoon sighs to himself, looking away.

"How're your folks?" Alex is addressing me again. "Your sisters?"

"They're good. I see Luna every day, and Zelda lives in Virginia now, but we're trying to talk her into coming home."

"And the baby? Well, I guess she wouldn't be a baby anymore, would she."

"Aisling'll be twelve in August."

He's blown away. "That's . . . how can she be eleven already?"

"Right? In my mind, she just started kindergarten."

"And how're your folks?"

I don't think he realizes he's already asked that.

"They're fine." I pause. "I mean, they got divorced, so *now* they're fine."

He nods as though he expected this news, and it's a struggle to shove down the memory of us in my childhood bedroom, late at night, after he snuck in through the window. How he'd hold me, speaking quietly in my ear about our wonderful future far away while my parents rattled the walls with their yelling and slamming doors. The steady rhythm of his heart, warm arms banding around me to keep all my loose pieces together, his eyes glinting in the dark.

"Mom's living in Dayton with her new husband. Still a divorce attorney," I tell him. "Dad remarried, too—Dawn's a folk singer. They live in California with her teenage kids."

The corners of his mouth curve into a smile, the too-rare sort of smile you see on somebody and think, *Oh, they truly mean that all the way down to the bottom.*

"And you?" I ask, cringing at my own eagerness. "I can't believe you're going to have a stepdad!" Alex's father died when he was little. Kristin never dated the whole time I knew her, still went by *Mrs. King*, still wore her wedding band. "What have you been up to?"

"You running your own daycare yet?" He leans forward just a fraction as if he actually hopes to hear I've done exactly what I used to say I would. The rest of the room begins to fill with voices that my ears register only as a low drone, life resumed.

"Ah." My voice hitches. "No. I used to work at one but not anymore."

"I can't get over your hair." Rough fingers pass through the white strands, briefly grazing my cheek, before shrinking back. He used to twirl my brown ponytail where it splayed across the headrest in his truck, seats reclined, other hand burrowed into the pocket of my hoodie to rest over mine. Fiddling with his class ring that I wore, with masking tape wrapped around the base so it would fit.

He slides the offending hand into the pocket of his jeans.

"Oh, yeah." All my words are getting stuck to my tongue. It's too warm in here. "I bleach it."

"She *fries* it because she uses box dye at home instead of getting it done by a professional," Trevor inserts.

"Is that any way to talk about your better half?"

We all turn to Allison, who's materialized from thin air.

Trevor blinks at her. "What."

"Hey, guys!" Another woman joins us—it's so crowded in our huddle that we have to move some chairs around.

Trevor's body language transforms immediately; he straightens up, dropping my hand. "Teyonna," he says.

I hold in a gasp. *Teyonna!* I've never met the legendary woman who bent Trevor's heart into a pretzel. I think she lives in Ingham, close by.

She smiles at him, a dimple popping. She's about my height, with deep brown skin, hair pulled back tight in a curly black puff. She's wearing flip-flops, silk basketball shorts, and a neon green shirt that reads ZANESVILLE VARSITY VOLLEYBALL 2014.

"Wow." Trevor exhales. "Hi. I mean, hey." His words are piling up on top of each other. "So, you still like volleyball?"

Teyonna cups a palm under her chin, knuckles against her mouth. Her liquid gaze darts from Trevor to me, a hint of a smile still hidden behind her hand. "Yeah?"

"Cool." He tries to lean against the table, but his hand misses and he flails, righting himself on somebody's plate of steak and fries. "That's cool." He wipes ketchup from his hand onto the back of my dress. I pinch the scruff of his neck like a mother cat handling her unruly kitten.

Teyonna laughs. "You're such a dork, Trevor."

He flashes a lopsided grin, as if being called a dork is the highlight of his day. "You are."

"Teyonna, have you met Trevor's newest girlfriend?" Allison announces loudly, gesturing to me.

Multiple sets of eyes swerve to mine, and my ears turn hot. Alex pales, then reddens. Kristin claps a hand over her mouth. At one time, Kristin and I were as close as mother and daughter. It takes a lot to throw her, and this particular expression is a De-Lorean back to her kitchen in another time and place, her son pacing circles around the table while I stood with my back against the closed laundry room door. I still dream about that house sometimes. I hear an echo of her voice from long ago: *You want to WHAT?*

"The two of you are dating?" she utters. "Small world!"

Trevor recovers faster than I do. He's sizing up Teyonna's re-action and seems to be bolstered by the faint notes of disappointment stirring above her head. "Guess you're not the only couple with shocking news," he says to his father, a bit haughtily. He's definitely taking it personally that he wasn't warned about this wedding. He squeezes me against his side. "Must be that Moon-ville magic at work. Love in the air, and all that shit."

Alex doesn't move but in a blink he seems to have traveled to the other side of a wall. A furrow in his brow deepens as he stud-ies Trevor and me. Trevor's casual drop of the word *love* echoes on and on: I watch the letters of *love* stretch out, *l-o-v-e*, vibrat-ing, forming circles that ripple outward.

"She works with me at the store that I own," Trevor informs everyone, pleased that he's captured so many people's attention.

"Which store is that?" Alex asks quickly.

"The Magick Happens."

"Your grandmother's?" A question burns from Alex's eyes right through my skin. I physically cannot bear to look at him, but focusing anywhere else when he's right in front of me is impossible.

"We lost the store," I explain, trying to keep my expression neutral. For a long time, I couldn't say those words without bursting into tears. "Trevor bought it a while back, and . . ." The sudden glower that crosses Mr. Yoon's face temporarily knocks me out of place. "And, um, we branched out from just being a candle shop into selling fantasy books and flora fortunes, too. As a matter of fact, we've recently purchased more property to expand onto, and we're seeking an investor . . ." I look to Trevor for a segue, remembering the reason we came here in the first place, but he's too brain-scrambled to throw out a life preserver. This isn't going at all the way we'd anticipated.

"What are flora fortunes?" Kristin asks, right as Alex asks, "So Trevor's your boss?" He lances Trevor with an accusing look but wipes it away when he notices me watching. Trevor nuzzles my temple with his nose; it requires all of my will not to break into strange, pealing laughter.

Alex pivots stiffly. "Excuse me."

"Trevor isn't my boss," I tell Kristin and Mr. Yoon, forcing myself not to watch Alex go. "He's the legal owner, but it's a team effort. No one's in charge of anybody."

Trevor makes a noise of disagreement under his breath. I know he's thinking about Luna's officiousness. She isn't at ease unless she's running the show, so in a way, she kind of is the de facto boss.

Kristin begins her quest to get to know her new stepson. First, she apologizes that this news was sprung on him out of the blue and assures him she's heard so many wonderful things about him. Trevor responds, "Like what?" and suddenly Kristin pretends to hear somebody calling her name.

Before she drifts away, she pats my shoulder. "You'll come to the wedding, of course?"

"Um."

"We've got fun activities planned for this week," she goes on. "We rented out all the rooms in the inn"—she points at the ceiling—"and Daniel and I are getting married on the river-bank right outside. Even though I haven't visited Moonville in years, when Daniel and I were discussing a wedding venue, all I could think of was Half Moon Mill. I always knew that if I ever got remarried, I'd want it to take place right here. Such a beautiful location, with the wooden waterwheel and all the pretty trees. You'll come to the bachelorette party, right?"

I am so astonished that I cannot possibly articulate my horror at the prospect of attending my ex-boyfriend's mother's bachelorette party. Before I can respond, she rushes on: "I'll send you the itinerary. We have so much to catch up on! What a wonderful coincidence, that you used to date my son, and now you're dating my future stepson . . ." I watch her try to wrap her mind around it. "We need to sit down so you can fill me in on everything that's gone on in your life. I've missed you so much." She kisses me, then Trevor. Pauses, studying me carefully. "It is really good to see you again, honey." And then she's gone.

Trevor and I lock eyes.

"Crap," we say at the same time.

Chapter Six

ASPEN TREE:
How could you leave me thus?

Luna's visibly struggling to lock in on one emotion out of the extensive menu of them we've offered her. For one, we did not come anywhere close to getting ten thousand dollars from Mr. Yoon, and fled the scene having forgotten about the money altogether, which had her so discombobulated that all she could do was gape at us. Her shock over our failure, mingled with anger relating to Aisling's antics, already had her teetering on a precipice. So when we filled her in on the rest of our interesting non-lunch at Half Moon Mill, she started laughing hysterically and hasn't been able to stop.

"I wish I could have seen your faces!" she howls. "Pretending to be a couple! Oh my god! And then you go in and *Alex* is there! Both your exes!" She doubles over. "You're both so stupid."

I throw back the rest of my coffee, which is the last thing my nervous system needs. Stupid, indeed. "Shut up."

"I love that we're able to laugh about this now," Aisling tells her mom, beaming. "Ha-ha, look at us all having a good time!"

"You're not having a good time for at least a month," Luna replies, and it's impressive how quickly her tone catches heat.

Candles are an apt magical conduit for Luna. In the stories Grandma used to tell us when we were little, the fire fairy's other form is a firefly. It brings light to others but tries not to get close enough for capture, and strives for harmony with nature. Although a wise, pacifist creature, if provoked it will respond with quite a temper. Grandma gave young Luna a pair of yellow nylon wings, which she wore until they were bent and shredded; to Zelda, who loved to hear about water sprites (mysterious creatures with creepily smooth faces and an appetite for human bones), she gifted a necklace of shells and driftwood. Sometimes I saw myself in characters who were gnomes, sometimes in mischievous pixies or damsel princesses, so I didn't quite know what to make of it when Grandma gave me a magic wand. I think maybe it was for changing myself into whoever I wanted to be, once I'd made up my mind about who that was.

Aisling slumps into the chair behind the cash register, lower lip jutting out. Her efforts to be cute and sad are fruitless: Luna is a steel pillar. "I only wanted to flavor her tea."

"Don't give me that BS. Nobody uses nettle for the taste."

Aisling's focus darts to the middle of Luna's forehead. She braces herself. "Okay. I was trying to perform an exorcism." We all holler. "But!" She waves her warms. "*But* Mrs. Davis is awful. I'm not even exaggerating. She said I can't go on the end-of-year field trip to Columbus Zoo because I turned in three assignments late this quarter. Which isn't true, either. How is it my fault that she lost my homework?"

Luna buries her face in her hands. Gusts a heavy sigh. "My child. Tried to perform. An exorcism."

"She needs one!" Ash cries. "That lady's evil."

I have to turn around to hide my spurt of laughter. Trevor tugs the collar of his shirt over his mouth.

"Stop it, both of you," Luna snaps at us. "And *you*!"

I turn again; she's glaring viciously at Morgan, who's pretending to be working on his laptop. (He isn't—he's trawling Etsy for vintage fits. He likes to dress like it's the 1980s and today is wearing eyesore acid-washed jeans and a fluorescent purple shirt.)

"Me?" He points at himself. "What'd I do?"

"You're a terrible influence."

The shop is Aisling's second home—she even took her first steps here—and she spends a lot of time with us, probably overhearing too many adult conversations, to be honest. She vents about her many preteen nemeses when she comes in after school, and Morgan, who was a miscreant as a youth, is far too inspirational.

Morgan offers up his palms. "I've never in my life suggested that she try to purge the demons from her teacher." He jerks his chin at me. "The hex was her idea."

"Hey! I said that in confidence. As a joke."

"I think we're getting off track," Aisling cuts in hastily. "Remember how Aunt Romina and Trevor are pretending to date? Whew! That's wild."

"Take this and run to the market." Luna holds up a grocery list along with two twenties, waving them. "No stops. And no messing around in the store, because if you do, Ron will tell me." Ron's the manager. Luna makes it her business to know absolutely everybody in Moonville on a first-name basis. "When you're finished, you're going to go read two chapters in *The Modern Witchcraft Guide to Magickal Herbs* and write a five-hundred-word essay on the importance of using herbs responsibly, on top of your regular reading-up on tarot and homework. After that, you're on dinner duty."

"Pizza?" Aisling says hopefully.

Luna crosses her arms. "Eggplant rollatini."

Ash falls to her knees. Shakes her fists at the ceiling. "Stell-laaaaa!"

Luna snaps her fingers. "Get busy. Tonight, expect a long, super draining heart-to-heart about why it is not acceptable to poison your teachers, which is not something I ever thought I'd have to say out loud. I hope you know that you will not enjoy a single minute of your suspension this week."

Ash grabs the grocery list and scampers off, with the promise to be miserable while she's gone. As soon as the door's closed, Luna sighs. "Mrs. Davis really could use some of our special teas, though. That lady's got the worst energy." She pounces on Trevor and me. "What next? I assume we're going to go back and pitch to him tomorrow?" The subject change gives me whiplash.

"We haven't thought of a new plan yet," I admit. "After we heard about the wedding, we drove here to freak out. And it was clear that Mr. Yoon didn't invite us there to discuss the loan, he and Kristin just wanted to surprise Trevor with the big news. So . . . still not sure what we'll do on that front. But if he's going to be in town all week, we'll have more opportunities to talk to him about it. Maybe we can invite him to the shop? Show him what a great job Trevor's doing."

"Yes." Luna's already taking notes. "Good. This can be good. Next time, I'll be there to help, so it'll go correctly."

"Excuse you!" I cry. "You said you had faith in us!"

"And where did that get me? You two drove back here without mentioning the loan to him! We're going to have to sell the lot for way less than we paid for it and the space next door will be turned into a Yankee Candle store. That'd be just my luck. Losing money on top of losing money."

"Oh, it's not going to be a Yankee Candle store," I tell her.

"You always jump to the worst conclusions. If we have to sell, maybe it'll become a Sonic or something."

She grips her pencil, face white. "It'll be another witchcraft boutique, I bet. This town is mentioned in too many witchcraft blogs; it's only a matter of time before some of these tourists decide they want to stay and make some tourism money of their own."

Since it's her turn to freak out, I shove my worries aside and pat her head. "It'll all turn out okay."

"My dad's getting remarried," Trevor says, mostly to himself. He shakes me like I'm a rag doll. "To someone I don't even know! She could be the mafia."

I cackle. "*Kristin*? Yeah, sure. She could be the tooth fairy, too."

His eyes narrow. "It's been ages since you knew her. You don't know what she might be into these days."

"You should have seen him when Teyonna walked over," I tell the other two, smirking. "He was like a cartoon wolf, jaw on the floor."

"I was not! I did not!" He springs up onto an armchair, fingers wrecking his coiffure. "Was I that obvious?"

"Sorry, but yes, you were. What about me? How'd I come across? Smooth, I hope."

"You were a disaster. But I knew you weren't over him, so maybe I was only seeing what I already knew."

"You didn't know that! That's not true."

"Everybody knows," Luna says soothingly, massaging my shoulders. I try to swat her away but give up because it feels nice. "Even when you were with Spencer, I could tell your heart was still Alex's."

I feel my face contort, a blush flooding. "Was *not*." I'm furious at my transparency, for being this wound up when it's been years since we were together, and I've had other relationships since then. By all rights, he should have been packed away in a long-forgotten box like everything else from high school. Damn him. He's so stubborn that even as a memory, he's refused to be scrubbed out.

Trevor crows. "Was *so*, and still is. And *his* eyeballs, by the way, were sparkling at you like cocktail juice right up until Allison paused drinking the blood of virgins and sleeping in her daytime coffin long enough to tell everybody we're together." He uses air quotes for *together*.

"Who's Allison again?" Luna divides a puzzled look between us, pausing her note-taking. The headline, ominously underlined, is *Don't take no for an answer*. "She's the cousin, right?"

"Cousin and archenemy. Told Teyonna I wasn't good enough for her. T didn't understand. I stole the helium tank to *impress* her, not because I'm some delinquent."

"I'm dying to know why you stole a helium tank."

"To blow up a hundred green balloons with," I explain. I've heard this story before.

Trevor is ripping off pieces of my florist's tape to give himself a tape beard. "Green's her favorite color. I was going to release them in the sky over her house, then shoot them down with a bow and arrow to celebrate her doing so baller in pharmacy school."

"Aw, what a sweetheart." Morgan spins his chair.

"Right? But Allison was all like, 'My cousin's immature, you can do better, you should go out with my boyfriend's best friend instead.' T said she was gonna stay with me anyway, but after I showed up at her house with squirt guns, she said she didn't think I was cut out for serious relationships." He broods over this. "I thought the squirt guns would be fun. She'd been under so much stress, you know? From school and working. I just wanted to see her laugh."

"And you?" Morgan turns to me, eyes glinting intently. "How'd it end with you and King?"

"It ended in a garbage can. Literally. He threw away all of our mementos—stuff I gave him during our two years together, anything that reminded him of me."

Morgan and Trevor wince. Luna's turned murderous; she was with me when we walked past Alex's house and discovered him making a trip to the garbage bin with my homemade presents in tow. As if *he* had any right to be mad at *me*! Him! I'm steaming just thinking about it.

"A mess!" I smack my own face with a bunch of freesia. "How are we going to rewind all of this and tell your dad it isn't true? I don't want to lie to the guy I'm trying to get a loan from. Not the right way to start business."

"Romina, you naïve potato," Morgan interjects with a tut. "You're not going to tell the *truth*. The truth never helps."

Luna throws a pencil at him. "Quiet, you. You've done enough."

"Isn't it obvious?" Morgan grins devilishly. "This is an opportunity to make them writhe in jealousy."

"Alex isn't going to be jealous," I deadpan. "He's the one who ended it, right before we went to college. If he wanted me, he could've kept me."

"Then let him see what could've been his. Make him sorry for what he lost."

"Ooooh." Trevor pitches forward. "Yes. You're on to something. Did Teyonna look a little flirty to you, Ro? She looked a little flirty to me. I think I've still got it."

"Don't." Luna slashes her arms in the air. "Don't make this worse by lying more."

"The idea . . ." I ruminate. "Is appealing."

"I'm not involved." Luna busies herself straightening candles that were neat as a pin to begin with. "I don't want to hear about it, I don't want to know a thing. This is how you wind up with bad luck."

"If I tell Teyonna we only pretended to be dating because of that shit Allison said about me not being able to keep a girlfriend, I'm going to look pathetic," Trevor says darkly. "Not to mention, that guy Alex? My new stepbrother? He was giving me the dirtiest look! I wanted to pop him in his pompous face."

"He *is* pompous," I agree heatedly. This is what happens when you receive too much praise from authority figures throughout your life. Alex actively worked to make himself the favorite student of every single teacher. The principal, too, who'd been good friends with Alex's dad when they were young. I've long suspected that when Alex and I started dating, Mr. Schneider phoned Mrs. King to discourage it. Unfortunately for Mr. Schneider, the only thing Alex loved more than his mentors' approval was a girl who flouted all the rules he lived by and made him feel like a big strong hero.

Trevor shakes his head. "We can't go down like this."

"And what would your dad think?" I point out. "If we turned around and were, like, 'Never mind! Just kidding!' We'd look like idiots. He'd never give us the money. And we *desperately* need this money. There are fliers all over town about the night market starting on May first, which seems impossible to pull off right now. We've got vendors on the line already."

The shop is silent as Trevor and I give this ruse serious deliberation.

"I think Morgan's right," he says at length. "This is a golden opportunity. To make Teyonna realize that I'm a fantastic boyfriend, actually."

"How dare Alex invade my life again," I spit. "I've been counting on him never coming back here. He's been gone so long, I was *this close* to putting him out of my mind for good. I'd been doing so well, too! It took forever to get over him."

Morgan punches the air. "Yes! Go get under their skin. Make them sorry."

"I'm a catch, aren't I?" Trevor is irate. "I'm not all that bad."

"You're not," I assure him. "You're a great catch."

"And so are you."

We high-five. "We're great catches!"

He nods energetically. "They're going to see it. They're going to *know*."

"Okay, we'll keep the façade up, but you've got to be convincing." I slant him a threatening look. "Don't go mooning over Teyonna, all right? You'd better kiss the ground I walk on, or else."

He falls to my feet, kissing the floor.

I nudge his elbow with the toe of my shoe, laughing. "Ew, Trevor. That's disgusting."

"I believe in gestures. And I believe in us!" He gathers me into a crushing hug, lifting me a few inches off the ground. "I can be a good boyfriend, Ro, I swear. You won't regret this."

"Y'all are tempting some ugly fate," Luna mutters.

My inability to forge deep, serious, lasting connections with the men I've dated throughout my twenties might stem from the fact that I am not, as is painfully obvious to my family and friends, all the way over Alex. And I don't like the effect he had on me when we were young, either, so I'm sore about that, too.

When we started dating, I was a wild, self-centered, carefree young thing, and he stunted my development with his pretty, hypnotic eyes and slow, deep, *"There's my girl."* Now I weep at diaper commercials, I invent distinct personalities for each of my crocuses, I chalk hopscotch boxes on the sidewalk for kids to play on. I am overly emotional when I watch videos of babies reacting to eating lemons. It is entirely his fault. He brought all of my nerve endings to the surface, when life would've been smoother if I'd remained feral.

If my heart hadn't been hollowed out after our breakup, it wouldn't have been such easy prey for Spencer to take advantage of. If you think about it, really, Alex is where it all went wrong for me.

I need to get some face time in with Mr. Yoon at Half Moon Mill this week, anyway, to hopefully persuade him to give us a loan, so wouldn't it be serendipitous efficiency to accomplish a second task alongside this one? Willingly putting myself in Alex's physical space again is like realizing the doctor accidentally sewed his scalpel inside me during surgery. It'll hurt to open the incision site back up again, but we have to get that scalpel out. This time, I'll heal properly.

And if regret just so happens to eat Alex alive while I'm receiving my closure and securing our funding? If he sees what he could've had and rues every day of the past eleven years without me?

Then so much the better.

Chapter Seven

BASIL:
I cannot like you.

I dream that I'm back in Spencer's living room.

He's seated opposite me, body language relaxed, sandy hair so gelled that it appears to be wet, his shirt ironed. He once told me he didn't know how to iron shirts, which is why I've been doing it for him, but he's suddenly picked up the skill to impress his ex-wife. I stare at the gold fibers in the love seat, on which I must have changed a thousand diapers. Little feet jump around in the playroom just on the other side of the open door. My heart rate kicks up so fast that the walls press in. I'm being buried alive.

"Please don't take her away from me," I beg.

"Romina." That horrible, false smile twists with false concern, and this is the moment I know he was never serious when we had all those talks about me legally adopting his daughter. "She was never really yours."

I sit up in bed, pulse slamming, pillow soaked in sweat and tears. I haven't had a bad dream in ages.

Remember the positives, I hear my therapist say. *List them one by one*. I flip my patchwork quilt off me and stand up, legs shaky. My carriage house is essentially a studio apartment, with a kitchenette along the eastern wall. I've painted it bright colors to cheer myself up: Everywhere my eyes land, there is soft fabric, Follow Your Heart thyme candles, monstera plants, tapestries of fairylands.

I riffle through herbs in my cabinets, forcing a change of mental direction.

I no longer have to pick up after a grown man.

I am no longer excluded from his family functions.

In hindsight, I can see exactly where I should have kept my boundaries firm, should have kept the relationship professional.

"Can Adalyn and I take you out for dinner sometime?" I didn't recognize his intentions then. He must have clocked my obligatory, wary smile, but pressed anyway. *"I hope that isn't crossing a line. Am I allowed to ask you to dinner? As friends, and mutual Adalyn fans?"* He'd bounced Adalyn on his hip, knowing I wouldn't be able to resist her smile. *"You want Miss Tempest to hang out with us, too?"* Then, leaning close to her as she burbled. *"What's that? You'd* love *to spend more time with her?"*

I'd said I wasn't sure, but somehow ended up at a restaurant, the focus of Spencer's charming attentions, and he made me feel special. Spencer tried to feed Adalyn in her high chair while applesauce dripped off the spoon. He asked me for help, and when she ate for me, he was effusive with praise.

"You're so good at that. Such a natural."

He didn't try to feed her again, raising his hands as if he didn't trust himself.

"Let's not jinx this. Adalyn will only eat for you, it seems. I don't want her to go hungry."

And that's what had captured my heart. Aside from being charismatic and handsome, Spencer made me feel needed. Of course, that twisted itself around eventually and became what I resented most.

While preparing chamomile tea, I pull out jars of dried juniper, lavender, and bay laurel, then dig my old dream pillow out of a chest. I haven't had to poke herbs into the small satin case and sleep with it beneath my regular pillow in a long time. It can't be a coincidence that a figure from my past drops into my life again and now my subconscious is in upheaval.

My house is quiet save for raindrops pitting the roof, the hum of my oscillating fan, the low whir of a car engine. I peel a scrap of diaphanous curtain from the window that faces the back alley, where a black truck is idling, puffs of smoke juddering from the tailpipe. It's just before six in the morning, gloomy night rain beginning to abate as a diamond of rising sun sputters through the trees. Farther down the road, a trash truck's *beep, beep, beep* helps to tug me into the present.

When I push my door open, I hear the black truck take off, which prompts my chickens to cluck lowly as they toddle down from their coop to explore the garden. I scatter their feed, collect their eggs, murmuring softly. My chickens are Silkies—sweet, fluffy, domesticated birds that are perfect as garden pets because they're happy to be kept in confinement and they're gentle with my plants. They also love cuddles and attention. I say hello to Rosemary, Chickpea, Violetta, Suki, and Miss Fig, giving the ever-demanding Suki a disproportionate amount of nuzzling. For now, I'm a bird and flower mom.

I perform my morning garden inspection, pruning spotted leaves, counting blooms, dreaming of a someday in which my home is loud with voices, footsteps, noisy toys. When I'm all alone, I allow my little envies to pass over me like clouds: the parents who send their kids off to preschool with their shirts on backward because they're busy with so many kids, and perhaps their job's calling them about a problem they need to fix, and maybe they've got to tidy up because their in-laws are about to pop by with little notice, while two dogs are going wild with zoomies.

I know I've probably idealized this, that busy parents probably wish they had more quiet time alone, so I'd never voice these thoughts aloud (I know *exactly* what Luna would say), but I'm wistful for it, anyway. I do love my life, and it certainly isn't dull. It's rich and wonderful even without children. It's just that . . . I want kids so much that it's a bit like sitting in a waiting room or being on hold for a really long time, waiting for my favorite part of my life to begin.

Whenever I voice my desire for a good, solid, dependable man (usually in the most detached tone I can muster, so that I'm not perceived as desperate), the replies usually roll in like this: *What's the rush? Love arrives when you're not looking. Date yourself! You don't need a man to be happy. Just get some sex toys.* As if it's such a bad thing, wishing I were in a relationship, that I had someone I could be close to all through the night, who would trust me with their secrets, their fears, their happiness, and who I could entrust with my own. It's the same whenever somebody asks where I see myself in five years, ten years, or what I want the most—the answer is to be a mom. I have other desires and interests, of course, and I've started to reply with those instead—that I want to branch out in my fortunes, maybe at Ohio carnivals and fairs, as well as putting together a family grimoire. The sort of goals that I could achieve on my own. Because whenever I admit that I want to be a mother most of all, the responses to this, too, can be awkward.

What's the rush? Enjoy being single and not having kids, because once you have them, you're locked in it for life! Basically telling me to be grateful for not having what I really, really want. And almost always, this unhelpful retort falls from the mouth of a parent. Only other nonparents, ones who *want* to be parents, tend to validate this deep longing. Even Luna, who I love with all my soul, slings back a sarcastic "Take mine" whenever I mention wanting kids. I know she's just joking, but she can only joke about it because she's lucky enough to be a mom already. We are a vast population of hurting hearts that miss people who haven't come into our lives yet.

I want to give my little ones piggyback rides and play hide-and-seek with them and teach them how to tend a strawberry garden, help them trace the letters of their names, take them on nature walks, listen to their dreams, show them the best parts of the human experience and help them to navigate those parts that aren't so light and easy. I want a family that is loud, goofy, exuberant at home because they know this is *their* place, where they can be themselves through and through, and be loved for it.

Someday. For now, I still have today, and I will make it a lovely one.

The next few hours blur: *Good morning* and *I'll give you a dollar if you bring me a bagel* to Aisling; *Yes, I took those to the post office yesterday* to Luna; *Put that down* to Morgan; *You're late* to Trevor. My thoughts cut into a dozen facets—the little girl in her playroom, the man who stared directly at me and said it was all for my own good; and of course, a different face that's aged a decade somehow, with thick, lowered eyebrows, a questioning air. A mystery, when I used to know him inside out, translucent as a glasswing butterfly. I'm concentrating so hard on that face, trying to dissect it, that I must summon his image from memory, transplanting it onto the sidewalk outside The Magick Happens.

When my eyes connect with Alex's through the window, it's a lightning bolt hurled from the sky, directly down my spine, radiating outward to every bone. His chin is tilted down, face forward, a grim set to his mouth. His mother stands at his left, fiddling with her purse, eager stare devouring our sidewalk sandwich board, our sign, our hundreds of candles on display.

When Alex sees me watching, he automatically opens the door for Kristin, both finally entering. I've been taping primroses to florist's wire for a customer who called the shop to tell me about two men she's torn between, and she's hoping for a flower crown that will help bring clarity.

"Hi, there!" I gesture to a familiar black truck parked out front. "Did you happen to drive down the alley earlier?"

"No." Alex cuts our eye contact, focus shifting to Dottie's crystal ball on the mantel, the dusty purple candle beside it.

"Really? Because that truck looks exactly like—"

"The roads here are ridiculous," he interrupts. "Too narrow. I'm going to get a mirror broken off."

My nose wrinkles. Moonville born-and-raised, and after a few years away, he thinks he can insult our inconveniently narrow roads. Who does he think he is?

"Is that a cat?"

I follow Kristin's line of sight to a black lump with yellow eyes, curled up in a loaf on top of a shelf. She extends her fingers, but Jingle backs away, hackles raised.

"Jingle's not much of a people person," I tell her. "Our people person is Snapdragon. Don't worry, he'll find you and force you to pet him. We have another cat, Mellow, but he's a ghost, so you probably won't notice him. My niece says he mostly sleeps in the front window." I smile broadly at Kristin. "Good to see you again."

"I haven't been in this store since your grandma ran it." She cranes her neck to get an eyeful of everything. "Goodness! So many candles. How is Miss Dottie doing, anyway?"

I feel Luna's eyes on my back, from where she sits in quiet conversation with a customer.

"She passed last year."

Kristin hugs her purse tighter. "I'm so sorry to hear that."

I nod. There aren't words that pay justice to Dottie, to how badly she's missed, so I don't insult her memory by offering paltry ones. The truth is that it feels like she's been gone for much longer than a year. By the time she departed this world, the only person she could consistently recognize was Luna.

My grandmother taught us that the world is more than it seems, and so are we. That we all have a little bit of stardust inside of us.

Trevor springs from out of nowhere. "Crystal! What's up!"

She doesn't know what to do with his proffered fist bump, so she closes a hand around it. "Kristin."

He casts around. "Is Dad here, too?"

Alex and Kristin exchange a loaded look. "Unfortunately, he was busy," Kristin answers with a polite smile. "But he'd love to stop by at some point while we're in town."

"Excellent. Well, let me give you a tour!"

I follow them awkwardly while Luna reintroduces herself, her eyes two round globes, flickering to me every other second to assess my reaction. She prattles on for a bit about how tall and mature Alex looks, until I realize there's no reason for me to hover and I return to the sunroom to work on my flower crown. I'm so addled that my nervous fingers keep snapping the myrtle in half.

Trevor's voice drifts in my direction, footsteps nearing. "Zelda does all the book stuff. Even arranges book signings with other paranormal mystery authors—we're part of Catriona Boyd's virtual book tour next month, which'll bring good business."

My ears perk up. Trevor's either mentioned the loan already and is trying to talk us up, or he's leading to the subject.

"Right this way, you have the Garden." An arm in the doorway gestures, and the second Alex enters my personal haven, my hands forget how to work. A roll of tape and sprigs of lemon leaf fall to the floor. Trevor hides his laughter behind his sleeve, but Kristin and Alex barely notice. The former has buried her face in white dittany, breathing in its fragrance; the latter's face is a smooth void.

"You're pretty much like a florist, then?" Kristin says.

"I'm a practicing magical-floriographer, or *flora fortunist*." My speech is well-practiced. "Meaning, if a customer tells me a little about their romantic state of affairs, I create a custom flora fortune for them that helps coax their needs and wishes to life. While I can brew teas and put together charm bags promoting health, prosperity, peace, et cetera, my specialty within flora fortunes is romance."

Kristin blinks. "Do you . . . but do you *actually* think you're a . . . ?" Her voice falls to a hush.

"A witch?" I prompt. "All the Tempest women are."

Alex frowns. "You believe in that now?"

"Yes," I reply primly.

"My Romina is the real deal," Trevor boasts, poking my cheek. I slap his hand away, before remembering that I'm supposed to be head over heels in love with him. Faltering, I give him a lively pat on the bum.

"She knows all the local folktales, too," Trevor continues, once he's recovered from that. "Some are even folktales about Romina herself."

I send him a questioning glance.

"The moths!"

"Oh." I fiddle with my plants, then fill up a watering can. It isn't a watering day, but I need to keep busy or I'll detonate. I can't believe Alex is in my shop. This is my *sacred space*. "That one's about my sisters, too."

Alex's words are hot, dragging down my skin. "I thought you didn't believe in that."

"I was narrow-minded."

"Your mind seems to have . . . *expanded* . . . quite a bit."

I glare at him, because I can tell that isn't the word he wanted to use. But I make myself say, pleasantly, "It has! I've grown up, embraced my identity. Turning into exactly the person you see standing before you was my destiny."

Kristin divides an odd look between Alex and me. "I don't understand. What's this about moths?"

"My grandma had prophetic dreams. Her dreams almost always came true—that my dad would step on his glasses and break them, that Luna's child would be a brown-haired girl, that Zelda would be stung by a bee on her thirteenth birthday. She dreamed that my sisters and I would someday, all in the same year, fall for the men we're meant to spend the rest of our lives with. We'll know it's our year of finding *the one* once we see a silver luna moth."

"Which you didn't used to believe in," Alex inserts, "not only because those moths aren't silver, they're green, but also because when she had that dream, you were already in love." Something in his eyes shifts. "You never saw any strange moths at the time."

"The prophecy wasn't about falling in love with just anybody, it was about falling in love with the people we're going to spend the rest of our lives with." I give him a bland smile.

His mouth tightens. I watch shadows roll over Alex, a coolness settling in their wake. "Have you seen the moth since you started dating Trevor? Because if you haven't, apparently, then you two aren't going to last."

"Alex," Kristin chastises gently under her breath.

"I'll take this," Morgan announces, reaching around foliage to pluck a small herbal sachet from Alex's hands.

Alex's forehead furrows. "Luna said that was a free sample."

"You don't have the right aura for this one, sorry. Doesn't work for nonbelievers."

Alex is disgruntled. "You used to say you didn't believe in magic, Romina. I don't understand."

I tamp down my own aggravation. Yes, I used to not believe, but that was a long time ago. I'm tired of people walking into our magic shop and questioning it, demanding we defend and explain ourselves. "There is a lot about this universe you do not understand, Alexander. You have to open your mind."

"He won't, with an aura like that," Morgan adds loudly, from elsewhere in the shop. The man reads one pamphlet and now he thinks he knows all about auras.

"I'm not surprised you're a skeptic . . ." I give Alex a slow once-over, filling my expression with palpable disappointment. "Little boring of you, though."

He recoils. Stands up straight and tall, which for some reason reminds me of videos of raccoons, who stand on their hind legs when threatened. I try very hard not to laugh. "If logical is *boring*, then yes. I live in reality."

I take a forward step, watching his eyebrow raise an infinitesimal fraction. A twitch. "What's that supposed to mean?" Is this the same person who hugged me yesterday, who couldn't stop staring? It's like he evolved into a different species overnight.

He shrugs.

My eyes are slits. I blurt the first thing that pops into my head. "It's a crime that you cut all your hair off."

He's unfazed. "Like it better this way."

Kristin steps between us, but she isn't tall enough to block our burning gazes—both of us offended, trying to pretend like we're not. "Your flowers are lovely," she tells me. "The shop looks like it's doing well; I'm so glad to see it. So glad to see you and Trevor are both happy and successful. But I wanted to drop by for another reason, too."

Alex scrubs a hand over his face. That momentary stomach drop I can feel from feet away, his internal *ugh, please, no* has my lips involuntarily curling into a feline grin. "Yes?"

"Remember those wedding festivities I told you about? I made up a scavenger hunt for wedding guests who're staying in the area. I thought it'd be fitting, what with celebrating our love, and this being such a romantic little town. You know? Isn't it just the most romantic little town? Daniel doesn't believe in any of that stuff, calls it nonsense, but I confess that while I don't totally understand all the stories myself, I think they're fun. Anyway, I remembered how much you used to love games. Do you still?" She claps her hands together, hopeful. "How about another game, for old times' sake?"

Chapter Eight

ANEMONE:
Your charms no longer touch my heart.

"You could've said you were busy," Alex mutters venomously.

"I'm not."

"You were at work."

"I dictate my own hours." I can't help but gloat. "Does being around me make you uncomfortable?"

He scowls. "Do whatever you want. I don't care." Then he pulls out the list of items we need to find around town, ignoring me while his eyeballs burn through the paper, making sure he holds it at an angle that makes it difficult for me to read. He and I had the misfortune of drawing the same color paper out of a hat, because the universe is being a big old donkey, so now we're shackled together as Team Yellow for the next twenty-five minutes. As Kristin mentioned, I love games, so I should beast this thing pretty quickly, and I'm always motivated by a prize at the end. Whoever wins gets a dozen cupcakes from Wafting Crescent.

"Aye-oh!" Trevor yells at us as he swaggers out of Half Moon Mill, hands cupped around his mouth. Half Moon Mill was the game's starting point. "Already got one, suckers!" Teyonna, Trevor's partner, is happily eating one of Ms. Vaughn's waffles and mirroring Trevor's celebratory dance moves. Her shirt reads DOGS AREN'T LAWN DECORATIONS. THEY BELONG IN YOUR HOUSE.

"Damn it," Alex mutters. I grab the paper from him, accidentally tearing off a corner.

These moons are good with syrup
Get something sugary for your sweetheart
What lovebirds! He built her a house and decorated it
Bring a flower of the gods to the ghost of Downigan
Take a picture where the town begins

At a glance, it looks easy enough.

"You and Trevor . . ." Alex says under his breath, watching Trevor and Teyonna advance in our direction.

"Are adorable," I finish for him.

"I'd love to know how that came to be."

"Well, I've always been adorable. Trevor grew into it quite recently." He lowers his head, gazing at me dead-on in that probing *You will tell me all of your dark secrets* way that he has, and I remind myself I have no reason to be flustered. I can lie to this man easy peasy. "We work together. Over time, we fell for each other."

"He's your boss. Seems unethical."

"Colleague. Not boss."

"Wouldn't have pegged him as your type." As in, *How could you possibly want anyone who isn't me?* The arrogance is astounding.

"I've changed a lot since we knew each other," I reply, allowing acid to coat my words. "And I don't have a type. I like all sorts of men, not just ones who wear leather bracelets." A quick glance at his bare arms informs me that he isn't that type anymore. It also informs me that he isn't married. No tan line where a wedding ring might ordinarily be, either.

His expression is indecipherable. I used to be able to guess his thoughts easily, but he's gotten good at screening them.

"How's it going, elder bro?" Trevor asks Alex, seeking my hand. He grabs it like it's an apple he's picked out of a supermarket bin. "How's business?"

"Fine."

"Fall into any bushes lately?"

Alex scowls. "I've never fallen into bushes. I've never fallen, period."

"I don't believe that."

I feel my face scrunch. "Why would he fall into bushes?"

"Isn't that a common hazard of the job?"

I bark a laugh. "Of being a neurologist?"

Alex is watching me with a strange expression, like he almost wants to smile. As if he thinks he might have misheard me, and what he imagined I said is hilarious. "I can't believe you still remember."

My mouth opens.

"I'm a roofer," he clarifies. "Not a neurologist. Didn't make it a full year through med school."

I have nothing to say. He nods as though my stunned silence confirms a hunch.

"Isn't that wild?" Trevor exclaims. "Dude could've been rolling in money. How much do you make a year? Forty-five thousand?"

"Be nice." Teyonna elbows him. He elbows her back, that goofy smile returning to his face.

Alex rolls his eyes. "How much do *you* make? Curious to know what it pulls, pretending to be witches."

I try not to smirk. Ooooohh, that *bothers* him.

"Oh, I'm not a witch," Trevor replies. "I just support the witches. Let them do their witchy thing, while I run all the marketing. Which I am amazing at, thank you."

I lean against him. "*So* amazing. And supportive. Hands down, the most reliable, dependable man I've ever had in my life."

"Isn't that nice," Alex says flatly.

"What she does is legit," Trevor tells him. "You staple shingles. How's that more valuable than bringing true loves together?"

I think Alex is going to be insulted, but instead he flashes a lazy grin. "I also clean out gutters, if you ask real nice." His eyes snap to mine. "Changed your mind about working with kids?"

The sideways attack spins me off-kilter.

I wave it away. "That was the dream of a teenager. What I wanted then wasn't the fate my stars had in the works for me."

"Hm," Alex replies at length. I don't appreciate the judgment wavering at the very top of his tone. He slides his hands into his pockets, leaning against a tree.

"You're not doing what you thought you'd be doing when we were kids, either," I point out snippily.

"True. I'm just surprised, is all. You always had a way with children."

I pen in the flood of emotional bile I could dump in response. "What one is interested in changes as one ages," Trevor observes sagely. "For example, one's taste in significant others. Looking back, the girls I was with when I was eighteen . . . what was I thinking? I'm sure it's the same for you, Romina."

"I can't imagine still being with the kind of person I'd date at eighteen," I agree.

The corner of Alex's mouth slides halfway between smirk and irritation. "Subtle."

"Oh, right!" Trevor snaps his fingers. "I forgot. You two used to go out, didn't you? My bad. Hope that doesn't stir up any nasty memories, Alex."

"I'm very over it."

"Good, because Romina might end up being your stepsister-in-law someday."

For a moment, Alex's impassive stare glitches. His jaw tics, but he says nothing. Trevor decides to cap off his direct hit by leaning in for a kiss. I startle and swerve, his lips landing on my cheek. To save face, I try to kiss Trevor, but he chooses that moment to initiate again, attempting to kiss my other cheek, like we're going for a French thing. We end up with three weird cheek pecks and one on the mouth, which tastes like waffles. Alex is poker-faced again when Trevor withdraws, arm slithering possessively around my waist.

Teyonna is quiet, fixating on a mound of dirt.

"Aren't you going to congratulate us for being such a pretty couple?" Trevor wheedles, and Alex *laughs*.

Laughs!

I hate him for it. Who does he think he is, pretending to be unbothered? He has to be bothered. I would be, if my ex were presumably sleeping with my soon-to-be stepsibling.

It is infuriating that he might not be bothered.

"Come on," Alex tells me, and begins walking, expecting me to fall in line. "I'm not losing to that guy."

❧

After finishing our waffles (which involved a lot of poking and prodding from Ms. Vaughn, who wanted to know if we were single. Alex confirmed he is—not that I care or anything), we walk quickly to make up for precious time. Our second destination is an obvious one.

Moonville isn't your average town. You can walk our streets at high noon in August and not need to shade your eyes, everything a few degrees cooler beneath dense trees and shrubbery, a high, leafy green enclosure that blots out half the sky. Our brick roads are more than a century old, so narrow that street parking causes chaos and locals prefer walking or biking. Vallis Boulevard is interrupted here and there with snaking creeks, waterfront shops painted up like spring tulips. Between buildings, we have lush, ancient gardens, greenery climbing brick, swaying over your head.

To the west, East Falls plunges into Raccoon Creek, which threads off into wooded hills. By the end of next month, all those hills will be blue with love-in-a-mist flowers. Back in the 1920s, a circus train crashed somewhere up there, and allegedly there are still a few exotic beasts hiding out in the wilderness. I've heard campers and hikers swap stories about nearly being mauled by lions, showing blurry cell phone pictures to anyone who would look.

In the opposite direction, there's the dilapidated train station from Moonville's days as a mining town; Pit Stop Soda Shop and its sign's revolving malted milkshake nicknamed Scary Larry due to the chilling number of teeth in its smiling face; and Our Little Secret, a murder mystery dinner theater.

And across from my shop, brother-sister duo Zaid and Bushra are in the business of selling *something sugary for your sweetheart*. Wafting Crescent Bakery is an apple-green Queen Anne house, the second floor of which is an apartment rented by Morgan. Like

The Magick Happens, Wafting Crescent plays into town folklore, their windows a pink carnival of cupcakes. Someone recently proposed to his boyfriend by sticking a ring in a cupcake from that bakery, like a frosting decoration, so Zaid and Bushra have been trying to capitalize on the attention by pretending that using their cupcakes to propose is an old tradition. Now half of their cupcakes come with plastic rings on top.

For a tiny dot on the map, we get a steady trickle of tourists thanks to ghost-hunting blogs touting our history, our popcorn drizzled with pink chocolate and crushed sweets, and of course, the big one: the legend that there's love magic in our air, in our streams and trees. Visit our town with the person you're sweet on and come away engaged to be married, or so they say. You can trace the roots of this story back to *As Evening Falls*, an anonymously authored book of poems, country sayings, and short tales written about this area in the mid-1800s. The author must have fallen in love here, romanticizing their experience into a whimsical ninety pages that sank teeth in our foundations, legends only strengthening with time. Some of my neighboring shop owners believe the stories, truly. Most don't. But all of them welcome the tourism with open arms.

I look at the lore of love magic in the air sideways, from a cautious distance lest it ever reach out and try to gobble me up again. Twice, I have given my heart to someone in this town, albeit different halves of it, with different types of love. Both times, it was handed back to me broken. At any rate, there's nothing in the legend's fine print about the love being *lasting*.

"Hello, hello!" Bushra chimes as we walk through the door, heavenly scents (many of them common in Bangladesh) curling up to greet us. Key lime pie. Chomchom. Rosogolla. Kheer Mohan. Balushai. Shondesh. Cocoa brioche morning buns, banana fritters, and every flavor of bread. She spots the paper in Alex's hand. "You're the third team to show up so far."

"Because you took so long flirting with your boyfriend," Alex mutters to me. "We could've been first."

"We would've been first if you hadn't insisted on *arguing* with my boyfriend," I counter.

Bushra's smile takes on a nervous energy as her eyes swivel between us. "So . . . something for your sweethearts, then?"

"Nothing wrong with third place!" Zaid pipes up, shuttling a tray of dough into the oven.

Alex and I both grunt. We used to play games together all the time, and it could get . . . fierce. At the time, we had affection for each other to round out our competitive edges.

Not so, anymore.

I study him sidelong, wishing he weren't so good-looking, trying to find fault but unable to come up with any. Physically, anyway. He's a little above average height, average build. He's got strong arms (probably a result of his career) but isn't ripped, his torso is a little thicker in a way that I like. And then, of course, there are those stupidly attractive eyes rimmed with dark lashes. A hard jaw. A pouty mouth that makes him look like he's simmering on the inside.

"Let's hurry it up," he says, as I pore over the selection of iced, colorful treats. To Bushra: "I'll have the Danish."

"You'll have the Danish, *please*," I add tartly.

He mumbles a *please,* throwing me an irritated look for calling out his lack of manners when he used to call out other people for *their* lack of manners, and I'd bet anything he still does.

In spite of wanting to speed this up so that we can advance

to number three—*What lovebirds! He built her a house and decorated it*—Alex trying to rush me while I choose my sweet is a cheese grater against my nerves.

"Hmmm." I tap the glass display case. "What do I want . . . what do I want . . ."

Alex opts not to give his food to a sweetheart and practically swallows it whole, like a snake. "Have the Danish."

"No, I don't think so . . ." I glance up at Bushra in her lilac headscarf and matching lipstick, taking pains not to meet Alex's burning stare. "What's your special of the day?"

She brushes the flour on her palms onto her apron. "Cherry turnovers."

"Mm. Hm hm hm, la te da te da." I tap the glass some more, drumming a tune. "I'm not in the mood for cherries. What about pineapple upside-down cake? You got any of that?"

Alex shifts his weight from one foot to the other. "For the love of god."

Bushra bites her lip. "No, I'm afraid. We do have pineapple-cherry dump cake, but . . . it has cherries in it."

I beam. "Sounds perfect!"

Alex provides a dramatic backdrop, stare withering, as I stab a plastic fork into my dessert and eat it one tiny bite at a time. I'll be my own sweetheart today, too. I circle the bakery at a leisurely pace, stepping one tile at a time, chitchatting with every customer who comes in. Finally, he has enough. "Can we get moving now?"

"Sure, I've been waiting on you," I reply brightly, pointing at the gooey contents of my bowl. "This is delicious. You want some?"

He makes an exasperated noise, pushing out the door.

Chapter Nine

SCARLET GERANIUM:
I do not trust you.

Mr. Pike?" I guess as we walk. "He builds houses."

"For a living. Not for someone he loves, and he doesn't decorate."

"Well, I don't hear you throwing out suggestions."

He clasps his hands behind his back, surveying the road with airy haughtiness. "That's because I already know the answer."

I wait for him to tell me what it is.

"Well?"

"No, I think I'll give you a chance to catch up. See if you can guess correctly."

I stare at him. He keeps his gaze even, features terse. Almost *daring*, like he hopes I'll argue with him some more. "Are you kidding me?"

"What?" He lifts a shoulder. "Just trying to go at your pace, since you took all the time in the world at the bakery."

"Yeah, but I was only doing that to annoy you."

The ghost of a smile threatens at the corners of his mouth. I nearly stomp my foot.

"It's only all right when I do that!" I cry. "Come on, just *tell* me."

Alex refuses. He maintains gloating silence while I wander around aimlessly, foraging for ideas. He probably doesn't even know the answer to number three. I tell him so.

He shrugs again.

"Fine, I'll carry this scavenger hunt on my back," I snap. "Sounds great. How lovely that I got stuck with you as my partner."

"Thank you, dear."

"Shut up. Tell me the answer."

"How can I tell you the answer if I'm supposed to be shutting up?"

"Tell me the answer, *then* shut up."

He pretends to consider it, taking a good long while. His pace has slowed to a crawl. One of his defining traits used to be his speed: jogging instead of walking, constantly moving, fidgeting. When we were teenagers, all it took was one whiff of my perfume floating into the room to get him going, and he was notorious for not being able to resist touching me. My dad teased him about it all the time, because you'd never see him without his arm around me or seated right next to me on the couch like we were attached at the hip. During dinner he'd rest a hand on my knee or try to hold my hand under the table, which could make eating tricky. He'd bounce a leg with perpetual nervous energy, glancing sidelong at me with liquid stars in his eyes.

Smitten, my dad had said. And now the smitten boy stands before me starless, wholly unaffected. "No, I think I'll watch your brain run in circles for a while longer. How was your pineapple-cherry dump cake? I hope it was worth it."

My hands ball into fists.

He lets me lead the way down a narrow alley, pushing aside

tree branches so that I don't get scratched, letting them whip back right into him. A stray cat follows us, darting across the tips of a yellow picket fence. "You know what," I tell him suddenly, turning around and pointing directly at his stony, cynical face. A mild breeze swirls around us, stirring the hem of his shirt. "I know the answer to number four, but I'm not going to tell you what it is. How do you like that?" Number four on the scavenger hunt is *Bring a flower of the gods to the ghost of Downigan*.

He scoffs, one hand on the back of his hat, the other on the bill. Kicks a foot behind him, taking a couple backward steps before circling around to stand closer to me than before. Gravel crunches beneath his shoes, shrubbery rubbing itself across his arms as he moves, tufting his arm hair with fine yellow pollen. "You do not."

"Oh, yeah?"

"Yeah. I think you're lying."

"Prove it."

(We are the height of maturity.)

"Want my proof? Right here." He bends his knees, nose to my nose. "I can see all your dirty secrets right here in your—" He pauses. Draws back as he studies me. Dons a smile so naughty, it's almost profane, which instantly has me on the defensive. "Ah, what's this?"

"What's what?" I touch my face, as if I might have scrawled messages across my own forehead without knowing it.

That self-righteous expression is shot through with curiosity now, and something else I can't identify. "Your pupils are dilated to fifty-cent pieces."

Adrenaline floods. "It's dim here, there are lots of trees blocking the light. Pupils get bigger when it's dim."

"Does your neck get red when it's dim, too?"

I clutch my neck, growing faint enough that he splits into twins. "It's too dim to tell if it's red."

"I should observe your vitals, to make sure you're all right." He clasps my wrist between his thumb and forefinger. I gawk at him, attention falling hard onto his mouth as he silently counts the beats. "Mm, just as I thought. Your pulse is fast, too. Why is your pulse fast?"

I yank my arm back. "It's always fast. I'm a medical anomaly."

He taps my nose. "You forget I went to medical school for a hot minute, honey. Your lies are futile."

My eyes narrow. "Your pupils are dilated, too. Explain that."

He pulls me after him, moving us along in the direction of nowhere. "It's dim out here."

Thought so.

Being stuck with him is the last thing I want, but while I've got him handy, I might as well satisfy a few of my questions. I could have googled them, but I've been firm on my no-cyberstalking rule. My fragile psyche has needed to believe he's been living as a monk all this time, dreaming about me every night and regretting leaving Moonville. In my mind, he's implemented the same rule about me, and that's why he hasn't reached out.

As we walk, I say, "Why'd you drop out of med school?"

"Because it sucked."

"But you got your bachelor's in biology?"

"Engineering, actually. Medical school was nothing like college. College was all right. Medical school made me want to shut my face in a car door."

"So you did end up going to Ohio State, then?" I venture carefully. This might be a dangerous topic, considering our history. Our arms brush as we walk, a little tingle of electricity zipping along between us. No! Bad electricity! I squint through the canopies, suspecting errant thunderclouds might be the cause. When in doubt, blame the weather.

"Yeah."

Unfortunately, we kept tabs on each other for months after our breakup. Otherwise, he wouldn't have seen what he saw and *I* wouldn't have seen what *I* saw, and what a load of ugliness that was. I have to flip the page to a different topic before I make myself mad all over again.

"Good. I'm glad you went."

This was probably the wrong thing to say. He grunts, the space between us pumped full of fresh tension.

"I did end up going to Hocking," I inform him. "For early childhood education."

"Good," he replies quietly. "I'm glad to hear it. They had the campus housing, right?"

"Yep." Which was rare for a two-year college, and extra appealing to me since I so desperately wanted to get out of the house. "I only ended up living on-campus for one semester, though." He laughs, which I expected. I plow on: "I moved into the carriage house behind the shop instead—paying close to three thousand dollars a semester to stay in a tiny dorm didn't make sense when my grandmother gave me free board twenty minutes away."

"There you have it, then." His words are heavy. "Everything worked out."

It's my turn to grunt.

Grandma and I did have a ball together—I didn't fully appreciate how stressful the last few years of my parents' deteriorating marriage made life for everyone in our household until I removed myself from it and awoke one day in an environment where my fight or flight instinct wasn't triggered by the sound of a door slamming.

I was breathing easier, surviving, but I wouldn't have called it living. Mornings were a fog, nights hell, a continual cycle of re-remembering that my strongest support was gone, off living his own uncomplicated-by-Romina dreams.

"Where are we going?" he asks, pausing for a moment.

"Bowerbird's Nest."

He turns his head toward me quickly. His mouth wants to grin, I can tell.

"What?" I prop my hands on my hips. "Gilda will know the answer. If there's someone in this town who built a house and decorated it for somebody else, she's gonna know about it."

His almost-grin breaks into a great big smile that looks achingly lovely on him, and very handsome. Infuriating, too. He laughs and laughs at me.

"What!" I sputter again. "It's a good idea!"

It is.

Boisterous busybody Gilda Halifax knows *everything*. She and Grandma were dear frenemies, each of them psychic, each calling the other one a fraud. Gilda passed out business cards at Grandma's Celebration of Life, and half the eulogy was an incredibly ballsy ode to her costume shop, Bowerbird's Nest, advertising discounts on palm-reading services when you sign up for her e-blast. She wears a locket that she swears Grandma's ghost is sometimes curled up inside of. Now and then, I see her talking to it.

And it turns out that I was right. When we push open the door to Bowerbird's Nest, Gilda scurries toward us with a loud "Well, it's about time!" squashing each of us against her in a hug. It's Gilda's signature. Whether you haven't seen Gilda in one day or in ten years, when she sees you, she's going to hug you, and your eyes will water from all the hairspray holding her stiff red barrel curls together. A white woman in her seventies, Gilda reminds me a lot of Dottie. Not just because of the psychic thing, or because Gilda wears the same blue eyeliner Dottie did, but because Gilda is so woven into memories of my grandmother. Lots of bickering, but I think each always secretly considered the other to be her best friend.

"I was starting to worry you two didn't know your Moonville history," Gilda exclaims.

Alex laughs at my confusion. Over the next minute, I discover that *apparently* male bowerbirds build nests for their potential mates during their bird courtship, and decorate those nests with brightly colored things. He claims to have known this already, but I don't see how. That is simply not a common piece of trivia. The man is a liar with an ego and a half.

"All right, I'll stop torturing you," Alex hums to himself after Gilda checks off Team Yellow on a clipboard and we go on our merry way. "I know the answer to number four."

"Yeah, so do I."

He continues as though I hadn't spoken. "*Bring a flower of the gods to the ghost of Downigan.* Obviously, the ghost of Downigan is referring to Downigan Cemetery, and that one lady from back in the day."

"Lovisa Coe, who haunts the town."

"She doesn't, because there's no such thing as ghosts, but anyway, that's the spot. The first half of the clue was easy to figure out. Just popped it into Google, which says that *flower of the gods* is the symbolism for dianthus flowers."

I laugh. "You are so off track."

He determinedly heads to Budding Romance, anyway. In his mind, there is no way he could be wrong. This is going to be delightful.

"Dianthus, please!" he booms as soon as we get inside the flower shop. I poke him.

"Calm down."

"Calm down? Did you hear Gilda? *It's about time.* We're going to lose, Tempest!"

"We're going to lose because you're wrong. You won't even consider the possibility that you're wrong."

"It's statistically unlikely that I would be wrong."

My eyes roll for eternity.

He gets his dianthus, and we amble on our way to the cemetery. We've been dawdling so long that the sun's run all the way across the sky, and it strikes me that we probably could have won this if he'd been more forthcoming about clue number three, and if I'd been more forthcoming about clue number four, but there you have it. Neither of us can pass up the opportunity to make the other one flail.

Gilda's daughter, Millicent, is dressed in an old white Victorian gown, waiting for us next to Lovisa Coe's weathered tombstone. I don't care what Alex says; that woman (Lovisa, not Millicent) has been banging cupboards and opening locked doors all around town since 1885.

Alex proudly presents his dianthus to Millicent, who shakes her head.

"This is for the scavenger hunt," Alex tells her, as if she might be here for some other reason. Which, honestly, she might. We get a lot of cosplaying ghost hunters in these parts.

"Thaaaat's not the ooone," she responds in a ghostly wail. "Tryyyy agaaaiiin."

Everything that Alex thinks he knows explodes. His brain shorts. He stares at me, takes in my smile, and my pupils that are hopefully not doing anything untoward. Sighs.

"All right. Just tell me."

I tip up my chin, skipping around him. "No, I think I'll let you run in circles for a while."

"Oh, come on."

"But you were so *sure* you were right," I sing. "How can I, a mere squirrel, know the answer when you, All-Knowing Wizard, do not? How can this be?"

He crosses his arms, mouth flat. When I still do not give in, he starts walking again (in the wrong direction, I might add) and motions for me to hurry up. "Fine. You can lord your secrets over me while we get something to eat."

Chapter Ten

HYDRANGEA:
Why are you so fickle?

Mozzi's Pizza doesn't have any empty tables, so we take our food to go and stop at a campsite area, four logs situated around the charred remnants of a fire. "So," he says, seating himself on one, patting the spot at his side. I opt for my own log. "Why fortune-flower-thingies?"

"Why roofing?"

He huffs a laugh, picking at his extra-mushroom pizza. "Why defensive?"

"It's a long story."

He studies me. "I see that."

"Oh, pah. You and your supposed *seeing*. What do you know?"

"You," he returns simply.

I take a bite of pepperoni calzone, rolling my eyes. "Afffilfionshershago!"

He correctly translates *a million years ago*. "You're still really easy to read. And you still talk with your mouth full. Ew."

I glare at him. "I was going through a . . . difficult time. Before flora fortunes found me."

The gleam in his eyes goes flat. "What happened?"

When my life was in shambles after leaving Spencer, a friend of my grandmother's dropped by the shop to give her a fern. Grandma's health was declining, so the fern sat neglected for a while. I happened upon it when the pitiful thing was half dead.

I'm still not sure what possessed me to care. To whisper hello as if it could hear, picking dead, shriveled fronds out of the pot, offering its cracked soil a long drink. To my shock, it mattered. The plant responded to my attention. I still wasn't good at nourishing myself, forgetting to eat at times, but I nourished the fern, so it grew tall, vibrant. I started to feel the hugs Luna and Aisling provided, a slow-acting medicine, the nuzzles from the cats, the fist bumps from Trevor. I started to reciprocate, slowly emerging in a softer, kinder reality. I covered myself in flowers and came back to life.

"I had this fern, of Grandma's, that was dying. After I revived it, I started planting more things. Luna kept giving me seeds. I was looking for a job, not knowing what I wanted to do—I wasn't interested in candle-making and I didn't want to go back to the daycare I used to work at. My newfound interest in plants led me to pick up a book called *Garden Spells: The Magic of Herbs, Trees, and Flowers*, which led to creating little posies out of flowers whose symbolism I thought would complement each other. A lady came into the shop one day, talking about her boyfriend, how she hoped he'd propose soon. Luna had a candle to help with that, of course, but I threw in some flowers. Gardenias and orchids. I'd been reading up on the floriography, so I thought—who knows? Maybe it would bring about a marriage somehow."

"Let me guess." He scratches his chin, smiling wryly. "The boyfriend coincidentally happened to propose."

"It wasn't a coincidence. I could tell by the feeling that over-came me when I put those specific flowers together for another person that I had . . . created magic."

He studies me closely. "What sort of feeling?"

I tip my head back, filtered sunlight warm on my face. How could I possibly describe it?

Magic brought back a memory of Zelda and me splashing in puddles, galoshes dirty. Bangs dripping wet under rubbery hoods. Smiling teeth, stained cherry-sucker red. I saw Grandma strolling across a windswept street toward us, a paper bag of surprise treats from Half Moon Mill in hand. Her ribbons of white hair streamed sideways, and she was radiant, absolutely spectacular with our mirrored joy. I saw her painting the dot of the letter *i* on our curved front windows, *The Magick Happens*, to look like a crescent moon. Part of me will always envision the shop name the same way I did when I was small, before I could read: back-ward, the way it looks from the interior side of the window. A bunch of symbols that felt mystical.

"Unconditional love," I say finally. "The first time I made magic, when I heard the click of a door and felt this rush of wild wind with petals on the air, it was the first taste of joy I'd known in a long time. I discovered how to manufacture happiness where there had been none, and all I wanted was to keep doing it, again and again, until I felt alive."

His stare, while remaining skeptical, softens just a little.

I look away, remembering what it had been like to lie at the bottom of darkness. The hope I clung to when magic blossomed, providing me with joy and purpose. Flora fortunes saved my life. I chased that feeling all the way to where I am today, creating magic now not only to bask in vivid feel-good sensations or re-capture old memories, but to help others find happiness. Much of the time, my flora fortunes act as tokens of courage: People just need that push to go for it, to let themselves love and be loved.

"The business side of my magic ignited almost overnight. When customers walked in for Luna's candles, they left with complimentary flowers that addressed their specific romantic desires. Before I knew it, customers were walking in purposefully to visit me, and *boom*. Flora fortunes became my living."

When Zelda got wind that we were selling flowers in addition to candles, she wanted to be involved somehow, to contribute her own passion to the mix, so the fantasy/witchcraft book collection was born. We cleaned out basement rooms that had previously been too creepy to visit, transforming them into the Cavern of Paperback Gems.

Alex stretches out a leg, slapping a mosquito away. "Hmm."

"Go ahead and doubt all you like," I tell him mildly. "I'm secure in my magic. I make a real difference in people's lives."

His expression is frustrated. "Are you calling yourself psychic, then? Like Gilda? I know that woman makes shit up. She tried to tell me I was captain of the *Titanic* in a past life."

"No. I'm a flora fortunist, like I told you."

"Okay, but that isn't a thing. You *invented* that."

I smile. "Somebody invented roofing, too. Does that mean it isn't real? Should I not believe in roofs?"

He leans back, gritting his teeth. I can tell he wants to laugh, wants to prove me wrong. This is the sort of conversation that must make him absolutely *lose* it internally. It isn't enough for Alex King to believe he's correct; he has to make the other party acknowledge that he's right. "That is . . . not equivalent."

I squint up at the treetops, which flutter side to side in a sweet spring breeze. "A daylight new moon." What I'm about to say next is going to annoy him. "Indicates a hidden truth will soon emerge. Maybe it's *your* truth. Are you hiding anything?" I fasten my eyes on his.

"You can see the moon in daylight every day."

"Not during a new moon, you can't."

He opens his mouth to argue, but I cut him off. "Are you a witch? I did not think so."

A laugh that is half cry lodges in his throat. "And you are?"

"Yes, as a matter of fact."

"You defy all science. Congratulations."

"Thank you. I don't care how you mean your congratulations, I will take them however I want to."

I watch him struggle to form a reply, then turn away. Shake his head. "I don't see it. Makes no sense, the two of you together."

"What?" My mind's still on flora fortunes.

"You and Trevor. Did you see him in there at Mozzi's? I watched him drink ranch out of the bottle."

"He's fun. Why do you care? Who would you pick for me instead?"

"You should stay single." Alex molds his hand into a fist. "Female empowerment."

"How empowered are *you*?"

Alex leans on one elbow, analyzing me. "You asking if I'm single?"

"No. Ew." I jump to my feet, rounding the campfire.

"Where are you going?"

My legs have unexpectedly developed a jittery condition. Walking is involuntary. "Wherever I want."

His features turn sly. Calculating. "Does Trevor know about your jumpy heart?" He spreads his fingers like a firework exploding. Chants lowly, *"Ba-boom, ba-boom, ba-boom."*

"You're not as much of a know-it-all as you think." I'm itchy all over. "You—" I stop. My phone is resting on the log, screen lighting up.

He sends me a mildly censorious frown, as though I am betraying Team Yellow somehow to receive a call from Team Red (Trevor and Teyonna). I don't have time to work out the inner mysteries of Alex's mind, though, because he answers my call before I get the chance to, then taps speakerphone. "What do you want?"

"Let me talk to Ro," Trevor's overly loud voice demands. "Y'all've been gone for hours. I want to make sure she's still alive." A woman is giggling in the background.

Alex lifts the speaker close to his mouth, each word deliberate. "Bring a box of fresh donuts to the red bridge in fifteen minutes or you'll never hear from her again."

"What's taking you so long? Kristin won't hand out prizes till everybody gets back. T and I got second place, which means we scored gift cards for Shoe Sensation. I want to see if they make insoles that massage your feet as you walk."

Alex makes a face at me, like, *This guy? Really?* His lips purse as he sweeps me from top to bottom. I think he partially dissolved my bra with his eyes. "Maybe we're taking so long because I'm busy seducing her," he replies at length.

A weird burble of laughter emits from my throat. "As if you *could*."

Alex wings a brow. "Let's not pretend I can't."

"Hurry up!" Trevor chirps. "And just so you know, T helped me break into your truck and we ate your bag of Rolos. Why the hell you keep Rolos in a hot car, son?"

In the background, Teyonna releases a giggling scream. "Why'd you tell him?"

"He deserves it for mistreating chocolate." Then to us, Trevor says, "T and I are going back to see if there's any more candy in the truck. Don't let him seduce you, Ro, or I'll respect you less."

The screen flashes. *Call ended.*

Alex closes his eyes, pinching the bridge of his nose. "Please help me understand, Tempest."

"Nothing can be done for you. I'm afraid your skull is too dense."

"Are you two serious? Do you live together?"

"Yes, we're serious. And no, we don't live together." His barrage of questions is throwing me off my game. "I'm moving in with him soon, though. Into his house."

"You two are wrong for each other. There. I said it." He slaps his left thigh. "As your old friend, it's my responsibility to tell you when you're with the wrong guy."

It's interesting, how much this statement chafes. I'd expected to feel gratified by Alex's irritation over me fake-dating Trevor, but I'm surprised by my resentment. He lost all right to judge if other men are wrong for me long ago. That memory is still a rush of cold in my lungs, that sensation of falling, clawing for someone no longer there, despite all his promises. So I turn my face away from the one who makes my stupid heart still jump.

"What else is new? I've always picked wrong."

Chapter Eleven

LARCH:
Only he who presses his suit with spirit shall win me.

After our early dinner, we end up running into Trevor and Teyonna, who have taken it upon themselves to add more items to their scavenger hunt: *a purple shoe, somebody bald, a REAL unicorn, an overflowing toilet*. They claim they're just trying to pass the time while they wait for the remaining two teams to finish, but I notice that the handwriting switches up with each line and suspect they're doing this to entertain each other. They seem to be getting along a whole lot better than Alex and I are.

I'm slumped on a bench outside a gas station, where Alex is using the bathroom. Trevor bolts past into the building, sneakers skidding loudly across tile, scooping up an armful of snack-size Flamin' Hot Cheetos bags.

"Tell me about it." Teyonna says with a light groan as she drops onto the bench next to me, even though I haven't said anything. She rotates her right foot in circles until her flip-flop falls off. "These are not the kind of shoes you wanna wear for walking around all day."

A lady passes by and plops a baby onto Teyonna's lap, then heads right into the gas station. "Denise!" Teyonna shouts after her. "How could you do this to me?" She leans my way, dropping conspiratorially, "I've got baby fever."

"Who's that?" I ask.

"Denise is Trevor's cousin. She's here all week, like me. The wedding's turned into a family reunion."

"Look at those cheeks." I smile at the baby. "What a cutie."

"Wanna hold her?"

"Sure."

I take the baby, and when she snuggles up to me, a strange guilt tugs in my chest. I remember Spencer's cold expression, how he'd wanted to be Adalyn's favorite without putting in any effort. She'd wanted me to hold her when she was sick, tired, upset; she ran into my arms when she was hurt, she'd swallow the medicine when I pleaded. He didn't try. *What's the point when she prefers you, anyway?*

"Watch this." Teyonna blows raspberries on the baby's belly, making her squeal. "She's so freakin' adorable! I can't stand it. Ahhh, I want one."

"Me, too." I pass the baby back to her.

Teyonna slides me a look that is first empathetic but morphs into surprise. A spike of alarm. "With Trevor?"

"Um."

"Sorry, that was nosy. Now I sound like one of Trevor's aunts, always coming for my throat with those kind of questions." Teyonna claps her hands against her knees in a Miss-Susie-Had-a-Steamboat pattern, riddled with pent-up energy, tapping her feet in that quickstep way I've seen soccer players do during practice. "He's a riot, isn't he?"

"There is only one Trevor in this world, for sure."

She half smiles. "Don't I know it. I used to think he might be . . . not too much for me to handle, per se, but more than I could deal with at that time. He seems to have mellowed."

I don't think I could ever call him mellow, but at least he hasn't been stealing helium tanks recently.

"I don't think I've had near as much fun since then," Teyonna says wistfully. Then she straightens, as if she didn't mean to say it. "I'm glad he found you, that he's happy. You two are cute together."

Discomfort pinches my nerves. It's a lot easier to lie to Alex than to Teyonna, who's never done anything to hurt me. I'd have to be an idiot to miss that emotion in her eyes.

I hesitate. "Trevor . . . I haven't been with him long. He and I, it's not . . ."

I'm spared from blowing our cover when Alex and Trevor walk out of the gas station at the same time, interrupting us. Alex doesn't even break stride, just cuts a peculiar expression at Trevor and Teyonna, who are now whisper-giggling, heads bent together. He shakes his head. "Let's go, Tempest. It's time to tell me your secrets."

I feel it again—that electrical burst—and my breath stills. There's a strange spark in his eyes that tells me he isn't just referring to the fourth scavenger hunt clue.

A raindrop lands on my forehead. Another darkens the sleeve over his shoulder. I lead him across the road, into the woods, and he reaches for the list in my hand; as it passes from mine to his, a memory glows brightly between us.

◊

THEN

I reach an arm behind me, practically dislocating my elbow to sneak around the binder and stack of textbooks on the window ledge. I hate sitting in this spot directly after gym, wet from half an hour in the pool, cold air blowing from the vent above turning my stiff hair into chlorinated icicles. My skin's uncomfortably tight, eyes watering. Good thing this class doesn't have any hot guys in it, because I haven't reapplied my eyeliner yet. I'm naked without my eyeliner.

Elbow somehow intact, I manage to pass the note into Yasmin's hand without removing my gaze from the projector.

Mrs. Chevis is jotting notes in green dry-erase marker across the clear sheet, pad of her hand stained. *Why did the Ottoman Empire retreat from the* (she yawns and checks her notes) *Balkans?*

The door opens. Yasmin slinks inside, hangs the hall pass up on its peg, and begins to walk over to her desk, which is behind mine. When did she get up to go to the bathroom? I whirl around in confusion, but her seat's empty. If she isn't behind me, then who just took my note? The only other person nearby is Alex, who sits at my eight o'clock, cheeks rather flushed, eyes cast down, trying to hide behind his hair.

"Psst."

I know he hears me. He makes a jerking movement, as if he almost glanced up but caught himself in time.

"*Pssst*. Did you take my note?"

Alex has superhuman memory. He only has to look at the screen for half a second, then neatly copies down three full sentences. I forget the end of a word while I'm still writing it. "Yes."

Yasmin's eyes bug out. She leans, loud-whispering, "Took your what?" Her neck and eyelids are packed with pink roll-on scented glitter, so she must've been busy decorating herself in the bathroom.

That.

Is.

Not the response I thought I'd get, even though it's clear he could've been the only person to intercept my private business.

Right now, Alex King is suddenly interesting. Much more interesting than the Ottoman Empire, anyway. "Why'd you take my note?"

"You handed it to me."

"That was for Yasmin." I check on Mrs. Chevis. She's scratching her head with the marker's cap end now, the sound of her own voice putting her to sleep. She has newborn twins. At the beginning of the semester, she unloaded her frustrations about the "crap maternity leave this district gives to new parents" onto our class and has been trying to make us all forget what she said about the superintendent with Friday movies as bribes.

"Yasmin wasn't here," Alex points out crisply.

"I didn't *know* that, though. The note was obviously for Yasmin. You shouldn't have taken it. You—"

He looks up at me then, lasering me with the full force of his eyes, and it lands a physical blow. His curly hair's untidy on the left side, like he's had a fist propped in it, face tilted toward the right half of the room. He tries to replicate my triangular note-folding but gives up and goes for an old-fashioned square. His hand is much warmer than mine when his fingers pass the note back into my waiting palm.

I unfold it, scanning with a third-party viewpoint to gauge how bad I came off in this note between Yasmin and me.

Hey, Yaz! I am so BORED!!!!!!!!! What are you doing later? I have to work until 8 but I told my parents I get off at 9, so you want to get ice cream? I know Corey works there but if I show up alone I'll look like a creep.

I don't know I have to babysit my little brother while my mom works. Tomorrow?

Tomorrow I'm supposed to help my grandma at her store. ☹

Maybe I'll come by? I'll let you know. What's your number? My parents have my phone cuz I'm grounded so I'll have to call you on the house phone.

Below that, my cell phone number is as big as a traffic sign in sparkly gel pen, followed by a string of hearts. I gasp, flattening the note to my chest before stuffing it into my pencil pouch.

"Did you read any of this?" I hiss at Alex.

Without looking at me, he angles his notebook in my direction so that I can see my own phone number dashed across the top of his notes in neat handwriting.

The gall of this kid! Yasmin and I exchange exclamation mark faces.

My attention ricochets between Mrs. Chevis and Alex. Another detention will cut into my work shift, which will cut into my slowly accumulating savings. The day I'm legally an adult, it is *Goodbye, Ohio*! "Forget what you saw," I tell him ominously.

"Sorry, can't do that." He's doing that thing again, gaze flickering briefly up at the teacher's notes, then expelling an entire paragraph onto his paper. His handwriting's better than mine. Heat flares up my neck, tingling in the tips of my ears for some reason. Is Alex my nemesis now?

"But." I am at a loss. Yasmin's eating this up, and I admit I'm enjoying the end-of-the-school-day drama. World history is usu-

ally when I nap behind my binder. Or ditch to see a matinee. I
haven't been able to convince Yasmin to join me ever since we
wound up in the same theater as her mom when we were supposed to be giving an oral report I'd neglected to prepare for.
I'm hanging as far out into the aisle as I can brave without spilling from my chair, eyes intense on his every flinch, the way his
knee won't quit bouncing. High color slashes his cheekbones,
and a rapid pulse thumps below the hard angle of his jaw. "You
can't call that number."

"I'm going to."

He says it so firmly, and my god. Where has this boy's voice
been? All I can do is stare. He doesn't look at me again, but his
neck gets redder. He shoves his notebook into his backpack as
if worried I'll dive for it. The thought hadn't occurred to me.

Yasmin covers her mouth with her hands to stifle a giggle.

"Then I won't answer," I tell him.

"I'll text."

"I won't read your texts."

He holds my stare. "You will."

Holy shit, I think I'm blushing. It is the most horrible sensation to have ever happened to me. My skin is being dipped into
boiling oil.

"Romina!"

I whip around to face the front. Mrs. Chevis isn't too tired
to put me in my place, unfortunately. She's told me twice so far
this year that I am one of the "most inattentive and disruptive
students she's had the joy of teaching" to which I pointed out
that she's only been teaching for three years. Get back to me
when you're mid-career like Ms. Linden and *then* evaluate how
bad I've been.

The bell rings. By the time I've collected my stuff, Alex is already ducking out the door into the hallway's swell of students. A Milky Way sits on my desk.

I pick it up: The wrapper is warm, like it's been in his pocket, and I'd bet anything the chocolate inside is gooey and melted. I am not going to answer a strange boy's texts, but I suppose I'll take the candy.

Chapter Twelve

PURPLE LARKSPUR:
First love.

NOW

There's a story in *As Evening Falls* about a woman who picked a magic purple flower to give to a man she loved. After she accidentally dropped the flower on her way to see him, it was scooped up by a lark, who flew away. Every so often, she would see this lark, still with the flower in its beak, fresh as the day it bloomed. As the weeks went by and she gradually lost interest in the man she'd fancied, she enjoyed searching for the lark and her stolen flower. "Until one day," I tell Alex, "after she had fallen completely out of love, the lark transformed into a young, beautiful earth god. He'd been waiting for her heart to be her own again so that she could then give it to him. After she gave him her love, he returned the flower, which she wore in her hair, and its magic kept her young with him for hundreds of years." The story claims that they live together beneath the swift-moving waters of Twinstar Fork, which is why larkspur grows in such abundance along its banks.

The sun is a low fireball flinting off the water of Twinstar

Fork now, trees losing their green as they darken to silhouettes. The cooling air clings to my lungs.

I bend forward, plucking a stalk of purple larkspur. "Not symbolism," I tell him. "A story."

He shifts closer, examining it. His eyes, haltingly beautiful, slide to mine. He has dark limbal rings, and looking into them, I feel as if he takes something; as if, every time I meet his gaze, he siphons off a little piece of me to keep.

I don't have time to stand here on a riverbank and pick larkspur with him. Don't have time to eat calzones with him, or snipe at each other.

Next Monday is May Day—Beltane—one of my busiest workdays of the year. I have hundreds of artificial flower crowns to make in advance (fresh flowers for an occasion like this would take up all the room in my fridge). It's also when the night market is supposed to launch, which we're not nearly prepared for. Which begs the question: What the hell am I doing?

"My mistake," Alex says softly. His gaze is sharp and glittering as the night. "I suppose I have you to fault for flower symbolism being on my mind."

I can't breathe as he holds my stare. "Of course you would blame me."

His head slants as though he heard me say something completely different. "When we were in the gas station, Trevor told me that you two live together. That you both live in the little house out back behind your shop."

I blink away my stupor. "Right. Yes." Lovely of Trevor to not run this by me first. How are we going to keep our story straight? "That is true."

"Then why'd you tell me you didn't? Why'd you say you were going to move into his place soon?"

I shrug, uncomfortable. "Let's go give this flower to the ghost."

He steps closer, facial muscles tense. "What kind of shampoo does he use?"

"What? Why?"

"Which side of the bed does he sleep on?"

I hesitate, turning and beginning to walk. "Left."

He keeps pelting questions. "What does his alarm ringtone sound like?"

I speed up my gait. "What's with the interrogation?"

"What's with the deflection?"

"I've spent all day on this scavenger hunt. I'd like to wrap it up." I thrust the larkspur at Millicent Halifax, who glares.

"You took a really, really long time," she tells me stiffly, then picks up her bag of flowers and marches off.

The fifth and final scavenger hunt clue is *Take a picture where the town begins*. This one's simple. The town begins at the Moonville tunnel.

I hurry as fast as I can, trying to leave Alex behind. "You're suddenly very motivated to finish this hunt," he observes, appearing at my side like an apparition. "Almost as if you're trying to dodge my questions."

"Trevor and I aren't any of your business. Now focus, please. It's starting to rain."

I hear a low growl in the base of Alex's throat. All the tiny hairs on my body stand on end.

I hurry faster.

"Oh, I'm focusing, all right," he says darkly. "What's Trevor's middle name?"

I figure my best bet is to throw him off his guard. "Our physical chemistry more than makes up for a lack of information."

"More lies." He seizes my wrist, bringing me toward him, and

I'm mesmerized by the heat flare from skin-on-skin contact. I got a good look at those hands earlier when they were busy fondling my plants; they've got calluses and at least one scar, which runs from the base of his index finger around to the knuckle of his thumb like a large letter L. I hate that I noticed this. I hate that I've been dying to know what it would feel like to be handled by them.

His voice is heavy. Pressurized. "You don't have any chemistry with him."

"You don't know everything, believe it or not."

His fierce gaze bores into mine. "I know one thing," he says quietly, breath ghosting over my lips. "I know one thing for absolute certain."

Our mouths are an inch apart, breathing labored. My heart thunders. I'm dizzy from the smell of sweat and soap and rain, the fresh-cut grass clippings mushed to the soles of our sneakers, and the last time we were this close he probably had a hand up my shirt. His thumb slides an inch down my wrist, pressing a little as if remembering, too. I shiver. He turns my wrist over, exposing the pale underside with its gleaming indentation. I can't believe he remembers my old injury.

Raindrops fleck his shirt, gliding down his temple, close to the corner of his mouth. I stomp out the urge to lick them, alarms flashing blue and red in my brain.

"What, then?" I hear myself murmur. "What's the one thing?"

My attention moves from his eyes to the stubble on his jaw-line, to his throat. I watch his skin respond, goosebumps appearing along his neck, a flush of color rising. I trace a finger down the bumps, flattening them. The movement is wholly involuntary and an instant mistake I can't bring myself to regret.

Then my hand wraps around his throat. Applies light pressure.

I don't know what prompted me to do it. I stare at my hand around his tanned neck and he takes a step forward until our fronts graze, his eyelids lowering. He swallows against my palm, skin blazing hot. I've definitely touched him before, but not like this. Not with a touch that feels like a word. We never got the chance to try having sex because between my parents, my sisters, and his mom, everybody conspiring to keep an eye on us, we never got any privacy. I would have been fine with a tumble in his truck bed, but Alex insisted our first time had to be special . . . we waited and waited for that perfect moment that never came.

I let go.

A birdcall filters through the bright red haze pulsing around me, blood slow, thick, and roaring in my ears. It drowns out the river.

He still doesn't tell me what that *one thing* is, his analytical stare flaying my nerves. Alex releases my wrist.

Even when standing utterly still, he is all movement. I see it crouching inside of him, a whirlwind storm of energy he's holding back with everything he's got; and if he were to release it, he doesn't even know himself what he might do—kiss me, curse me, tell me he wishes me eternal suffering, pin me to a tree. It's painful to not touch him where his pulse beats, sweat limning the bridge of his nose. His gaze searches mine with a near-frantic intensity, and when he speaks at last his voice is like cement. "We'd be a lot further ahead right now if you'd just been honest."

I take a step away from him. "You knew the answer to number three and took forever to tell me what it was. You're just as much at fault."

His head tilts. Something almost sad hides in the way he

looks at me, but his smile is all amusement. "Come on, then. Even though we lost, might as well finish what we started."

⟡

By the time we return to Half Moon Mill, the rain's let up to a sprinkle and the other hunters have collected their prizes and left. I approach Kristin, who's surrounded by a gaggle of ladies in hot pink visors. Suitcases are strewn all over the grass.

"There you are!" she exclaims. "Those clues must've stumped you, huh? I thought for sure you'd be the first ones back here— remember all the board games the three of us used to play together? You two would go for the throat, every time."

I see a brief flash of my hand against Alex's throat, unmistakable desire darkening his eyes.

"Sorry for making you wait." I school the wobble out of my voice. This is absurd. I am not allowed to find Alex attractive, and more importantly, I have forbidden myself from being attracted *to* him. It would be too humiliating to survive. "Good night, bride-to-be," I say. "Thanks for inviting me to play today. I had fun."

"Oh, I'm so glad!" Kristin hugs me.

Kristin seems much more relaxed now. I remember when she worked two jobs to make ends meet, her house a shrine to her husband, who died in a car accident when Alex was six. Everywhere you looked, there was a picture of grinning, gregarious, practical-joke-lover Alex Senior: candids with Kristin—him with a bushy mustache, her with hair teased to heaven, laughing hard, trying to shield her face from the camera; wedding photos; family portraits with baby Alex and his cute right-cheek dimple, toddler Alex in scarlet and gray overalls and a matching Brutus

Buckeye hat, nostalgically backlit with his chubby hands on his knees. The trio's succession of photos stops abruptly after kindergarten-graduation-Alex. Their house used to be loud with laughter, the hub where aunts and uncles assembled to drink and play games. Alex Senior and Kristin had intended for Alex Junior to be the first of many.

There are knots in the heartstrings that connect Kristin and me, but I still love her dearly.

"Here's Marcy," she says. "Marcy, did you ever meet Romina? She used to go with Alex, but she goes with Trevor now."

"Romina gets around," Marcy says with a smoky chuckle.

My chin falls. "Uh."

"Don't listen to her, she's joking." Kristin waves a hand. "Marcy, I didn't think you were going to make it! I can't believe you brought so many friends with you." I watch her attempts to be chill and stress-free for this wedding disintegrate before my eyes.

"We're on our way to the Wild Turkey Festival," one of the ladies pipes up, swaying. She's sipping a margarita with four neon straws. "In McArthur."

"Hope you still have room for us," Marcy says brightly.

Kristin presses two fingertips against her lips. "Ah . . ."

"No worries, Mom." I jump at the sound of Alex's voice, landing directly on top of my head at close range. Just as I revolve to face him, he steps forward, bumping our bodies together. There is a zero percent chance it wasn't on purpose. "You can give them my room."

"Yours? But then where will you stay? There are no other hotels in town."

Alex wraps an arm around my shoulders, his smile genial. A raindrop slides along his hairline, landing on the collar of his shirt. "I'll stay with my new stepbrother, Trevor. This would be a great chance for us to bond."

Horror leaps up my throat when I realize what this means for me. "No way."

"Oh, c'mon, it'll be fun."

I snarl at him.

Kristin bites her lip, but the drunk pink visor ladies are already wheeling their suitcases inside, so she grips my hand. "Thank you, honey. I appreciate this so much."

"Can't you just drive home?" I whine at Alex.

"Nah, I live all the way in Oreton. I want to stay close this week, so I can help Mom out. Get to know Daniel." He's putting it on. Oreton isn't all *that* far. The meaner my scowl, the bigger his smile gets. "Arrangement works out for everyone. Fantastic."

Chapter Thirteen

PASSIONFLOWER:
I am pledged to another.

A bewildered Trevor and a smug, pleased-with-himself Alex follow me into the carriage house; I just know that if I turn around and peer at the upper windows of The Magick Happens, I'll see my sister and niece with their noses pressed to glass, cackling gleefully. Right after I texted Trevor to tell him what was happening, I texted Luna, and she had the brilliant idea to run over to Trevor's with her spare key and grab some of his stuff to stash in my house. The problem is that Alex beat her here, so now she can't plant Trevor's belongings where they'll look natural.

Alex stands in the middle of the room, my lumpy, modestly sized bed perfectly visible from the squashy yellow couch where he will be taking up space uninvited. He appraises my red cabinets, the tiny round dining table with mismatched chairs, the soothing parchment-colored walls with framed botanical posters. Pictures of El Paso, New Orleans, and Minneapolis that Zelda's sent swarming the fridge. A zillion pots bursting with greenery. Turquoise throw pillows. A stack of tabbed, highlighted books on the limited counterspace, devoted to garden witchcraft. He can't tamp down his curiosity, nosing inside my fridge and freezer to see what I've got in there (vegetables and soups, mainly).

"Make yourself at home," I tell Alex nervously, rubbing my arms to flatten the goosebumps (which are caused by the rain and nothing else). It's *The Twilight Zone* in here. He doesn't acknowledge me, conducting an investigation of my nightstand, my board game shelf, even my chargers. When he swans out of the bathroom, half of his mouth is ticked up into a smile that thinks it knows something.

I can't stand it.

In recent years, I have transformed myself into a character from a Little Golden Book, a country mouse in a flower bonnet who drinks dew from acorn cups, enveloped in my cozy comforts. Which is precisely how I like it.

But Alex's loaded silences, his probing stare, his smirk, the way he ends certain sentences with an aggravating upward inflection, just sets me the hell off. And that soft creature who's burrowed deep down into a basket of fluffy sun-warmed clover pops her head up like an angry meerkat.

"What?" I snap.

He shakes his head, still smiling. "Nothing. Not a thing, Romina Romina. You've got a beautiful place here."

My hands curl. "Yes, I do. We do. Trevor and I."

He juts a thumb at the bathroom door. "Mind if I use your shower? It's been a long day."

I mutter my permission, even though I've been looking forward to showering myself. As soon as he closes the door behind him, I seize the front of Trevor's shirt. "This is a nightmare. Wake me up."

He lightly slaps my cheek.

"Damn." I rub my skin. "Didn't work."

"Try me."

I slap him.

"Nothing." He checks himself out in a hexagonal mirror. "Nice slap, though."

I turn in anxious circles, hands wringing. "What do we do?"

"We make popcorn, obviously! It's a slumber party. And you're in for a rough one, sugarbobs. I snore."

"I already knew that. Hey, what kind of shampoo do you use?"

He doesn't bat an eye at the non sequitur. "Ro, I'm relieved you finally asked. I use PK's Perfectly Bright shampoo. Say goodbye to brass forever—this is going to change your life. We're talking shine that lights you up like the angel you're meant to be."

"Not an angel," I reply reflexively. "Get on the other side of the bed. I told him you sleep on the left." I pause. "Wait. Maybe I said you sleep on the right side. Bah! I can't remember." And Alex will *definitely* remember. I loathe his computer brain.

"Correction: I sleep in the middle."

"How about we wait for the lights to turn off, and then you move," I suggest. "You can starfish all you like on the floor."

"Listen, you might be the love of my life for the week, but I'm no gentleman. This fine ass sleeps on memory foam only." He presses hard into the mattress. "Hm. Memory foam topper on junky old springs. I'm going to have the full peasant experience, I see."

"*I'm* not sleeping on the floor."

"Did I ask you to?" Trevor climbs under the covers, wriggling to make room for me. "Grow up, Ro."

"Fine, but if I wake up in the middle of the night to discover you gazing soulfully into my eyes, I'll go get Snapdragon and let him sleep in here, on your face. He'll suffocate you to death with his love."

"What a simple-minded little button! Thinking I'd be gazing at your *eyes*."

I zero in on his dirty shirt touching my sheets. "Get out of my bed with those outside clothes, you monster."

"It's my bed, too."

"Trevor!"

"You're always excluding me from this relationship. We should consult a couple's counselor." He ducks to miss my assailing pillow.

"Speaking of relationship troubles," I tell him. "You were being awfully friendly with Teyonna today. Should I be jealous?"

"Oh, absolutely you should. She's so hot, I can't stand it. Did you see those shorts? Holy *shiiiiiit*. When she bent over, I almost passed out."

I snort-laugh. "You're a weak man."

"No argument there. But, like, on top of that, she's still the nicest person on Earth. I can't think straight when I'm talking to her, all that's going through my mind is hoping I don't sound like an idiot. But then again, whenever I say idiotic things it makes her laugh, so." He releases a groaning sigh.

I glance at the bathroom door, from which an odd electric noise buzzes. "Jeez, what's taking him so long?"

"You know." Trevor waggles his eyebrows, miming a jerking-off hand motion, and this time my pillow connects with his face. He hops up, reheating yesterday's tomato soup. "Damn, I could go for some raspberry silk pie right now."

I'm exhausted. It's been the longest day in history, my bones are heavy from walking all over town, I've discovered about a dozen new muscles, and they all hurt. I want to wash this day off me before the hot water runs out.

"Hurry up," I call to Alex, knocking.

"Room for two in here," he calls back.

"Ew."

The door swings open; I stumble back, hitting the wall. "Ew?" he repeats, voice deep. Closes in on me. "*Ew*. Really." He's in soft gray sweatpants, rolling a fresh shirt over his head. There are tiny stray hairs clinging to his neck, and I realize what that buzzing noise had been. He trimmed his hair again. It's now one quarter of a millimeter shorter.

"You did that on purpose," I say, poking my tongue against my cheek so that I don't laugh.

"Did what?"

"Made your hair even shorter just because I mentioned it was a crime to cut it."

He skates a hand over his scalp. "You and my hair. Leave it alone, woman. Trevor has long hair. Go run your fingers through it."

"I *will*." I slide past him into the bathroom, coughing on the hot, humid cloud of various bodywashes from my predecessor. Look at him pretending he didn't do this to make a statement. Oh, yes, he just *had* to bring a razor over to my house and trim off a microscopic sum of hair. What an urgent priority.

"Your fingers won't be able to get past all the hairspray," he throws over his shoulder.

"He washes it out at night. Which is when we do *it*, anyway! Sex, I mean."

I pause; it's a short-lived death. Behind him, Trevor buries his head in a pillow. Ten years from now, Trevor will still be haunting me with that line. *We do all our sex at night! After I wash out my hairspray!*

The complete shower experience goes like this: I stand under a pour of lukewarm water, eyes squeezed shut, knowing that the last person to stand in this spot was Alex. An unclothed, wet Alex. Who is about to spend the night in my house.

Breathing my oxygen. Smushing his face against my couch pillows. Wrapping my shaggy blanket with the strawberry print around his shoulders. I've rubbed blessed thistle into my furniture (protection against evil), so we'll be testing the limits of its power tonight.

At some point I accept that avoiding the intruder is fruitless, so I reenter the real world to find Alex relaxing on my couch, one ankle resting atop his knee, arms stretched comfortably along the back. He surveys my home with primal satisfaction. This is fine. This is totally a normal and okay thing to happen.

"Finally," Trevor grouses, heading into the bathroom.

"You could've showered together," Alex points out.

I'm running a brush through my hair as he watches, the ends dripping onto my burnt-orange caftan. "I don't trust you in here unsupervised. You might be a thief, for all I know."

"True. I see all sorts of things I'd like to steal." He regards me closely. "It's good manners to offer the bed to your guest, you know."

"I must not have good manners, then."

"Your couch is on the smaller side." He plumps one of my throw pillows dubiously, as if unsure whether it will support his huge, arrogant head. What's gotten into him lately? When seeing each other again for the first time, he was friendly, warm. Then in a snap he became aloof, surly. Now, he's not only cocky but *annoying*.

"You are more than welcome to sleep in the chicken coop."

He hums under his breath. "The couch will do, I suppose. We'll renegotiate for the bed tomorrow."

Tomorrow?

Oh, jeez, I think he intends to stay here until the wedding's over.

"Chickens as pets," he muses, getting up and wandering over to my cabinets. He starts opening them, poking around. "Is that allowed? You'd think there'd be codes about that. Livestock within city limits, et cetera."

"My chickens aren't livestock, they're family. What are you doing? What are you looking for?"

"I'll know it when I find it." He glances at my counter, then does a double take, swiping my small suede notebook from the top of the pile.

I lurch forward. "Give me that!"

"Why? What is it?" He spins so that he can snoop through my notebook, holding it aloft. "Is it a diary?"

"Stop it right now. Give me that or my very sexy boyfriend is going to fight you."

Trevor exits the bathroom in my baby blue terry-cloth robe, a dark mood, and I suspect, nothing else. I can guess the source of his aggravation: my cheap array of hair and skin products. He's constantly bragging about the fifty-dollar moisturizer he uses.

"Romina," he calls, sulking. "Where is that waterproof wall mount shower phone holder I bought you for Christmas? I was going to listen to Sleepytime FM, and the acoustics of leaving my phone on the sink are atrocious."

I clap a hand over my forehead, a headache beginning to pulsate. My phone rings.

I glare at both of them, swiping across my screen to answer. "Yes?"

"Hey, how are *thiiiings*." Zelda's joy radiates. "Are you going to sleep between them and be a Romina sandwich? Sounds *cozy*."

"No, thank you for asking," I respond through clenched teeth. "I don't need any ice cream."

Trevor gasps. "I do! I want some! Is that Luna? Tell her I want peanut butter chocolate."

"This is hilarious." My sister's gloating is surely payback for the bumper magnet I slapped onto her camper van the last time I visited: HONK IF YOU LOVE ASS. Also, she evilly enjoys other people's discomfort. "I would hate to be you!"

"Feeling's mutual, pal. That ocean air has made you salty."

"Ocean?" Trevor halts in the act of pulling on a pair of my fuzzy socks. "Is that Zelda? How is she going to get us ice cream?"

"What's Alex wearing?" she teases. "What are *you* wearing?"

"Why?" I ask. "Are you hitting on me?" Alex and Trevor both swing weirded-out looks in my direction. "I'll call you back."

"Chrysanthemums and purple roses to nurture a love pegged at first sight," Alex reads aloud. "Sunflowers to signify you wish for a long relationship with your present significant other. Liatris for when you want to try to make a troubled relationship work. Hm. Strange diary you've got here."

"Trevor, are you going to accept this?" I wheel on him. "You're taller than Alex, go get my book."

Trevor, who's lying in my bed, shows me his hands, gold polka-dot polish drying on his nails. "Babe. Look at me. I can't do anything, or it'll smear."

Alex flips several pages. Clears his throat. "Cyclamen and

butterfly weed help drive away an unwanted admirer. Well, that's not very nice. Just use your words."

"I wouldn't expect you to understand."

"You shouldn't. Ferns encourage your one true love's secret feelings to come to light. Oooh, sexy. And sneaky. Is that why you've got a fern tattoo?"

"*No*, I—"

"White clover," he trails on merrily, "will bring your face to the mind of your OOA . . . Your OOA?"

"Object of affections," I growl.

"Your OOA," he continues, insisting on pronouncing the acronym *ooo-ah*, "over and over, so that they can only think of you. Yellow hyacinth wards off jealousy when your OOA might share their heart with another. Mock orange declares that you know someone is trying to deceive you." A loaded pause. "Interesting!"

"I hope you're enjoying yourself."

"I am." He stretches out on the couch, holding my notebook over his face. "Quiz time! What do variegated tulips communicate?"

"I'm not playing this game."

He makes a buzzing *Ehhh!* noise. "Come on, Romina, you should know this one." He flashes a grin. "It declares to your OOA that you find their eyes beautifully bewitching. Okay, next question. What's viscaria for?"

"I hope it's for you shutting up."

The group chat on my phone is going wild without me.

Zelda: LOOK AT THE PHOTO OF THIS
SNACK. Kristin posted him on Facebook

Luna: You're not allowed to call our sister's ex-bf a snack

Luna: We're still mad at him, remember!

Zelda: I know, but he's hot. I remember when he was
twee. He is twee no longer

I turn my phone on silent, climbing into bed. I roll onto my
side facing the fan, drawing the quilt up to my chin, and switch
off the overhead light.

Alex automatically turns on a lamp beside the couch, continuing to read. I huff loudly. He huffs back.

Even with the loud whir of the fan close by, riffling pages of
a shopping list magnetized to the fridge, and the faraway chirrup
of crickets, all I hear is Alex's breathing. I sit up on my elbows,
watching his eyes quickly scanning the contents of my notebook. I hate that his memory is so strong that he'll be able to
instantly recall everything he's reading. Nearly three years as a
flora fortunist, and I still regularly have to look up meanings.

Trevor's snores rip through the air.

"Dear god," Alex mutters. I cover my smile with one hand.

"Regretting staying the night with us yet?" I ask.

"Not at all. It's been quite enlightening. Out of curiosity,
how can you be so confident that the people who came up with
the language of flowers knew what they were talking about?"

"How can I know they didn't?" I get up and unplug his lamp
from the wall.

He taps the flashlight function on his phone, aiming it at my
face. I shield my eyes from the harsh blue-white star. "That's
your argument?"

"I'm not arguing."

"I am."

"Then argue with yourself."

He returns to his reading. I can see, by the glow of his phone, a furrow between his eyebrows. Alex is all about facts and reason, which travel downstream while the supernatural tends to flow upriver. I can hear his mental processor hissing like water droplets on a hot stove.

"Hm," he says quietly. "Fine, I will."

I know I won't be getting any sleep tonight. Burned into my eyelids is that picture Zelda was ogling. Alex sent it to his mom directly after we took it, posing in front of the Moonville tunnel with his arm draped casually around my shoulders. My body unconsciously turned in toward his like Ash's pair of cuddling stuffed monkeys with magnets in their arms. I wince thinking about it.

I pull my phone back out just to study the picture again, staring until Alex's eyes become two shadowy pinpoints, features distorted into unrecognizability. I can't get over how different he's become, yet how familiar, and way more beautiful than he has any right to be. I frown at my appearance on the screen, upper arms squishier now.

Well, of course you're going to look different now, I tell myself. *You were a teenager.* I refuse to feel self-conscious about aging, metabolism slowing down. Change is movement, as my therapist tells me, and the inverse is stasis. I'm evolving because I'm alive.

I save the picture to my phone, knowing I'll hate myself for it tomorrow. I try to quiet my breathing so that Alex won't hear it, so that he'll think I'm asleep, while I stare wide-eyed at nothing and grip my blanket so tight that my fingers lose sensation. When I close my eyes, I rewind back to that moment in the woods: Alex's tense shoulders, his wolfish gleam. Greed and want and an ache pounding deep within me. Rain sliding over skin. *We'd be a lot further ahead right now if you'd just been honest.*

But when my eyes reopen, everything but the here and now melts away, and my senses cast out to find Alex, lingering over every inch of him. It's as if I'm homesick for a person lying fifteen feet away.

Out of anyone I could possibly feel this way about, why did it have to be *him*?

Chapter Fourteen

PINK GERANIUM:
I await your explanation.

I wake up to the harsh slap of my own arm hitting my face.

"Ow."

"Keep your hands to yourself," Trevor mumbles. "You keep flinging your arm over me. Ro, if you fall in love with me this is going to be so awkward."

"Shh!" I sit up in bed, one eye open, panning the couch. It's empty. Alex must have left, or maybe he's in the bathroom.

I plant a foot on Trevor's lower back and kick, propelling him onto the floor. He takes the blanket with him, howling. "Turn around! Don't look."

"Why?"

"Because it's first thing in the morning, and I'm wearing nothing but a robe. It's the Apollo Thirteen launch over here."

This is all the motivation I need to scramble out of bed. The bathroom's dark, door open. When I'm finished doing my business, I find that my notebook has been returned to the top of my bookstack.

"Oh, thank goodness. He's gone," I tell Trevor, body flooding with relief.

"Who's gone?"

Alex's face pops up on the other side of the open window. I scream.

"Sorry, was I interrupting your cozy couple time?" Alex leans against the ivy-clad exterior of the house, tranquil as a rose. "Y'all sleep in *late*."

I check my clock. "It's not even six."

"Six a.m.?" Trevor exclaims. "That's not a real number." He dives back into bed, yanking the covers up over his head, feet sticking out. "Nobody talk to me until noon."

I scuttle outside to meet Alex, closing the door behind me. "I'm a morning person, for your information."

"Not as much as I am. I've been awake since five."

"I actually woke up at four, but kept my eyes closed."

"I've been awake since five o'clock, *yesterday*."

"Well, I haven't slept in eighty years. I'm a vampire."

Laughing, he sits down to pet a chicken. "Roxanne is my favorite."

I run my fingers through her downy white feathers. "This is Suki."

"Why'd you name her that? She clearly looks like a Roxanne."

I take in his change of clothes (jeans and a plain T-shirt— naturally, he refuses to wear anything fun), a plate sitting nearby with the remains of his breakfast (toast and an orange). A thermos of coffee. The coffeemaker is near the bed, which means he's been bustling around me while I slept. The thought is jarring. "Don't you have a job you should be heading off to?"

"I'm on vacation. Why are you trying to get rid of me?"

"Stop answering questions with questions, it's annoying," I reply. He's got bruise-like circles under his eyes, I notice. "Late night all alone with the darkness of your thoughts?"

"Wasn't alone. Hard to sleep, with the racket you made tossing and turning. I bet you were torturing yourself thinking about me. *Oooh, that Alex, so sexy right out of the shower. Oooh, he's got such nice biceps.*"

He isn't far off the mark.

I rear back. "What's with the southern belle voice? Is that supposed to be me? You don't sound anything like me." I only have a hint of twang going on, as does he—comes with growing up in the boondocks—but I'm not full *Gone With the Wind*.

He keeps at it. "*Oh, Alex King, you've got the prettiest eyes on this earth, makes my legs just tremble.*" He laughs to himself. "That's why you're flustered this morning."

"Nobody would say that about you except yourself." I leave him behind, trotting into the store's sunroom. I try to shut the door behind me, but he squeezes inside too fast. This room quite literally isn't big enough for the two of us—he bumps into everything. "You did not come close to entering the sanctity of my fantasies last night, and my legs are stiff as a corpse's, thank you."

"Liar."

"If that's what your massive ego needs to believe." I sit down primly on my workbench, conscious that I should be changing out of my caftan pajamas, applying deodorant, eating breakfast, that sort of thing. But the idea of Alex watching me eat is oddly disconcerting. I wish he'd pin his attention somewhere else. "Try to keep it in your pants, will you? You're in town for a *wedding*, for goodness' sake. Weddings are sacred." I begin assembling my florist's wire in neat rows, wire cutters and sharp scissors at the ready. "You don't have any biceps, either."

He lifts an arm to inspect himself. "More lies."

"I want you to know," I say in my sweetest voice, "that I forgive you."

"For what, exactly?"

"It was harder to get Trevor to come around, but he forgives you, too."

"I'd simply *love* to know what I did to Trevor. I hope I do it again, whatever it was."

"You once shattered his girlfriend's heart." I lift a stalk of silk roses out of a container, pairing pink with myrtle and yellow with ivy.

"Do you think I'm an idiot?"

"Couldn't say." *Snip, snip.* I weave together flowers first, then wrap them to wire with tape. "Don't know you well enough to be sure, but I have a hunch leaning in that direction."

He laughs as if he's so unbothered when he obviously *is*, tugging on the bill of his red Ohio State ball cap so that it slides around backward. I think I've just discovered one of his tells.

I smile to myself.

"You need a bigger space. It's way too crowded in here."

"If you think it looks bad, imagine how it feels. All the magic going haywire." But even as I say it, I notice the magic has taken up a different attitude today. Today, every plant's energy has turned toward Alex, inspecting him curiously. It feels like low, breathy chatter, appreciative murmurs, raised eyebrows, and devilish grins. I kick that energy out of my way and refuse to pay attention to it.

Alex fingers the crown I just finished. "Who's this for?"

"A tourist, most likely." I don't glance up, feeling my forehead pinch in concentration. Second crown of the day finished, on to the third. My fingers will give out after twenty, and I'll take a break for a couple of hours to go mash up some herbs.

"You get a lot of tourists here?"

"Yes, but I'll have more than usual next Monday. People

flock in from all over on May Day." Saying the words *May Day*, ironically, brings the appropriate surge of panic. *Magickal night market opening May first* flashes across my mind. How hopeful we'd been when we printed those fliers and paid for ad space in the newspaper.

"What's wrong?"

It takes me a moment to realize my feelings must be showing on my face. I wave my hand dismissively but explain the situation anyway.

When I'm finished telling him everything, his focus moves to the wall, as if he can see the lot next door through it. "Ah."

"I don't want to think about that right now, though."

"Okay." His attention zips back to me. He leans forward. "Prove you're magic."

"What? No."

"Because you can't." He sounds so sure of himself, so exacting. But just a *smidge* disappointed, as if he'd prefer to be wrong.

"Because I don't have to." He's right, though: I can't prove it. *I smell my great-aunt's spaghetti Bolognese when I mix stems correctly* is not concrete evidence.

I look at him now, and this time my smile is genuine. I can tell it frustrates him. "Anyway, it's obvious. *In a garden where tea roses bloom with the snowdrops, there must live a witch.* That's common knowledge." I gesture to my tea roses, then my snowdrops, both in full bloom. "You see?"

"Anyone can make up anything, that doesn't make it so," he counters. "I could say that if you sit in a yellow chair at the exact coordinates of the South Pole, it will start raining licorice."

"That's absurd," I reply amiably. "There's no such thing as the South Pole."

"What?"

When I don't reply, he lays a hand over my crown-in-progress and slides it toward himself, to get my attention. "What did you say?"

"The earth is flat. There is no South Pole."

I watch horror dawn in his (*variegated tulip*, I can't help but think) eyes, and it's excellent. I hold his stare for a full ten seconds before laughter bubbles out. "Kidding."

He mops his forehead, arching backward. "Don't scare me like that."

"I had you, didn't I?"

"How could I have known you were kidding? By the way, you control when your snowdrops and tea roses bloom. You have them in pots on your porch, circumventing their natural life cycle."

"Go outside and check the rest of the garden. You'll find all sorts of plants that aren't supposed to bloom until late summer, and they'll be bigger and prettier than any you've ever seen. Explain that."

"Illegal fertilizers." He lays yellow roses together with ivy, and pink roses with myrtle, like I'm doing, to help me along. I push a wire and tape toward him. He begins to assemble. "Tell me how your magic works, at least."

"Witchcraft is a mix of respecting basic cornerstones and intuitive improvisation."

He laughs again. "That is some vague word salad you're trying to get me to eat, there, Mother Nature."

"This right here?" I point to my Wonder Wall, which is loaded with Polaroids of customers holding up the flora fortunes that changed their lives. "When I finished that talisman right there, it felt like a kitten on a tree stump, pouncing on a butterfly." I indicate a woman and her posy. "This one felt like the last page of a dark fairytale." I gesture to other bouquets. "Solving a mystery. The first lick of ice cream in summer. The strike of midnight on New Year's, when the person you want to kiss suddenly appears, backlit by fireworks. And *that* is how I know magic is real."

His expression is exactly what I would have guessed. It's impossible to convey the sensation of magic flowing through my hands without sounding bananas.

"You mean you don't even have any magical amulets that light up when you chant at them? Spooky spells that shake the ground? You're giving me nothing."

"There're plenty of places to sit," I say, plucking a spotted leaf and flicking it playfully in his direction. He closes his fist around the leaf just before it makes contact, scrunching his nose with a smile. "You don't have to stand directly on my nerves."

"Hey, just trying to understand you."

Why bother? I think. I glance sidelong at him again, catching him staring. "What is it?"

"You're so calm here. This is your happy place."

"Yes, it is." I wind a finger. "And the rest?"

"The rest of what?"

"I can tell you want to say something else. Other words are hiding in there for me."

His smile is a flare of genuine wonder, pleased that I pegged him so accurately, but then he softens. "That something else is . . . the way you . . ."

I wait for him to finish, but he changes the subject instead. Traces one of my flower tattoos, half of its buds closed, just beginning to bloom. He swallows. "What kind of flower is this?"

"Lily of the valley."

He thinks. *Return to happiness.* Alex's thumb brushes the pink outline of another flower that grows on my arm, one of its petals in an everlasting process of falling away. "And this one?"

"Carnation."

His mouth pulls, flattening.

"Would you like a flora fortune, Alex?"

"Huh?" He's still puzzling over the pink carnation, which symbolizes a mother's love. He's probably thinking about my relationship with my mother, whom I've never been close with. Wondering if that's changed. (It hasn't.)

"You're awfully curious."

"I like to know things." He returns to his crown, which is coming together clumsily, half the quantity of flora I'd typically use taking up twice the space. Painfully visible gaps of wire. "I like the tattoos, too."

Our heads are bent close together as I loop ribbons along his effort. "The fern is a reminder that I can always start over. That I can let go of a life that isn't working and begin anew."

His attention is so keen, it's a brand. "Is that what you did?"

I nod.

A pregnant pause follows.

"Is that what *we* did?"

He absorbs my surprise, which appears to satisfy him in some strange way. I hate that I keep telling him things without meaning to. He's good at reading between the lines. I have no clue what Alex is playing at—outwardly, it might *look* like he's interested in me, but this could be explained by his deep-seated need to solve for X. He likes riddles, puzzles. He likes to be proven right. Whatever it is that he's searching for right now, it's because he's got a question in his mind, a strong guess as to what the answer might be, and is working to confirm his accuracy.

Thankfully, I'm spared when Luna appears. She does her best

to not make it apparent she's been eavesdropping, but I know better. She keeps trying to catch my eye, her expression significant. I ignore it. "Morning, Luna."

"Morning." She nods coolly at Alex, not quite rude, but certainly not rolling out a red carpet. "Hello."

His reply is warm. "Hello, Luna."

"Where's Trevor? Out getting breakfast for you again?" Before I can say "Hm?" her eyes flash. "He spoils you rotten. So doting."

Alex slowly pushes his crown aside, then crosses his arms over his chest. Tips his chin down, trying not to smile.

"He's sleeping in," I tell Luna robustly. "But I think he has a date planned for later. Knowing him, it'll be somewhere special."

"The corner table at Mozzi's," Alex adds. He gestures his arm in a wide arc, admiring an invisible corner table. "You'll gaze into each other's eyes over the shaker of chili flakes, elbows sticky. Share a breadstick like the spaghetti from *Lady and the Tramp*."

"A picnic in a meadow," I retort lightly. "He'll have a rose between his teeth, and I'll wear nothing but a dreamy smile."

"Naked in a meadow. Just you, Trevor, and a thousand brown recluse spiders."

I stick out my tongue. He narrows his eyes, but there isn't any heat in it. I don't know how we got to a place where we can tease each other in good fun like this so quickly.

It's alarming.

"Trevor give you that necklace?" Luna interjects, motioning at my throat. "Looks new."

My necklace is at least four years old. Luna bought it for me herself. Just look at this meddler, Miss I'm Not Getting Involved.

"Isn't it beautiful?" I preen.

"He knows your taste."

"Oh, yes. He's unparalleled."

Alex stands to his feet. "Thanks for letting me crash at your place," he tells me, then runs a finger across the rim of a pot of black dahlias. Considers it for a moment before pushing it an inch in my direction. "See you tonight."

Luna eagle-eyes his trip from the Garden through the shop, front bell chiming as he leaves. Then she pops her hands on her hips. "You're *welcome*."

"For what?" I'm still staring at the black dahlias, which symbolize *dishonesty*. It was too marked an action to be coincidental. The man is toying with me.

"For reminding you of what you're supposed to be doing."

I pick up Alex's clumsy crown, settling it over my head. Even though his hands didn't infuse it with magic, a fuzzy vision appears in my mind, wiping out Luna, the shop. In someone else's body, I see myself, and I'm wearing white orchids in my hair and smiling up. It feels like five-petaled blossoms of vervain, a forest of them, blooming simultaneously. Like the purest adoration. The vision fades away, but the adoration lingers, and now it is *my* heartbeat that thumps wildly.

What is it, exactly, that I'm supposed to be doing? I can't seem to remember anymore—with these flowers on my head, all I can think about is Alex's dimple, his thumb caressing the petals of my tattoos, his gentle strokes through Suki's fuzzy feathers. His wavering line left unfinished: "*The way you . . .*"

It'll come to me, I'm sure. What I'm supposed to be doing.

Chapter Fifteen

RUE:
Do not annoy me with your unwelcome attentions.

few hours later, Trevor, Luna, and I are huddled in the entryway of Half Moon Mill, watching Kristin and Mr. Yoon from across the room. It's raining again, so the happy couple is entertaining themselves with Parcheesi. My stomach clenches.

"I hate being rude. How can we interrupt them?"

"What choice do we have?" Trevor murmurs. "They're leaving for Paris on Monday for their honeymoon. It's now or never."

Luna clutches the business plan tightly. "Why couldn't we have just won the lottery? This is mortifying."

Alex passes by. Halts abruptly, then turns.

"Look who it is." His slow, satisfied grin freezes when his eyes fall on Trevor. "Oh. You."

"Yes, the son of the groom. Shocking of me to be here."

"And me, colleague of the son of the groom." Luna gives Alex a pointedly insincere smile, teeth bared.

His eyes flick to her, then back to Trevor. "Hello again, Luna."

She makes an *I am not impressed* tsk. We all wait for Alex to go away, but he hangs tight, close enough to hear what we're talking about. We decide to pretend he isn't there.

"Beltane's the ideal time for business ventures," I remind my colleagues. I am All Business in my peach dress with ruffled sleeves and large pearl buttons. I reach up to adjust my hat, before remembering I'm not wearing one. I'm still wearing the flower crown Alex made.

"Right." Trevor draws a bracing breath. The three of us link arms. "Let's do this."

Alex tails us over to Mr. Yoon. Trevor clears his throat twice before his father says, without looking up, "Would you like a drink of water?"

"I was—we were—we're hoping to talk to you about a business proposal," Trevor forces out.

Mr. Yoon is instantly guarded. "A business proposal."

"Sir, if we could just have a few minutes of your time." Luna slides a copy of the proposal in front of him. Kristin moves the Parcheesi board aside, her gaze conveying polite interest.

Mr. Yoon heaves a sigh, then begins to read. Flicks to the next page.

"You see, we purchased property—" I begin, but he holds up one finger. Continues to read.

"I seem to recall giving you a significant sum of money, Trevor," Daniel says. "Surely you can use some of that?"

Trevor shrinks.

"Ah, yes, that would be impossible, because you've already spent it all. Stitch and Turn Shoe Emporium. Ken's Barbecue." He ticks them off on his fingers. "Mighty Fitness. Two of them figuratively burned to the ground, one of them literally. You purchase properties without thinking, and that is why you find yourself in these unpleasant situations. If you had actually gone to business school—"

"I told you, I'm *sorry*. Everybody makes mistakes! Remember that golf course you opened?"

"The golf course situation was different. Nobody could have anticipated that many gophers. Anyway, your financial history is not my only hesitation here. *Moonville's famous love magic*," he recites, four pages later. "Pardon me if I don't quite believe in that."

"Sir?" I prompt nervously.

"It's cute," Mr. Yoon concedes. "I understand why local businesses keep that story alive; there's money in it. But there is no such thing as a one true love."

Luna pales. "I disagree."

I bump the toe of her shoe with mine.

Mr. Yoon stacks his hands on the paper, creasing the page. It took us weeks to fine-tune this, and our dream is currently sopping up water pooling around the base of his drink, a grayish ring right over *The Magick Happens is a favorite stop with tourists hoping for* . . . "Do you see this woman?" He reaches for Kristin's hand. She lays her palm up for him. "She lost her husband many years ago. She loved him. I lost my wife, too, and I loved her. But Kristin and I love each other also. There is no such thing as a one true love, because one can have many loves."

I lower my head. "You're absolutely right. I think what we mean to say, is that Moonville has a special way of revealing the person you're meant to be with here in this moment, in your present stage of life."

"Exactly," Trevor inserts smoothly. "It's a whole thing. And the candles and flowers do that, too. They create a road of clarity, which leads you to the person you're meant to be with." He is speaking verbatim from the proposal.

"Is that what you two are to each other?" Mr. Yoon inquires seriously, his black eyes switching back and forth between Trevor and me. "You are meant to be?"

I can't help glancing at Kristin. It's a mistake.

It's that damned windbreaker tripping my nostalgia land mines: This is the woman who paid for my homecoming dress junior year, who helped me apply for scholarships, who baked a three-tier birthday cake when I turned eighteen, who gave me a ride to the doctor when I missed three days of school with a fever that peaked at a hundred and four. Afterward, she took me to her house instead of mine, tucked me into her queen bed with the soft white comforter, and lay beside me while we watched TV Land. Maybe it's wrong to say, but I loved her more than my own mother. I cannot lie to her face.

I look down at my shoes, reflecting sunlight peeking through the forest beyond the windows, allowing Trevor to answer. "Yes."

What other choice does he have, but to say that? We sell romance. It stands to reason that Luna and I both ought to have been happily paired off with our meant-to-be's long ago. And perhaps Luna would be, if Grandma had never uttered a word about silver luna moths, which she's been holding out for. As for myself, I just haven't met anyone who wanted to hold on to me, or who I wanted to hold on to. Zelda at least has the comfort of not believing in soulmates. She doesn't believe in prophecies, either. Or magic.

Mr. Yoon stares into my eyes. Kristin's gaze is fixed on a spot right behind me. "I'll think on it," he says crisply.

He stands up, grimacing. Grabs a newspaper. "Excuse me." He nods at us as he leaves, left leg limping. The packet we gave him is left on the table.

Luna, Trevor, and I exchange worried frowns. We're all trying to hog the blame for this—Trevor's the one who cut the check and waived the inspection; I'm the one who suggested we buy the lot because I needed room; and Luna is usually the voice of reason who talks us out of risky ideas, but she encouraged us to go for it because she feels guilty that her candles take up most of the store.

I'm the first to break the silence. "That didn't go so great." It's probably time to face the music: We are not going to be able to fix the sewer line and asphalt in time to put up the night market, and if we want to be able to pay ourselves, we might have to re-sell the lot, probably at a loss. Which means no expansion, and I'll need to cull my plants to make the magical climate bearable again.

"He didn't say *no*, though." Trevor begins to loosen up. "That's a good sign, trust me. We've got a shot."

Alex leans in, lips close to my ear. "Meant to be? And you don't know his middle name?"

"Mind your business," I hiss.

"I think I see your angle here." His eyes dance. "I underestimated you."

I glare. He breezes a short distance away, whistling.

"Your business plan looks very nice," Kristin tells us diplomatically, sparing an extra twinkly smile for Trevor. "You did a good job!"

I think I speak for Trevor and Luna when I say that this compliment makes us feel about six years old.

"Thank you, Kristin. Excuse me." Luna pulls out her phone, checking the barrage of missed messages from Zelda. Zel keeps complaining that she's out of the loop. Secretly, Luna and I are hoping she'll grow so exasperated with her out-of-the-loop-ness that she'll decide to remedy it by visiting. She rarely ever comes to Moonville—the last time she was in Ohio was for Grandma's Celebration of Life.

Zelda is like a water sprite: elusive, mercurial, and deeply private; most comfortable in solitary darkness but easily lured by something sparkly. We do this dance where Zelda invites us to wherever she's living, and Luna and I invite her to Moonville instead, and we end up putting off vacation for another year.

Alex drops several boxes onto a table, which I recognize straightaway as my favorite board games.

Wait a minute.

Those are *my* games! The Monopoly lid is taped together, and I'd recognize that Hungry Hungry Hippos anywhere. It's covered in a child's marker scribble.

"Hey!" I shout. "You took those from my house!"

Alex doesn't acknowledge me. "Memory Mayhem?" he suggests to his and Trevor's relatives, holding a red box aloft. Then he lifts another box, balancing them like the scales of justice. "Fact Carnivore?"

"Fuck you," three different people reply.

"There's no guarantee I'll win." He can't keep a straight face as he says this. "Fine, you bunch of babies. Here's one I don't have an advantage in: The Newlywed Game."

I squint. "I don't have that game."

The expression he turns on me is unreasonably snobbish. "I printed it off. Downloadable questions."

I'm immediately suspicious. Alex never brings a game to the table unless he believes he'll win and is a sore loser on the rare occasion that he fails. Such a sore loser, in fact, that he'll nurse a grudge forever.

"Not all of us are newlyweds," Allison deadpans. "Or dating anyone."

"I think these questions can apply to all relationships," Alex says. "Pair up with whoever you feel you're closest to."

"Bet you've already memorized the questions," I tell him. "Not fair."

"I'm not playing. I'm hosting." He takes an unnecessarily out-of-the-way route to a particular table, just so he can skirt by me and whisper in my ear. "Thought I'd give others a chance to show what they know."

"Whoever we're closest to," Kristin repeats. Points at herself, then at her husband-to-be, who's standing along a wall and hiding behind his newspaper. "Okay, so Allison and Teyonna. Me and Daniel. Trevor and Romina. Or maybe Romina and Luna?"

My sister is talking on her phone, too far away to hear us.

I clutch my purse. "Afraid I can't join you. I should go back to work."

"Sit," Alex replies cheerfully, prodding me into a chair. He pushes it in, looping my purse handle around the back.

"I don't have the time." I shoot Trevor frantic glances that he is totally oblivious to, clicking and unclicking the pen Alex passed him.

"Trevor, don't you think you and Romina deserve a break from working?" Alex says to him.

"What? Yeah." Trevor laughs at my alarm. "We work too much. Got to get that R & R, baby." He taps my nose.

Alex drops a card in front of me, littered with questions and spaces left blank for filling in answers. Winks. *Winks!* "Have fun."

Chapter Sixteen

ELDER:
My efforts will remain unremitting.

That asshole.

"Phones here." Alex thumps the center of the table. "I don't trust any of you not to cheat. Then I want Daniel, Allison, and Trevor to head onto the patio to work on yours, where I can monitor you."

"Bossypants," I mutter, refusing to surrender my phone. Alex has never wormed his way into a debate club or Model UN he didn't eventually seize captainship of, so he's in his natural habitat here.

"Stop thinking about my pants and do your homework." He confiscates Trevor's phone, which renders mine useless, now that we can't compare notes.

ROUND 1

How many kids do you want?

Do you have allergies?

When's your birthday?

What did you wear on your first date with your significant other?

I would like to have at least three kids, but Trevor's not going to know that. He's going to make a dumb, overplayed joke about me having twenty cats someday instead. *Twenty cats*, I write with a sigh.

And Trevor better know the answer to the allergy question. He brought in curry to share with Luna, Morgan, and me, but neglected to mention it contained mushrooms. He then watched hives break out all over my face.

Trevor might remember the *month* of my birthday. He definitely isn't going to remember what I wore for our first date, as we've never been on one, but I know what answer he'll give for that, anyway: a blazer with gold chains draping from shoulder to shoulder. Trevor found one online, became obsessed with how *powerful and commanding* he looked in it, and purchased a dozen others for his friends. I removed the gold shoulder chains from mine to repurpose into an anklet, which he still complains about, many months later.

"Come along, come along." Alex excitedly gestures the others back inside, harvesting all their cards, his smile obscene. "Sit, sit, and don't talk to your teammate! First question is for Daniel. Daniel, if your partner was an animal, what kind of animal would she be?"

He contemplates. "An armadillo."

"An armadillo?" Kristin repeats. "Why would you say such a thing?"

"Armadillos are beautiful creatures, and they have a protective outer shell."

"Aww." Kristin smiles at him. "I want to change my answer."

"Too late," Alex replies briskly. "You said Clydesdale, so no points." He's ruthless. "Allison, if Teyonna had a superpower, what would it be?"

"Flying," Allison answers at once.

Teyonna frowns.

Alex booms, "Wrong! Teyonna would be able to restore all the rainforests."

"Everybody answers *flying* to that question," Allison huffs. "Come *on*, Teyonna. We're not going to win if you give obscure answers!"

"It's not obscure! We discussed this when we watched one of the X-Men movies."

"Trevor," Alex forges on. "How many kids does Romina want?"

"At least three," Trevor replies, and I throw up my hands.

"Why're you looking at me like that? Isn't that what you've said?" Trevor ticks them off on his fingers. "Girl, girl, boy. You'd call one of them Louise."

"Louis," I correct, a moment before thinking better of it. Louis is Alex's middle name. It has nothing to do with him—he doesn't have exclusive rights to that name.

"Exactly!" Trevor preens. "I should get an extra point for knowing that."

Alex and Kristin are both staring at me. "Wrong," Alex responds finally. He's a live wire, radiating a strange, crackling energy that makes it difficult for me to focus. "Romina says she wants twenty cats."

Allison laughs, then tries to sputter it out, making herself cough. "Gross, Romina," Trevor utters. "That is too many cats."

Mr. Yoon goes again, followed by Allison. "Trevor," Alex continues. "What is Romina allergic to?"

Trevor purses his lips, studying me. I can tell by his blank stare that he has no idea. "Nail files?"

"For crying out loud!" I yell.

"Ro, there is no other explanation for those jagged edges."

"Gardening causes breakage." I examine my nails, which aren't *that* bad.

"So does scrubbing your clothes on a washboard, *Little House on the Prairie*."

"I don't hear you complaining about my washboard when you come begging with your bags of clothes," I reply hotly. "*Ro, please do me this solid. I can't trust a washing machine with my Merino wool.*" For the record, the only reason I got into handwashing my clothes is that the carriage house doesn't have a washer/dryer hookup, and Luna's washer is at the top of her apartment, in a cramped, dark closet. Lugging my laundry baskets up there is a trial.

"Let's continue," Alex rolls on. Trevor gets the next question (my birthday) wrong, as well.

"December . . ." Trevor lets the word stretch. "First."

"October ninth," Alex swiftly corrects without consulting his notes.

"December first is *my* birthday," Daniel inserts.

"Well, that's gotta count for something."

He's gotten three out of four questions wrong so far. The last question of the first round doesn't give me much hope. I wish Luna would come over here and pretend there's a candle emergency. She can say they all caught on fire, heaps of melting wax with screaming energies all crying out for love—

"Trevor, you're falling behind," Alex reports to the room, barely containing his glee. I imagine him in a suit and tie, microphone in hand, like Bob Barker from *The Price Is Right*. "For five points: What did Romina wear on your first date?"

"A pistachio blazer with yellow gold shoulder chains and mulberry silk lining in mother-of-pearl," Trevor replies without giving it any thought whatsoever.

"Uh." Alex is quiet. "That's correct."

Trevor whoops. He requests a fist bump, then when he catches the murderous expression our game host is giving to an innocent box of Scrabble, slips his fingers between mine, drawing my wrist to his mouth. He plants a kiss there. I don't miss the heat that flashes in Alex's eyes as he follows the movement: from Trevor's grinning mouth to an opalescent scar on my wrist imprinted with the ghosts of hundreds of kisses that all belong to Alex. Every particle of oxygen in the room sucks flat against the floor for a moment, a sharp sigh, before the atmosphere stabilizes.

The next question for my team is worse.

"Romina." Alex wheels on me. All of my blood starts rushing in the wrong directions. Alex's stare is hunting. "Where did you and Trevor first have intimate relations?"

"Gross!" Allison exclaims. Mr. Yoon throws his head back, face pained.

"Alex, that's vulgar," Kristin scolds gently. "Where did you find such a lewd game?"

"We're all adults."

"You gonna ask your mom where she and Dad have had relations?" Trevor retorts.

"Shh." Alex's eyes haven't left mine. "Answer the question."

I look at Trevor. Alex moves, blocking my view. I tip up my chin, defiant. "The back of his Nissan Cube," I declare.

Everybody screams. Kristin shields her eyes, then her ears. "Ohhh noooooo. I wish I hadn't heard that. Someone please find the wine and bring it to me."

Alex pales. The glittering amusement in his eyes recedes, card lowering. He stares at me. "Correct."

It's the only response Trevor could have given. I've heard him mention it countless times as his dream sexual fantasy, which, incidentally, none of the women he's been with has yet to indulge.

Trevor is making keening noises. "We're at ten points! Who'd have thought?"

Alex rereads his card as if he forgot where he left off, where he is in general. We cycle through more questions: Kristin, Teyonna, then me. Alex blinks. "You . . . what's Trevor's favorite color?"

"I didn't get that question on my card," Trevor interrupts. "The next question should've been asking what Romina's most irritating bedroom habit is."

I raise my eyebrows. "Really, now?"

"Good lord, Alexander," Kristin says faintly.

I twist my mouth, hazarding a guess. "Something about orchid bodywash." He hates the smell of it, made from Lady of the Night orchids.

"You did Romina and Trevor so dirty with their questions," Allison snickers.

"Correct, he hates sleeping next to your flowery soap," Alex says quickly, moving on. He fires off the next few questions, and when he comes back to me, he's talking faster but his tone is flat. He isn't having fun anymore.

Play stupid games, win stupid prizes, I think. But I don't get that checkmark of satisfaction that I thought I would, to see him rattled like this.

"What's Trevor's middle name?"

Ha! I asked Trevor this question after he woke up this morning. "Joseph." *Take that.*

"That's right. Congratulations, lovebirds." Alex turns stiffly, marking up the scores. Trevor and I didn't win, but we performed better than I thought we would, and obviously better than Alex had predicted. I can't help but notice that Teyonna isn't looking too happy about what this game revealed, either, and small victories dissolve tart on my tongue.

🍃

"I don't think so," I growl, following Alex outside. He's rambling at a brisk clip through the downpour, red Buckeyes hat tugged low over his forehead, down the rocky path to the wide gravel lot. The driver's door of his black truck slams shut.

I open it back up while he's yanking the seatbelt across his body.

Alex starts, seatbelt rewinding. "Agh! What are you doing?"

"What the hell was that back there?"

He glowers. "You need to move."

"You didn't give anybody else bullshit questions like *where they've had sex* and *what are their bedroom habits*. Were you trying to embarrass me? Because it didn't work. Or are there any other details you'd still like to know? You want to know what color bra I've got on right now?" I yank my collar aside so he can view the lavender satin.

He flushes, brows knitting together as he turns away to stare through the windshield.

"You better fucking open your mouth and tell me what you were thinking back there."

"You know what I thought?" He rips his hat off, rubs a hand all over his head, then slams it back on again. Its color brings out the blood burning under his skin. "I thought you and Trevor weren't actually together. I thought you were pretending to date Trevor because you wanted an excuse to come to the wedding, to see me. Be around me."

"I didn't even know there was going to *be* a wedding when we showed up! Trevor's dad was in town, and we were going to have lunch with him, do our pitch. That's what we thought."

"Something about it felt off. Maybe the two of you saw me before I spotted you, and you cooked up a story about being together. To rub it in my face that you were with somebody else now, or to piss me off because you were with the guy who's going to be my stepbrother. I don't know."

"Because everything I do must revolve around you?"

He flinches. Doesn't meet my eyes. Then grips the steering wheel, hard, shaking it a little. Laughs without humor. "The back of his car. Goddamn."

"Why do you care?"

"I don't," he replies, razor-sharp. "Just surprised at you."

"You're not allowed to judge me." He tries to close his door, but I wrest it open wider, rain pitting off the dashboard, the steering wheel, darkening his jeans. His knee bounces uncontrollably. "It was fine for me to take my clothes off in the bed of your truck at eighteen, when we *almost* went all the way but you changed your mind—but I can't do the same with somebody else when I'm damn near thirty?"

"Not with him, you can't. He's going to be my stepbrother. How could you do this to me? How would you feel if I slept with one of your sisters?"

The words are a physical slap.

"For the last time, I didn't know you and Trevor were going to be stepbrothers. Neither did he! Or you!"

"You and Trevor don't act . . ."

"Like what?" I press.

"You don't look at each other with any kind of deeper feeling."

My hands clench. "You just think I'm incapable of wanting anyone other than you."

His eyes are piercing. "Yes. And I don't give a shit if it makes me sound conceited. Yes. As long as I'm alive, how could you be satisfied with anybody else?" He looks genuinely perplexed at the thought. "It doesn't make sense that you're over me, when every signal you send says otherwise. I thought you had to be lying about being happily in love with him; that you were sorry you dumped me and wanted to make sure I missed you back. I don't understand how I got it so wrong. Will you please let me shut my door now? I cannot fucking breathe with you here."

All I see is red. His pulse and mine, adrenaline, fury. The betrayal he exudes, the self-righteous indignation, the shock that he might be wrong about anything, ever, is an itch inside my skull that I can't scratch, inflamed by my embarrassment that he's right about some of it. I had hoped that enough time had passed, that I had changed enough, that I had become unreadable to him. It never occurred to me that he'd figure me out all over again exactly like he did the first time. He's even more perceptive now. And three times more persistent. I can't tell if Alex wants *me* to want *him* because *he* wants *me*, or if he simply craves the satisfaction of knowing I never got over him. He drives me up the goddamn wall. I don't want to be affected by this man! I hate how wildly out of control he makes me feel, and how unfair it is that I'll never be able to look at him without the floor giving out from beneath me.

I'll never be *over it*. I don't know why. I don't know what it is about this person—who I half despise right now—that has me in such an iron grip. As I stand here, allowing this cold truth to slide over me, I want to scream at the unfairness.

"Get over yourself," I reply instead, and slam his door shut.

Sure wish I could.

Chapter Seventeen

YELLOW ACACIA:
Let us disclose our hearts to no one.

Trevor bursts into my house, where I am swaddled in soft knits and cupping a mug of hot tea, *Unlikely Animal Friends* babbling on the television in an effort to drive Alex's frustrated voice from my thoughts. "We have to break up."

I snap my neck so hard toward the doorway that it pops. "What?"

"I think Teyonna's into me. She's been acting down since I kissed your arm. Which I regret now, and not just because I had to taste your flower soap. Please, Ro, I bought you that kiwi smoothie body butter for a reason. You want to smell *edible*, trust me."

I sit up, *The Green Witch's Garden* sliding off my lap. "Wasn't the plan to make Teyonna regret what she could've had?"

He thumps the ceiling with the flat of his hand. "Bro, she can HAVE it."

I picture Alex's expression if he gets wind that Trevor and I have broken up. He'll come to the conclusion that (1) he was right all along and I've been longing for him pathetically, (2) he was right about Trevor and me not being a good match, or (3) nobody wants to be with Romina.

"Trevor, if we break up *right* after we told your dad that we're each other's one true loves, he's never going to take anything else we say seriously. Do you think he'd still give us a loan? He didn't seem to be leaning in that direction to begin with."

His face falls. "Hm."

I collapse back against my pillows, exhausted. "If you have serious feelings for Teyonna again, if you see a future with her, then you should explain what happened. Tell her we only said we were dating because Allison was taunting you, that it got out of hand. Hopefully she'll keep it under wraps."

"She will."

"You think you'll get back together for real?"

"I hope so." He jumps into bed beside me, helping himself to my bowl of apple slices. "It helps that we've got a wedding coming up. Women love weddings. They get emotionally horny."

I flick his cheek.

"By the way, Kristin wanted me to pass along that the bachelorette party is tonight."

I groan. "No way. Tell her I'm sick. I can't think about anything but the fact that it takes two days to install a new sewer line, and May first is, like, two seconds away. I'm very busy sitting here feeling anxiety about things out of my control."

"See, that's *exactly* why you should go. There's going to be a masseuse. The ladies are doing a spa thing, real tame shit. Dad's got a guy coming in to teach us manly menfolk how to laser our initials into wooden keychains, so you're getting the sweeter end of the deal. Dad and Kristin originally wanted to do a joint potluck in a church basement instead of traditional bachelor and bachelorette parties." He rolls his eyes. "This was the best I could talk them into."

A massage sounds amazing. My tense muscles deserve some love. Alex won't be there, so how bad could it be? "Maybe. What time?"

"I'll find out and text you." He lands a kiss on my cheek. "Thanks for giving the all clear to tell Teyonna what's up. This doesn't mean I love you any less, you know."

"I'm bereft."

"The two of you can be sister wives, if you want. There's always room for more love."

"Stop. Your sweet talk is seducing me too much."

He laughs, helps himself to a sip of my tea. "Get outta bed. You should be over there making King miserable, not over here making yourself miserable."

"Eh, what do you know?"

"How to pull off Hammer pants." He slaps a hand against the window as he flies past it, then is off to throw himself at Teyonna's mercy.

Godspeed, my friend.

I do get up, to huff a hot breath onto the glass. An exhale, a wipe of my shirt, and the handprint smudge is gone. The motion takes me back to other smudges I wiped, from hallway portraits, in someone else's house. Sweeping up crumbs from kitchen counters, cleaning the oven, dusting cobwebs from where wall meets ceiling, scrubbing grape jelly from a refrigerator shelf. Invisible work that nobody noticed, that nobody said a thank-you for, but that if I were to cease doing it, someone would certainly notice *then*. And then I'd hear: *What do you even do around here all day?*

I happen to glance down, noticing a white flower laid across the doorstep, half trampled from Trevor's shoe. I twirl it in my hand in wonderment. Wherever this flower came from, it wasn't my garden.

♦

You know, it's interesting, the situations we will tolerate for ourselves but would hate to watch our loved ones endure. Reading the transcript of my relationship with Spencer is a sprawling kingdom of red flags, even if at the time I thought, *This is probably the best it's going to get for me now.*

If you were to ask Spencer, he would absolutely tell you that we broke up over Kleenex. *She's crazy! She dumped me with no warning, over some tissues. Who does that?*

What really happened was this: Spencer never picked up after himself, ever. And while this mess was not restricted to our bedroom—he would routinely walk over toys left lying on the floor rather than pick them up, and leave his dirty plates on the coffee table, and get aggravated with me when he had no clean underwear (which he wouldn't put in the laundry basket or wash or put away)—it was the small trash can next to his side of the bed that was ultimately my last straw, atop a Matterhorn of straws.

While emptying all of the little wastebaskets throughout the house, one day I paused before emptying his, and wondered how long it would take for him to simply do it himself. I watched as the days passed and it overflowed. When the three of us caught a cold, and he was being pathetic—*I'm so, so sick, Romina.* As if I wasn't, too!—his trash can got so full that he didn't bother aiming used tissues at it anymore, letting them pile all around it. I was already disgusted with him, but it was *this* that tipped me over the edge. This disrespect, this laziness, this refusal to be a partner, to be responsible for himself. I'd been holding out as long as I could, for Adalyn, but I could not put up with his shit for one minute longer. And Spencer, who'd been banking on me tolerating it because he was Adalyn's gatekeeper, was completely shocked. Everyone in our social circle couldn't believe that this kind, generous, sweet man had been left by a partner *twice*. Either he hadn't been listening when I asked him twelve million times to help out more, or he had decided, twelve million individual times, that it was easier to not do anything and hope I'd eventually wear myself down enough that I'd stop asking for help. I'm sure he thought, if he thought about me at all, *She'll learn it's just easier to do it by herself.*

And you know what? He was correct. Everything was easier without him.

We'd discussed ironing out a custody arrangement, because that forty-year-old child had no interest in parenting, but he reneged when Adalyn's bio mom reentered the picture. So, yes. Very easy to hate him.

Conversely, at the end of Alex and me, I couldn't summon any anger. In spite of how we ended, pain was what burnt me up because he had taken himself away from me, and the absence of Alex was *hell*. It was hell.

I am so skull-poundingly angry with him right now, though, that it rises off my body like fever, curling into the steam that wafts from the hot towel lodged behind my neck. Green goop rests heavily on my face, cucumbers cooling my eyes. We're in Kristin's bridal suite, ten massage tables crammed in wherever they can fit (two are in the hall, along with some furniture that had to be removed). A heavy-duty essential oils diffuser is expelling a mist so pervasive that even my saliva tastes like lemongrass. The masseuse has permeated the room with whale noises meant to relax us until our "bones turn to gelatin." But I'm lying here tense, stewing. My bones are brick.

How dare he leave in the middle of an argument.

How dare he think I'm here for *him*.

How dare he leave me a flower—and I'm certain he's the one who did—that, upon my research, is a tuberose, which expresses that one feels wounded. He must have bought it at Budding Romance. Every time I picture Alex striding into that shop for the sole purpose of buying a nasty little woe-is-me message and then driving over to my house, deliberately placing it on my doorstep—I am livid and astounded in equal measure. Of all the overdramatic nonsense! I returned the gesture by leaving a basket of dandelions with Half Moon Mill's reception, his name written on an attached card. I've never scavenged for dandelions so viciously before. Only wish that I could've seen his face when he recalled the meaning behind them: *Your pretentions are ridiculous.* He's got to be so vexed right now.

I've always found his boldness appealing.

"Not anymore," I mutter to myself. "I miss when you were a freshman and too scared to talk to me." I was intimidating as a fourteen-year-old, probably due to the dark eye makeup. Now I'm a pip-squeak. I wear milkmaid braids and petticoats. I spend time thinking about what type of butterfly I would be (I want to say *sunset moth*, but let's face it, I would never be a butterfly at all because I might get caught in somebody's net; nay, I would be a toadstool. Hunkered down in an unreachable cave).

"You say something?" Kristin asks drowsily from the next massage chair over.

I open my eyes, thin green slices slipping off. From my other side, Teyonna replies, "She said she misses scared freshmen."

"Haven't had a man get fresh with me in a long time," one of Trevor's aunts laments.

"Romina," one of Trevor's cousins calls. "Tell us more about you and Trevor."

Allison groans. "Tell us less. Remove what I already know. I'm still recovering from the Nissan Cube revelation."

I look over at Teyonna, expecting to see her laid out like the rest, eyes closed. But she's playing on her phone. When she notices me watching, she offers a small smile, then turns her attention back to her screen. Types on it, then shows it to me.

Trevor told me the truth.

I get out my phone, drumming up the notes app. I'm sorry for lying.

She replies: I understand. Kinda. He asked if I want to date him again.

I type: Not to be nosy, but . . . ??

She makes a so-so gesture, half-smiling, half-grimacing. I don't know, she types. He's so much fun and I've missed that, to be honest. Every time Trevor and I have seen each other one of us has been in a relationship so we've been on different pages. But this time it just felt like we clicked again, like it was the right time even though it should've felt like the wrong time bc I thought he was your bf. Does that make sense? I've been trying so hard to suppress my feelings! So now they are exploding out of me! And he's SO HOT, right!!!

I'll give him that. Oh, he's beautiful for sure. Not to persuade you one way or the other but the second he saw you here I could tell he was really into you.

I watch her eyes brighten as she reads, then she falls dramatically backward and hugs her phone, gazing dreamily up at the ceiling. Kicks her feet.

Ok yeah that's what I wanted to hear, she types, then looks sideways at me.

I text Trevor: Hey how's it going with Teyonna? When he replies immediately, I lean over so that she can watch the frenzied fleet of messages roll in.

I DON'T KNOW IF SHE LIKES ME MAN

I TRIED TALKING TO HER

I TOLD HER EVERYTHING

SHE LOOKED SUSPICIOUS WHAT DO I DO

WHY ARMPIT YOU ANSWERING

*ARENT

ARE YOU THERE WITH HER

RO IF SHE TURNS ME DOWN I'M THROWING MILF
INTO A HOLE

*MYSELF

DON'T TELL HER THAT THOUGH, TELL HER I'M WELL
ACCOSTED

*ACCOSTED

FUCKING SHIT MAN ADJUSTED I am well adjusted

We giggle madly.

"What are you people *doing* over there?" Allison calls from across the room, propped up on her elbows. Then I laugh at Teyonna, who's snapping a picture of my phone to save a copy of Trevor's texts.

"Please don't judge me for wanting documentation of this."

"It's adorable."

"*He's* adorable." She sighs. "Just *stupid* gorgeous, I swear. Makes my brain cells trickle out of my ears when I talk to him. And there's more to him than everybody sees. I know he comes off as this goofball, which he is, but there's depth to that goof-ball. I notice more of his layers as we get older."

"Plus, he's so well-adjusted," I point out with a grand sweep of my arm.

She laughs. "Okay, I need to lie back and let this facial do its work. Gotta be hot later."

I lie back, too.

"Romina?"

It's Kristin, speaking softly.

"Feeling pampered?" I ask.

"Like a baby." She frowns. "That's a lie. I can't enjoy any of this because I'm stressing over the arrangements I'll need to make if it's still raining on Sunday."

"I'm sorry. Anything I can help with?"

"Oh, honey, you're sweet." She pats my arm. "But I wanted to ask, how are you? How's it going?"

I try not to squirm. "I'm doing good."

"You've been talking to Alex again. Has it been . . . Is this the first you've talked since . . . ?"

I'm torn between a compulsion to confide in her and holding every Alex-related detail private. I settle for an island in-between, responding honestly before changing the subject. "Yeah, it's been a long time. What does your dress look like?"

"Simple, you know me." She gestures down her front, features expressive. Kristin talks with her whole body. Alex used to wave his hands wildly all around, eyebrows dancing in an exaggerated imitation while she regaled us about her day over dinner, which she'd then pretend to be insulted by. "Still don't know how I let that consultant talk me out of sleeves, but I guess it's too late now. I hope nobody criticizes me for wearing strapless."

"Why would anyone criticize you?"

"I'm an older bride, I've been married before. I asked my pastor if it's dishonest for me to wear white, and he didn't think it was a problem at all, but I still worry. Do you think I should've picked a different color? There was a champagne dress I saw, maybe it was at Georgina's Bridal up in Toledo—you ever been to Toledo? They have great seafood."

"Kristin." She has not changed a bit. "No one's going to judge you for wearing white. Almost every bride in the country wears white, regardless of how many times they've been married."

"I know, Alex thinks I'm being old-fashioned, too. My first dress was beautiful. Alex thinks it was heinous, with the big puffed sleeves, but I *loved* that dress." Her gaze is far away.

"Your new one's every bit as lovely, I'm sure."

"It is, it is. Better suited to who I am now, but it's a good thing I've got a red jacket to go with it. Strapless! Who am I, Madonna?

But anyway, that's not what we were talking about—we were talking about you and Alex, together again. The universe works in interesting ways, doesn't it?"

A jolt wracks me; it only lasts a second, but I'm positive that Kristin sees. "Uh."

"You and Alex . . . I know that was long ago," she says gently, trying to be discreet. "But I hope you don't mind if I say you and he were wonderful together."

All of the sweat on my body cools. I open my mouth, then close it. My throat has gone so dry that my eyes water with the urge to cough.

I think about Kristin and Alex holding me while I cried after getting my rejection letter from OSU.

"*We've only been dating two years,*" I had told him. "*I don't know if we can survive so much distance, hardly seeing each other. You'd barely have time for me even if I did go to OSU.*"

Alex had cupped my face in his hands, eyes bright with panic. "*Don't talk like that. I don't care that we've only been together for two years, Romina, I have loved you since I was fourteen. Nothing's going to come between us. I won't go to OSU. I won't go. We both got into Hocking. We'll go there. Being together is more important to me than where I get my degree from.*"

I recall Kristin's bloodless face. Her shock painted in stark black and white for me that, as much as I knew she loved me, she'd want what was best for Alex even if it damaged our relationship, because he could go on to have any number of girlfriends in his future but he only had one shot to get into his dream university. *Their* dream university.

Her son, her perfect angel who was going to be valedictorian, who hadn't gotten a B on his grade card since sophomore year. And me, the girl who climbed onto his lap to make him forget all responsibilities while he was trying to study, who kept him tied up on the phone late at night, who was going to derail his immaculate future because he was young and in love, and unable to appreciate the long-term ramifications. In hindsight, I know Kristin must have been thinking about her own high school boyfriends, how fleeting love is when you're a teenager, even though in the moment you think it's serious; you think it's forever.

But she couldn't verbalize this, because she wasn't the number one woman in Alex's life anymore and she knew that if she pushed him too hard she would end up being the one he alienated, not me. I was the girl he'd loved since he was fourteen, long before he ever registered on my radar.

I'd never deserve him. I would always win.

Wonderful together. If we were so wonderful together, then why'd she try to break us up?

A month after we decided we'd go to Hocking together, Kristin pressured us to change those plans, putting Alex back on the Ohio State path while I settled on Columbus State Community College. But since Columbus State didn't have dorms, we announced we'd get an apartment together. Kristin flipped out. Said he was going to get me pregnant, that we'd both end up dropping out. And that was when she started telling us we were too young to be so serious about each other, that we hadn't seen the world yet, that we should go experience life separately and, if it was meant to be, we'd find our way back to each other again someday.

I've been imagining all this time that she celebrated our breakup with champagne and confetti—surely it was a relief for her, to send him off to Ohio State without me there to distract him. Telling me eleven years later that she thought we were good together is a shove backward off a cliff.

"You and Trevor are serious, then?" she goes on. I force myself to meet her stare with neutrality. She's rooting for information, and that gleam in her eyes tells me she wants to hear *no*.

I stiffen. It requires all of my control not to snap at her.

"I hate to pry, but . . ." She drifts off, whatever she was about to say overshadowed by my jerky standing. "Are you all right?"

"Yeah, I have to use the bathroom." I pat her arm and fix on a smile. It feels like swallowing blood. "Thank you for inviting me! So relaxing. I really needed this."

Chapter Eighteen

GLADIOLUS:
Your words have wounded me.

I don't see Alex again until the following night.

It's eleven o'clock when a fist knocks heavily on the door. I'd been lying in bed dwelling on how much work the greenhouse needs, and how I might not get the chance to use it. The abrupt noise has me jumping out of my skin. I already know who's knocking.

I open the door. He stares at me, haunted and transfixed, almost as if he sleepwalked here and can't believe where he's woken up.

"You are my worst nightmare," Alex says. Then he moves past me into the house. Falls onto the couch.

I turn, processing this. "No, sure, come right on in."

"I wouldn't be here if I had anywhere else to go. I slept in an armchair in my cousin's room at the inn last night, but he found himself more attractive company for tonight."

He could certainly go home. Oreton isn't *that* far away. I'm about to point this out, temper rising, when he mumbles, face buried in a pillow: "Why do you think I haven't been back to town since I left for college? The worst thing that could happen to me would be running into you while you're with someone else." He laughs tiredly. "Figures."

He pulls the strawberry blanket over himself and doesn't say anything else.

I stomp over to my bed, switching off one of the lamps. Before I turn off the other, I glance back at him. His eyes are closed, brows lowered as he wills himself into unconsciousness. I almost take pity on him, but then I think about his parting words before he peeled off in his truck.

I march back over, grab the pillow from beneath his head, and bring it down over his back. His eyes fly open. "How dare you say that I dumped you," I snap. "How fucking dare you, Alexander King."

He straightens, twin spots of red flaring on his cheekbones. *"Me,"* he returns, low and deadly. Stabs a finger into his chest. *"Me*? How dare *you*."

I'm so mad that my mental functions begin to shut down, feet carrying me in a rote pattern back to bed. He stands up, brutally outraged, as if I'm the one with the audacity here, and he's standing over me in an instant, peeling the blanket back.

"Get away from me," I seethe. "How dare you make me love you like that, then act like the breakup was all my doing."

"You were the one so scared we'd break up that you said we should get married, and then at the first sign it would be a challenge you left me anyway."

"Me? *You're* the one who ended it."

"The fuck I did!" he yells. "Do you have any idea how badly it destroyed me to see how fast you moved on? It had never. I never. I still . . ." He lifts his hands to his head as if to fist his hair in clumps, then drops them because there's nothing to yank.

"Your texts," I throw back at him.

"I apologized for those texts. I was spiraling when I sent them."

"So was I!"

We're both breathing heavily.

"Here is what happened, and correct me if I'm wrong. Which I'm not," he begins, endeavoring to keep his tone measured. "We weren't final on where we'd go to school. You suggested we get married because you thought it would make it harder for us to break up if we found the distance difficult. Then you changed your mind. Left town after a half-assed explanation. Is that right?"

"You weren't excited about getting married. I was doing you a favor."

"We were eighteen years old!"

"I know, I know." I cross my arms, irate with myself. "I don't know what I was thinking. It felt like I . . . I freaked out because I thought I was going to lose you, so I suggested we get married, and I thought you'd react differently. With more excitement."

"I don't think my reaction was all that bad?" He's moving around the room, dazed. "I wasn't jumping up and down with euphoria, but, Romina, the logistics of that—I was thinking about the cost, where we would live, whether I could give you a nice enough wedding, whether you really meant it. It would've been one thing if you'd told me you wanted to marry me when we were older, more stable, when everything was fine, but that's not where we were. You were speaking from a position of fear."

"I meant it."

"If *you* were allowed to mean it, how could you accuse *me* of not meaning it when I said I'd make it happen? If you meant it, how could you turn around and take it back?"

"Because I realized I'd pushed you into getting engaged!"

"You did not." He bends forward, digging his hands into his eyes. I think he'd like to hit a wall. "I knew why you asked to get married. I knew you were disappointed when I wasn't immediately ecstatic. But I didn't have to be talked into it. I'd already known that I was going to end up marrying you someday. I didn't plan on it being so soon, but I loved you, I would've done anything you wanted—"

"Exactly," I interrupt, getting heated. "That right there. You would've done it because I wanted it."

He makes an animalistic noise. "You're not hearing me."

"Yes, I am. You were right to have been hesitant at first. I was offended, I was hurt, but then I realized that was my pride talking. I needed to be more pragmatic like you. Getting married wasn't the solution."

"There were better ways to deliver that revelation other than 'I'm calling off the engagement,'" he throws back.

"Your mom was right. We were too young, and you would've ended up dropping out of school. You were considering it. Kept mentioning maybe you'd like to go into construction instead—"

"I had been thinking about doing that, anyway."

"No, you weren't." The tension in here is so tight that I open the door to release some of it. Before I can storm out into the garden, he blocks the doorway with an arm across the frame.

"Oh, *please*," he spits sarcastically. "Romina, I would've picked up the sun with my bare hands and moved it if you didn't like the position of your shadow, but consider that not everything is about you. I was genuinely torn between devoting so much of my life to school, to a career that frankly was starting to scare me, or going down a different road, one that required fewer years of school, that allowed me to work with my hands in a more personally satisfying, less life-and-death way, that could support us faster, and if you don't believe that, you're being purposefully obtuse. Am I a doctor? Am I a doctor right now? *Hm*?"

"Don't you *hm* me." My hands are fists. "Oh, I hate it when you *hm* me."

He snakes an arm around my waist, faster than I can draw a breath. Brings me flush against his body.

"You're mad because you went and became a martyr so that I could attend OSU. Then I blew up your false version of reality when I told you I quit med school. I bet that just eats you alive, doesn't it?" His voice is so low, so heavy that when words fall from his mouth, they immediately hit the floor. His eyes are ferocious, black. I can't hold myself upright; he squeezes tighter to pick up my slack. "That you dumped me, thinking it would force me to do what *you* thought was best for my future, so eventually you could say you did the right thing. Guess what? You can't, because you didn't. Breaking up with me was a mistake, and you know it. We could've been together the whole time. I finished my bachelor's just to have a degree—which I could've gotten at Hocking, by the way—and hated med school. Absolutely fucking hated it. Easiest decision in the world to quit."

I flinch, but he isn't done.

"I moved to Oreton to join a buddy's renovation business, then got into carpet installation for a while before I started putting up and fixing roofs. Which I like doing. You didn't factor into any of those choices, by the way."

"I didn't break up with you," I tell him, curving back around to the beginning of our dispute. "I ended our engagement."

"Same thing."

"It was not. Right there—that's your whole issue." My chest aches. "You wouldn't listen when I tried to explain—"

"Where's Trevor, anyway?"

"What?"

It takes me a second to figure out what he's talking about. My bed is empty because Trevor and Teyonna are out late canoodling somewhere.

He's got me all mixed up, unable to lie. "It's late. I'm not arguing with you right now." I shut the front door, then march back to my bed. Switch off the remaining light. "Good night."

His voice is close in the darkness. "Where is he?"

"Go to sleep."

"You don't know? It's nearly midnight."

"I'm not his keeper. He's allowed to have a life."

Alex mutters his way to the couch. Bumps into a table.

"Anyway," I continue, once I've heard him tussle a throw blanket from the back of the couch over himself, "you were so irrational when I said we shouldn't get married, you were all 'You're gonna regret this, you broke my heart, if you come crawling back I won't have you—'"

"I did not say that!"

"Paraphrasing."

"*Exaggerating*. Because you can't stand that this might've been your fault, too. I'll admit that I shouldn't have sent those texts. I know they pushed you away. But I was *hurt*, Romina. You'd broken up with me."

"You keep saying that, but I did *not*. I only broke off the engagement. We still could have dated, you idiot, I tried to tell you that! Why did it have to be marriage or nothing when marriage had only been on the table for two seconds? But no. You didn't want to listen, and immediately started throwing out all the stuff I'd ever given you."

After I told him that we shouldn't get married, he purged himself of everything that reminded him of our relationship. CDs of playlists he burned for us, notes I'd written him, the empty container of a heart-shaped box of chocolates from Valentine's Day, the papier mâché dog I made in art class, a tribute to Lacy, his sweet old childhood dog who'd passed away over Christmas break. And, theatrically enough, even his yearbook that I'd signed and decorated. I remember pulling our junior yearbook off his shelf once and it falling directly open to the page with my picture on it, having spent its life opening to that page so many times that it remembered what the viewer wanted to see.

I was out walking with Luna when I saw him toss it into the dumpster next to his house. My sister started telling him off—which, maybe it wasn't her place to do so, but she is a very protective big sister—and Alex had never looked at me that way before: like a wounded animal, like I was the enemy who'd shot him in the leg. Later, he tried to call me, but I turned my phone off.

"I dug all of it out of the dumpster later, and believe me, I had regrets. *You* moved away without talking it out," he counters.

He came by my house the next day wanting to apologize, miserable, dark half-moons under his eyes, while I was packing my car to go stay with my great-aunt in Cuyahoga Falls. I refused to talk to him, wouldn't tell him where I was going. He watched me drive away, and that was that.

I feel his emotions pumping into the air. He falls silent for a while, long enough for my pulse to calm. But then he says, startling me: "You posted that picture."

"That wasn't what I made it look like." I might as well admit it, now that so much time has passed and it doesn't matter, anyway. I can't pretend I don't know which picture he's referring to—I posted it specifically to make him mad: Me kissing the cheek of an older boy with cheekbones as sharp as talons. I'd captioned it Muah! xoxo

"What do you mean?"

"It was just some random guy I saw at Hocking. I asked if he'd take the picture with me. He said sure. Didn't even care to know the details. I think he might've been high."

Alex is silent for a full ten seconds, then thunders, "Are you kidding me?" Light floods the room—he's standing on the other side of my bed, face tight and shadowy in the glare of the lamp.

"It was stupid." I roll out of bed, back to the wall, defenses rising even though I know I'm in the wrong here. For this bit, anyway. "You sure paid me back, though."

We stare at each other, gazes burning.

My palms are sweating. I clench my fists, unclench them. "I didn't move on as fast as you think, Alex." My voice weakens. "I didn't date anyone seriously the whole time I was in college. But you did."

Three days later, he posted: POLL: Our Little Secret or Half Moon Mill for a first date?

When I saw it, I stopped breathing for a solid minute, then let out a horrible, inhuman scream. I can still remember my mother passing by in the hallway, how she'd snapped at me. *"It's good you and that boy are over with. You were attached to each other more than was healthy."*

"I can't believe you took another girl to Our Little Secret." It's asinine to still be stuck on that after all this time, but the imagery of him and a random girl together in our favorite booth still threatens to burst a blood vessel. And I know that Our Little Secret feels like "our little secret" to everyone, to all the local couples who get lovey-dovey there on anniversaries, but when

you're a teenager in first love, it really does feel like *your* little secret. "That's where we ate dinner before prom, both years, you
asshole."

"So, you're telling me," he winds on faintly, "that you posted
that picture to make me jealous."

"Yes."

He just stares at me for a beat, crazed. Then, all at once, the
fight leaves his body.

"I posted the restaurant thing to make you jealous," he blows
out in a ragged rush, then slides down the wall to the floor. "I
made it up, too."

No.

"*No.* You didn't. Tell me you didn't."

His lets his head thump gently against the wall. *Tap, tap.*
"There was no girl." His eyes are tortured. "Of course there was
no girl. You were always the girl."

A fuzz creeps into my ears. "But that. That's why I . . ."

"Please." He shakes his head. "Don't. That makes it worse."

I can't speak. I sit down on the bed as the room spins around us.

After he posted that update, I lost it. Went on a five-day
bender, engaged in some destructive behavior that was very unlike me, including a one-night stand with some guy called Rob
I barely remember aside from the fact that he had black lights
and a ton of iguanas and was skinny as a yardstick. I left Alex a
voicemail telling him everything, half-shouting, half-crying. I
never heard from him again. That night, that voicemail, so many
other decisions I'd made, ate away at me for a long time.

He gusts another sigh. "I wanted that to be me."

I can't bear to look at him, my fingers reaching out to snatch
up a pillow, clutching it to myself for something to ground me.

"That should have been *us*. I shouldn't have waited so long . . .

that night when we almost . . . I wish . . ." His voice breaks. "I just wanted it to be special. For our first time. I thought you were worth better than the back of a truck. I wanted to give you more."

This quiet pain is unbearably worse than cursing, shouting. There is nothing more awful than Alex rolling up his sleeves to show me all the wounds I left on him, and him reckoning with the ones he gave to me.

"Please don't," I whisper. "I can't believe you lied."

"I can't believe *you* lied."

"I can't believe neither of us suspected the other lied."

"We were stupid," he says after a while. "Our brains weren't fully developed yet. Lying just to make the other person jealous? Stupid." He can't stop shaking his head. "I am so ashamed of myself. My only excuse is that we were young and dumb, but . . . Christ, what a way to treat the one we loved."

My gaze snags on the empty side of the bed where Trevor's been sleeping, and I hear an echo of Morgan's words drift in from a few days ago: *Let him see what could've been his. Make him sorry for what he lost.*

My heart breaks all over again for us. I now know, without a doubt, that he's sorry.

It doesn't feel as satisfying as I'd imagined.

Chapter Nineteen

BRAMBLE:
I was too hasty; please forgive me.

I don't want to think. I just want to forget.

But I don't. It's four a.m. and he's asleep, after what I suspect was at least an hour of pretending to be. Even in the full darkness, I could sense that he was facing me rather than the back of the couch, and in my dizzy, floating state of sleep-deprivation, interpreted it as a sign of vulnerability. Forcing me to face him and all we have done to each other, bleeding hearts on sleeves, emotions drip drip dripping onto my floor. It is entirely out of order, that we've been apart for this long, that we've reconstructed our own adult identities with a chasm between us, and yet, a handful of days together is enough to wreck all of our load-bearing beams. Or maybe I stuffed too much lavender into my dream pillow and it's making my head wonky.

Ah, the age-old question: Is it a breakthrough of clarity, or an incorrectly measured witchcraft recipe?

I end up in my garden, observing patches of starry sky between treetops that swish like black clouds, my senses settled all the way down into the pit of me, in an eerie calm as I replay the past from a new perspective, with new information. I want to think it would have changed nothing, to have better known Alex's side of our catastrophe. I badly need to believe that.

I recall Alex's face, every pixel in clear high definition when I suggested without preamble, *"What if we get married?"* His shock, pause, as he sized up whether I was serious. I couldn't be serious, could I?

But as though a different memory has been stuck to the back of that one and forgotten, the page flips to one July night at the Moonville Fair, sparkling grit of sweat on his cheekbones, our lips tasting of soft pretzels and a shared Coke, Alex's curls sticking to his temples. I was in a silky green halter dress, perfect for a summer date. A full Thunder Moon loomed close enough to distinguish every crater; the town was so warm that heat scattered off Vallis Boulevard, smoking upward, buildings wavering like mirages. Nothing felt real except for him, hands sure on my hips, treasuring me close as the evening cooled to night, until goosebumps prickled on my arms. He watched me like he'd never grow tired of it, like he was the luckiest boy to have ever lived.

"We're going to dance to this song at our wedding," he'd said in my ear. While he worked to keep his emotions level, his hand on my waist tightened, and I felt it, all of it, everything he tried to keep hidden below because he felt *so much*. So much that it stunned me, made my shoes fuse to pavement.

How had I forgotten the hitch in his voice, how deep it slid, when he threw out that casual remark? Why had I not taken *that* into account when I decided not to marry him after all? All I could think about at the time was his initial shock—understandable!— and Kristin's marriage statistics, how we were too young, hadn't seen the world yet. How she likely thought I was trying to trap him, and I loved her dearly, almost as much as I loved Alex. I wanted to prove to her that my intentions were good, that I was worthy of him.

I still haven't seen most of the world that he and I broke up for. I visit the Netherlands via Google Earth because I don't have travel-the-world money, but I flew to visit Zelda once when she was in Roanoke evacuating a hurricane. We holed up in a hotel room for three days, watching *Hart of Dixie*. I adopted five baby chicks. I can recite twenty uses for a quill of cinnamon bark. I can fix a mean tea that helps with both the common cold and the heartache that follows crushing mildly on a handsome man who walks by your store every afternoon, then one day vanishes, never to be seen again. I have yet to meet a ghost, but I *have* caught orbs on camera. I've earned a degree and found magic. I've been a mother. Romina Tempest has lived.

I must have met hundreds of men along the way. None of them made me feel the way Alex did. Too bad I messed it up, then made sure I couldn't fix it by trying to teach him a lesson.

My face burns with shame, regret. I know only one thing for sure anymore—this stupid stunt with Trevor is going to the grave with me. Alex must *never* find out I've been lying again.

Luna, Trevor, and I fret all morning at work over our diminishing time available to secure a loan from Mr. Yoon.

"We should wait to ask him about it on the wedding day," Trevor suggests. "He'll be in a great mood, and more likely to say yes."

"We can't ask him for favors on his wedding day!" I exclaim.

"Ro, my love." He settles a hand on top of my head. "You

need to get a whole lot sneakier if you're going to survive in this cutthroat world."

"I feel plenty sneaky already."

I think Trevor and Luna hear my guilt, because they exchange a concerned glance before advancing on me. Before they can dig in, however, our prayers are answered. Or perhaps, our bad news is expediated. Depends on which way this thing rolls.

Mr. Yoon stands in the doorway of our shop, face impassive, flanked by Kristin and Alex. "Dad?" Trevor jumps to attention. "I wasn't expecting you to come by today."

Mr. Yoon's lips press together. Alex's eyes flash to mine, and I read his thoughts easily. This was Kristin's idea, and Mr. Yoon wasn't thrilled to be dragged here.

My stomach drops but is swiftly caught by an unexpected net: Alex went out on a limb for me, and for Trevor by extension, coaxing Mr. Yoon to do this. He wanted to help.

"I'm Morgan." Morgan sticks out his hand. "You look like a sensible man. The Magick Happens is an amazing business opportunity you'd have to be stupid to pass up."

We all throw him evil looks.

"Don't listen to him," I cut in quickly. Morgan frowns at me, like, *I'm trying to help!*

"Does he work here?" Mr. Yoon asks, unimpressed.

"No," we all hurry to say. Except for Morgan, who replies: "I'm a volunteer."

As Luna launches into the specifics of the store, beginning with her candle-making process, I sneak a look at Alex, who's watching me. We quickly avert our gazes.

"Here's where you can find lighters, matches, natural oils to dress your candle, and votive holders," Luna tells them, showing off her favorites. "I create batches of my love oil on the Friday before a full moon."

"Oooh. Any particular reason?" Kristin wants to know.

"Friday belongs to Venus, and the moon rules passions such as love." Next, she leads them through the step-by-step of practicing candle magic; each candle in the store comes with a brief instruction card of how to dress the candle, when to light it, how long to keep it lit, how to properly extinguish it without affecting the magic at work, and how to read flames. Candles with two wicks, for twin flames, are marginally more complex.

Kristin picks up a red seven-day candle called Make Your Wish and waves it under Mr. Yoon's nose as if admiring a wine's bouquet. "You'd like this one, Daniel. It smells like cinnamon."

Mr. Yoon makes a noncommittal noise. He keeps his hands balled behind his back, not touching anything.

Trevor proudly educates them on candle disposal—if you don't dispose of a candle responsibly after using it for magic, your spell might not work right, or it might draw curious or dark energies to the scene where the spell was conducted. You can either bury the candle in your front yard, bury it in a riverbank, or leave it next to railroad tracks. There are certain ones you can drip across the road outside your house or anoint your doorway with, for protection, before they're deactivated.

"That's Maxima," Trevor tells Alex, whose gaze is locked on the crystal ball on the mantel. "It's good luck, if you want to touch it."

"I remember."

I feel an ache in my ribs—the happy, yearning sort with a three-second delay of pain—remembering right along with him. Grandma referred to Alex as *that boy*.

That boy came by the store looking for you again. That boy needs a haircut. That boy better keep his pants on. You better be treating that boy right.

Alex's gaze flickers from Trevor to me, assessing our proximity to each other; he looks swiftly away again, one hand resting on the carved wooden sign with arrows pointing in three directions: CANDLELAND, THE GARDEN, THE CAVERN OF PAPERBACK GEMS.

"How charming!" Kristin exclaims, rubbing Grandma's crystal ball. "Daniel, isn't that charming?"

He grunts. Luna and I cut each other nervous smiles, then I follow Kristin's focus to our whiteboard, with a fundraising meter drawn on it. Thanks to Zelda generously adding more of her book royalty money to it yesterday, all we need at this point to fix the sewer line is two thousand dollars, which would surely be a drop in the bucket to the wealthy Mr. Yoon. As for fixing the greenhouse, that doesn't look like it's going to happen anytime soon. I'll be lucky if we manage to tuck enough away to get that running before the end of the year.

I show them to the Garden, my fridge stocked with ready-made pieces (talismans for luck and love, mostly), the Wedding Bells wreath I was working on before their arrival. It's outfitted in Canterbury bells, bluebells, bells of Ireland, white ribbon, and an actual bell, small and silver. The tour group is squeezed in due to the limited space, and all the heady scents mixed together makes Mr. Yoon sneeze.

"How cute!" Kristin gushes, accidentally knocking over a bottle of root hormone I use for propagation. When she replaces it, the neem oil goes tumbling. "Are you online, too?"

"Yes," Luna responds before I get the chance. "We get a lot of business through our website. Fairly diverse business, too.

While physical traffic comprises mostly women, roughly half of our online demographic is actually men between the ages of thirty-five to sixty-five."

"I'd like to see the lot," Mr. Yoon interjects, clearly not interested in my flowers or Luna's stats.

"Oh. Uh, it's this way." Trevor glances at me, and I nod, feeling a bit outside of my body because this is our best shot, and I can't tell if it's going well or if I'm going to have to start downsizing. How will I choose between sea holly and red-hot poker plants? Blue poppies and Amethyst in Snow?

Luna droops after the two of them leave. I pull her close to my side, cheek against her shoulder. She tousles my hair. I already hear the conversation we'll have tonight, in which she'll insist on getting rid of some candles to make more space for my flowers, which I'll refuse. Around and around we'll go, but in the end, I shouldn't have gotten carried away planting all this stuff in the first place when I didn't have proper room, so I'll be the one digging up inventory with a trowel.

"What is it, exactly, that you need to do to the property?" Alex asks me.

"New sewer line, then repairing the asphalt afterward. The greenhouse needs a couple of panes replaced, and its floor is completely ruined thanks to backflow."

"What sort of flooring are you looking to get?"

I shrug. "That's kind of up in the air right now. I asked a contractor how much it would cost to pour concrete, and at six dollars per square foot, it comes out to almost seven hundred dollars, not including labor. But he also said that a rush job will cost more."

Alex makes a face.

"It probably doesn't sound like that much, but we're a little in the red after pooling all of our money to buy the lot," I tell him, rambling, "as well as other night market expenses. Farmers market tents, tables, industrial fans, heavy-duty extension cords, that sort of thing. Our priority right now is a fixed sewer line, so that we'll have a paved parking lot to put all the booths on. Which is why we're hoping Mr. Yoon helps us. *If* he says yes, we've got a guy who promised he'd get in here right away to work on it. We'd be able to launch the night market like we advertised, by the skin of our teeth. We wouldn't break contracts with vendors." We were quick to get business in motion, contracting all sorts of promises before we realized the full extent of sewer line damage.

"The night market," he repeats, brows furrowed.

"Yes." I can feel my eyes grow starry as I imagine it. "We want to create a labyrinth of outdoor tables and potted trees decorated in fairy lights and moonflowers. Colorful rugs, those little pouf things you can sit on. Other vendors can bring their own pieces to sell, for a fee, all of it magic-related. There isn't any nightlife in this town except for Moonshine, the bar, so we think it's an untapped market. Ours will be family-friendly. And then later, once I'm able to use the greenhouse, I'll make it pretty and open it up for people to walk through. I can do special midnight flora fortunes."

A smile spreads across his face as I chatter on. "What?" I hedge, self-conscious, but he just shakes his head, still smiling.

"These are *lovely*," Kristin remarks, jolting us out of our bubble. She lifts a yellow carnation to her nose. "Do you think I could have one?"

I smile at her, taking the carnation. "This one," I say conspiratorially, tapping her chin with it, "wouldn't suit you, I'm afraid, unless you're planning to jilt Mr. Yoon at the altar. It means *rejection*."

She claps her hands. "Really! What would you pick instead?"

"For you?" I hum, perusing our options. "For you, I would pick lily of the valley, because you've found happiness in love again. Stephanotis, for marital bliss. And . . ." My fingers hover over a vivid orange bloom, waiting for my intuition, either a sticky sensation or one that sparkles. "Bird-of-paradise."

"Ohh." She peers at me with round eyes. "What made you pick that one?"

"In any flora fortune, one particular stem usually stands out to me above all the rest, sort of a lynchpin for the magic, which I call the queen. This is your queen—romantic with a dash of excitement. Love arrived unexpectedly for you." I select grevillea as the greenery to fill out the arrangement, but magic responds with a phantom cicada hopping along my left wrist. Shuddering, I put it right back. I pluck purple statice instead and, having arrived upon the right combination, am immediately overpowered by vivid sensation.

Warm winds ripple over my skin, carrying a looming shadow I instantly recognize. I look down at the floor, and where hardwood is supposed to be, there's asphalt, a puddle of rainwater reflecting a bold pair of eyes that know me all the way to the end. Instead of hearing his voice, I'm given the visualization of it— drizzling honey, each letter that spills from his mouth linked together, lovely amber words glittering in the sun. I see the notes of Alex's laugh swirl around me, hear my name tumbling through his mind, desperate and heady as a kiss, and swallow hard against the thud of my heart in my throat.

When it all fades, I blink rapidly and catch myself before I swoon, hoping that none of what I just experienced is scribbled across my flushed face. To magic, I give my fiercest side-eye. Absolutely none of that was necessary! Or wanted! *Please just give me tasty desserts.*

Magic hums from leaf to leaf in my bouquet, satisfied and balanced. The energy I pick up from it is *I'll do what I want.*

I clear my throat. "What I would do, ordinarily, is get some wire and—"

"Mom?"

I look up. Alex isn't watching me, thankfully. He's watching Kristin, who's gone misty-eyed.

Oh, no. "Did I do something wrong?"

"No, no." She shakes her head, dabs her eyes with her sleeve. "It's . . . the bird-of-paradise. Daniel brought me those on our third date." She fans herself to dry the tears. "It was a special date, at a little diner in Hillsdale, Pennsylvania, the halfway point between Sandusky and Philadelphia. We're going to be living in Hillsdale, did I tell you? The diner has amazing French toast, and I just think it's so romantic how we fell in love halfway between my city and Daniel's. I knew, then, at that third date, that he was somebody I needed to know better. Somebody who would become important to me."

I melt. "He has excellent taste in flowers."

"And these." She taps the statice. "These were in my bouquet when I married Alex's father."

My mouth goes a bit wobbly. "They mean *remembrance.*"

"I didn't know that." A fluttery laugh. "I picked them because I liked the color." She reaches for the flowers, which I pass to her. "You've got a real eye, you know."

Kristin crying makes me want to cry, and her proud words

certainly don't help. I pull myself together. "Thank you. What sort of flowers did you pick out for your bouquet this time around?"

She hand-waves, frowning. "Originally, I thought I wouldn't need any, that I'd just keep it simple since this wedding is so last-minute."

My thoughts zigzag. I'd assumed that, like her cake and venue, she'd already had her floral decorations squared away. Very carefully, I venture, "Originally? Does that mean you've changed your mind? Because, if you have . . ." I gesture to the arrangement I made for her, letting the unspoken offer linger in the air.

I've never done arrangements for a wedding before, partly because I don't have enough inventory for big events, but also because brides would naturally want to choose their own flowers, and I'm not an ordinary florist.

But this is different. This is *Kristin*.

Her mouth opens, eyes shining with hope. "It wouldn't be too last-minute?"

It's *extremely* too last-minute. Plus, an event like this one would clean me out—between this and May Day, my garden will be empty, which means no more flora fortunes until it all grows back. I glance at the fundraising meter on our whiteboard, recollecting Mr. Yoon's skepticism. Our investment in the lot has left us hemorrhaging money and we need to recoup our losses before we collapse.

I decide to seize the chance.

"I'll do your bouquets and boutonnieres. I can do aisle flowers that double as reception table flowers, the arbor if you have one." I try to think of other wedding necessities. "The flower girl basket."

She plasters a hand over her mouth. "You will? You're sure?"

I nod. "Absolutely."

"I know it's a lot to ask for with such short notice, and I'm willing to pay extra—" She stops as she reads my face, a small smile forming. She knows exactly what I want. "Would two thousand cover it?"

Luna gasps.

I grin, reaching for Kristin's hand. Give it a firm shake. "It's a pleasure doing business."

I'm afforded a brief glimpse of Alex, watching us with unbearable tenderness in his expression, before his mother throws her arms around me and pulls me in for a hug. I close my eyes against the brush of her hair on my cheek, her familiar scent— Happy, by Clinique, and cocoa butter lotion. Although I can tell that Kristin sincerely loves my flowers and wants me to provide this service, there is something else in this hug, too. It feels like atonement. Regret for pushing Alex and me apart. Love flares inside me, so much of it that some escapes through my tear ducts; I wipe it away with the back of my wrist as we finally part. She wipes away her own, sniffs, then pats my shoulder in silent communication that she knows I understand. That she loves me, too.

"We match." She feathers her lily of the valley against the one inked into my skin. "Tattoos!" She tosses a short-lived, knowing smile up at her son. "Alex, I bet you like those."

Alex is devastated to be called out like this. He scratches his jaw. "Mom."

Luna is fairly vibrating at the news. "Thank you so much. Oh my goodness, thank you, I can't—wow. This is amazing. Romina will do the best job in the history of jobs with your wedding, I swear. You will not regret this."

I give her a look. "Why would you even say that? Why would she regret it?"

"She won't!" Luna's eyes are two spinning UFOs. "I have the utmost faith in you."

I appraise her narrowly. "You'd better."

Kristin only laughs. "I have no worries. I know Romina will do a marvelous job."

Mr. Yoon and Trevor return, Trevor shaking his head in exasperation. Mr. Yoon, interestingly, is regarding the store with begrudging respect. "He's a hard sell," Trevor grumbles to us. "There should be a statute of limitations for how long he's allowed to be upset about me spending my college money on businesses."

"That isn't it," Mr. Yoon replies simply. "Actually, Trevor, I think you've done a terrific job here. I'm quite proud, even though you should have done your due diligence and gotten an inspection first." He holds up a finger. "*Always* get an inspection before you purchase property."

Trevor begins to build his defense, but Luna grabs his arm and whispers in his ear. He shouts, "Holy shit! Thanks, K!" Then he squeezes his soon-to-be stepmother. "Never mind, Dad. We don't need you to invest anymore. Unless you wanna give us money for the hell of it—we've got a tip jar by the cash register."

As Mr. Yoon and Kristin wander back into Candleland, Luna grabs her phone, rushing off to call the plumber. I give Trevor a bear hug, squealing. "We're going to be able to open the night market!"

"Look at me!" His grin is huge. "Making Moonville less boring."

There's a heaviness in my chest at the thought of not being

able to do many fortunes for the next couple of months. But this was the best decision. "Woo! Go you."

Off to the side, Alex watches the two of us celebrate. I notice his profile turn away when Trevor kisses my cheek. At some point before everyone leaves, a sprig of yellow hyacinth is tucked into my hair, behind my ear, which I discover when I'm all alone again, leaning over my worktable. The soft, buttery blossoms fall upon a scattering of wild rose. Magic surges, encircling them in a vibrant glimmer that can only be felt, not seen.

I have to hunt for it in my notebook, because I'm so overcome with night market excitement that I can't recall the meaning of yellow hyacinth off the top of my head. When I find it, my heart tumbles.

Jealousy.

Chapter Twenty

MOSS:
How sweet is the bond
between mother and child.

One day before the wedding, the weather finally breaks, sunshine creeping between clouds that thin in the heat, dissolving.

"This weather better hold," Kristin has repeated to everybody at least twice, with a grim edge that indicates she will hold us each personally responsible if it doesn't. "Do you think the ground will be dry by tomorrow? Is there anything we can do to speed that up?"

"Yes, Mom," Alex tells her evenly. "We'll blowtorch it."

"Do you really think—?" Kristin smacks his arm. "Don't tease me! I'm getting *married* tomorrow! How would *you* like getting married in wet grass?"

Alex meets my eye for a split second, then continues his task of tying ribbons to wreaths. The two of them have returned to the shop to watch me sort out wedding flowers. I'm so busy already with May Day preparations that a Very Big, extra, short-notice task is frazzling, to say the least. I think that's partially why Alex has volunteered to be my assistant. (The other part is that we've got a crew making quick work of the sewer line right now, and Alex enjoys offering them unsolicited advice on how to do their job.)

"Sorry, Mom."

"You can make it up to me by hunting down some place cards for the reception. They were supposed to be here by now! Romina, I know you've got a lot going on already, but . . ."

Alex says to his mother, "Mom, I think she's busy."

I should leave it at that, because he's correct, but some part of me will always want to impress Kristin, make her pleased with me. "What is it? Do you need something?"

"My maid of honor was supposed to fly in yesterday, but her daughter just had a baby. A C-section, she was stalled at two centimeters for forty-eight hours, poor thing. The baby was eleven pounds! I can't imagine delivering an eleven-pound baby. Alex was seven pounds and came out in two pushes."

I'm not sure where she's going with this. "Oh . . . ?"

"Patricia will be here tomorrow, but I'd like a stand-in for the rehearsal, so that I can see *exactly* how it'll go, where everybody stands, all that. Would you mind? I know you're Trevor's plus-one, you're already helping me out so much with these flowers . . . I don't want to put you through any trouble . . ."

"I'll help out however I can."

She beams. "Oh, thank you! You won't have to do much. Just walk a few steps, stand next to me, so that we can make sure everything looks right. Short and breezy, then we're off to dinner."

"I'd be happy to."

"Wonderful! I'm so glad you're a part of this, Romina." She hugs me, tears fountaining. She's been crying nonstop today—over the flower girl's dress, because it's tiny and cute, and over the sunshine, and the new earrings Daniel surprised her with for the bride's *something new.*

A couple of hours later, Kristin has returned to check on our progress, making a sad sound over the place cards Alex has been working on. "What are these?"

"Place cards. I bought a downloadable template."

"They didn't have any with a salmon, white, and green design?"

He scratches his head. "You didn't say you wanted that."

"Those are my colors!" More tears. "Nobody cares about the colors except for me. Everything's such a mess."

"Sorry," Alex says wearily, half dead from running around all day. I've put him to work snipping things from the garden whenever I need it, as well as packing wedding flowers into biodegradable cartons that are speedily filling up not only my work fridge and my home fridge, but the one in Luna's apartment upstairs as well. "Do you want me to find different ones?"

"They're fine, they're fine. I'm sorry. Am I doing the bride-o-saurus thing? I didn't think I'd become one of those people."

"Bridezilla," Trevor supplies, struggling with a heap of string lights that Kristin's tasked him with untangling. She also bought the kind that blink on and off, but wants the lights to remain steady.

Kristin has a minor breakdown over the lights, which is only resolved when Daniel calls with his hourly update on tomorrow's weather forecast: "Seventy-two and sunny! They're saying less than forty percent chance of rain." Her mood does a one-eighty.

"All right!" Kristin claps. "The pastor's going to be at Half Moon Mill in twenty minutes, so it's time to jet. Romina, are you ready?" She smiles beatifically at her son. "I'm sure Alex will give you a ride."

He cuts her an evaluating look.

"Uh, sure." I'm at loose ends already, and the prospect of sitting in a car alone with Alex has me even more flustered. "Just let me change real quick?"

I flee the sunroom, across the courtyard. I go tearing through my wardrobe, under my bed, in my closet. "Black shoes, black shoes, where are my black shoes?" I can't ever find anything when I need it! And I swear Trevor has been stealing my perfume. This bottle was full a few days ago.

I track down my shoes, then forage for a nice pair of socks. I can tell that Aisling's been rummaging through my stuff, because older clothes I don't normally wear have turned up at the surface, like an archaeological digging site. Frog-patterned stockings. Fishnets. Socks with holes in the heels, but that I can't throw away because I might teach myself how to darn them eventually. I sit down on the bed and begin yanking on a fancy white pair with silk polka dots in dove gray. The left sock has a weird lump in the toe.

I turn it inside out, revealing a much smaller sock, white with tiny pink hearts on the ankle. Small enough to fit in my palm. It's stiff and crinkled from being scrunched into a ball throughout the drying process, my sock one of the Bermuda triangles where her miniature garments perpetually disappeared to. I stare at it, light-headed.

Adalyn.

Sometimes, I trick myself into thinking I'm all the way okay. I don't know if such a thing exists.

After I moved out of Spencer's house and he told me I'd never see her again, I turned avoidant, mapping my world around triggers: certain aisles in the store, songs Adalyn and I listened to during car rides, television shows. I was caught in a riptide of references to parenthood that crashed from every direction—until I lost the girl who'd practically been my daughter, had there been this many Pampers commercials? Every car at every stoplight showcased a sticker family on the rear windshield with a passel of scribbled children.

I put in a great deal of work to recover, at least as much as anyone could recover from something like that. At the urging of my therapist, I coaxed myself to walk by purple bottles of Johnson & Johnson nighttime baby wash at the store, Garanimals onesies with colorful animals. I can't avoid "The Wheels on the Bus" and tiny house slippers with bunny ears and washcloths ("Washclosh!") and bubbles and *I Can Learn to Read* books forever. Reminders will always appear, because Adalyn was not a splinter that could be easily excised, leaving no mark. She is all over my heart; I could probably take any object in the world and find a way to connect it to her, I loved her so completely.

One day, a few months after I moved back home, Trevor brought strawberries into the shop. When I saw the plastic carton, I immediately stumbled back in time—Adalyn loved strawberries, had a permanent red juice stain around her mouth. Trevor tossed them up in the air to catch between his teeth, and the most wonderful, ordinary thing occurred: I threw another strawberry at Trevor's while it was tumbling upward—a collision—resulting in both of them hitting Luna. I'd laughed, a shock of a noise I hadn't heard from myself in a long while. From that point on, whenever I've seen a strawberry, the dominant link is laughter. One memory's power superseding another. I'm not sure how long I'll continue to remember Adalyn's strawberry grin, but it's been pushed further back, my brain rewriting over scar tissue with a scene that makes me smile.

This sock smells like Dreft detergent. I bought this, I washed it, I dressed her in it. Peeled it off a sweaty foot at the end of the day after I carried her in from the car, tromping over dandelions in a grassy yard, dead autumn leaves, snow, my boots crunching through the top layer of ice, Adalyn and I joined at the hip from before she could crawl until she was five years old. Sliding with her on the icy walkway, balancing my purse, a shopping bag, those legs kicking, mittens a lost cause. Into the laundry basket went the sock, into the washer, dryer, back onto her foot, then onto the floor of the living room, into the washer and dryer again, her dresser drawer, under the couch, at the bottom of her toy basket. I was eternally cursing how easily they'd vanish.

I can hear *Peppa Pig* blaring in the background while I'm on my hands and knees digging under the couch, *Where'd it go?* She crammed stuff under there on purpose. Half of a rice cracker, the whole set of *Blue's Clues & You* toys she couldn't sleep without only last month. And there it is, in an alphabet bus toy. A thin pink line at the seam, the row of delicate hearts.

You are not going to fall apart right now, I tell myself harshly. Not over a wrinkled lump of cotton. But in my mind's eye, I see my hands rolling that sock over a little foot. I hear a voice proudly saying, *"Toes,"* as a chubby hand reaches toward them.

"Toes," I repeat encouragingly. "Nose. Where's your nose?"

She points.

"Good job!"

She claps, grinning.

"Where're your eyes?"

She pokes her eyelids, making me laugh. "You're so smart!" I fasten the Velcro buckle of her shoes, sit her up, finger-comb her fine blond hair. "So pretty, my sweet girl. Are you ready to go bye-bye?"

"Bye-bye!"

"Yes, bye-bye! We're going to spend the day with Aunt Luna so that Daddy can get some work done."

My eyes burn. I can't discern anything in front of me. "Romina?" someone asks, and I turn, my eyes hot and wet. Alex stands in the doorway.

"Oh, no." Another scent sweeps in to overpower the Dreft: eucalyptus, which he's been weaving around wire crowns. Calming eucalyptus is all over his hands. I feel the strangest blast of gratitude, that with this new smell, I have snapped back to the present and my chest has loosened, able to breathe again. "Romina," he repeats softly, taking me in his arms. "What's wrong?"

I sniffle into his shoulder. When I lay my cheek against it, I see his gaze shutter for a moment. "Thank you" is all I can say.

I feel him trying to puzzle out what's going on, why I'm crying. He takes the sock. "What's this?"

"It was Adalyn's."

"Who?"

I shake my head.

"Will you tell me why you're crying?"

"Because you smell like eucalyptus."

He nudges me. "You smell like a garden. Naturally."

"It's my soap. Brassavola nodosa, Lady of the Night." I stretch my socks on, finally, too dazed to be embarrassed that he wandered in here and caught me crying with a baby sock in my hands. I'm going to make him late. I'm going to ruin the rehearsal, and all I'd wanted to do was help.

"I like it." He watches me, concern deepening. "Romina. Talk to me."

The silence stretches.

"I met someone," I say slowly. He hands me a tissue, waits

while I blow my nose. "When I was twenty-one. He was thirty-eight, he had a baby. His wife had left them, and . . . he needed a lot of help."

He lowers to the floor, wordlessly sliding a black ankle boot over one of my feet. Then the other. My fingers fist the blanket as I watch.

"He kept asking me out. I'd say no, because it didn't seem like a good idea to get involved with the parent of one of the kids— did I mention that? This was at the daycare. When I worked at Over the Moon Daycare. I had Adalyn every weekday from morning till evening."

Alex listens, not interrupting.

"He was so sweet, at first. I still don't exactly know how it happened, the shift from me taking care of Adalyn to me moving into his house, taking care of both of them. I . . ." There isn't enough time to sift through all of that mess right now, and he's only being polite. He can't sincerely want to hear about this. "Anyway, the relationship ran its course, obviously, but I didn't realize that in leaving Spencer, I would be forced to lose Adalyn. I taught her how to walk and talk. Losing my role as her mom killed me."

He rests a warm hand to the side of my face. "I'm so sorry."

"I'm doing better now, but sometimes a reminder will hit me out of nowhere, and it's as if not a single day has passed since I was with her, and I start to miss her so much, it's the worst pain imaginable."

"I can tell my mom that you aren't feeling well, if you want. It's not *that* important to have a stand-in maid of honor at the rehearsal." He draws me upright, then close, clasping me into a hug.

I relax into him, but only for a heartbeat. Then I wipe my eyes. Remind myself how far I've come, how much progress

I've made, how I can wheel my shopping cart past the pacifiers without being sucked back into a nursery in my memories, fumbling in Adalyn's dark crib for a glow-in-the-dark handle. Adalyn is eight years old. By now, her memories of me must be blurred past the point where she'd recognize me on the street. She probably associates the vanilla fragrance I used to wear with birthday cakes celebrated with her dad and biological mom, her family singing to her. Loving and cherishing her, I hope. With every passing year, the little girl who once called me "Mama" and loved me more than anyone else in this world will write over all of our memories together until someday she won't remember me at all. If I made a difference in her life, she won't be aware of it. I don't get to be a part of what happens next, who she becomes. But I can take heart in knowing I did my very best in the short time we had together.

In time, a strawberry can just be a strawberry. Life goes on.

I draw a deep breath, squeezing his hand. "Let's go."

East Falls scents the air like puffs of woodsy perfume, mist pearling in the treetops, and walking beneath is like wafting through a gentle, continuous rain. Alex's left arm is an anchor as we march to the spot of grass where, tomorrow, an arbor will be crowded with bird-of-paradise and Magical Moonlight buttonbush. The pastor, who works an aggressively firm handshake, is leading Mr. Yoon and Kristin through the *And then this happens, and then that, and afterward* . . . When it's time for me to join Daniel's brother (the best man) as we glide down the invisible aisle, Alex removes his arm as anchor but gives me his eye contact, steady and centered. He accompanies his mother, as he'll be giving her away, but his gaze is trained on me. I'm situated on one side of the arbor; he joins the other, next to Trevor, third in line among groomsmen.

If anyone notices my face is blotchy, at least I don't stand out—Kristin's weepy, too. Mr. Yoon keeps fondly teasing her about it. She responds by burying her face in his shoulder.

After Kristin and Mr. Yoon exchange their practice "I do's," Alex snaps back to my side like a rubber band, arm sliding behind my waist. Trevor skips away, Alex's eyes following him with an unmistakable shine of outrage.

"I'm going to talk to him," he mutters darkly.

"About what?"

"I found you crying, and where was he? He should be here with you, not me."

"It's fine." I wave dismissively.

Alex slides in front of me to block my view of everything else, watching me carefully. "Why doesn't that bother you?"

"I'm all right, Alex. Seriously."

He looks up at the sky and sighs. "You're about to be annoyed with me."

What else is new. "Can't wait to hear where you're going with this."

"I have circled back to my belief that you and Trevor are not a couple."

"Oh, boy. This again."

"You're not in love with each other, that's for sure."

"Why would we pretend to be in love if we aren't? That's absurd. Also, our relationship is a very relaxed sort, which is exactly what I want. You're in denial."

"First of all, *you're* in denial, and you're bad at it. And yes, it *is* absurd to pretend to be in love when you're not, but call it a gut feeling—I know something's up. Secondly, there's no way that if your relationship *is* real, you're satisfied. You barely even look at him, you never walk over to stand next to him whenever he comes around. You look at me *way* more often than you look at him, I've noticed."

"Notice less, please. Your mom's getting married tomorrow, so you should try focusing on that instead."

"I'm a solid multitasker." His head tilts, tone curious. "You're blushing."

"No, I'm not."

"Why are you blushing?"

He isn't going to let this go. "I'm sunburnt, probably. Be useful and go get me some aloe vera."

"Is it because of this?" His hand flexes on my waist.

My breath catches.

"Interesting." He trails a finger up my arm, chucking me beneath the chin. "Shall we experiment?" Mischief dances in his eyes.

"Hands to yourself," I hiss.

"You first."

I frown, then look down. To my horror, my hands have found their way to his sides, tips of my fingers curled into his waistband. I leap back with a start.

Heat rushes to my face, my ears, between my thighs. Alex laughs a quiet, knowing laugh. Strolls off without a care, offering an elbow to his mom, kissing her cheek, and when he glances back at me, he winks.

Chapter Twenty-One

CORNFLOWER:
Be not over-impetuous;
my heart cannot be stormed.

R ehearsal dinner at Our Little Secret!" Kristin announces. "Chop-chop, let's go, everybody. Remember to give our name at the door. *Yoon*." She squeals. "I'm going to be Mrs. Yoon."

"Would you like some ice?" Alex asks comfortably as I climb into the passenger seat of his truck, concentrating anywhere but on him.

"For what?"

"You're looking all hot and bothered." He meets my scowl with a pleased smile. "Might help."

"Bothered as in *annoyed*."

"Bothered as in *indecent*." He clucks his tongue. "Pull down the mirror and take a look at yourself."

"I will not."

"All right, I'll look enough for the both of us." He lets out a whistle. "Whew, all this just from a hand on your waist."

My scowl deepens as he shuts my door, rounding the front. Laughing! He's trying to get me riled up. It's working.

"So," he says as he starts the engine. "What're your plans for after you're done with Trevor? Got anybody lined up?"

I snort, allowing my gaze to drift out my window. It's an awfully bouncy truck; I don't know the terminology but I'm pretty sure something is wrong with his shocks. I have to hold my door handle for dear life as we rocket over the large rocks half embedded in the parking lot, and again he has the nerve to hum placidly, all cool, easy amusement. "You love to hear yourself talk."

"You hear my voice? Rich as sin, honey, you love to hear it, too." He grins as he checks behind him, backing out.

I watch his hands on the steering wheel. Palms on the torn vinyl, fingers raised. "Like smooooooth whiskey."

"So into yourself." I reach for the music.

He bats my hand away from the dials. "No, you don't."

"Why?" I press a few buttons, howling when a CD ejects. "You still buy CDs! That's so old school."

"It's classic," he corrects, even though this isn't a proper CD. It's coated with a silver sticker, a label he didn't bother filling in.

"They have this thing called Bluetooth now," I tease. He grabs the CD from me, throwing it onto the narrow bench seat behind us.

"Hey! I wasn't done snooping."

"Don't worry, you won't run out of stuff to stick your nose in before we get to the restaurant."

So true. I page through a battered copy of *BirdWatching* magazine. He's got more of them rolled up in the glovebox.

He glances. "Reading material for my lunch break."

"Into birds, are we?"

He twitters a rapid, musical birdcall. "Was that a house wren? You'd think so! However. It was actually me. Realistic, eh?"

This successfully steals a laugh from me. I try to cough it away.

Motivated, he imitates a different birdcall, this one akin to a machine gun drill. "Chipping sparrow." He swings a look at me. "I know what you're thinking right now."

"Please tell."

"You're thinking, *Ooh, Alex is soooo good at birdcalls*, but you won't tell me so, because you don't want me to know how impressed you are."

"I'm actually thinking, *Ooh, Alex has the biggest head in the universe.*"

"Biggest, and most irresistible."

As I shake my head, his smile grows. And then, because he makes it too easy, I say, "Paul McCartney's kind of overrated, don't you think?"

"Excuse me?"

I nod toward the radio, which is playing "Bohemian Rhapsody." "Paul McCartney," I repeat, as though he's missing something obvious.

"What does he have to do with anything? This is Queen."

I squint. "Uh . . . no. I don't think it is."

He accidentally steps on the brake, then corrects. "Are you serious?"

"I'm pretty sure this is Paul McCartney. The guy from the Rolling Stones."

"WHAT?"

Alex passionately lectures me on the three different bands, their members, their songs, the fact that calling any of them overrated is an insult to the arts—nay, to all of humanity—until he catches my smirk and then completely loses his mind.

"Raising my blood pressure for fun," he grumbles.

I try to whistle. "This is a barn owl."

"It is *not*."

In a delightful stroke of fortune, the next song on the radio is "You're So Vain," which I sing directly into his face. "Look, Alex! They're playing your song. *Aww.*"

"I bet that to you, *all* songs are about me."

He grins, never removing his eyes from the road, as I sputter in response. I hate how he does that, hate it so much I lose the ability to speak. Turning all my arrows around in midair and redirecting them at me. But on the other side of that coin is another talent I can't be mad at: his ability to distract me into a better mood. Making me forget I was crying not all that long ago.

We veer into the murder mystery dinner theater parking lot, a stream of cars ahead of us and behind us all belonging to the wedding party. I hop out, refusing to make eye contact with Alex due to some principle I haven't determined yet, which he barely acknowledges, sliding right into step with his cousins, chatting with them. Trevor waves from the restaurant door, which he opened for Teyonna.

"Ro! Why'd you ride with him for?" To Alex: "King, you flirting with my girl?"

"No," he returns with a lazy dazzle of a smile. "I'm flirting with mine."

I bristle, hurrying past him. "You wish."

"Oh, Ro," Trevor whispers when we're alone, his voice pained. "Please, no. One of us was supposed to be successful with this 'make them sorry' thing! I'll never be the strong one. It had to be you."

"What show are they doing today? I can't watch *Winds of Auberville* one more time. Ted's a sweetheart, but the man couldn't reach high notes with a ladder."

"Not Alex. You deserve a man with more style than that— do you really want a guy who wears jeans and a plain-ass T-shirt every day? The same jeans, too. It's like he found one that fit right and bought twenty identical pairs. Or worse—he only has one pair! Let me set you up with my boy Keith. He's got an albino snake big as your thigh, named Amber, and the most incredible collection of slim-fit chinos."

I decide I do not hear him.

The Yoons reserved half the restaurant, long gleaming tables pushed together. The recessed lights are dim, walls aglow with neon steins and signed *Moonstruck* movie posters. Joan Finkel and Wanda Horowitz, two ladies who are in a perpetual state of 1950s dress and have been doing these shows for as long as I can remember—yet never seem to age—are moving set pieces around onstage, prepping for the show that begins in a few minutes. Judging by the men's mining clothes and the ladies' long white nightgowns, we're being treated to *The Lavender Lady*, an embellished re-creation of a local ghost story.

I wait for Trevor and Alex to pick their seats, then choose a spot far from both of them. Trevor stands up and walks directly over the empty chairs, dropping into the one beside mine.

"I know your father did not teach you to act like that in restaurants," I snip, darting a glance at Alex. He's watching us with transparent displeasure. We don't look away from each other until the lights are killed, vanishing him. Yellow hyacinth flashes through my mind, bright in the black room.

I shiver.

"Calm down, Mother." Trevor recites his order to the waitress, I give mine (manicotti with two-pound bricks of cheese inside. I'm talking cheese that wants to make a tender loving home inside your arteries), and the show begins. Twenty minutes later, I'm only just beginning to cool off.

Trevor borrows a swig of my lemonade. "Ro," he whispers, "give it to me straight. Are you boinking Alex?"

I dip my fingertips into my glass. Flick him in the face with lemonade.

He blinks the droplets away, unfazed. "As your ex-lover, I'm entitled to know."

"We have never been lovers."

"We've been bro-lovers. Brolos." He tilts his head, thinking. "If you're going to boink Alex, that makes you and I step-lovers."

"I'm not boinking anybody."

"You should, it would give your hair better body. What do you have against volumizing mousse?"

He flits away to go bother Teyonna, and at one point lets himself into the kitchen. It's astonishing that he doesn't get kicked out, but, even more astonishing: He returns with a slice of pie for me. I don't have room, sadly. You could drown somebody in a river by tying this manicotti to their ankle.

I take the opportunity to set him straight. "Trevor, I need you to grasp that if I wanted to have sex with Alex, I would," I mutter, keeping my volume down. "You don't get an opinion on it."

"Ew, it sounds so much worse when you phrase it like that. Ro, as your brolo . . . your *Robrolo*, if you will . . . I think I should get a vote on your boyfriends, and the reason I bring this up is that Keith thinks you're cute. He wanted me to pass along that he lays excellent pipe—"

"Keith, the guy with the snake?"

He pauses. "Yeah? I told him you want three kids and twenty cats. He's cool with it. I mean, you'll have to be careful with your cats around his snakes, and one of his pythons could potentially try to eat one of your kids, but—"

"Goodbye."

I get up, searching for a different spot, only to discover with a horrible jolt that Alex has relocated. He's one chair removed from Trevor now, back ramrod straight, eyes on his untouched dinner. He slowly sets down his fork. Looks up at me. He's rolled open the doors to his thoughts and is letting a rainstorm out; his eyes say *I was correct all along*.

Pulse a painful gallop, my mind drains of all language except for *Well, shit*.

I trip, lemonade sloshing over the table, and sop it up clumsily with a napkin. The cast is belting out a tune about a woman who was out collecting lavender, then got flattened by a train. I reject the possibility that Alex heard Trevor and me through all this din. I wouldn't survive the humiliation. The judgment. The *Romina Tempest, you are so pathetic*.

"Trevor." I grab him. "Let's go."

"What? The show isn't over."

"I need to get out of here, now, and I need someone to drive me away like they've just robbed a Tiffany's. How fast is your Cube?"

He jumps to his feet. "I'm in. Hang on, gotta get T. She rode with me."

"Hurry." I bustle toward the door, checking over my shoulder. My stomach flips. Alex has abandoned his seat and is walking up the sloped floor in my direction. Kristin will have to send me a picture of the wedding, because by the time she and Mr. Yoon exchange vows, I'll be building a new life in Canada. If there's anything I'm good at, it's escaping a confrontation!

Trevor tugs along a befuddled Teyonna, and it's Go Time: We fly across the parking lot, throw the doors open, and jump in, car already shifting gears before I've got my door shut.

"Lock 'em, lock 'em!"

Teyonna howls, clicking her seatbelt. "Aghh! Who'd you kill?"

"My pride! Hurry, hurry!" I grip the back of the passenger headrest hard, and we peel out of the lot, around the corner. I am exhilarated, electrified, terrified. A wobbling pair of headlights in the dusk swings toward us, twin stars rapidly approaching, rebounding off our mirrors. I detect a dark shape in the driver's seat wearing a ball cap, left arm draped out the window, idly tapping the metal body of the car.

Trevor presses the gas until the engine keens, peering over his shoulder. "What'd you do to him? Is this a sex thing? Do you like to be chased? I did not consent to participate in your kinky shit, Romina."

"I'm pretty sure he overheard us talking."

"I don't remember what we were talking about. Anything good?"

"It was clear from our conversation that we're not dating."

Teyonna *oooohhh*s. "Alex still doesn't know?"

"I was planning to take the secret to my grave."

The speed limit marker changes, and Trevor's a bullet from a barrel, firing ahead—the road out of town is barren, nothing but empty, winding highway flanked by forest, wildflowers bleeding into navy pools. I check for exits we could take, then turn around to monitor Alex's location. Teyonna shrieks with laughter. "What's he doing? Where are we even going?"

Alex appears beside us in the other lane. He meets my wide-eyed gaze with one that promises to scorch the earth, then speeds up. Passes ahead of us, sliding in front.

"Oh my," I say faintly.

Trevor's phone begins to ring in the car. He answers it, hands-free. "What up."

A familiar voice pours through the speakers. "Pull over."

Alex disconnects the call.

"Don't pull over." I'm sweating through my clothes. "How much gas is in this tank?" I lean forward from my spot in the backseat, up between them, to scope out his gauge.

"Got me in a car chase while I'm trying to digest a skillet cookie!" Trevor bounces up and down, checking his mirrors. "I *knew* you two were doing it."

"This isn't a sex thing!"

Trevor narrows his eyes at me in the rearview mirror.

Ahead of us, Alex gradually drops off in speed, slowing to fifty miles per hour, then forty-five, then forty. Thirty. At this point, I can count every fence post that streaks by, trees no longer blurring together. Thanks to all the hills, we're stuck in a no-passing zone.

Twenty miles per hour. Fifteen. Ten. Trevor honks. Hangs out the window. "Move your ass, son!"

Then we stop. Alex switches on his emergency flashers.

"Oh my lord." I clutch my seatbelt, nervous system blowing up with adrenaline.

Teyonna's phone rings. "Hello?" She cranks around to look at me. "Mm hm. Mm hm." Nods. "Got it." Calmly returns her phone to her pocket.

"He says he isn't going anywhere till he's got Romina."

"Couple of perverts," Trevor's complaining now.

I grip Teyonna's arm. "Never let your consequences catch up with you, Teyonna."

A knock at my window makes us both shriek.

I turn slowly to see Alex, leaning on the door all casually, like he could wait around all day for me to give up, face angled toward the violet sky.

Trevor rolls my window down. "You're insane," he tells him. "Maybe we'll get along better than I thought."

Alex's eyes cut to mine. His hand makes a quick dart inside my window, unlocks my door, and opens it. "After you," he says amiably.

I glare up at him. "This is extremely questionable behavior. I will get out of this car, but only because I want to, and it is my idea." I purse my lips. "Trevor drives too fast."

Some colorful language booms from the driver's seat.

"Come with me, we're going somewhere to be alone."

I grumble, stalking after him to his truck. "You're an overbearing asshole," I mutter. Alex slides behind the wheel.

"And you're a damn liar."

I press back into the seat to ground myself, stare locked on the road. I feel his loud inner dialogue hitting off every surface of the car.

He swings down a gravel exit, rumbling slowly under an overpass of laced treetops. Cuts the engine in a grove that faces the narrowest section of Foxglove Creek, our backs to the field and a narrow strip of woods.

I jump out, sprinting through the field before Alex can blink.

"Get over here," he growls.

"In my defense," I begin loudly as he slams his door and regards me, "I started pretending to date Trevor approximately five minutes before I knew you were in town. It wasn't personal."

"Feels personal."

I feint left, dart right. "His cousin was giving him a hard time for not being able to keep a girlfriend. Trevor's my friend;

my job is to wingman in whatever way is necessary. I won't apologize for that part."

He walks backward, circling, tone suggesting mere, mild curiosity. "What part are you going to apologize for?"

"You finding out."

"I see." He moves faster, a quicksilver streak in the semidarkness, and I realize he's been pulling punches with his speed.

My steps falter, but I pick back up, dancing around the truck. He loops opposite. "Maybe I didn't think it'd be the *worst* thing in the world . . . if I were to make you a little bit jealous." I lick my lips. He follows the movement, torment racing just below his skin in a sharp electrical zigzag up to his left temple.

"A little bit jealous," he repeats. "Got what you wanted yet?"

I raise my chin, searching for the thread I can pull that will make him grin, make him scowl, make him tumble to his knees at my mercy. "Yes," I reply archly. "I'd say that I certainly have, Alexander."

His head dips. "My turn."

Then he runs.

I fly for the truck, but I don't have time to open the door, he's a blaze on my heels, lighting me up from behind—I vault over the tailgate into the back instead, no plan, just the instinct to stay in motion. Alex lands with a heavy thud behind me, the whole vehicle rocking. I whirl, uncertain where to go now, strong hands landing on my upper arms with a touch that's impossibly tender. A body braces mine against the roof of the truck, coaxing me slowly backward until my vision is filled with starlight. Trevor might be on to something, because I think I enjoy being caught.

Alex pursues what he wants with thorough, willful dedication. I'm weak for it.

"You'd better be single," he grits out.

I unleash a terrible, rotten grin up at Alex that's going to eat at him, bite by bite, for days. Weeks. Years. "Too bad, I'm not. I have fifty men waiting for a piece of me."

"Fifty-one."

He bites my neck.

Chapter Twenty-Two

TIGER LILY:
My passion burns like a firebrand.

Not hard—but not so gentle, either—and I'm learning that I like that. I gasp, arching into him, and Alex swallows the gasp, mouth moving against mine. It isn't a sweet kiss. It's an explosion of relief, frustration, pressure, reprimand. Desire. My hands track up his chest, greedy, squeezing his shoulders, nails skating over his scalp. He shivers.

I tug the bill of his ball cap. "I hate how hot I'm finding you in this hat. Why is it so sexy?"

"Welcome to my world," he mutters roughly against my skin, punishing me with bites, then soothing them with his tongue. "Everything about you. You're a real fucking tease, and I like that, too." He raises his arms so that I can tug his shirt over his head. "Wish I didn't."

I trail a finger from his lower lip down his chin, throat, chest, stomach, which jumps back from my touch, muscles constricting. He watches me fathomlessly for a moment, then returns his mouth to mine again, hot and demanding, tongue sliding me open. We kiss like we want to destroy each other, take over the other person's body. "Lying on your couch, thinking about the two of you in bed," he's saying, crumpling the hem of my shirt in his fist, riding it up. "Torturing me on purpose."

I palm him between his legs and he moans, pressing closer. I squeeze. "Get down here and touch me," I command through clenched teeth.

"Tell me what you want."

"I want you to do whatever it was you were thinking about while lying on my couch."

Alex picks me up and hauls me over his shoulder, so fast that all I can squeak out is an "Oof," then jumps down from the truck. Carries me into the field and lowers me onto the long, soft grass.

Alex rolls my shirt over my head, unclasps my bra. Pins his hips against mine and slowly thrusts upward. He fills his hands with my breasts, eyes dark with frenzy, the hard length of him insistent against the seam of my shorts. I unzip them and shove them down a few inches, and he makes another deep groaning noise. My hands slip into the back pockets of his jeans to bring him closer, closer, riding him against me to the rhythm I want. "Yes," I sigh. "*Yes.*"

His tongue swirls around one of my nipples. I hold his head in place, unbearably turned on by the sight of his tongue gliding over my flesh, beading the pink crest until it's hard and swollen. His other hand is at work on my other breast, rolling my nipple between his fingers. Then he's sucking, and I see stars, his hot mouth torturously slow, dragging it with careful teeth into the cooling night. Goosebumps scatter. Then he's sucking deeply again, timing his thrusts so that he notches his hard length against my clit right when I'm already delirious with pleasure.

He cups me through my panties where I'm throbbing, making my legs jump, go watery. "Please," he rasps. "I'm dying to watch you come."

I can't think, undulating.

He grits out another "Please."

"Yes."

"Hands or mouth?"

I barely hear him, I'm so narrowed in on chasing the pleasure. "Yes."

Before I know what's happening, he's rolled us so that he's beneath me, guiding me astride him, lifting me higher up his body, fingertips digging into the backs of my thighs. I raise a questioning brow when my legs are clamped around either side of his neck.

"Come here," he says, pitch low, sliding the wet cotton strip of my underwear aside with one finger, another dragging up my center. He carefully inches me forward, guiding my body down, down, until I'm hovering over his mouth. "You'll come *here*." I don't want to apply all of my weight but he demands it, and the first lick of his tongue has me concerned I may not survive this night.

"Don't you dare be gentle," he orders when I rise back up so he can spread me with his fingers. "I've waited for you, for this. You'd better ride me like you mean it."

His hooded gaze falls between my thighs, where the heat rushes, and I do what he says.

I seat myself on his mouth and begin to move, and it's a good thing we're hidden by the grass, by the night, because I might be too far gone to care if we're visible from the road. My nipples are achingly hard where his mouth made them wet and then exposed them to the cooling air. A breeze stirs, ears freezing, lips full, warm, and roughed up from his stubble, clit throbbing. I don't think, don't see, don't hear. There's only Alex and his tongue, the pleasure he wrings, his hands guiding me up and down, back and forth.

When I'm close, I clench, and stop. Ease off.

"What are—" he begins as I tear my underwear off and turn around, unbuckling his pants. He jerks involuntarily when my hands skate across the hard ridge in his jeans. "Romina." He can barely speak. "If you—"

"Do you want me to?"

"Yes, if *you* want to. But you don't have to. I don't want you to feel—"

I unzip him, shove his jeans down to his knees, and take him into my mouth.

Alex hisses. Thrusts. Moans. I suck, and his tongue finds my body again. He adds a finger. I work faster. We turn onto our sides.

Another finger.

I wrap a hand around the base of him, silky and pulsing. Alex pumps gently into my mouth, as restrained as he can achieve when I know he wants to go deeper, faster, while I rock against his tongue and hand. He's thick and hard, so hard, I can feel he's ready, trying to hold it back.

Three fingers, and I nearly black out.

My lips are a tight seal around him. I hear his heavy breathing as he bumps the back of my throat; his fingers curl deep inside me, hitting that spot with wonderful rhythm as he begins to suck my clit, steady and relentless. I swirl my tongue around the head of his shaft one last time and he tenses, then shudders. Releases. Knowing I made him come is what sends me over the edge completely. We're gripping each other's bodies tight, tight, pressing so hard, *oh that pressure is delicious*, I am tethered to him, I am *floating*.

His eyes are fever-bright when I twist to face him again. He stares at me, then up at the stars. There's a deep pang that sparks alive in the center of my chest, radiating outward. He catches my hands when I sway dizzily, interlocking our fingers. I have missed him terribly, I have expended so much energy suppressing it, and I can't suppress it anymore. Emotions dear and tender and carried close to the heart are flowing over uncontrollably, streaming everywhere, from me into him.

I swallow, blinking back tears. Alex says nothing, only watches. Lifts a hand to my cheek, stroking softly. "*That* escalated fast. What are you thinking now?" I ask, voice a little wobbly.

"That I was going to sell this truck," he replies, "but now I can't. We put a dent in the roof."

I laugh. He grins.

Slips his fingers into my hair. "That you're beautiful," he says, delicately. "That what we're doing is probably illegal because we're naked on private property, and I'm pretty sure there's a speed trap by the bar a mile down the road."

Nothing wakes you up quite like the prospect of a cop shining his flashlight at your bare tits. I remove myself from him and go hopping around for my bra. "I am so out of shape," I lament. "My butt muscles are going to be feeling this for a while."

He has the nerve to look proud.

I shove his jeans at him. "Look at us, in the middle of nowhere, getting each other off. Who'd have thought?"

"Anybody with eyes. Leave the underwear," he says.

"In a field? Why?"

He snatches my underwear before I can step into them, stashing them in his jacket pocket.

"You've turned into a real deviant, King." I shiver, wishing I'd brought a cardigan to dinner. "It's gotten cold."

"All of my blood supply went to my dick and now I can't feel my hands or see colors anymore." He ties his shoelaces. "If you ask me what my middle name is, chances are I can't tell you."

"Louis."

He hauls me against his chest, chin on top of my head, and I reach up to pat his face, feeling the skin stretch with a smile. "Tell me what you're thinking about," he hums against me.

"I'm thinking about how good I feel. What a fan I am of your arm muscles. That I'm *freezing*." I full-body shiver. "The last time I was this cold, it was when Luna, Morgan, Trevor, and I went camping, and the floor of my tent turned out not to be waterproof. Woke up at three a.m. soaking wet."

"I can't imagine camping with Trevor." Alex's tone is grim.

"Nah, it's a lot of fun, actually. I mean, he *never* comes prepared with the usual camping equipment, completely forgets food and bug spray and all that. But he's the first person in a situation to jump into a lake with all his clothes on, first person to explore a random cave that may or may not be safe. Never a dull moment."

"And *Morgan*," he adds dryly. "Camping with Morgan, mm?"

"Oh, don't be jealous, we're just friends. Besides, I'm sure you've been camping before. You know there isn't anything sexy about mosquitoes and the smell of dead fish in the air."

"It would still be sexy for me," he says, eyes sweeping my face. Regarding me like I'm a star that fell to Earth and crash-landed in his backyard. "Name any condition, and I would still want to be all over you."

"Okay. Imagine we're in a sewer."

Alex barks a laugh. "Yeah, sure. Bring a few candles and the dripping water sounds could almost be romantic." He taps my nose. "Nobody makes me laugh like you do. You know?"

I do.

"Remember when it started to rain while we were doing the scavenger hunt?"

His eyebrow lifts a fraction. "Yeah?"

"You were looking very delicious, and I was mad about it. I wanted to lick the raindrops off you."

Alex's hold on my waist tightens. He blinks, leaning away slightly so that he can gather his bearings. "Wow. That is . . . that is hot." He pauses. "I would not have stopped you, if you'd tried. I wanted to kiss you so bad, Romina. It was physically painful to hold myself back. Even in the bakery, when you were trying to antagonize me, I would've happily had my way with you." He gestures, envisioning it. "Rolling all over the cupcakes."

I take it a step further, trying to make him smile again. "I would have mauled you on Lovisa Coe's grave."

Success! His roaring laugh makes me swell. "With Millicent Halifax watching."

"She needs new material to gossip about, anyway. And it might scandalize Lovisa enough to get her to stop disrespecting everyone's windows. She loves to slam them."

He toys with my hair, my necklace, the strap of my bra beneath my shirtsleeve.

With our sexual frustration blunted, I think we'll climb back into the truck, but he grabs me by the hips, straddling me over his thigh. Kisses me slowly.

"I like this," he murmurs. I can tell it costs him to admit it. That he's afraid of my reaction, maybe a little bit afraid of me.

"What took you so long?" I reply, and he punishes me with a nip of my earlobe.

Kissing Alex is unbelievable, in more ways than one. I'd thought the Alex chapter of my life was long-closed, never dreamed I'd have his skin on mine again, feel the brush of his mouth. *This is right, this is right* echoes neon in my bloodstream. My palms coast up his jaw; his eyes shine, heart jumping. I can see traces of the boy I fell in love with, but the man he's grown into has spun my heart like a top. He's so good at handling me, it's scary. I might be a little afraid of him, too.

The break in our timeline hasn't dulled what we had together. If anything, it's left me ravenous.

Chapter Twenty-Three

PRIMROSE:
My heart is beginning to know you.

What are you thinking?" Alex wants to know, driving down the lonely highway at a quarter to ten, moonlight a web between flecks of dirt on his windshield. "I know I just asked you that, but I like to refresh my data every two seconds, so I've gotta ask again."

"That you're cute. Ugh. It stresses me out. Do you know how hard it's been to ignore your face?" I angle toward him, cheek on the vinyl seat, and smile at his posture: relaxed, fluid. He's been tense this whole time, every minute we've spent together. I never knew exactly how much he was holding in until he let go. "You have the *best* face."

"I don't want to hear about it. You only had to suffer for a few days." He goes silent for a moment, thinking. "I always had a crush on you—can't remember a time when I didn't—but the crush grew into this uncontainable monster freshman year. I stared at you in biology while you stared at Corey Muskingham, feeling like my skin was so hot that it would start peeling right off me."

I pat his cheek lightly, my face cracking into a smile so wide that it hurts. "If it makes you feel any better, I spent so much time memorizing your profile in eleventh grade that Mr. Broeckhart wrote a note of concern to my parents in my report card. In pencil, thankfully. What a snitch."

"Corey sent me a friend request a couple years ago. I ignored it."

"Haaaa! You did not!"

"Didn't want to decline because it wasn't as if he'd personally done anything wrong to me, but I couldn't forgive how many pencils you loaned him that he didn't return. Even your fuzzy pink one with the charms on it! Asshole. I couldn't stand it. I remember walking about fifteen feet behind him one day after baseball practice, glaring at the back of his head, so jealous that I felt waves coming off me . . ." He talks with his hands, fingers spread. "Radioactive. I didn't know what to do about it, so I threw my baseball into the creek as hard as I could. Then I had to go get it, like an idiot. Mom asked why my jeans were soaked. I told her the grip of my shoes was bad, that they made me fall into the creek. Brand-new shoes." He sighs. "She made me wear my dad's old sneakers until she could buy me a different pair—these ugly, bulky ones with ridiculously bumpy treads. My new terror became, *What if Romina thinks my shoes are ugly?* Which would be even worse than my usual terror: *What if Romina never notices me?*"

"Young Alex and his new hormones." I laugh and laugh. "I forgot all about Corey. Hmm. Maybe I ought to look him up. You think he's still got that hot pink skateboard?"

He slides me an amused grin, then returns his focus to the road, shaking his head. His left hand drums the door handle continually. And then, much too quickly, we're rumbling down the alley behind the carriage house.

After he parks and the headlights shudder out, we sit in the pitch-black car for a quiet, loaded minute.

I turn toward him. "Tell me honestly." Alex's finger-drumming stills.

"Do I look like someone who just sixty-nined in a field?"

His eyes are sparks in the darkness of the cab. A flash of white teeth. "Nah."

Before I can say anything else, he unbuckles and springs across the seat, lips crushing mine. He kisses me until my mouth is swollen, one hand roving up my shirt, cupping a breast, lightly pinching a nipple, his touch desperate right up to the point when I begin to reciprocate in frenzied kind—and then he withdraws instantly, leaving me disoriented. Out of my mind with need.

He musses my hair until it's scandalously sexed-up. "There. Now you do." Then he jams the button of my seatbelt, opening my door for me from the inside. Starts the engine again.

"You're not coming in?"

He smiles at my disappointment. "I want to give you time to miss me."

"Where will you go?"

"Home." He shrugs. "Oreton isn't *that* far away."

I shove his shoulder. He laughs.

I slide out of the truck, smoothing my clothes. "Not even gonna walk me to my door. I see how it is."

"Walking you to your door is boyfriend business. You want me to be your boyfriend, Romina Romina?"

I'm so flustered by this blatant teasing that I bump my elbow into a telephone pole. *"No."* Before I unlock my back door, he calls my name.

I turn.

He leans his head out the window. "You never answered my question."

"Which question is that?"

"What's viscaria for?"

I stare at him, open-mouthed, trying and failing to remember. Before I can come up with an answer, he drives away.

It's the day of the wedding.

"Croissants," Kristin says to Daniel, standing shoulder to shoulder in Half Moon Mill's empty restaurant, gazing out onto the patio. Rain sheets down in end-of-the-world waves.

He takes her hand. "Gelato. Macarons."

"Toast," Trevor chimes in, unaware of what they're talking about, as he spreads jam on his snack. Next to him, Alex is doing the same. When he catches me watching, he licks jam off three of his fingers while holding my gaze, and I have to quickly look away before someone asks why I'm flushed. Outwardly, I'm trying to maintain my composure. Inwardly, I don't think I've stopped freaking out.

Did last night actually happen? Did I make it up? If not, what does that mean? Is Alex the kind of guy who partakes in one-night stands, and if so, am I one? Is *he* a one-night stand for me?

All I know is that I can't think about him, or anything remotely related to him, without feeling like my brain has been smushed into a juicer. But also, excessively turned on? I want to sit in a closet and stare at a wall for a few hours until I can get it together, but instead I end up in the corner with ten kids ranging from three to eleven years, most of whom are making it their mission to stain either their own nice clothes or someone else's.

"Romina, you're a lifesaver," Kristin calls. "Thank you so much!"

"No problem." I'm doling out printer paper and crayons. One of the kids gets ahold of glitter markers, which are swiftly removed. "We're going to draw pictures for Kristin and Daniel to open on their anniversary next year," I begin to explain when I notice a little boy lurking behind a nearby chair, jacket still zipped up, boots shiny with rain. He's watching us, gripping a kids' tablet in a blue safety case, looking unsure.

"Hey, there." I smile at him. "I'm Romina. We're drawing pictures for Kristin and Daniel. Would you like to color one?"

He shakes his head.

"Oh, he loves to color," a woman pipes up. "Miles, don't you want to color?" To me: "He's a little shy."

"Everyone here is super nice, I promise." I hold up the drawing I'm working on for Miles to see as the woman shifts aside to allow a few other people by. It's starting to get congested in the restaurant, but there isn't anywhere else for us all to congregate ahead of the ceremony. "I drew Kristin in a wedding dress that looks like a cupcake. What do you think?"

"I drew poop," a little girl announces, giggling.

The woman kneels to the boy's eye level, unzipping his jacket. "Coloring sounds fun," she whispers, with a rapid tickle over his belly that finesses a smile from him before he leans to the side and subdues it, rubbing the back of his hand over one eye. "You want to draw a picture, too?"

He shakes his head, retaining a white-knuckled grip on the strap of her tank top. Whispers in her ear.

She hugs him tight. "It's all right, buddy. You're going to

have so much fun today, and you can eat as much cake as you want! I love you bunches and bunches. Be good for Daddy, all right? I'll see you in a few days."

He adheres himself to her leg when she tries to leave. Side-eyes me as if to say, *No sudden movements, you!*

"I didn't see you come in," Alex says, joining us.

"I've been—" I begin, then stop.

He isn't speaking to me. The little boy wraps his arms around Alex's waist right at the moment I realize who his golden-brown ringlets remind me of, and he says in a quivery voice, "I don't want to be here with so many people, Daddy. Can we go?"

PART
TWO

Chapter Twenty-Four

LEMON GERANIUM:
There will be an unexpected meeting.

When I was eleven, I jumped a chain-link fence and fumbled the landing, snapping my right wrist. I recollect the moment I launched myself off the metal pole, how it felt like I was thirty feet up in the air—the swoop of my stomach lifting, everything inside of me rising, the peak timeless—right before the drop. I came crashing down so fast that I didn't realize all of the green blurring around me was my body rolling over grass. Three flips, then confusion. Wondering how I got all the way down there onto my back. Followed by searing pain.

Alex meets my stare and that's when it all drops. He has to know how stunned I am, but he merely smiles and says casually, "This is my son, Miles. He's a little shy at first, but chatty once he opens up." He makes Miles's arms do the wave. "Aren'tcha? Miles, this is my friend Romina."

My heart sprains.

Miles's mom points at me, eyes widening. She's pretty, with carroty hair, transparent lashes and eyebrows. "You," she gasps. "Did you used to have brown hair?"

I've lost control of my faculties. A stranger inside my body responds: "Yes."

The woman's nose scrunches adorably when she smiles. "When I met him, he had a picture of you on his fridge."

Alex reddens. "I did not."

"You did so! I told you I thought she was cute. Then you got all moody and took the picture down, hid it somewhere. Weirdo."

Alex gestures from me to her, bemused. "Romina, this is Kelsey. Miles's mom."

Kelsey's husband doesn't have to introduce himself as her husband when he appears—I know straightaway, because they're the kind of couple who look like a perfect pair. Both are heavily tattooed, from their knuckles all the way up to their necks. He's in a ribbed white tank that sticks to his amazing physique as if it's been painted on. He's got shiny black hair that cascades down his back, light brown skin, and either his left eyebrow has a scar in it where hair no longer grows or he intentionally shaves a line through it, but the effect is quite something. Kelsey pats his chest. "José, this is Romina. Alex used to have her picture on his fridge! He's embarrassed about it."

José and I nod hello.

Kelsey's eyes dart from mine to Alex's and back again. "You look kinda freaked out," she observes.

Alex tries to move closer to me, but Miles is still hugging his waist, so he arranges Miles's feet on top of his own and awkwardly side-shuffles over. Miles buries his face in Alex's side so that he won't have to look at me. "We recently reconnected," Alex tells her. I try very hard not to think about all the dexterous ways we connected. I am conscious of what my face is doing, how it keeps slipping into a deer-in-the-headlights stupor when I need for it to remain blank until I figure out how I feel. To me, Alex explains, "She and I were together a few years ago."

Kelsey slaps a hand over her chest. "Not *together*, together. We weren't even exclusive."

My mouth is dry. I try to nod along, unsure how to participate in this conversation. "Oh. Okay."

She hoots at the look on my face. "Sometimes, life goes *boom*! And you've got a Miles. And you didn't even know you *wanted* a Miles, but then you find out, and it's like, wow. I kinda really want this Miles." She tousles her son's hair.

José presses his lips to her shoulder, holding back a laugh. Kelsey pats his head. "He thinks I overshare. I'm sorry."

"It's fine," I manage, somewhat faint.

Alex seizes my waist, yanking me close to his side. I can feel the low vibrations of his contained laughter.

"Okay, so." Kelsey squints, aiming two fingers at us. "Alex, I trust you, so I don't know what *this* is but I know you're gonna do what's best for Miles. And, Romina? It was nice meeting you in person, sweetie." She hugs me. "I'm a hugger," she explains happily, squeezing.

"Yeah, you are," I rasp. "You're so strong."

She steps away, curling a bicep. "I don't wanna be one of those people who tells everybody their Peloton changed their life, but legit, Peloton changed my life."

"It's her whole personality now," José adds.

"We better get going, but thanks for the extra day," Kelsey tells Alex, trying to sneak toward the exit without Miles noticing. Miles has unburied his face and is watching the other kids curiously but hasn't yet detached from Alex's leg. "Didn't think you'd want Bert here, too much chaos, so we'll bring him next time. We got these awesome Dole whip meringues for you, though. Left 'em on that table over there!"

"I'm allergic to pineapple," Alex replies, half a second before I can.

"Whoops, my bad. You want them, Romina?"

"I'd rather she didn't." Alex slants her a meaningful look.

Her eyes widen. "Oh. Oh! Right. Yeah, don't eat those." Kelsey waves goodbye to us in the same way I've seen moms at daycare wave, imitating their toddlers—four fingers together, tapping their palms, *bye-bye*!, while holding another finger to her lips. We both assess Miles, who's shuffling cautiously toward the herd of children. Then she tiptoes away in her chunky combat boots, José following behind.

Alex turns to me. "I have him every Saturday and Sunday, but they took a vacation to Disney World, so it was either he went to the wedding rehearsal or he got an extra day at Disney."

"Yep," I say, bobbing my head. A more intelligent response cannot possibly be expected from me right now.

"Wedding rehearsals are boring when you're four. Figured he'd have more fun on tiny roller coasters."

"Yep."

He beams winningly. "I have a son."

I sit down. "So I have learned."

Miles doesn't look back at him; a boy is showing him a picture of a turd he drew (I'm pretty sure they're all drawing turds— what a fun surprise that will be for Daniel and Kristin) and Miles is showing his tablet to the boy, so Alex is basically a piece of furniture now.

Who is watching my reaction closely.

I know I have to say something, so I grapple for words. "You didn't mention you have kids."

"Kid. Only one." He holds up an index finger. "The best kid in the world. And he's *so* smart, too. He has, like, thirty dog breeds memorized and can tell you their countries of origin. He plays T-ball and has this little jersey with his last name, Hoffner, on the back, it's the cutest thing you've ever seen in your life." He's very proud. "He'll tell you he can do cartwheels but really, he just bends over and puts his head between his legs. When he grows up, he wants to work both as a veterinarian and also at Long John Silver's, his favorite restaurant."

The more I analyze Miles, the more slap-you-in-the-face-obvious it is that he's Alex's. Not just the hair, but his side-to-side dancing reminds me of elementary-age Alex. He used to get in trouble in second grade for climbing out of his seat without permission, wandering to the bookshelves, messing with building blocks. I let out a long, hissing breath. "You're a dad. You're a *dad.*"

"I know. Great, isn't he?" Alex is smiling affectionately, and there's a wistful tug in my ribs—a fervent wishing that I'd gotten to see the love in his face when he held his baby for the first time.

There's a noise in my eardrums like a snapping wind, my equilibrium off. The world tips onto its side, everybody in the room walking on the walls, across the ceiling, totally oblivious to it.

"Kids, go find your parents," Alex announces. "Miles, you're with me, little man. Are you excited to wear a special suit?"

"No."

"Won't it be fun to carry Grandma's ring in a box?"

"No."

"It's a special job. You get to be ring bearer! Remember when we asked you about being a ring bearer?"

"No."

"Wonderful! This'll be fun."

They disappear upstairs together, to get ready with the other groomsmen. I flatten myself against a wall downstairs, attention darting to the door every so often, panic quickening my pulse. I feel *deeply* strange. Out-of-body strange. It's just now hitting me: Kristin remarrying, Alex thundering back into my life, Alex's son. Why am I here? What is the point? I've already set up Kristin's flowers, so I could easily leave, nobody would even notice.

Alex has a *son*.

I fiddle with the tulle flower petals stitched to my mint tealength dress, tears rushing to my eyes. I wipe them away, hoping nobody notices. Reach into my purse for my charm bag. I turn the malachite—a beautiful, deep green stone—over in my palm, repeating its magical properties in a mantra. *Protects. Grounds and centers. Keeps the heart open.*

Alex reemerges in a suit sharp enough to draw blood. He spins. "How do I look?"

I swallow. "Very handsome." I try to help him with his tie but only succeed in creating a knot that takes five minutes to detangle. Somehow, Allison's the only one who knows how to tie a tie besides Daniel, who's busy, and she's been going around assisting all the other men. She threatens to start charging for her services.

"I'll just be down here." I try to sidle away, but Alex catches my arm.

"Ah, ah, ah. You'll just be right here."

"I can't hang around you," I whisper. "People will notice."

"So? What's wrong with hanging around me?"

I press the malachite against my breastbone, hard.

"Hey, Miss Skittish." Alex bends to look me in the eye. "You all right?"

Miles troops downstairs, slowly, one step at a time, clutching the rail. I try to leave again, but Alex takes my hand.

"I don't want to intrude. This is a special family moment."

"You're not slithering away, Romina Emily. I know your modus operandi. If I let you escape, I won't see you for the rest of the day."

"You have other things to concentrate on." I hug myself, smoothing my hands over my arms, exposed nerves. *Remember to breathe.* "Kelsey's pretty nice."

"Yeah, she's cool."

My mind leaps from lily pad to lily pad. "You had my picture on your fridge."

He grunts, helping me untangle my earring from my hair. He's standing very close, those beautiful eyes fixed on me, knowing entirely too much, fingers brushing my skin. It's unfair, his way of turning me inside out, upside down. It compels me to babble nervously.

"How long ago was this? Four years, nine months, something along those lines? Wow. The choke hold I must've had on you."

"I had loads of pictures on my fridge, since I didn't have anywhere else to put them. Figures that she noticed the one with you in it." He takes a break from pretending to adjust my jewelry to remove the choker necklace from my throat, silk weaving between his fingers.

"Do you still have it up? My picture, I mean."

A stern glance. Then he loops the ribbon around his wrist, fashioning it into a bracelet. "No."

"I bet you know where it is, though. What on earth are you doing?"

"Stealing your ribbon."

"Get your own."

"That defeats the purpose of stealing yours."

Before I can ask why he needs my ribbon, he continues, "Initially, I thought you were with Trevor." He briefly pins me with a fierce look. "Because you said you were. For a while, though, I suspected you weren't. Then, I thought you *were* again, and then after that I thought, no, I was right to have been suspicious. It's been quite a ride. I haven't had you alone to myself nearly enough until last night. I wasn't sure how to say it, how to introduce you to Miles. As a friend? *Am* I your friend?"

"I have no idea," I reply honestly.

Alex finger-combs Miles's hair. "Your pants are on backwards. Let me help you fix that."

Miles's forehead puckers as he surveys himself. "No. I want it this way."

"All right, then." Alex gives him a thumbs-up. "You look great."

Miles gives a thumbs-up, too, his small face serious.

"I don't want to be ring bearer," Miles says, and Alex inhales. Squats down.

"Why don't you want to be the ring bearer?"

"I don't want to walk, I want to sit with you."

"I'm not going to be sitting. Remember? I'm going to walk with Grandma down the aisle, and then I'll stand near Grandpa Daniel."

"Can I walk with you, too?"

"I don't see why not. Would you help us out and hold onto the ring box, though? I'm going to be holding Grandma's arm, and she'll be holding her flowers, so we need a big helper to hold the ring."

"Okay." Miles admires himself. "I like my shoes!"

"You look very nice," I hear myself say, distantly.

"Thank you. You, too." Miles isn't looking at me, and his reply is perfunctory, but Alex beams.

"She does, doesn't she?"

I am a hanger-on, uncertain of myself, my presence, my role here. All I know is that I don't like the way this uncertainty feels and it makes me want to hide.

Chapter Twenty-Five

GREEN LOCUST TREE:
Affection beyond the grave.

Patricia, the maid of honor, arrives at the last second. She and Kristin ruin their makeup crying over how beautiful the other looks. I hitch a ride with Teyonna in a car full of wedding gifts for the bride and groom, two miles away to the barn where the wedding's now going to be held. When I leave Half Moon Mill, Alex is calm and smiling. They're going to take pictures with the rest of the wedding party, then head over.

When Alex shows up at the barn, however, his eyes are bloodshot. I don't mean bloodshot as in *got a little teary during the photo shoot*. At some point between my leaving half an hour ago and now, he had to have truly *cried*. I grab his arm, startled. "You okay?"

He nods but can't bring himself to speak.

"You wanna talk about it?"

He shakes his head. Leans in to study my hand. I'm wearing six dainty rose gold rings. He slips one off my thumb and pockets it.

A few other relatives flock, asking him if he's all right. He either nods or shakes his head, depending on the question, clearly wanting to be left alone. I hear somebody whisper that he's probably thinking about his dad today, and I could smack myself, I am so dumb for not realizing that myself.

I can't imagine how hard this must be for him. Even though he seems to like Daniel and is happy to see his mom happy, he grew up in a house plastered with his parents' wedding photos. His mom is changing her last name. His dad's absence is tangible today, reminders everywhere he looks that Alex Senior is gone, that the shape his family has held nearly all of his life will change today. In less than an hour he'll gain a stepfather he barely knows and a stepbrother who hasn't been his favorite person thus far.

I monitor Trevor as he mills about, accidentally knocking a few chairs askew with his long legs. He lost his mom when he was little, too. He isn't teary, but he's more solemn than I'm used to seeing him.

The barn wasn't Daniel and Kristin's first choice, but it's gorgeous. Edison bulbs swing from the rafters, along with four elegant chandeliers. The aisle is trimmed with coral peonies, the tables and archway with bird-of-paradise, Magical Moonlight buttonbush, pale green spray I spent hours fixing together this morning. Blown-up photos of Kristin and Daniel in black and white adorn the walls; toward the back, a naked red velvet cake studded with white candy pearls is the crowning jewel in a sea of cupcakes. Bushra from Wafting Crescent is arranging them into hearts.

I find my seat in the second row on the groom's side, right next to the aisle, one of the first guests to sit down. All of the bride's and groom's relatives are still scattered, voices echoing.

This is where the reception was going to be held, and the wedding planner's flapping around, working out the logistics of setting up reception tables behind the folding chairs. A few folks in pink aprons are adding finishing touches to a candied popcorn bar. The deejay's testing the equipment. "We can't wait until after the vows to set up the reception, it follows immediately afterward," the planner's saying to a caterer. "Three long tables along the back for the buffet. We'll have to get rid of the photo booth or find a different spot for it. Food is the priority! Has anyone seen the flower girl's basket?"

Soon, all of the seats have filled with people and Pachelbel's *Canon in D Major* starts playing. Daniel in his black tux and salmon vest walks with casual ease, waving to family and friends. Trevor walks slowly, distractedly, messing with his boutonniere. The bridesmaids are decked out in stiff curls and pale green floor-length dresses, the flower girl in white with a salmon sash. Miles has changed his mind about walking with Alex at the last minute after watching everyone oooh and ahhh over the flower girl, deciding to forge bravely ahead by himself.

I feel a mixture of strange sorrow to know the life Kristin led in my warmest memories is gone and joy to know that she's found love again, and somehow I am a part of it, too, serendipitously. Before I can get carried away, the music swells and there she is, not a tear to be found for the first time today, vibrant in an organza mermaid gown with a cropped, long-sleeved red jacket, on the arm of the most incredible man I've ever known.

He's fine until he sees me. Then he presses his lips together and looks away, chest swelling. His eyes are red. Shining.

It's so distressing to see him upset that I want to stand up—he quickly wipes his eyes with his free arm as they pass me, Kristin sweeping the tips of her bouquet along my shoulder in hello. I smile back, then switch my attention to Alex. I can't see his face again until they reach the front, when he lifts Kristin's short veil and smooths it back. He tries to let her go, but she grabs his face, forcing him to bend down so that she can kiss his forehead. It leaves a big raspberry mark that everyone laughs at, which helps ease some of the tension in his body. He makes his way next to Trevor, and once I see Daniel with hearts in his eyes for Kristin I remember that I'd meant to keep my eye on him the whole time. That's what the wedding planner advised me to do: *Look at the groom while he watches the bride waltz down the aisle!*

I keep forgetting to look at the happy couple, I keep forgetting to listen when they deliver their vows. I try, especially when gentle laughs pepper the audience, but Alex is an irresistible beacon, head bowed, one hand settled atop Miles's thatch of curls while the other flexes into a fist at his side.

As soon as the couple says *I do*, there's a curious silence as the rain abruptly stops beating down. Kristin's head tilts back as her eyes run across the roof, and I know her well enough to hear exactly what she's thinking:

That this is Alex Senior and Trevor's mom saying hello, their way of blessing the day.

Chapter Twenty-Six

VISCARIA:
Will you dance with me?

Happy anniversary! I hope you've made each other smile at least once every day.

I'm poring over a station with note cards and a large vintage milk can to deposit them in. We're supposed to jot down wise marital advice (as if I'd have any) or congratulatory sentiments for Kristin and Daniel to read together next year. Most of the guests who've contributed so far have tossed in white envelopes containing money, as well. I feel a presence at my back. The tiny hairs on my neck stand on end.

"Have I mentioned that I like you in a suit?" I say without turning.

Hands smooth up my arms to my shoulders, where they rest. The clasp of another necklace is unhooked, a slight weight lifted as the cool chain snakes across my chest and disappears. I twirl.

Alex's face is innocent as he drops the chain into his pocket.

"Care to explain why you're stealing my jewelry?"

"I'm undressing you very slowly. Watch out, your dress is next."

I glance at Kristin and Daniel, who are pouring tea at the head table and serving it to their siblings. Pouring tea and serving it to the bride's and groom's parents, Kristin told me, is traditional at Korean weddings. Since their parents have passed away, the bride and groom are serving their siblings. Another tradition they're sort of incorporating is the practice of having relatives toss dates and chestnuts at them. When you're a younger Korean couple getting married, you're supposed to catch the dates and chestnuts with the fabric of your clothes. If you catch dates, you'll have sons; if you catch chestnuts, you'll have daughters. Kristin and Daniel won't be having children together, so Kristin asked me to add chestnuts and dates to her bouquet for the flower toss, to let somebody else catch the fertility.

"Are you okay?" I ask Alex. "You sure you don't want to talk? Or need a hug?"

"I'm fine, but I'll never say no to a hug."

I try to embrace him with minimal squeeze action, like how you'd greet an old family friend you haven't seen in a long time and don't remember too well, but my body loves the way he feels and I find myself sniffling into his suit, thinking about his father and Alex's feelings, which must be very mixed. He bites back a smile.

"Are you crying on my behalf?"

"Shush." I half-heartedly shove his shoulder. "Yes."

"That is . . . incredibly sweet. But I'm fine, Romina. Better than fine."

He regards Kristin, who's raising her bouquet above her head, getting ready to throw. Megan and Allison run away from the spectacle. "Not gonna try to catch it?"

"I'm pretty sure you need to have sex first in order to have kids."

He coughs into his arm, eyebrows high. "What?"

"The dates and chestnuts? Fertility."

Teyonna catches the bouquet. The room explodes with claps and cheers.

"Oh." He backs up a step, hand on his heart. "I forgot about that part. I was referring to the whole 'catch the bouquet and you'll get married next' thing."

I purse my lips. "Alexander, I don't even have a boyfriend."

"Darling, if you want one, all you have to do is ask. It's your turn to do the asking."

I shoo him aside so that I can plunk my note card into the milk can, then wander to the popcorn bar. I'm still full from dinner—the buffet was enormous—but Alex is observing me intently, which makes me nervous. I have to keep moving.

He's still hovering at my back when I grab a cupcake, hesitating with it halfway to my mouth. "You're following me."

"I'm getting up my nerve."

"For what?"

Alex sets my cupcake back down on the table. "I believe you owe me a wedding dance."

He swallows, pupils so wide that I can see myself mirrored in them. Sweat gleams at the hollow of his throat where he's unbuttoned his shirt, tie loosened.

I'm not the only one who's nervous.

Relaxing slightly, I offer him my hand, which he grasps. But then he doesn't move.

"Are we going to dance?" I prompt.

"Uh, yeah, in a . . ." His gaze slides to the deejay. "You ever think about colors and themes and that sort of thing? I mean, back then? Probably not."

"What are you talking about?"

The song changes. He says hastily, "Never mind, let's go," then captures my waist and tugs me toward him, tight against his body.

"Easy, tiger. We can't be *this* close."

"Why not?" His firm hold on my lower back agrees with his question. Then, a rumble in my ear, "You're so beautiful that it kills me a little. I'm putting you in my pocket next, to take home."

I blink at a floral centerpiece nearby, the barn fluttering soft and out of focus. I think I am being properly romanced?

We dance to "My Girl," which I am certain he requested, as we've danced to this song before, long ago at the Moonville Fair. The slow tempo is followed by a more upbeat number, one of his mother's all-time favorites, "Lay Down Sally." I try to spin him; he tries not to elbow anyone. Lifts me off the ground and holds me close, our heartbeats a rapid clip. I am half delirious.

"Fifty men," he muses, coiling a lock of my hair around his finger. "They're going to be jealous when they hear about me." He nuzzles my neck.

"No neck kissing," I say quickly. "Not here."

"So mean."

Kristin dances by with a giggling Miles standing on her shoes. She throws us an interested look, and it's automatic, how deeply I blush. Alex is being so *obvious* about . . . whatever this is. I'm not one hundred percent certain what he's up to here, and I don't like the idea of other people taking guesses.

"Look at me, Daddy!" Miles calls. He is utterly unfazed by the sight of his dad and a woman he hardly knows with their arms around each other, leaving no room for the holy spirit between them.

"You've got great moves!" Alex tells him.

"I'm dancing better than even you!"

Alex laughs, says under his breath, "Doesn't take much." Then louder: "You having fun?"

"Yeah!"

As Kristin and Miles whirl away, we edge closer to the wide-open barn doors, moonlight slanting through. One song flows into another, another, and I know when I climb into bed tonight that my feet will be killing me, but right now I could be swaying on a cloud. A few aunts have been casting *looks* at us, at Trevor and Teyonna, plainly wondering when this development occurred. A drunken, dreamy magic threads its way into the fabric of time, slackening its stitches; the longer he holds me, the less real reality becomes.

"Yo, everybody! Listen to me, I gotta get something off my chest!"

We all whirl to see Trevor in the deejay booth.

"Oh, no," I groan.

"I love Romina Tempest!"

I wave.

"But just as a friend!" He extends an arm and points directly at me, forehead damp and glistening. "Girl, you're my number one bro!"

I cup my hands around my mouth. "I love you, too, Trevor Yoon!"

"Teyonna Johnson!" he shouts at the top of his voice. I pan the crowd for Teyonna's face, finding her frozen in shock under the flower arbor. "I fucking love you! *Not* in a bro way! I wanna be with you all the time! I'm sorry to everybody I lied to about dating Romina, she and I are just pals. Allison, you suck so hard but I love you, too. I love everyone in the world, except for murderers and people like that, obviously. But everybody else!" He spreads his arms. "Circle of love! I've gotta be real!" He jumps into the audience, absently passing off the microphone to Alex, who doesn't seem to know what to do with it. Trevor high-fives me, then grabs Teyonna and kisses her. Screams of delight spark the air. Most folks are extremely drunk by now.

"Well, uh." Alex taps the mic, laughing awkwardly. "If Romina is unattached, I think I might go ahead and try to capture her for myself." He returns the microphone to the booth. Smiles shyly at me on his walk back. My heart flips on a balance beam. Misses the landing.

"Your mom's going to be upset." I fiddle with the hem of my skirt.

"Nah." He doesn't say it like *No, she won't*, but rather like *I don't care*.

But *No, she won't* turns out to be accurate. Kristin dances with Alex, possessed by happy-go-lucky wedding spirits who forgive all transgressions. Trevor steals me for a fast song. Then Miles and Trevor dance until Trevor tires him out and Miles curls up beside Patricia on a bench to fall asleep. Somehow, I end up dancing with Daniel. Kristin guides me over to him, insisting that we "must, as family." Trevor is busy rocking Teyonna in his arms, staring at her with a goofy, lovestruck grin.

"No hard feelings," Daniel says to his son. "Love makes you do strange things." Not that he has anything against me, but I think Daniel's always preferred Teyonna for his son above anyone else.

Kristin's veil is ripped. She's red-cheeked, glasses askew, curls on their last hurrah. Frosting's melting off the cupcakes, which were positioned too close to a speaker that's been hooked up since this morning and has overheated. Both of her hands are in the air. Daniel's hair is a mess from dancing with his brothers.

"Kristin, I'm sorry," I confess. "I didn't mean to trick you . . . it was a little white lie that got out of control."

"I know that, sweetie, I overheard Trevor explain it all to Teyonna days ago. He doesn't have an indoor voice." She twirls a hand. "Life is short! Have fun."

I'm still dumbstruck when Alex finds me again—it's an automatic *snap*, our bodies locking into their proper positions. His hands go *here*, and mine go *there*, and it was always meant to be that way. How does one possibly fight fate?

But how does one trust it, when fate has burned them before?

"I dreamed this up," he tells me, pulling back just enough to admire my face.

"Get your own dream. This one's mine." I stretch on tiptoes, so close to kissing him—I think he waits for it, eyelids lowering. But I hold back, because this doesn't feel like it did during our last kiss, when I was only aware of what was *between* us. This time, I'm distracted by all that's around us.

He's framed by filaments of hot gold shooting from sparklers that guests are passing around. Trevor flies by with two in each hand, high overhead. Someone wreaths glow-in-the-dark hoops over our heads like necklaces, mine red, Alex's blue. My senses buzz with the fire and laughter, the impossibility of those hands skating all over my skin, burning me through my dress. He thieves one of my diamond flower earrings, adding it to his collection.

"Mmm, don't think so," Alex tells me. "From this angle, I can see down the top of your dress. This dream's all mine, gorgeous." His sinful dimple, which appears only when his guard is down, was surely designed by a female higher power.

"That may be so, but *this* . . ." I drag a fingernail down his tie. "Is *my* fantasy, thank you very much. I want to strip you and tie up your hands with this."

Alex stiffens, and down low I feel him instantly harden against me. His hands stroke languidly up and down my spine, the curve of my hip. "You can't talk like that," he murmurs, eyes glittering black. "I'm in dress pants. We're in public."

"That's the best part."

"You evil creature." But even as he says it, he begins to dance us outside, away from witnesses.

"You started it."

He carries me out behind the barn and pins me to the smooth wood, music reverberating through the boards. We're invisible in the cool shadows, safe from prying eyes. Alex positions his hands flat against the barn on either side of my head and bends his head close, hips aligning with mine. I arch to feel him, nails digging into his back.

"Shhh," he half laughs, burying his lips against the base of my throat. Releases a tender little sigh that sweeps over the swell of my breast. The straps of my dress are well past my shoulders, traveling south. I didn't say anything to earn a *shhh*, but I know what he means by it and try to rein in my enthusiasm.

It's a struggle.

"Don't think I'll ever get enough of you." Alex groans. Slips his fingers in my hair, dropping kisses on my cheeks, jaw. Then his eyes fall closed and his mouth is covering mine, my head spinning with a delightful combination of the new and familiar; I can taste his eagerness, but I also taste his resolve. He's being methodical about this.

His touch is a slow burn, tongue exploring my mouth with the agonizing sweetness of someone who knows his power but knows how to dampen it, too, slowing time. An intoxicating rush pounds through me, fading to gray, to quiet, to feel these arms, and these lips, right where they belong.

He strokes a finger along my spine to make my back arch. Smiles against my skin. I make a noise of desperation, moving against him again. Alex laughs. *"Romina."*

"Sorry."

"Let me enjoy you without losing my ability to focus. Keep going like that and you'll lose another pair of underwear."

I consider it. "I'm fine with that. You undress me too slowly."

He bats my hand away from his belt. "Let me kiss you. Kiss me. I want you to kiss me."

"I can do that." I hook a leg around his hip, sucking his lower lip between my teeth. Let it go. He brushes the hair away from my face, mouth curving.

So we kiss, long and slow. *We have all the time in the world*, his touch says.

But I'm not sure if that's true.

He hums with pleasure, deep down in his throat, unaware that I'm not entirely present. Kissing him like this is tumbling through a void, tethered to him with nothing to find purchase on, not knowing when or where we'll land, how punishing the impact will be. I'm going to crash. It's going to bruise.

I hook my fingers in his belt loops, pinning us together, and although his eyes remain closed, his forehead furrows like he's clinging to grounding forces, mind made up. "Tomorrow," he says, eyes flashing open again, words fluttery, "we'll have break-fast together, play Go Fish with Miles. I'll look the other way when you cheat." Then he kisses me again, blazing trails of heat. "I've missed you. I've missed you so much, you have no idea, I can't describe it. It's like I'd forgotten what it feels like to be warm." His words are breaking. "I thought I'd never get to touch you again."

I peer up at him, his words sinking into the earth around my feet. I feel as if this moment sits next to our real lives without overlapping. I feel like I'm compressing into a tight coil that could spring up in surprise at any moment. A ticking clock strapped to dynamite.

He unhooks my other earring; I watch it sparkle in his palm before it joins the rest.

"Touch me now," I whisper, but he takes me by the hand abruptly, tugging me back into the barn, into the lights and the noise. It's as if he only peeled off one of my layers when he led me away, and the other half of me is still leaning against the back of the barn, staring up at the stars, that knot of dread drawing tighter, tighter.

Chapter Twenty-Seven

BLACK MULBERRY TREE:
I shall not survive you.

It's late when Alex takes me home. He can't stay long, because he has to get back to Miles, so he drives off with a smile curving his lips, anticipating the morning, when he plans to introduce me to Miles in earnest. They'll be staying at Half Moon Mill—a few wedding guests left right after the reception, which opened up a room for them.

I'm in the courtyard behind The Magick Happens, prying up stones buried in the four corners of my flower beds. Amethyst, rose quartz, moonstone, jade, all planted with the hopes of growing love. In their places, I leave black tourmaline, citrine, tiger's-eye, carnelian. For protection. My haven is fragrant with fresh rain, straw from the chicken coop. Dark, moist dirt. The pavers below my shoes are eternally wet from a hose—not only from watering my plants but also from Aisling coming back here to play with it. I can tell by a thick wedge of twigs, petals, and leaves turned to mulch, caked into the crevices along one wall where the ground dips. Indicative of water flowing down there, time and time again, carrying loose debris. I close my eyes to breathe it all in, grounded in this sanctuary where I feel the most at home, where I know what I'm doing, that my choices are *right* because they are often guided by ancient forces.

I love flowers. They're beautiful and predictable; some are capricious, some are hardy. They bring all different scents— woody, fresh, clean, earthy—and all different textures. Caterpillarish chenille plants, waxy heart leaf philodendron, velvety purple passion, papery cupid's dart. I like putting them to bed in soil and watching them slowly rise, knowing I helped create life, that I've brought loveliness into the world. Closing my eyes as I run my fingers over a plant, feeling every cell of it from root to leaf, responding to my touch. I should have just stayed in my garden and minded my business. I should have declined Kristin's invitation to participate in the scavenger hunt.

The charm bags tied to our witch hazel tree, weeping higan cherry, and royal purple smoke bush are turned out next, cinnamon and crushed rose shaken loose into a dustbin. What was I thinking, filling my home and garden with such dangerous requests? I've done nothing but draw trouble.

It was horrible enough when Alex and I broke up the first time—if we break up again, I don't think I'd ever recover. The fact that he has a child makes it riskier, because I don't know how to have a child in my life without making them part of my family.

I'm tired of losing family.

I'm not the only one who would end up hurt, either—how will Miles feel if he gets attached to me, and Alex and I break up? It's horrible, at any age, to have someone you love and depend on suddenly disappear from your life. But it's more confusing for children, who don't understand *why*, who might blame themselves.

I have only one hard and fast rule for dating. *Nobody with children*. I've never voiced this out loud to anyone, because it might make me sound insensitive. But I can't go through what I did with Adalyn, again.

And yet? Do I have a choice? It's *Alex*.

Yes, I have a choice, I argue with myself, washing my hands under the spigot, rinsing off my trowel and gloves to prevent mixing magics with their next use. Cross-pollinating protection spells with any other, such as spells for weather, could result in any number of small calamities. *End this now, gracefully, before you get in too deep.*

I'm overwhelmed. I need help. With *what*, exactly, or from whom, remains unclear.

Up above the pergola embroidered with purple wisteria and soft, tiny lights that twinkle like fairies, a window in the apartment screeches open. A head of blond curls leans out. "It's midnight, little garden elf," Luna observes, fresh-faced from a bath. "Wanna talk about it?"

I sigh. "Maybe."

She shuts the window, waiting for me up in her apartment.

Jingle and Snapdragon are stretched out on Luna's bed, engines purring, their paws curling and uncurling. Snapdragon contorts himself to rub the top of his head against my knee as I climb under the covers beside my sister.

Luna's bedroom is a nest of treasures: suncatchers hanging in the big round window, glow-in-the-dark cat eyes painted on the wardrobe doors. Rows of books by Tamora Pierce. There's a gold birdcage hanging from the rafters, stuffed with dried Spanish moss and a plush fox from our childhood that we believe might hold a two-thousand-year-old sleeping demon. Glass-front cabinets display such riches as falling-apart vintage spell-books, our grandmother's perfumes, special editions of *Tributales* books, quartz known as "witch's fingers." Jareth's crystal ball with Sarah trapped inside, from *Labyrinth*, which Luna won in a contest she found on the back of a cereal box. Harmonicas. A Disney World viewfinder souvenir of a vignette featuring us sisters barreling down Splash Mountain; every time I hold it up to my eye like a pirate's spyglass, I'm immersed in sunscreen and ocean, the music of Main Street, USA, and the awe of watching fireworks boom over the parade.

"The silver moth prophecy needs to hurry up and play itself out," I say, reaching out to spin the mottled blue plastic ball of a world globe. Antarctica rolls face up like the losing number on a die.

Yes. That's exactly where I should go to escape my mess.

"Why do you say that?" Luna closes her door, revealing an old *Death Becomes Her* poster taped to this side, the corners curling. She removes her septum ring and earrings, which fall with *clink*s into a dish, then rubs lotion onto her hands and elbows as she pads to the bed. Moves aside a bowl of milk with three Froot Loops floating around the spoon's handle as if magnetized by it, which she must have set down when she heard me in the garden. Peculiar, since I don't think I was making much noise.

"Once I meet my one true love," I tell her, "I won't ever think about Alexander King again. And then I won't have to feel this way again." Desperate. Unmoored.

"Ahh." She snuggles beside me. "Unless you're the *in over her head* sister."

I make a face. "No."

She taps my nose. "Have you considered that maybe—"

"Rawrrghhhh!" a small shape shrieks, throwing open the bedroom door and diving at us like a flying squirrel. Jingle's a quick flash of ebony, diving under the bed.

"Ash!" Luna and I cry.

"You're having a party in here without me. How cruel!"

"We're not having a party." Luna ruffles Ash's bangs. "Go back to bed. It's a school night."

Aisling burrows under the quilt like a mole, tunneling her way up to the pillows to make herself at home between us. She closes her eyes and breathes heavily, pretending to be asleep. Luna and I lock eyes, amused.

"Just keep talking like I'm not here," Ash whispers, eyes still closed.

"We were discussing what sort of summer school we should send you to," I tease. "Math camp? Or maybe one especially for . . . *dodgeball*."

"I bet you two were really gossiping about *boys*," Ash reports sourly. "Mom, I heard you on the phone telling Great-Aunt Misty that Aunt Romina is still in love with—"

Luna muffles the end of Ash's sentence with her hand. "Shh! You little eavesdropper."

I smack Luna with a pillow. "She gets it from *you*."

"Well, she gets her big mouth from—"

"Shut up." Now it's Luna's turn to have her mouth covered. I slap a hand over it, sitting up. "Did you hear that?"

"Hear what?" Both of them still, ears perking.

And there it is again—

A gentle *crash* emanating from the direction of the kitchen.

"The cats?" I suggest hopefully, as Ash exclaims, "Serial killer!"

We count the number of cats in the bedroom. Snapdragon's

still asleep at the foot of the bed. I get down on my knees beside it, spotting Jingle's effulgent eyes beneath. "She's under here."

Ash darts to the doorknob, locking it, as Luna rolls off the bed and draws a long sword from the depths of her closet. It's foam. She made it to wear with her costume for *Tributales* conventions, dressing like her favorite character, a troll called Byorgilaf, from her favorite fantasy series. While Zelda favors werewolves, hobgoblins, and giant raven-spider hybrids in her fantasy, Luna's tastes are more of the medieval dragons-and-swordplay variety in which everyone has really long names with lots of vowels.

Aisling wields the remote control. I grab a hardcover copy of *The Tributales Three*, which is so dense (both literally and figuratively) that it doubles as a weapon.

"Stay in here," Luna orders her daughter, unlocking the door. Ash doesn't listen, creeping behind us down the hall. I try to gently kick her back into the bedroom with my foot, but she dodges.

"Do you want me to call 911?" she whispers.

"Shh."

"I wouldn't be messing around in a house full of witches if I were you," Luna calls out, voice even. I'm quaking in my gingham socks behind her. I want to be Luna when I grow up.

"Witches, eh?" We turn the corner into the kitchen, where a redheaded woman is rummaging through cabinets. "What are you going to do? Make me fall in love to death?"

We've been shrieking and babbling nonsense for the past five minutes. Zelda treads water in the chaos of our arms. "Not a single normal decaffeinated tea bag in the whole house! Nothing but weird stuff that's supposed to meddle with my future."

"Decaffeinated?" I repeat. "Who are you?"

"Aunt Zelda!" Ash cries, attaching herself to my sister's waist. "You're here! Just in time. These two are trying to make me play dodgeball, and they won't tell me *any* gossip. I have to hide on the stairs to hear anything good."

"Very rude of them," Zelda agrees, eyes narrowed at Luna and me. "No one's been responding to my texts. Do you have any idea how annoying that is?"

"Yes." I beam at her, my arms around her neck.

"Monsters, I say. Both of you."

"I knew you were coming, I could sense it," Luna gloats.

Zelda rolls her eyes. "You could not."

Hm. Come to think of it. "I must've subconsciously known, too. I swear magic's been planting echoes of you all over the place. Every closet I've opened this week smells like the ocean for some reason."

Zelda turns to Luna. "Well done. You've brainwashed her."

"She's brainwashed me, too! Save me." Aisling's unzipping Zelda's bag, rooting through it. "Oooh, Pringles! Can I have these?"

I peek through the blinds onto the front street, where a station wagon is parked. "What'd you do with the camper van?"

"Esmerelda was on her last legs, so I had to send her off to the great junkyard in the sky." She picks up Luna's foam sword, pokes her with it. "What if I was a robber? What's this gonna do?"

"Distract you while I get *this*." Luna opens the freezer, retrieving a box of three-year-old freezer-burnt asparagus. A jagged dagger tips out.

I jump back. Aisling tries to grab for it. Luna frowns, rolling the dagger from hand to hand. "Ouch. Keeps sticking to my skin."

"I'm glad you didn't attack me in the dark," Zelda tells us, "or I'd be on the floor right now, dying. From laughter. Luna, it took you, like, six minutes to open that box." She tears off her jacket and lays it over the back of the couch, revealing a floor-length black dress that makes her look like she's in mourning. Her fashion sense is self-described as "goth Emily Dickinson meets art curator who's going through a divorce and trying to rediscover her fun side"—all black with a tiny splash of color. Pearl cameos featuring zombies, miniature cereal box brooches, hot pink panda earrings. Striped pointy boots with spurs. Today's color pop is a sparkly Pusheen hairpin. "By the way," she tells Luna, "we need to clear all of your junk out the attic, because I'm moving in."

Luna blubbers at Zelda that she's insensitive when it comes to people who just really love to collect stuff and we've missed her tremendously. Zelda expels a sigh at the ceiling while we jump around her in a tight huddle. "Curses, misery, bother, blast," she mutters. (When Zelda is excitable, she becomes a glitching thesaurus.) She stiffens and raises her shoulders up to her ears, but once we've disbanded I detect a microscopic gleam in the corner of her eye.

Ash leads our small parade back to Luna's bedroom. With so many Tempests in Luna's bed, we have to lie in it sideways. "I can't sleep without a fan on," I complain.

Ash whines. "I can't sleep without the TV on."

"I can't sleep, period," Luna replies, "because my bed's full of other people."

We ignore her, Aisling hunting for *The Dark Crystal: Age of Resistance* on Netflix while I plug in a box fan. Then I snuggle close to Ash, tousling her hair until her eyes grow heavy. The familiarity of my loves—Aisling wearing her mother's tie-dye maxi skirt, fabric bunched together at the waistband with a scrunchie because it's too big on her; Zelda's river of orange-red hair, scented with sea, sunlight, and coconut; the sunflower tattooed on Luna's shoulder, the small bump on her narrow nose in profile—all combine to form a thick lump in my throat. No matter what happens, where I go, how badly I mess up, I'll never lose these three.

"So," Zelda mentions finally, with a careful eye toward her sleeping niece, "what's all this gossip I've been missing?"

At last, I tell them both about Alex. How right it feels, being close to him again, and how terrifying. I tell them about Miles. The subject wanders to kids in general.

"I love being able to get up in the morning and work all day long if I want to," Zelda says, kneading a knot in her calf. "Not fitting my day around others' needs. I love the freedom of knowing I could jump on a plane tomorrow, fly around the world, stay gone as long as I want."

"Mm," Luna and I both hum.

"Sometimes men lie to me. Say they'd be good with not having kids, but then it turns out they thought they could change my mind. I'm tired of always feeling like I have to justify my reproductive choices."

I tie a gold thread at the end of a thin braid I've woven into her hair. I've always loved playing with Zelda's beautiful hair. When I was little, she cut it to chin-length and I actually cried, which she and Luna teased me for. Such are the woes of being the baby sister. "I'm sorry."

"Oh, and a favorite pickup line," she goes on. "*You'd look so good pregnant with my baby.*"

"Ew! Has someone seriously said that to you?"

"An old landlord. All credit goes to him for my transition to the camper van lifestyle."

"Gross." Luna makes a face. "Give me his name and address."

"Feels like everybody thinks they know what I want better than I do, trying to convince me my life has a hole in it. That it doesn't have enough meaning unless I'm a parent, that I won't know real love unless I have children, and I'll change my mind sooner or later. Like I have to have kids in order to be a whole, fulfilled person."

Understanding crosses Luna's face. "Something happen with Zeke?"

Zelda releases a long, slow exhale. "It's over."

"He do something to you?"

"No, he was perfectly wonderful."

Luna and I exchange glances. "Then what happened?" I venture. Much like her penchant for moving restlessly around the country, she's swift to end relationships before they've truly begun.

"*I* did," she replies darkly, emotionally zipping up. "I happened."

When she doesn't elaborate, I sense her desire for a change of subject. "You're whole just as you are, Zelda," I tell her. "I love your life for you. I love Luna's life for her. Both are equally worthy."

"What about yours?" Luna's looking at me.

"I love mine for me. For now. But you both know I want kids. It's so weird, the peer pressure we get, to have them when you're young and energetic, to have them when you're older and more settled—"

"To have another one the second you've popped out your

first," Luna cuts in. "I get that from Dad and Dawn sometimes. *When are you going to give Aisling a sister? She must be so lonely!*"

"Boundaries!"

"There aren't any." Zelda folds her pillow in half, punching it to get comfy. "Why do I have to justify myself? What's wrong with being fulfilled by working and traveling?"

I like to stay busy with my work, but I'm a homebody. "Whenever I'm away from Moonville, I spend the whole time thinking, *This is nice, but I can't wait to go home.* I find traveling stressful."

"You'd have to pry me out of this town with an ice pick," Luna declares. "You know, at this stage of my life, I can't see myself having another baby. I used to be eaten up with guilt over that, not giving Ash a sibling, like she was missing out, but if I'd had another kid, I wouldn't have been able to give Ash as much time and attention. Now, Ash has everything she wants, so I don't regret it. I think society makes women second-guess their choices no matter what they are."

"Give me all of the babies," I declare. "I want five."

"Five!" they crow.

"I thought the magic number was three?" Luna props her chin in hand.

"That was before I held one of Trevor's baby cousins the other day. Every time I see a baby, the number grows."

They laugh.

"Good." Zelda grabs her contacts case, removes her lenses. "I'll get to snuggle your babies for a while, then give them back to you when they start crying."

"The best arrangement," Luna agrees. After a long look at Aisling, she switches off the TV. "I *cannot* sleep with the television on. I don't know where she gets that."

Mutually validated, we all wind down. Some time later, I break the silence. "Zel?"

A few beats pass. "Hm?"

"Why're you here?"

She pats my head sleepily. "To help with the night market, silly. And, I'm tired of missing out on everything that happens around here, watching Ash grow up." I sense an undercurrent to her words—maybe she's running from something. Zelda's told us a hundred times that she had no interest in moving back to Moonville.

On the other side of Ash, Luna reaches across to grab my waist, shaking me just a bit in a silent show of excitement. *This means she's here to stay!* I feel her thinking.

I'm in a cocoon of safety—my sisters, my niece, Snapdragon. Jingle, too, judging by the set of small, careful paws sinking into the mattress near my feet. The hum of a breeze through the cracked window and corresponding flutter of pale curtains, the smell of wooden bowls with blown-out floating candles, the soft old carpet, the half-paneled walls, and Luna's house slippers discarded on a rainbow rug. This place is my constant.

I cannot risk it.

Chapter Twenty-Eight

STRIPED CARNATIONS:
I can't be with you.

"I can get you over here." Trevor herds a gaggle of women, their arms laden with candles and crowns, to a second cash register that's only necessary on the holidays. The Magick Happens is a friendly clamor of bells chiming every time the door opens, Southwind's traditional Celtic music, hot paper curling from receipt printers, and exclamations. Every doorway's vibrant with May flowers—pansies, forsythia, yarrow, lilies. Streamers in white, dark green, and red cascade from witch bells, light fixtures, the stairs, every flower coronet. It is May Day, my favorite twenty-four hours of the year.

"You write a wish on it," I'm telling a young couple visiting from upstate, pressing a scrap of cloth into their palms. "Then tie it to one of those trees." I indicate the hawthorn, ash, and sycamore trees growing out of the sidewalk out front, roots unfurling deep below the road. Our town was built to accommodate nature as much as possible, some of our buildings shaped irregularly to fit around the trees that laid claim first. "Those trees right there are the best ones for wish-casting." They're each home to a dozen wishes apiece.

"Oooh," the lady breathes. "How fantastical!"

It's so crowded in here that it's getting hot, and multiple people have complained about the lack of space on my porch. Doing the flowers for Kristin's wedding has opened my mind to the idea of offering baby shower services and birthday parties someday. When I have space.

At lunchtime, we engage in the traditional May Day trading of gifts with neighboring shops, passing out herbal blends and packs of candles in exchange for hot cross buns, lavender and lemon shortbread, and margherita pizza.

I carry a slice with me into the Garden, stopped every so often by patrons with questions or excited remarks, wonderfully dizzy with the aromas of delicious food and spring magic.

"Which ones should I get for my wife and daughter?" a middle-aged man asks me, picking through a crate of premade posies.

"Lavender, alfalfa, and peppermint for the daughter." I sort them so that he can see. "Primrose, woodruff, and birch for the wife."

"What's this one mean?" A lady holds up a corsage.

"Ahh. White violets are for taking a chance on happiness."

She examines it. "Suppose I should. Why not?"

"That's the spirit!" I'm a filthy hypocrite for saying so, as my flower crown is made of striped carnations. I've got a veritable razor wire fence on my head.

"Romina!" Trevor calls. "This guy wants to know what kind of rocks are in the May Day charm bags?"

"Bloodstone."

A new, and unexpected, voice responds. "Hey, missed you at breakfast."

I spin. *Alex.*

"Oh! Sorry. I wish I could've come, but it's a busy day for us." I scoop up Snapdragon, who isn't allowed in the Garden and who was supposed to stay upstairs today. Nosy cat. Some of these plants are toxic.

He scoots aside to allow a customer to squeeze by. "I see that." He opens his arms for me to deposit the cat into. "You need help?"

"Nah, we've got it." I avert my gaze, sweeping loose leaves. "Thank you, though."

"I can . . ." He casts around. "Water something?"

"Where's your son?"

"Miles is with a cousin of mine, and her son, who's his age." He follows me through the store. "What's going on out there?" Nods through the open door, where two people stand next to the green-and-white-striped maypole erected in our yard, joining their wrists with a long red ribbon. Luna's conducting their steps.

"Handfasting. Not a real one, just for fun."

His brow crinkles.

"It's a tradition rooted in the god and goddess of spring. They were kept apart for a winter, then were able to come back together in spring."

"Separated for a period, then reunited, hm?" His tone is light.

"So the story goes."

His eyes travel to the top of my head, clocking the flowers. I watch his cogs spin. A frown develops. "Romina?"

"Sorry, I just . . . It's not a great time right now." I try to paste on a smile. "There's a lot of work to do."

"Of course. Yeah. I'll come back later, then? Is that okay?"

I don't meet his eyes. "Yeah, that's okay."

I feel him watching me for several moments before he turns and disappears.

That evening, I'm facing a small bonfire glowing in our night market, which I still cannot believe we put together in time, watching fireflies arc and dip while I pop a third fairy cake in my mouth. Behind me, voices clatter and bodies move from booth to booth: Gilda Halifax is reading palms in her spookiest voice, a gauzy blue scarf wrapped around her head; a local jewelry artist is selling druzy gemstone earrings; a fantasy author and friend of Zelda's is signing copies of her book that hit shelves last Tuesday. Here, at our magical night market, one can discover things they might not find in our shop by day: mystical candles that can only be lit on the full moon, scrying bowls, popcorn-filled cauldrons. Your very own Book of Shadows starter kit.

As proud and happy as I should feel, I'm stiff and antsy instead; nothing tastes right. This is only partially due to the phase of the moon—the moon is void-of-course tonight, meaning it's stuck in a transitional phase until it enters Libra tomorrow. When the moon is void-of-course, it can provoke feelings of doubt, restlessness, and low energy, so it's unwise to make any major decisions. But I'm going to, anyway. I can sense my muddled thoughts creeping toward resolution. I am going to bruise a heart tonight in order to prevent a broken one down the road.

Smoke and cinders funnel into midnight-blue dusk. A figure skirts the flames. Even with his features bathed in shadow, I'd know him anywhere.

Sometimes, I wonder. If I could rewind to the moment I called off our engagement, and tap *undo*, what would have happened? Would we be married now?

He stops before me, expression guarded. "Hi there."

I run a hand through my hair. "Hi." It's all I can manage to say. Face-to-face, all of my *it would be for the best if . . .* convictions evacuate.

Alex nods, as though I've confirmed a suspicion with only one word. "Come on." He leads me away from the crowd, across Foxglove Creek, not stopping until we're enclosed in a thicket and there's nothing else to see or hear except each other. "I knew it. I started getting a bad feeling yesterday. You're trying to slither away, even though I'm still holding all your jewelry as collateral. Quick, give me your shoes."

I flick him a half smile. "They're not your size."

He lightly grips my waist, persuading me to stand with my back against a mossy tree trunk. Above, black foliage towers. "Talk to me," he says softly.

I don't know where to start. So I blurt: "I can't do . . . whatever this is, with you."

The color drains from his face. He's inhumanly still, moonlight tracing cheekbones, and I sense a diversion in the flow of his focus—usually so riveted on me, now turning inward. It shrinks back inside of him to a dark, vulnerable place I can't see.

"Why."

I know it would be cleaner to keep it vague. *I'm not looking for a relationship right now, I've got too much going on*, or even something like *I think we'd be better as friends*. But I can't lie to him. He doesn't deserve it.

"It's . . ." I wipe my eyes. Concern flashes through him, but he doesn't make any motion to step toward me, to comfort me. "God, it's even worse on May Day. Celebrating love and fertility! The best time to conceive a child. Always gets me extra emotional." I try to force a laugh, but I don't find this situation funny at all.

He waits.

"Do you remember what I told you about Adalyn? The daughter of a man I used to be with? How hard it was for me when we broke up and I never got to see Adalyn again?"

"Yes." And then it clicks. "Oh." All of his rigidity melts. *"Oh."*

I hold up a staying hand just as he begins to move. He halts at once.

"It's not that I think it would be the same experience all over again. You and Spencer aren't the same person. Part of me knows that. But he was so kind to me until I moved in, kept calling me Angel. Which I thought was a sweet pet name, but there was a dark side to it. *Angel* became an expectation: *Do whatever I want without complaint.* After I moved in, the difference was night and day. I wanted to leave, but Adalyn came down with a fever—I know this is going off topic, but I'm just trying to illustrate— anyway, Adalyn came down with a fever of a hundred and three, but Spencer wouldn't do anything about it, said she was fine. Turned out, she had an ear infection."

He slides his hands into his pockets, listening. It surprises me, because I thought he would interrupt, try to change my mind before I've explained myself fully.

"Not long after, I went away to visit Zelda. When I came back, Adalyn had awful diaper rash, painful red blisters. There was dried snot all over her face, her clothes were a mess, the same clothes she was wearing when I left. I asked how Adalyn ate for him, because she was fussy, you'd have to be patient and wait for her to come around to it, and he said she 'wasn't hungry.' That he tried to get her to eat but she only took a couple ounces and was full. That man did not try. I knew he didn't."

Alex nods, once.

"I didn't trust him to parent this kid, so I thought, fine, the responsible thing to do was to stay for a couple weeks until Spencer got his head straight. He hadn't been single that long, maybe he was still reeling. Maybe he could see a therapist to help him bond with the baby, help with his traumas. I let him get away with a lot. I tried to track down the ex-wife, get child support if nothing else, but Spencer said no, she'd made her choice and didn't want them, so he didn't want anything from her, either. He worried that if she started paying child support, she'd end up with visitation, too, and would take Adalyn away." The words are spilling out faster and faster. "His ex-wife was obviously unreliable, neither of them wanted anything to do with that baby. I'm the only one who gave her any attention. I missed so much work when Adalyn was sick that I had to quit my job—"

"You had to *what*?"

"Spencer wasn't going to stay home. I intended to go back to the daycare center eventually, but they replaced me. I got used to being with Adalyn all the time, taking her shopping, to the park. Spencer insisted on referring to me as the mama, so that's what she called me."

Grief breaks over his face. It hurts me just as much as my own grief, to see his reaction.

"It was Adalyn's first word." My voice is shaking. "I loved being her mom, Alex. I loved it so much. I know that I shouldn't have stayed with Spencer for as long as I did, but that's . . . that's how it went, and I didn't see the situation clearly to understand that loving Adalyn wasn't reason enough to stay in that relationship, until much later. Eventually, I told him we were over and moved out. I said that I'd raised his daughter as my own and would like to adopt her, split custody. Things were looking like they might go in that direction, but then his ex-wife came back around, said she was finally ready to be a family. I had no legal claim, so they cut me out of the picture. Didn't even let me say goodbye, didn't let me explain it to Adalyn—I have cried so many nights, imagining her confused, not knowing where I am, why I went away. Calling out for me. I still feel so much shame for not leaving earlier, but at the same time, regret for leaving *at all*, because of what I lost."

He can't hold himself back anymore. Alex folds me into his embrace, and it doesn't feel like falling, like it felt last night when we danced. This feels like being caught, an unbreakable net of understanding and warmth, like he's tucked me away inside of his own heart for safekeeping.

"I loved that little girl," I sob.

He murmurs my name, his hand rubbing circles over my back.

"I begged him to let me visit her and explain that I didn't choose to leave her, but he acted like I was being unreasonable, like I was being selfish. Said it would be better for everyone if I never contacted them again."

"That's terrible. I don't even know what to . . . I'm so sorry."

"I'm sorry for getting your shirt wet."

He shakes his head. "I can't imagine how painful that must have been. The whole time you were telling me about this, I was imagining Miles and José. José has helped raise Miles with Kelsey, loves him like he's his own. If things went south in their marriage, I'd be devastated if he got shut out of Miles's life. My heart breaks for you. I know you must have been a wonderful mom to Adalyn. But I think I can see now, that my suggestion of having breakfast with my son today probably brought some feelings back."

I nod.

"When I said we'd have breakfast together, that's really all

I meant to happen. I'd intended a friendly thing, nothing seri-ous, I wasn't going to tell him we were dating or anything like that at this point, that's not how I operate as a dad—"

"Of course." I feel like an idiot. "Yeah, that's . . ." My voice fades away. I keep trying to grasp for language and fail. "I don't know how to explain it. I just want to feel stable. If I start dating anyone again, I want to feel *sure*."

"Can you ever really be sure of anyone, in the beginning?"

He has a point.

"I know I sound irrational, not to mention presumptuous. We're not even dating and here I am, demanding a guaranteed, seamless happy-ever-after."

"What you sound like," he tells me lowly, gently, "is some-one who's been badly hurt before, and you want to avoid be-ing hurt again." He lifts a shoulder and lets it fall. "Makes perfect sense. I don't know what the future holds. We've got so much ahead of us. But stable? I can show you stable."

Alex King: incorrigible problem-solver.

"You and me . . ." He pauses. "Do you want to be a *you and me*? Does any part of you want that? Even though another part of you is afraid?"

My heart flutters, betraying me. "Yes," I whisper.

"I need to hear you say that you want me."

This man is a sorcerer. I tried to end things between us, and yet here I am telling him I want to be a couple. "I want you," I admit. "I want you so bad, I can't stand it. But this isn't like the first time around, when it was easy. Our lives aren't in sync. I've got emotional damage and am terrified of taking risks. I'm scared I'll lose you again, that it'll hurt even worse this time. I'm scared to love someone else's child the way all children deserve to be loved, wholeheartedly, as if they're my own, then to suddenly no longer have them in my life. I don't see how . . ." My thoughts unravel.

"Leave that to me. I'll show you how." He's solemn. Steady. "You and I will get on solid ground together. We'll move slowly. The foundation of your last relationship was built upside down, sounds like. I can promise that until we're sure where this is going, we'll keep Miles out of it, and build the foundation right. You and I need to spend time together alone first."

My gaze drops from his eyes to his chest. "It sounds a little less scary, the way you say it."

He chucks me under the chin. "Anything is possible if you plan it right."

"How is it that you always know exactly what to do? It's annoying."

"I'm going to remember that you said I always know exactly what to do. It's so close to admitting that I know everything."

I laugh. That's such a sneaky trick of his, making me laugh. Making me let go of my worries, if only for a moment. "The muscles in your neck must be like steel cables, to hold up such a big head all the time."

He winks.

We wander back to the market, night settling in earnest now, our hands not quite wrapped together but not quite lonely. A deliberate brushing of fingers. Chemicals have been added to the bonfire, flames of every color ripping from the logs like party streamers. Just a little ways away lies a three-by-three-foot square of hot coals, which Luna and I arranged earlier. "Care to give it a go?" he asks.

The old tradition is for couples to hold hands and leap over the coals together. If they land on the other side still holding hands, they become honorary May Majesties.

"Don't let me burn," I tell him. "I like these shoes."

I lace my fingers in his, looking to him for reassurance, and his fingers tighten in mine automatically. I know a ferocious pleasure when we leap and land together, closer than we were before; like magic has sealed the warm and fluttery feelings within us.

"My queen." He bows low, one arm outstretched.

I remove the flowers from my head, settling them on his.

He makes a face. "Striped carnations? Sends the wrong message. I'll be needing snowdrops. Grow any yet in your new greenhouse?"

"The greenhouse is out of commission," I remind him. "Needs a new floor, remember? And a couple of windows."

He scratches his jaw, eyes mischievous. "You sure about that?"

Imparting a suspicious look at him, I turn toward the greenhouse. I haven't been able to bring myself to look at it lately. "Yes, I'm—"

Right away, I can see that missing windowpanes have materialized. "How!" I shout, making a beeline for the door. "How did you do this? And the—oh my goodness! You didn't. You *didn't*."

"Oh, but I did."

I hear the grin in his voice, and I could kiss him. I could shake him. But I can't do anything at all because the rotten hardwood is gone, replaced with gravel, and the moldy shelves are gone, replaced with nice metal ones. I'm going to cry. Over glass and gravel and metal.

I lift my hands to my cheeks, totally at a loss. "Alex King."

"I hope you don't mind that it's not concrete. Did a little research and gravel should work just fine for now. It's much cheaper and quicker, too."

I stare around me in amazement. "I can't believe you did this. And again, *how*? I've been in the yard all evening, prepping for tonight. I should've heard something."

He leans back against a shelf, arms crossed over his chest. My focus is irresistibly drawn to the lines of his body, graceful but firm. The hard sweep of his jaw, shadows beneath, the rise and fall of his chest as he breathes. "I did it this morning, while you were busy inside the shop."

"I just . . ." My hands fall limply at my sides. "Thank you. So much. You have no idea what this means to me. I don't even know what to say, or how to thank you properly."

He taps the rim of an empty flowerpot resting on a new shelf. "Just don't forget me when you're famous." He checks his phone. "I've got to get back now, though. Glad to see you like it all."

He awaits my response, but since I can't grapple for any, he throws his head back on a laugh. "Boy, you are *shocked*, aren't you? Clearly not used to surprises. Think I'll have to change that."

My heart can barely take it. I'm going to *expand*. I'm going to grow and grow, with nothing to stop me. I'll stretch my roots out all over Ohio. More people will hear about my flora fortunes, and they'll come to visit the shop. They'll leave with armfuls of flowers, candles, books. I'm going to dream a garden so beautiful that it'll spawn legends; tourists will be able to *feel* the promise of true love in every leaf. I'm so swelled up with joy that I could burst.

"I'll walk you to the fire station," I finally manage to say. It's the halfway point between here and Half Moon Mill. Although

I need to get back to work, I don't want to send Alex off on his lonesome just yet.

I check his hands furtively, every so often, wondering if he'll try to hold mine. But he doesn't. I can't blame him. My emotions are an unpredictable seesaw between the desire to run for the hills or to drag him to my bed. Finally, when I can't stand the silence anymore, I stop walking and burst, "Why did you do it?"

"Do what?"

"The greenhouse!" It's all I can think about. Who *does* that? Who just sneaks into a woman's yard and fixes broken things? I can't wrap my mind around it.

He shrugs. "You needed it done."

"Yeah, but you don't even believe in flora fortunes, in what I do for a living."

Alex takes a step closer to me. Tilts his head down so that our noses are close to touching. "What you do for a living is one of the surprises about you that I like the best. Me not understanding it only makes it better."

I just stare at him. "What." That does not compute. Alex is *all about* understanding things. It's what drives him.

"It's like a puzzle," he goes on. "I love puzzles. The harder, the better. Nothing about magic makes any sense to me, but you seem to have it all figured out, and I admire that. I admire your passion when you talk about what you do, the ambitions you have. Frankly, passion and ambition are downright gorgeous on you. I'll be your biggest customer and I don't even know what the hell all this shit is—I'll be here all the time buying things I don't understand, just to see you in all your hot witchy businesswoman glory."

Once again, he's rendered me speechless. When we continue walking, I tentatively reach for his hand. "I like your passion, too," I admit. "Just throwing it out there—I wouldn't mind seeing you in a hard hat. I've thought about it a lot."

"Noted." He clears his throat. "To be honest, I compulsively fix things. Those missing windowpanes have been bugging the hell out of me. I have a dent puller tool in my truck so that I can offer to pull dents out of people's cars. And it isn't to be nice. It's actually selfish. I just really fucking love pulling dents out of cars."

Alex's arm becomes a beam of support to hold on to while I laugh. It's one of those laughs that makes your whole body go slack, that fiddles with your vision and makes it seem like all the lights around you flare brighter. "Of *course* you do."

"Hey, we've all got our weird things."

"Yeah. You've got that, and I've got you."

He nudges me, smiling. Then, a minute later:

"Romina?"

I peer up at him, but his eyes are fixed straight ahead. "Yeah?"

"I need you to know that I'm coming for you. Okay? Making my intentions unmistakably clear. I'm not going to play games. I know what I want and I'm not stupid enough to let you go twice."

I nearly walk into a lamppost.

"That okay with you?"

It's the strangest phenomenon, when my tears haven't even dried yet but my mouth can't help but trip into a cautiously optimistic smile.

We reach the fire station.

"Yes. A slow, careful, looking-both-ways-before-we-cross yes."

"Good. Get ready."

I'm not sure if a relationship between us can work at this

stage of our lives, or if we'll end up hurting each other again. I guess there's no way of predicting which way we'll go. "Thank you. Not just for the greenhouse, but for being understanding, for comforting me," I say, voice thick. "For letting me cry on your shirt. Which is super soft, by the way, and smells amazing. What kind of detergent do you use?"

"Not telling."

"Why?"

He squints. "If you co-opt it, my smell will lose its special appeal."

He begins to head home. Revolves to face me while continuing to walk backward. "You'll be seeing me around, Romina Romina."

It's the first spell cast in his determined pursuit. I feel it take immediate effect, as if a fizzy tablet's dissolved into my limbic system.

I shiver with a mixture of terror and delight. Alex never throws his hat into the ring for any venture unless he knows he's going to win.

Chapter Twenty-Nine

SNOWDROP:
I make a fresh bid for your affection.

"Tomorrow, then?" Morgan asks hopefully.

"I think I'll be busy tomorrow."

"What about the next day?"

"Uhh, I think I have something going on then, too."

Poor Morgan is fighting a losing battle and doesn't even know it, because Zelda's evasive responses are keeping his hope alive. She wasn't back in town for three seconds before he cornered her, firing off twenty questions a minute, urging her to go on his podcast and talk about the magic system in her series. Zelda is antisocial and hates talking about herself; she's been very tight-lipped about her books these days. But she doesn't want to seem ungrateful, so she's decided that avoiding him is the best course of action. Morgan has been increasingly persistent.

"Step-lover," Trevor trills, heading my way with a small package. "You've got mail."

"Thanks, and stop calling me that."

"We also got more packages meant for other people. Why does everybody's mail end up here? I accidentally opened an envelope with a HitClip of Shaggy's "Angel" in it. Old-school! Not gonna lie, I'm keeping that one." He shows off the HitClip attached to his belt loop.

After Luna lectures Trevor on why he can't keep other people's mail, her nose is instantly in my business. I try to open the package with my hands, but she gets impatient, procuring a box cutter. Inside are two men's shirts: one a jade cotton, the other charcoal, with white lettering: MITCHELL HABNEY ROOF-ING LLC.

"Sweetie, where'd you order these from?" She pokes the peeling letters. "They're used."

"Alex's?" Zelda guesses, popping up at my left. "Why is that gorgeous glass of excellently aged wine sending you used T-shirts instead of making dirty, dirty love to you right now?"

"I have no clue." I hold one of them against me. Shaking it out releases the smell of his fabric softener, tropical and delicious. I am abruptly devoured by homesickness for Alex. He left Moonville on Monday, and now it's Friday. All week, I have mostly been doing fine. Mostly. I've only thought about him every other minute, wondering what he's doing, if he's thinking of me. Being in a relationship with him scares me down to my bones, but *not* being with him is an equally scary prospect. It's an emotional cocktail that's hard to swallow.

I bury my nose in his clothes and breathe. "Mmm."

Trevor backs away slowly.

"A wise move," Luna muses. "*Plant the seed of love on the Flower Moon with a gift, and your heart's desire will blossom with the Strawberry Moon.*" I freeze. May's full moon, which will rise tonight, is called the Flower Moon. It holds personal significance for me. For obvious reasons.

"There's no way he did this purposefully to coincide with one of Moonville's bizarre sayings." Zelda laughs. "That boy's sensible. He doesn't pay any attention to love magic."

Despite Alex's "I'm coming for you" declaration, Saturday passes without a word from him, and then Sunday, and Monday. The rest of the following week crawls by. I am beginning to miss him to a degree that is both surprising to me and also embarrassing: I have, for the first time since the summer after our breakup, googled him, and Sharon from Ingham had a LOT to say about (1) what a great job he did putting on her new shingles, and (2) how she hopes a storm will destroy her roof again so that she can have him, and his blue jeans, back in her life.

Me, too, Sharon. Me, too.

I've now degenerated to the point where I'm watching YouTube videos of birdcalls, familiarizing myself with the sounds that interest him. It's patently unfair that I can't whistle. But did you know that sunflowers attract northern cardinals and black-capped chickadees? I spend half of my waking hours cursing the existence of bugs, but this research presents them in a fresh light: insectivorous birds love to eat the bugs that prey on flowers like goldenrod and purple coneflower. I may hate the bugs, but they bring the birds that Alex loves.

In the middle of the month, he finally texts me. He sends a picture from up on a rooftop, a landscape of blurry houses and blob trees. Look at this view. Not as pretty as you, though.

And that, I kid you not, is literally all he says. I ask him how he is, what he's been up to, but I get nada. Maybe he isn't a big texter. Or caller.

On the twenty-fifth, I'm out for a jog (I am expelling my frustrations through exercise). When I pass a random man wearing a Buckeyes hat, I get so agitated that I whip out my phone and text Alex again.

Romina: You are being mysterious and infuriating and I have had it!

Alex: Not yet, you haven't.

Romina: I thought you pursuing me would involve a lot more pursuit.

Alex: I am pursuing you very hotly behind the scenes. Ducks in a row, et cetera.

Romina: ?????

Alex: ☺ ☺ ☺

This man has nerve.

I feel like an imbecile, wafting around yearning for him, but the longer I go without hearing from Alex, the more obsessed with him I become, to the point that I am completely useless at work. I know because my sisters have told me: "You are completely useless."

"Look at this pencil," I sigh. "Alex likes to keep a pencil in the pocket of his shirt." I pick up a pineapple cupcake and take a bite. "This would give Alex mouth sores." I look at the sky. "Alex's eyes are blue, too." Zelda locks me out of the store when I ride my bicycle back after lunch (at Half Moon Mill, because it reminds me of him).

"I'm sorry," she shouts through the door. "It's just that I really can't stand you right now. Love you, though!"

It's hardly fair, since Trevor and Teyonna have been just as bad. Teyonna hangs out at the store all the time now. They like to make animal crackers pretend to talk to each other and take turns finding "the worst picture of fruit." Doodle on each other's sneakers. Not to mention, *lots* of making out in the storeroom. Teyonna is warm and kindhearted, softening Trevor's energy without pouring water over it. An explosion transformed to a containable, brilliant ball of light.

◈

On Monday, the twenty-ninth of May, I begin to hear whisperings.

The gossips of Vallis gather in the shop, because that's where Morgan's stationed, and he has the sort of charm that oozes your secrets right out of you, as well as a knack for overhearing conversations he wasn't invited to. He absorbs all the juicy details about anything that goes on around here.

The whisperings go like this:

"Alex King is back."

"From the dead?"

"Not that one. His boy."

"Ohhh. *Romina's* Alex." A few faces swivel to stare at me, then flit away, pretending to act natural.

"I heard he's renting the yellow two-bedroom on Hewett Fork that's been sitting empty since the Pickards left."

"I heard he has kids."

"Two, I think. Heard him mention two boys. But no wife?"

"Mm-mm. No wife." More long, persistent looks in my direction, hoping I'll volunteer my knowledge. Hell if I know. I text Alex: You didn't move to Moonville, did you? and he replies with a picture of a beagle sleeping on its back, paws in the air. I don't know whose beagle this is. I ask if he has two sons, and he responds: Only one, unless a miracle happened on the night of the rehearsal dinner that you haven't told me about. Why're you asking me that?

I respond that word on the street is that he moved to Moonville with his two sons. He sends me a laughing emoji with no follow-up.

Gilda claims she saw him and another man lift a couch out of a moving truck into the little yellow house. I'm beginning to suspect folks are driving by that house on purpose now.

"I heard he's gunning for the mayor's job," someone mumbles. "Ran into her this morning at the general store, she was all nervous about it. Who does he think he is, running for mayor? Lives here for two damn minutes—"

"If you lovely folks are going to hang out on top of my desk," Morgan drawls, closing the lid of his donut box, "you'll need to chip in for snacks. Somebody ate my last cruller when I explicitly told you they were off-limits."

Ron, the manager of Moonville Market, is peeved. "He hasn't lived here long enough to be qualified, in my opinion. And being born and raised here don't get you ahead, neither. Where was he when we fundraised for the new playground? In *Oreton*. What about when all the pumps at the gas station stopped working? Where was he then? Did he have to deal with it like the rest of us when that cow wouldn't get out of the road? He most certainly did not."

Titters and grumbling scatter through the room.

"Graduates from college, then moves to *Oreton*. Way to turn your back on the people who helped you win that What I Love About My Ohio Hometown essay scholarship."

I know these rumors are absurd and also that Alex is the one who got Alex that scholarship, but I'm losing my marbles here. I'm chasing them all over town. I break down and text him: Are you running for mayor?

Alex: Where are you getting your news? Do they deliver? Where do I sign up?

Alex: You look glorious in that purple dress, by the way.

I gasp. Plaster myself to the window. Smush it right and left to peer down the street both ways. I don't see him anywhere.

Romina: How did you know my dress is purple? Where are you???

Alex: In your dreams, I'm betting.

Romina: ☹

Alex: ☺

I walk to Pit Stop Soda Shop that night after closing up. He sends me a picture of myself, arms distorted in motion, sipping my milkshake in the twilight. I jump out of my skin, then scour the neighborhood, but there's no sign of him. No truck, no Alex, nothing. He's in the wind. He is invisible!

I am unnerved.

I am so unnerved that I eat a whole bowl of spaghetti and meatballs for dinner without realizing they're the vegetarian meatballs I hate.

Luna points her fork at my face. "Ha! You see! Can't tell a difference."

"I can tell *now*."

"Only because I told you. You *enjoyed* them." She's so smug about this.

"I can't taste anything. My tongue isn't working right."

Zelda snickers into her food. "What have you been doing with it?"

"I'm right here," Aisling whines, waving a breadstick. "I'm eleven. Save your weird stuff for when I'm not in the room, please."

"Sorry."

I bang my head on a table until Ash complains that I'm causing her distress and Luna drags me away. I flop onto my belly on Luna's couch, distracted by Alex's spate of bizarre text messages.

Nobody even knows about this horse

Do you think there's such thing as sharks

How come a Pluto?

One small corn muffin

What?? I reply. When he doesn't immediately reply, I draw

the conclusion that these texts were sent by his Alexa, which is probably listening to the noise in his background and garbling it at me. But then, half an hour later:

Alex: I bet you're still thinking about How come a Pluto.

Romina: wtf

Romina: that was just to get attention?

Alex: Yes.

Romina: -___-

Alex: I have developed a plan and am holding fast to it. But please know that I miss your beautiful face! In addition to one small corn muffin.

Romina: Come see my beautiful face. You know where to find it.

Alex: Soon.

Romina: Are you playing hard to get, or what?

Alex: Honey, you know I'm easy. You're getting used to the idea of being with me, a little bit at a time. And look at you now, pining over me. SO sweet.

Romina: I never said I was PINING

Alex: You didn't have to. (I am pining too, naturally. That's my secret, Captain. I'm always pining.)

Alex is absurd. I am certainly not pining.

My phone buzzes with a surge of pictures he's sending one right after the other: the night sky, a blurry shot of the moon. A grinning selfie. He's a terrible photographer—the only fragment of the picture that's properly in focus is his broad smile. I think he's waving, arm a smear. He's wearing an ACTION LEAGUE NOW! shirt and looks so light and happy.

I decide it's a nice night for a bike ride.

"I'm going for a ride," I announce, very casually, as I slip on my shoes. "Nowhere in particular. The weather's nice."

Zelda sprints toward the stairs. "I want to see his house, too."

Luna shovels popcorn into her mouth, not turning away from the television. She and Ash are bingeing *Over the Garden Wall*. "Already saw it."

I gasp. The betrayal! "When?"

"*Forever* ago."

"Yesterday," Ash inserts. Luna pokes her arm. "We drove by on the way back from getting ice cream."

Zelda and I scowl. "Where's our ice cream?" We turn to leave when Luna hops up.

"Hang on, I wanna come, too. Let's take the minivan."

"You've already seen his place."

"So? If you're having a snoop party, I'm not missing out."

"I wanna come, too!" Ash pipes up. "I love snoop parties."

Chapter Thirty

PINK CLOVER:
Do not trifle with my affections.

And this is how I wind up in the driveway of a modest yellow house with a small front yard, right where the highway curves. In a cornfield across the road, a big silo painted up with MOONVILLE, OHIO welcomes tourists to our neck of the woods.

"Turn the headlights on, it's too dark to see," Zelda says, reaching between Luna and me from the backseat.

Luna twists around, stern. "Did you have your seatbelt on during the drive over? I've told you, I don't care if we're driving for a minute or an hour, you'd better buckle up."

"Yes, Mom. I unbuckled a second ago." (No, she didn't.) Zelda switches on the headlights.

"Hey!" I swat her hand, then quickly turn them off. Whoops, no, I don't. I accidentally turn on the windshield wipers.

"Stop it!" Luna turns the lights off, but then turns them back on again while trying to flick off the wipers. Everybody hollers. We're flashing our high-beams through the front window of Alex's alleged house. Gilda Halifax's information isn't always one hundred percent reliable.

My phone rings. "It's the cops!" Aisling yells. "Drive, Mom! Step on it!"

It's Alex. I stare at his name on the screen, then at the window, its curtains drawing apart. And there he is in his living room, presumably, one hand on his hip. We all duck down in our seats.

"Caught," I wheeze. "This is mortifying. We should have idled on the street. Why'd you park two feet from his window?"

"You can't see anything good from the street, Romina. If you're gonna be a creep, don't half-ass it."

I let the call go to voicemail, which he ignores, redialing.

"You gonna answer that?" Zelda asks.

I'm still hiding my face behind my knees, feet propped up on the seat. "No. Do you think he can see me?"

"You have white hair. It's kinda the only thing noticeable in a dark car. And the light from your phone is probably illuminating your face."

I drop my phone with a quickness. Luna laughs.

"Y'all are chickens." Zelda rolls her door open, vaulting out. "I want to see this thing over here. This a wishing well? Romina, your man bought lawn ornaments and everything!"

I join her. "Look! There's a tire swing in the back!"

Aisling and Luna come running, shoving each other aside in their bid to reach the tire swing first. Ash wins. "Push me!" she demands.

Luna notices that Ash isn't wearing shoes and lectures her on the dangers of running through strange yards barefoot. Then she pushes the tire swing with so much gusto that Ash almost swings upside down.

"Zelda, look." I'm crouched in a strip of mulch that runs along the side of the house. It would be the perfect area for a garden, but nothing lives here. I show her a squat, bearded figurine in a red dunce cap. "It's a GNOME."

It's a *family* of gnomes. With mushroom houses, a miniature bridge, and pebbles surrounding a shallow lake crafted from a yogurt lid. Two fairies and a few LEGO people sit at a small table, enjoying a feast of shriveled blackberries on acorn cap plates. "It's a fairy garden."

I clap my hands over my heart and fall back into the grass. "He made a fairy garden for Miles. That's the sweetest thing I've ever heard in all my life."

"My teeth are rotting out of my mouth," she remarks, handling a tiny birdbath with a Fisher-Price chicken roosting in it. "I can't believe he just up and friggin' moved here. That's bonkers. You realize that, right? I can't imagine *moving* for anyone—well, anyone except for you, Ash, and Lune."

"And here I thought Alex was normal!" Luna chimes.

"Oh, he's disturbed. A truly dark individual." Zelda flicks me. "All that trouble for *this* little elf?"

"Him moving has very little to do with me, probably," I say archly. "The real estate market is . . . doing things. Prime opportunity to move, perhaps. And he grew up here, after all. Who *wouldn't* want to live in Moonville?"

The window above us opens. I cross my arms over my head as if that will disguise me.

"Nosy Nancies," Alex scolds. "Don't eat any of those blackberries. Those are for the fairies." His gaze snaps up, past me, through the yard. "You don't have to drink from the hose, you know. You can ring the doorbell like a civilized human and ask for a drink."

Aisling grabs the hose that Luna's drinking from and sprays

it up in the air. Freezing cold droplets rain down on Zelda and me. "Aghh! Turn it off!"

Zelda, alight with malicious joy, pushes Luna into the stream of water. Luna wails.

Alex shakes his head.

I flash him a smile that I hope is charming. "I like your gnomes."

"She likes more than just your gnomes," Aisling hoots. "Your face is the background of her phone."

"It is *not*." I dive for her, but she skips away. I turn back to Alex. "It's not."

"Is it the same picture I uploaded to Instagram two years ago that you liked at four in the morning last week, then quickly unliked?" He's gloating.

"I was hoping you didn't notice that."

"I notice everything."

I glare. "Damn you, Alex King."

He smiles at me, eyes molten.

"Do you have ice cream?" Zelda asks, as I wrap my arms around her middle, lumbering her backward toward the minivan. I'm not strong enough to toss her inside, so I poke her ticklish parts until she surrenders and clambers in.

"Bye!" I call. "We were never here!"

"You saw nothing!" Luna picks up Aisling and piggybacks her to the car. My niece's feet are filthy, brown ponytail bobbing.

Alex vanishes from the window and teleports to the front door. He watches us leave, hands in his pockets. I turn in my seat so that I can make out his shadowy form until it recedes from view, then I yell nonsense at the top of my lungs. Aisling's laughing her head off.

"Think we scared him away?" Luna muses.

"Are you kidding?" Zelda rolls her window down, slipping her hand out to allow an early summer breeze to weave between her fingers.

The sky is indigo, trees inky scribbles. We soar into town like a homing pigeon, slowing at the empty stoplights, headed toward Pit Stop Soda Shop ("Yes!" Aisling and Zelda cheer). I rest my cheek against the car door, a smile tipping up the corners of my mouth, happy to exist in the midst all these little lights hiding in a sprawl of woods and hills in southern Ohio. I can't imagine living anywhere else. And now, it's finally acquired the few finishing touches necessary to render it perfect. "You remember how obsessed he was with Romina back then?" Zelda adds thoughtfully. "If anything, she's catching up."

♠

The following morning, Alex texts to ask if I have evening plans. No, I reply.

At six o'clock, I stroll into late golden sunshine to find his truck parked out front, two bicycles loaded into the back. One is my mint green Schwinn, the other a mountain bike I don't recognize. "Hey, sexy!" he catcalls, beeping his horn twice.

"Thanks!" Trevor yells back, doing a twirl on the way to his car.

Alex smothers a laugh, then says to me, "I wanna take you on a date."

"Will there be corn muffins?"

"Not telling."

"Sharks?"

"No more guesses."

"Bikes?" I try again, gaze sliding to the truck bed.

"How'd you know?" He waves me over. "Hop in. Can I have you for the rest of the day?"

I sniff. "Only if you make it worth my while."

"I wasn't going to, but all right. If you insist." He eyes my plaid pinafore, layered over a loose white dress with puffy sleeves. "I should've seen right through that lie about you wearing a blazer with gold chains for a date with Trevor. Look at you. You look like you're ready to go on a picnic in the Hundred Acre Wood."

I gasp.

"In a good way! I love Winnie-the-Pooh. Your style—it's very *you*."

I take my time approaching the truck. Once I'm close, Alex lurches forward five feet, then stops. Waits for me to reach for the door before lurching ahead another five feet.

"Alex*ander*."

He beams at the look on my face. "Darling."

Oh, that word does something to me, especially the way he rumbles it. I feel it in my knees. "You'd better stop that."

He stops. Goes. Stops. Laughs.

I cross my arms over my chest. It draws his notice to the area and his eyes get a bit glassy. "I ought to go home. I'll draw a bath and enjoy a lovely evening with myself."

He revs the engine, daring me, while holding my gaze. "You won't."

Chapter Thirty-One

PETUNIA:
I like you near me.

Y our eyes are like raindrops."
I continue walking.

"I would tightrope across an active volcano, just to fetch you a sandwich," he calls from his truck, inching along. Dividing his attention between me and the road.

I wind a finger in circular motions. "Keep going."

"You make my pants tight."

"Is that the best you can do? My while is not being worthed."

"For you, Romina Romina," he tells me, as someone walking in the opposite direction slows to listen, "I would move to Moonville, just so I can look out my window and pinpoint exactly where the sun rises over your house. So that you're never farther away from me than a few minutes. So that I might run into you in the grocery store, or get a glimpse of you circling the post office on your bicycle, or see someone walking by holding your magic flowers."

Well, damn. I climb into the truck. "Fine. I will allow you the pleasure of my company."

He floors it. I yell, grabbing his shoulder, and he slows to normal speed, laughing gleefully again.

"You're on my last nerve."

"Which one?" Without taking his eyes off the road, he starts poking me—my arm, ribs, thigh, stomach. I seize his hand in both of mine, waging a thumb war that I win by cheating. We drive to a gravel parking lot by Moonville Rail-Trail, a sixteen-mile path that spans from Zaleski to Mineral.

"Aw." I grin at him. "You're taking me for a bike ride."

He climbs out of the truck and gets our bikes down. "Found your bike in the garden and gave it some more air. You've been going around on half-flat tires!"

I shrug.

"Need to keep up on that, lady." He cuts into a figure eight. "Miles and I love biking at Lake Hope. I've got a tandem attachment I bring for long rides, otherwise he wants to give up at the first half-mile marker."

"I got chased by a wild turkey at Lake Hope. Somebody on a horse saved me."

"Yeah, they've got all those bridle trails, don't they? I'd like to learn how to ride a horse."

"Me, too. Take me along if you try it, will you? I want to make sure I'm better at it than you are."

"Does it have to be a competition?" But he smiles, the hypocrite.

I nudge the kickstand. Straddle my seat. "You're lucky my dress is a skort, or I'd be flashing my underwear on this thing."

"I don't think you know what 'lucky' means." He flies past on his mountain bike, speeding ahead.

I pedal harder to catch up. "We'll get ticks in here."

"I'll check you after."

Moonville Rail-Trail is paved in most areas close to town, but bordered with heavy foliage. Loads of trees. About ten zillion bugs. "Ticks are sneaky. They can hide anywhere."

"Then I'll check you anywhere. This date gets better and better." He pivots on his seat, squinting against a pocket of sunlight. "I don't remember this concern when we were rolling in a field, by the way."

I decide that I am going to make him eat my dust today, and also that I will hold him to his promise (*"Alex, you have to check under my bra, ticks looove bras"*). "So, we're on a date?" I ask, rolling alongside him.

"Coming on awful strong there, Tempest."

"Says the man who thinks he needs to know what the clouds over my house look like."

"We've been on tons of dates, you just didn't know it. Like the rehearsal dinner at Our Little Secret, when you refused to sit anywhere near me. That was a long-distance date. And the wedding was a date for sure, with all the dancing. Any time I've had you to myself? Honey, those were all top-secret dates. We had another one yesterday, did you know?"

I can't remember what I did yesterday. "Was it good?"

"It was fantastic. I drove past while you were collecting your mail. Drive-by date."

My mouth lifts into a smile. "What if somebody tried to flush a bag of cookies down the toilet in my store and I asked you to come plunge it? Would that be a date? Someone has done that before, by the way."

"Oh, big time. I get to show off my handiness *and* save the day." Figures. He still loves swooping in with heroics.

"What if I asked you to rob a casino with me?"

"The two of us making out on top of bags of stolen money?

Full of adrenaline? That's the kind of date that gets you to third base."

I can visualize it. "Hot. What if . . . we ran into each other at the pharmacy where you were buying constipation suppositories and I was getting medicine for a pus-filled blister in my eyeball? Is that a date?"

A laugh bursts from him. "You're coming up with such sensual ideas for what we'll do after this."

We barrel smoothly along the trail, sunshine dappling his arms with green and yellow flowers of light. I keep decelerating to let Alex cruise ahead so that I can observe him easier. He's wearing a yellow and black windbreaker with long black drawstrings. Jeans. The red hat that I'm learning is essentially a permanent fixture. He periodically checks on me over his shoulder, slowing when I slow.

We speed over a bridge, creek burbling below, then under a trestle, past train tracks overgrown with weeds. I yell at him to stop and look both ways. He turns down a deer path.

"Where're you going?" I skid to a stop.

"C'mon!"

"I don't wanna get lost."

"Girl, do you think I do anything by accident?"

I grumble, heading after him. "High-handed, cocky know-it-all. You make mistakes all the time. Like, the other day, I saw you driving the wrong way down a one-way street."

"Prove it."

"I bet you still call the hardware store Perry's, like all the boomers do."

"What else would I call it?"

"Newsom's Goods. It hasn't been called Perry's in ten years."

"Damn. Really?" He points. "Careful here, it gets bumpy for a minute."

"You're lost."

"You insult me. Listen, you hear that?"

I pay attention. "Hear what?"

"That's a tufted titmouse. Should've brought my binoculars."

I stare at him, bemused. Alex is a talented, intelligent man, but this is beyond the pale. "How can you hear a *mouse*? Do you have bionic eardrums?"

Alex almost falls off his bike. "A tufted titmouse isn't a *mouse*, it's a bird."

"How would I know that? Here's another bird for you." I make a rude gesture with my hand.

"Stop making me laugh, I have a stitch in my side." He clutches his ribs, accidentally kicking his bike chain instead of the pedal.

Another bird twitters nearby, *see-wee, see-wee*. "What's that one called?" I mutter. "A fluffy dickrabbit?"

"That," he tells me imperiously, "is a house finch."

I make him stop so that I can look it up on my phone. He watches in dismay.

I play a video for him. "That's not a house finch. *This* is a house finch. Totally different sound."

A muscle in his cheek jumps. "I meant to say *eastern phoebe*."

"You meant to say *I don't know*, but you're physically incapable of doing so."

"I can't hear you." He rides in circles.

"Did you know that if a bluebird lands on your windowsill, it means someone you miss is thinking about you?"

"Yes."

"A bald-faced lie. I just made that up."

He laughs. "Did *you* know you're in a YouTube video somebody from town posted? It's an eight-hour loop of one of the creeks. One of those nature videos people like listening to while sleeping or studying. Every twelve minutes, you flash by, walking across a bridge. Must've been from a while ago, because you had long brown hair."

"I had no idea. When did you find this?"

"Last year, probably. I'd been so careful to not google you, didn't want to know if you were happier without me. But I like listening to those videos, sometimes, to relax, and when I saw one called 'Moonville, Ohio' I couldn't resist. It'd been so long since I'd seen my home. Turned it on and after a couple hours, happened to glance at the screen and there you were. It was like being punched by the universe."

"I'm sorry."

"Then, first day I'm back in Moonville, you appear right in front of me." He thumps his chest. "KO'd."

"Me, too. I never looked you up online, and I never tried any dating apps, either, just in case you'd pop up. I'm too sensitive. I didn't want to see you out there living the ladies' man life."

"Ha! Ladies' man, my ass. I spend my Saturday nights building LEGO sets with a four-year-old. Oh, look! Here we are."

We taper to a halt at the foot of a broad blue lake, visible through a gap in the leaves. It flows endlessly, hundreds of thousands of love-in-a-mist flowers raising their faces to wide-open sky, the distant ring of trees a thick, dark smudge.

I abandon my bike with a squeal, rushing the field. "It's *gorgeous*!"

Alex grins. "I hoped you'd like it."

"How'd you *find* this place?" Sky like this is in short supply in town; everywhere you look up, you see leaves. "Are we allowed to be here? It's probably private property."

"This land belongs to a guy I did a job for. I've received all the proper permissions, no worries." He reaches for my hand. "There's supposed to be a strawberry patch somewhere, and a water pump to wash them with."

We wander through the meadow. "What sort of job?"

"I reroofed a barn." He points to a red blob nestled in a valley, the property a series of gentle swells.

I shade my eyes to see the roof clearly. "Is that a W?"

"Yeah, for Weyman. That's his last name. I like interesting projects like that, where I get to make designs. More of a challenge."

"Aren't you scared you'll fall off?"

"Nah. It was intimidating when I first got into it, but the height doesn't faze me as much as structural integrity. Sometimes I work on roofs that are badly damaged, so I have to be super careful."

I imagine him plummeting through the roof of an ancient house, landing on somebody's kitchen table. A woman who lives there licks her lips and says: *Is this feast all for me?* "Oh my lord."

"I don't mind those situations, because I get to come in and make them safe. I get to bring stability, eliminate the danger so that no one gets hurt."

"I hope you wear protective gear. Helmet, kneepads, gloves, all that."

He tousles my hair. "Absolutely. Safety goggles, too. My hard hat is full of *Mickey Mouse Clubhouse* stickers, to make it fashion."

We locate the strawberry patch, where we brush bugs off fat, bright red berries then rinse them under a water pump. Alex spreads his jacket in the meadow. We flop down, strawberries cradled in my pinafore. As we eat, he watches the clouds and I watch his face, evening sunlight gilding the shape of his nose, lips, shoulders. The weave of his shirt is thinner where it strains across the back, tiny holes from constant motion. I touch it, warmth seeping into my fingertips.

Alex turns his head, looks down at me. Considers for a moment, before gently pushing me down into the grass.

Drops a long, slow kiss to my mouth.

It's decadent. Rich, torturous, the thump of my heart so intense it beats into the ground. His mouth on mine has an explosive effect, my senses casting wide for a moment—picking up the wings of a bee settling onto a flower, each rustling blade of grass in a quarter mile radius—before narrowing tightly on every exposed inch of Alex's skin, to the texture of his clothes and the way his irises contract when they're above me. One corner of his mouth tugs as he watches thoughts rolling behind my eyes, but for once there isn't any playfulness in the expression, only a quiet adoration he doesn't try to hide. Emotion combusts in me without warning—my hand slides around the back of his neck to hold him to me, enjoying the slight weight of him that he allows to press down, a breeze stirring his scent through my hair. I think it's possible that we've tumbled off the earth into heaven, to a distant somewhere in which I don't have fears or insecurities; somewhere everything about this can be easy, and I can simply trust, let go. Before I get the chance to explore our heaven more thoroughly, however, he breaks away, fiddling with a lump in my pocket. "What's this?"

"My charm bag."

He drops it into his hand and stretches out beside me. "This doesn't look like the ones you sell."

"The ones I sell are more generic, one-size-fits-all. Tumbled red jasper for protection, gingerroot for prosperity, crushed rose geranium for calm, a quarter stick of cinnamon for luck. That sort of thing."

Alex empties the contents of my charm bag. "What are these?" He rolls a handful of round black seeds.

"Oh. Uh. Dicentra King of Hearts."

A slow grin spreads. "King of Hearts, hm?"

"I know what you're thinking, and no way. It has nothing to do with you."

"Sure, sure."

I sneak another glance at him, which is a mistake. He's *glowing*. He notices another item in the bag. "Is this . . . ?"

I cover my face. "No."

"It *is*!" An alexandrite gemstone flashes with sunlight as he throws it up in the air, catching it in his other fist. "I want a charm bag, too. Full of nothing but King of Hearts and alexandrite, so that I can think about myself all day long."

"You *would*."

Alex pauses, deep in thought. He plays with my hair and I admire his profile, every perfect feature. Birds are twittering, sunbeams dreamlike gold-dust swirls. I would like to slip into this moment and keep the door locked forever. "I like how driven you are in your career," he says. "Like me. But you're still family oriented, too. Tight-knit with your sisters. I've always wished I had a little more family around." He meets my gaze. I can tell this is a topic he's been thinking about a great deal. He's foraging for information in light, sensitive steps.

"Me, too. I have my sisters and niece, of course, but I've always wanted a house of my own that's full to bursting with family. *Happy* family."

My sisters and I don't enjoy a close relationship with our parents. Our dad is go-with-the-flow, happy so long as no one bothers him with wanting anything, a hippie with long Willie Nelson hair who likes weed and Harley-Davidson motorcycles. A total mismatch with our high strung, no-nonsense mom. It was opposites attract for them, and sometimes that dynamic works, sometimes it doesn't. At first, Mom found Dad's side of the family fun and refreshing, vastly different from her own. She thought it was interesting to have a practicing witch for a mother-in-law. For a while, Mom kind of wished she were the witchy type, too, and tried to fit herself into that mold, emulating Grandma Dottie until she decided one day that she was tired of Dad, tired of Grandma, tired of anything related to magic, which never worked for her anyway. The truth is that my parents are good, nice people, on their own, individually, but they were not good, nice people together, and neither of them are the nurturing type. I've known from a young age that I want to be the exact opposite as a parent. I'm going to call my kids every week, no matter how old they get, just to tell them I love them.

"*Exactly,*" he says with a nod, letting out a long, slow breath. I think he'd been holding it while awaiting my response. "Lots of noise. Laughter."

"Everywhere you look, somebody to hug. And pets."

"Oh, definitely. You like dogs?"

"I love all animals." I tear the leaves from my last strawberry and pocket them. "I'll start your charm bag with these."

"They have any meaning?"

"Things that come in threes are lucky." I lay a palm to his

jaw, feeling the muscle beneath loosen. "Strawberry leaves mean *a romantic rendezvous*."

His gaze flickers from my eyes to my lips, then away into the sky. "A rendezvous," he repeats quietly, turning the definition of that word over in his mind. *A meeting, a date.* Which technically is what we're engaging in right now—but the word also evokes brevity. Having fun for a while, before it ends.

I have the sinking worry that I might be self-sabotaging, letting my fears dictate the future. But I don't know how to stop. All I know is that whenever I catch myself basking in how good this life is beginning to feel, a cold voice slips between my ears, hissing *It'll all be snatched away.* Alex and Miles are the family, and I am the outsider, easy to dispose of after a while. After it ends.

Chapter Thirty-Two

WHITE PHLOX:
Tell me something about yourself.

We take a different trail on the way back, emerging on Bear Run, the road that cuts behind the library and the dentist office. Then we turn right, single file on the sidewalk. I used to ride my bike all over this town with Zelda—not so much Luna, thanks to the age gap—and a ride isn't complete without a race through the Moonville tunnel. This tunnel is our most iconic feature: fifty yards long, burrowing straight through a high hill. It's made of brick, the word MOONVILLE cut into the front, grassy slopes on either side blanketed with more of our signature love-in-a-mist. Alex hunts for the best-looking flower and picks it, then tucks it into my hair.

It's growing colder, especially in this haunted tunnel, and I shiver. Alex unzips his jacket without a second thought, folding it around my shoulders.

"You sure?" I ask, even as I zip it all the way to my chin.

"Think I hear a baseball game going on out at Coe's Park," he says, with a jerk of his chin. "Want to go watch?"

"Sure." My arm brushes the pocket of Alex's jacket, rustling something he's got in there. I reach inside, fingers closing around a folded page of notebook paper. A number of odd phrases are jotted down in his handwriting, in a combination of Sharpie, pencil, and a pen with its ink cartridge slowly easing into the great beyond:

RT AND ME
Running back to you (for the foxes)
4runner (this one especially)
Now & then
big fat mouth
From the back of a cab
Peach (islands something??)
Edge of town
You're so vain

My forehead puckers. "What's this?"

Alex's eyes pop. He dives for the paper just as I'm skimming the next line, *Can you feel the love to*—and I issue a reedy *"Hah!"*

My face is ninety-percent grin. His has gone terribly red.

"Alexander."

"No," he cuts in.

"Is. This."

"No."

"A playlist."

"No."

"*RT and me.* This is about us. This is a playlist about us, isn't it?"

He stuffs the paper into his back pocket, neck flaming. "No, it isn't, Miss Nosypants." Quite rich, after he rummaged through my charm bag. "RT is my girlfriend from Canada. You don't know her."

"*The Lion King*? Alex. *Alex*. Oh my goodness, that's cute. You're so cute, I can't stand it. I'm gonna take you home and keep you in a shoebox."

"Listen, if it fits my vibe, it goes on the list. No judging."

I kick off on my bike, piloting around him in circles. Around and around I go with a grin I can't tamp down. He stands still, watching. "Was I judging? No, I was not. I told you it was cute. Do you have this on Spotify? I want to listen."

"You don't have the required clearance."

I skid out. "Excusez-moi?"

"If you can't handle scores from *The Lion King* soundtrack, I'm not showing you what else is on there. Some of the songs will seem strange because the lyrics don't have a, you know." He coughs into his fist. "A romantic feel. Like I said, it's about the *vibe*. You'll tease."

"You *love* when I tease." I am dying to know. I've never wanted to know a thing more in my life. "Please oh please oh please oh please oh please, I'll marry you—" I snap my mouth shut. I should do that a lot more.

To deflect from my blunder, I reach up and switch our hats—his ball cap for my straw boater. "I'm into it," I say. "You look like a hot farmer."

Alex's expression is carefully neutral. He spins the ball cap on my head around backward, static in my hair reacting, ends standing to attention. "First my jacket, now my hat. You want my pants, too?"

"Yes, take them off, please." I rocket down the tunnel, determined to beat him to Coe's Park. Maybe by the time I arrive, I won't have cheeks so hot you could fry bacon on them. That "big fat mouth" song is probably about me. "Not that you have room to talk—you've still got all my favorite rings. Probably have them tucked away in a special drawer. Bet you take them out before bed and try them on."

"Hey!" He veers onto the sidewalk on the other side of the road, joining me. "You're supposed to cross at the stoplight!"

"Goody-goody."

"Hey, I can be bad if I feel like it. Watch this." He tries to pop a wheelie but almost falls backward; my hand shoots out to steady his handlebars.

"Calm down there, Evel Knievel."

We cruise the street Alex grew up on, riddled with potholes so deep you could crack your front bumper on them, slowing when we reach his grandfather's old house. He passed when Alex was away at college. I felt like an asshole for not attending his funeral, but I knew Alex would be there.

In my mind's eye, I can still see Joshua King loping out the front door in one of his argyle sweaters, waving hello to us as we walked Alex's dog, Lacy. If Zelda was with us, he'd shout out *Zelda, Warrior Princess*, eternally mixing up Zelda and Xena.

"Who lives there now?"

"Looks empty." The windows are smashed.

To wipe that somber expression from his face, I cry, "Race you!" and off we fly—I weave, which more or less forces him to stay behind me, ensuring my win. When we arrive at our destination, he picks me up off my bike and swings me around. I scrabble at him, shrieking with laughter; we end up sprawled in the grass. I roll on top to pin him.

"My poor legs are tired. You're going to have to carry me home," I sigh.

"Four blocks away."

"Yes."

He gazes adoringly at me, rosy-cheeked, stealing his hat back and replacing it on his head. "Okay."

I tug on the bill. "You and that hat."

"I'm only wearing it this often because you don't like the short-hair look."

I take the hat back off, casting it like a Frisbee. Shower his head with kisses. "I like you with *any* look. I like your look so much that I'm poaching your wardrobe. I'm Single White Female–ing you."

"You have leaves in your hair." He picks them out one by one, then kisses my forehead. "Why did you have to be so pretty? It's such a waste, whenever I have to look at anything else. The worst part is I've always known it, had to go too many years looking at too many other faces. Knew the whole time what I was missing. Knew that being satisfied with anyone else would be impossible."

When he talks like this, confirming that he was missing me all the while that I was missing him, how much time we spent without each other when it didn't have to be that way, an invisible hand wraps around my windpipe and squeezes. If I think about it too much, I'll pass out. "I'll give you my picture in a locket so you can wear me around your neck." I roll into the grass beside him. "We're so good at watching baseball."

He jumps to his feet, then grabs a metal bench to steady himself, dizzy. "Right! We're on a date. I need to feed you nachos. Lots of cheese, so that you keep coming back for more, like a stray cat."

We settle shoulder to shoulder in the second row, soft pretzels and nachos in greasy cartons across our laps. The sky is a rich cerulean edged with pink, just dark enough for the stadium lights to spring to life. The metal beneath my legs is slightly sticky and cold.

I look at Alex as the bat connects with the ball—*crack!*—and celebratory whistles erupt around us, his profile sharp and attentive on the game. My heart is breaking down, blood vessel by blood vessel. Everything about him is a wonder. The shadows of his eyelashes flaring over his cheeks, the sweat glistening on his hairline, the stubble darkening his jaw. The setting sun is a flame in his eyes, dusting his throat and arms with rose. He's perfect. *Perfect.* Every inch, designed for me. I'm not entirely convinced I'm not dreaming.

"Romina?"

"Hmm?"

His voice drops. "You're staring."

"Your fault. You're beautiful."

He angles his face to appraise me, a smile first lighting up his eyes before it takes effect on his lips. My leg begins to bounce up and down unstoppably. He holds it still with his hand.

"Probably about twenty minutes left of the game," someone in the bleachers behind us says, and Alex stands.

"Stay here," he tells me. "I'll be right back."

"Where're you going?" I watch him walk across the grass, picking up our bicycles. "Hey! Explain yourself."

"Don't move!" he shouts back.

He returns when both teams are jogging past each other, arms extended for high-fives. I like baseball, but not with the same enthusiasm as Alex, who *loves* sports—a religious football watcher, a casual baseball player and lifelong fan, collector of cards. It's disappointing that he missed the end of the game when, of the two of us, he'd have enjoyed it more. A familiar honk has me panning the parking lot.

He's leaning against the driver's door. Holds up a hand when I spot him.

I sprint over. "You missed the end!"

"Had to go pick up the truck. And I took your bike home."

"I could've gone with you."

"Your poor legs, remember?"

I say *thank you* with a kiss.

Once inside the cab, he drapes across my lap a throw blanket that he must've grabbed from his house. "Date's not over. Pit Stop, Mozzi's, or the deli from Moonville Market for a late dinner? I'm sick of Half Moon Mill's food, and Our Little Secret's doing their spaghetti western thing. They put too many onions in their spaghetti."

We grab calzones from Mozzi's and park on a hill overlooking the rushing current of Twinstar Fork while we eat. "So. Why Oreton, town traitor?"

He coughs on a meatball. "Sheesh. I don't know . . . Oreton's fine. Doesn't have you, that's about all that's wrong with it, though."

I pepper him with another question. "Who's the dog in that picture you texted me?"

"That's Bert Handsome. He's Miles's best friend and goes with him everywhere, which means I get weekend custody."

"What's your favorite color?"

"What color underwear have you got on?"

This man is impossible. "Give me a real answer."

He snaps up the bottom of my skort dress. "Black."

I pinch his leg. "What's your favorite song nowadays? Still Weezer?"

"Weezer's a band, not a song. My favorite song is '4Runner' at the moment. Changes with my mood."

I cock my head. "I recognize the name of that song."

"No, you don't." He rolls my window up and down in a weird bid to distract me.

"It's from your playlist!" I shake his arm. "The one you've forbidden me from listening to."

"Forbidding it was a mistake. Forbidding made it sexier."

"You're right, you should let me listen. Hey, what's your favorite movie?"

"I didn't study for this quiz, Romina."

"It's your favorite movie, not the Pythagorean theorem. Surely you have a favorite movie."

He casts around, as if the concept of having a favorite movie is totally foreign to him. "*Mamma Mia*?"

"Seriously?"

"It was on TV the night before Mom's wedding, after you scrambled my brain with your mouth. I don't remember a thing about that movie." His smile is wistful. "But damn, was I feeling great."

"You're playing this game wrong."

He crumples the foil wrapper from his calzone into a ball and stuffs it into a bag. "Sorry. These're the answers you're getting, I'm afraid. You wanna go back to my place for a while? I've got a cheesecake in the fridge I know you'll love."

"Ah." I twist the hem of my dress into my lap, fiddling nervously. "Maybe another time. It's getting late."

As we drive back to my house, I squeeze whatever juice I can manage out of our few remaining minutes left. "What are your nights like? What are you going to do when you go home?"

"Think about you."

"Okay, but what are you going to *do*?"

"Lie on my couch and think about you."

"Alex. I'm talking activities."

"Some of the thinking will take place in the shower. I will be thinking about you strenuously there."

I'm exasperated. "Alexander!"

"Romina!" he returns happily.

"You're talking about me. I want to hear about you. Talk about Alex."

His grin dissolves as he stares at me. Weeks ago, his eyes were intense, guarded whenever they landed on me. Now, they're wide-open, radiating perfect contentment. His entire body language has unwound, the tightness of his muscles, spilling from straight lines into easy curves, not a care in the world. The countenance of a man who thinks he's manifested exactly what he wanted.

"I *am* talking about myself."

"No, you're not. Come on, there's so much I don't know. I wanna know it all."

He leans back, scrubbing a hand over his hair. Snaps the seatbelt that crosses his chest. "Well, shit, you already do."

"No, I don't."

"You don't? How so? You know me. You know how to make me laugh, how to get on my nerves, how to bring me out of my head and into my body. How to make *me* fun, which I don't think I usually am—that's a side of me you bring out. I like *playing* with you. I can get kinda tense sometimes, and you loosen me up like nothing else. You make me feel . . . lighter." He parks his truck on the curb in front of my shop, unfolds the playlist from his pocket. Jots down whatever song is softly playing from the radio. Then he climbs out and walks me around the alley to the back door.

"I moved to Oreton," he continues, "because it hurt to breathe, being here, seeing all the places we'd been together, driving by those memories, seeing an imaginary younger me and a younger you at every turn. It's only bearable now because I badly want to make more memories with you rather than run from the ones that bleed."

He takes the key from my stiff hand and unlocks my door. I cannot seem to form a reply.

"You want to know what's going on with me? Then start thinking about Romina some more, because that's all I'm able to do. I can't talk about me without talking about you."

"Oh," I say, almost silently. You could knock me over with a whistle.

"Yeah. So you can go on and think about *that*."

I glance at my door, then back at Alex, and it's an electric shock. *Every time.* Every time I look at his face, I'm startled by a tug that begins in my throat, branching to my heart, my tingling fingertips, between my legs, to the soles of my feet. Even if we've been together for hours, all it takes is for me to move my attention away for a split second, then I meet his eyes again and it's like being slammed up against a wall.

On impulse, I take his face in my hands and kiss him. Hard.

He reacts instantly, gathering me up in his arms. My body seeks him out, curving to fit his. Eyes closed, pulse thrumming, his body heat flaring over me, everything else in the world falls to the void. He's so wonderful that it hurts. It *hurts.* Emotions likes these aren't sustainable. They're going to kill me.

When I let him go, he moves away slowly, breathing labored. I don't have to wonder if he feels that electric shock, too, because I see it burst behind his eyes every time I smile.

"You can think about *that*," I say. His eyebrows raise, an astonished, crooked grin unfurling.

He's halfway to his truck when I call his name.

He turns. His profile glows under the streetlight.

"I'm so glad you moved here," I tell him. "I go on dates with you that you don't know about, too. Probably going to have one tonight, and visit you in a dream."

He hits me with a big, beautiful smile that I feel like a meteorite to the chest. "I'll be waiting."

Chapter Thirty-Three

PERIWINKLE:
My heart was mine until we met.

I used to believe that I'd picked up a magical flower as a girl like in "The Bird and the Flower," a story from *As Evening Falls*. That the first boy I ever loved flew away with it, preventing me from giving it to its rightful owner. I thought he had cursed me. But I'm starting to wonder, as the weeks go by: Who else, in all the world, could I imagine gathering up my heart and giving it exactly what it needed?

Alex moves into my every waking thought and redecorates. He paints the walls summer-sky blue with rings of green-yellow, a reflection of his eyes. He furnishes it with pictures in large gold frames: the tiny dragon I added to his fairy garden to surprise Miles, which Alex said destroyed him emotionally; the two of us sitting on the curb, sharing a funnel cake; a picture he texted late one night, of the two of us dancing at the wedding. In it, my eyes are closed, and his are bright, glistening with unshed tears. He's whispering in my ear. The radio station is RT and Me FM, and in the breaks between songs it plays recordings of his voice: *I'm coming for you. I moved to Oreton because it hurt to breathe, being here. Why did you have to be so pretty? I dreamed this up. Fifty-one.*

We're inseparable for the two first weeks of June. Weekdays, we don't go more than a day without seeing each other; weekends, we talk on the phone. It's a careful peek into his life, listening to Miles and Bert Handsome in the background, the crickets that sing on both ends of the line. I leave surprises in his mailbox: a Rubik's Cube, a book of riddles. Gifts that will please his busy hummingbird brain.

After he finds the book of riddles, he texts a picture of himself and Miles side by side, Alex filling in the answers. Miles is a portrait of his father in miniature, with an ad-libs book across his lap. Movie night?

Biting my lip, I reply: On Monday, maybe? I'll look up showtimes.

I know he wasn't talking about going to an actual theater. The idea of hanging out on his couch with him and Miles makes me panicky. What if Miles doesn't like me?

If he notices I'm suggesting Monday because that's when Miles will be at Kelsey's, he doesn't say anything. After we go to the movies the following Monday, he brings up plans to take Miles to Kings Island, an amusement park in Mason, and asks if I want to join them. I make an excuse, citing the night market.

Most of our dates are local adventures—bingo night at the town hall, watching a community play, rolling around on the trampoline that we bought at a yard sale. He pushes me on the tire swing in his backyard, chatting about work, both of us rapidly filling each other in on what we missed, until it's so late that dew rises up the grass. Then we run to Pit Stop for Late Nite Sundaes—if you stop in at 8:59 p.m. exactly, you get an extra scoop of rainbow chocolate chip ice cream—which we lug back to my place to share with Luna, Zelda, and Aisling. We join my sisters on a tour of all the quilt barns in the county, and he buys me the softest blanket in the world at Bear Hollow Gifts N More.

We've been having so much fun together that I forget we were ever at odds.

"Come inside," Alex murmurs against my jaw on a hot June evening, while we're sitting on his porch swing. I'm straddling him, my mind consumed with kissing, never able to get enough. His hands are on my waist. Lighting up skin wherever his touch roams.

So consumed with kissing, in fact, that I hear myself say, "All right."

He pulls away, dazed and happy. *"Finally."*

"Wait." My lust fog begins to dissipate. "No, I heard you wrong. Never mind."

He strokes a lock of hair away from my face, expression meaningful. "Come on. Let me make you something to eat? We can put a movie on and then not watch any of it."

I try for a smile. "It's getting late. I think I should be heading home, actually."

Alex watches me for a few moments, then slumps back. "The house doesn't have asbestos."

"I never . . . ? I never said it did?"

"Or lead paint."

"Alex, I'm sure your house is lovely—"

"Then why? Don't tell me *it's getting late*, because you always come up with an excuse. You've been to my house twenty times but you've never once stepped foot *inside* my house. We don't have to do anything physical in there, you know. But I moved here so we could be closer together, and it's like . . . maybe you don't want this as badly as I do. Or at least, that's how it feels when you won't even come inside to get a drink of water after admitting you're thirsty."

My stomach drops. I climb off of his lap, hugging myself. "I want to be with you, Alex. It's not that I don't want to do anything physical, either—I do—it's just . . . It's hard to explain."

"Listen." He takes my hand but doesn't look at me.

Something between us shifts. A draft of cold air, and a deep, dark dread.

He's breaking up with me, I think, abruptly light-headed. I need to escape. I have to run.

"I know you're scared," Alex says. "But I am, too. I'm scared that you're not all-in. That you want me, but not the rest of the package. Which is Miles. He isn't even here right now, but you still won't step foot in my house. I'm not saying I want you to jump right into being his stepmom or anything, but if this is going to work out between us, you *do* have to develop a relationship with him at some point. It's integral. We can't really move forward without it."

I glance at his front door, paralyzed with fear. I want so badly to say yes, but I'm not ready for whatever lies on the other side of that door, what comes after I begin to pour some of my life into his personal space.

"Remember what you said about spending time alone together first?" I remind him.

"We have. We are. But." He scratches his jaw, still unable to make eye contact. It occurs to me that this probably makes him feel a little sick, like he worries he's pressuring me when all he's doing, really, is stating his needs. "I mean, look at it from my perspective. This is my son. He's a *huge* part of my life, part of me. Don't I need to make sure you're compatible with that? That you *want* that?"

"I want it," I say in a rush. "Oh gosh, Alex, please don't think I don't want Miles. I do. I wish I could fast-forward to a time when we're all used to each other, when we already feel like a family and all of my worries are gone."

"There's only one way to get to that stage," he tells me, gentle but firm. "Listen, I'm not trying to rush you." I squeeze his fingers in acknowledgment, because I understand. I truly do. "But you and I? What we talked about, getting on solid ground before introducing Miles? Honey, we're there. It's time to take the next step. I don't want anybody else, I want you." I nod to indicate I feel the same. "I only want to make sure we're both all-in. Are you all-in, Romina?" I hear the subtext. *Are you going to hurt me?*

Of course I'm all-in.

That's what I tell him, even though I still don't go in inside. After he drops me off at home, it's what I repeat to myself, until the words lose meaning.

Alex and Miles are a package deal, like he said. I can embrace that he's a father because he's a *good* father, but getting close to an already established family is terrifying. There's no pep talk on Earth to make it less so. There might not be room for a permanent third person in that unit, which can't be confirmed until I make an attempt to ingratiate myself. I've been drawing that out to avoid the sting of potential failure, rejection. Maybe Alex and I are puzzle pieces that used to fit together easily but have now changed shape.

Thinking in circles, I pace.

And pace.

I can't lose Alex, but I'm going to if I can't find some courage.

Even Alexander King, a god among men, isn't going to be patient forever.

♠

The following evening, I duck into Moonville Market to stock up on food from the deli, deciding I'll drop it off at Alex's. He's been a busy bird on his rooftop perches this week, which worries me sick—all day, I visualize him falling off roofs, which he thinks is funny. *"Romina, I've been doing this for years. I'm careful. Trust me."* I don't tell him that I've been researching safety statistics and that every year, there are fifty fatalities in the roofing industry. I want to trap him in a plastic ball like Bubble Boy, but I make myself feel better by bringing him food when he's too tired to cook a decent meal for himself.

The lot is deserted when I stroll out of the market with two bags looped over each arm. To my left, Moonville Market's digital sign is a bright rectangle against the deepening twilight, images flashing from the time of day to the temperature to a pixelated turkey. THANK YOU FOR SHOPPING LOCAL. My gaze skates along the powerlines, the contrast of black wires against sunset's fiery reds and purples, a sense of peace filling me all the way up. I can feel it in my bones, even if I cannot see it: a bird looping over my head, wings strong but tired, waiting for the invitation to land. A purple larkspur somehow still alive in its beak. *This.*

Yes.

It's Midsummer's Eve, a curious time-trap in which impossibilities bleed through layers of invisible planes into ours. When, if you lay your hand to the bark of a pitch pine, you can feel the revelry of elves and fairies within.

This is a night for magic. It crackles and hums all around me.

My gaze happens to fall upon a black truck at the Sunoco across the street. A man is facing away from me, hanging up a gas pump nozzle. My heart beats wildly in my throat, the future expanding before me like sunlight gilding the horizon, beginning on this day, at this hour, this minute. A future that depends on me summoning courage I don't completely feel yet, but that I have to trust I'll grow into. Because Alex has communicated clearly what he needs, and this relationship isn't just about me and *my* needs.

I reach into my pocket for my phone, tap the screen a few times, then hold it against my ear.

At a certain point, holding back doesn't merely protect me, it actively hurts him. When I bring that fact into the light, all of my concerns shrink to shadows. Because you know what?

He and I aren't doing the hurting-each-other thing anymore.

We're past that. If I believe that we belong together—and I do—then isn't he the safest place for all my fears? Isn't it safe to have faith that we will be okay?

I watch him look down at his hand, phone light illuminating a smile as he answers it.

"You again," he says.

Chapter Thirty-Four

ENCHANTER'S NIGHTSHADE:
You have bewitched my heart with your charms.

THEN

I quick-walk out the automatically opening doors of Moonville Market, face tilted up to catch the cool evening breeze.

This is my favorite time of day. The sky is a wavy purple smear on ocean blue, flares of ruby between the trees, the gas station and tire service shop across the street. The higher up it all goes, the darker it gets, stars twinkling. My ballet flats are pinching my toes after standing in one spot for so long, the cherry on top of an already bad shift. I hate it when kids I know from school go through my checkout. They're visibly awkward and won't look at me, as if I'll judge them for buying Kid Cuisine TV dinners.

I dance to the steep slope at the edge of the parking lot where it spreads onto Vallis Boulevard, high beams lighting me up. I clutch my purse against my side as I turn, tucking a long brown strand behind my ear. Down a ways, the revolving milkshake above Pit Stop Soda Shop smiles tantalizingly. If I turn right, I can be in a stool licking ice cream off a cone in ten minutes. Maybe Corey will finally notice me.

I press my lips together, considering it. Then my phone rings. I don't recognize the number, but I answer anyway. "Yes?"

"Hey."

He sounds different over the phone, voice deeper. This isn't Alex King in world history, it's Alex King, Normal Human Outside of School. He might even be in his *bedroom*.

I smile in spite of myself, other hand gravitating to my hip. I shake my head at nothing. "You again. I knew it."

"And yet you answered."

"You're really pushing it today." I once borrowed a pencil from him and he wouldn't let me give it back, even though the pencil was personalized with his name. This newfound confidence is exquisite.

"I'm across the street."

I spin, even though that's facing the wrong direction. Spin again. I hear him laughing, both loud through the phone and faint in my physical surroundings, farther away—and ah, *yes*, there he is. Blue-and-gold hoodie, our school colors. As he moves closer, sharpening into focus, I read the letters across the front: NATIONAL HONOR SOCIETY.

He checks both ways before crossing the road, and my brain snaps a picture of what this looks like: Some boy I've hardly ever spoken to before today walking across a Moonville street at five minutes after eight, wind ruffling his springy hair, hands in his hoodie pockets. The powerlines above him seem to shine for a moment, lit up neon with a wild charge, sky a magical blend of every color that drops with the night.

I feel as if I'm visiting someone else's life when he strolls over like we're good friends, like we do this every day. "Did you leave candy on my desk today?" I ask him.

He nods. "Milky Ways are your favorite, right?"

Actually, no. That was a lie I told my friend Brian in algebra so that he'd give me half of his candy bar. We're given an absurdly short lunch period—by the time I'm through the line with my tray and sitting, I've got six minutes to choke it all down.

Instead of correcting, I circle him slowly. He watches me, brows lowered the way they were earlier when he was writing Ottoman Empire notes. Nerves flicker in his eyes. My, my, those are some gorgeous eyes: blue, green, and yellow. He should cut his hair so people can appreciate them better. "How'd you know that?"

"Heard you say it."

He's in algebra with me? My mind blows with the wind.

I continue to watch him, biting a hair band between my teeth while I slick my hair back into a ponytail. "You're quite a conundrum."

That flicker shifts, nerves into amusement. The corner of his mouth tips up. "Yeah?"

"Yeah."

"Well." He twists his upper body, blush from an old streetlamp touching the edges of his profile. Evening cuts his figure into fascinating angles, and I stand up straighter. "I think we should go to the homecoming dance together." I didn't know this kid was in math with me? That'll be the last time I don't notice what Alex King is doing.

A car horn honks. We both jump out of the way, startled. "I'll walk you home," he offers, leading the way. He can't possibly know where I live.

Actually, he might. I forgot he came over once, to work on a group project.

I'm still delirious from his proposition. "Me and you?"

"Anybody else intending to walk you home?"

"You know what I'm talking about."

He grins, and oh, boy am I noticing that, too. He's got nice teeth. A shallow but long dimple curving along the right side of his mouth. I'll have to see if there's another dimple on the left, but so far it appears he smiles more to one side.

"What color's your dress?" he inquires. "I need to know what color tie and corsage to get."

I marvel at him. "We don't even talk."

"We're talking right now, Romina. I love your name, I've gotta tell you. Probably say it in my sleep, too: *Romina! Romina!* Love it so much, have to say it twice."

I don't know how to react to this except with laughter.

He gives me a cheeky grin.

"Wow, I . . ." I don't get flustered around boys. Around boys is usually where I feel most in command, a shameless flirt. "I don't get it. Where's this coming from?"

Alex lifts a hand into his hair, raking it through his curls. Then he extends his arm, pointing. "Know the tracks down there?"

"I've graffitied my initials on them." I shouldn't sound so proud of this.

He laughs at me, a loud bark that makes me think he doesn't let it loose enough. That he's not usually like this, either, but he tried something different and is liking the way it's working out for him. It isn't the reaction I expected from Mr. Honors Boy, but I find myself grinning back. I keep trying to shock him and the reverse happens instead.

I am delighted.

"This morning I was walking along those tracks to school, had my headphones on, almost got hit by a train."

My smile dies.

I'm picking up that nervous energy from him again, and he walks faster, has to double back for me because my feet hurt, so I'm progressing slowly. He glances down at my shoes like he can actually *guess* that. "Right? Crazy. Could've gotten my insides splattered all over the Moonville tunnel and I'd never even gotten up the nerve to ask you out yet. I would become a ghost with unfinished business; you'd feel cold spots following you all the time, but you'd never know what it was about. Wouldn't know anything about me, wouldn't miss me. I'd have been a memorial service that got you out of school for half a day, and that's all."

I stare at him. Air sticks to my lungs, unable to circulate.

His forehead creases, serious now. "I just wanted you to know who I am. I made it off the tracks with seconds to spare, and my first thought was, *Fuck! She wouldn't have even cared!*"

"I'd care," I force out.

"Listen, I didn't mean to freak you out. I'm not dead. Say no if you wanna say no, that's cool, no pressure." I hang back, so he returns, but can't stand still. His shoe taps the concrete sidewalk, fingers drumming against his thighs, reaching to muss his hair, base of his thumb skimming up the bridge of his nose. I can't stop staring at all the ways he's in motion even when he remains rooted to one spot.

"You'll have fun with me, I promise," he goes on earnestly. "I know you're more outgoing than I am, but I'll catch up. I'll be the most attentive date you've ever had. I'll carry your purse, your shoes, I'll dance the slow songs, the fast songs, I'll sit down with you when you want."

The dance is two weeks away. I have a dress but no date: I've had my sights set on Corey, but despite my lending him a stick of gum in third period every day all year, he's still going with LeAnne.

Andrew and Javier are my reserves. Alex from world history (and apparently algebra) did not even register. Until now.

I swallow. "My dress is pink."

His face transforms. And now he's the one who can't bring himself to speak, lips pressed tightly together as his mouth twists, fighting back a smile that I'm scared might change my life if he lets it free.

We've reached my porch. He halts. Butterflies twirl in my stomach.

"Night," I say, voice cracking.

"Is it all right if I text you?"

I nod. After a few seconds, I'm not sure what else to do—I think he was counting on hearing a rejection, and hadn't prepared for what would happen if the outcome went how he wanted—so I hop up the long, low, wooden steps to my porch. Our front window pours yellow light onto the narrow boards, making my slanting shadow wobble. I hear loud, furious voices inside. This house is where most of my stress lives. It blazes high and sweltering as I approach, ready to feast on me for hours.

He looks at the door, then at me. I don't want him to have heard, but I think he did.

"You can text me, too," he says, softer. "And call. Anytime."

I give him a small, embarrassed wave. "All right."

Before he gets too far down the sidewalk, he jogs backward, skidding to a stop in front of the house again. "Seriously, please call. I would fucking love it if you called." The lopsided grin is back. "Oh! Also! What shade of pink? If I show up in a hot pink tie and you're in, like, coral, I'm gonna look stupid."

I smile into my hand. "Dusty rose. I'll send you a picture."

"Great!" He gives a thumbs-up. Begins to run again.

"You should watch your step."

"I love that you want me to watch my step, Romina Romina."

"Hey, Alex!"

He stops dead, arms melodramatically flailing as if he almost dive-bombed. "Hey, what?"

I wrap an arm around the porch column, leaning. Where has this boy been? Good lord! "I'm glad you didn't get hit by a train today."

His laugh is a sharp arrow slung upward into the night sky. It gets stuck up there, morphing into a glittering star. "Hey, Romina!"

His laughter is contagious, overtaking me. "Hey, what?"

Even from half a block away, I can still see that grin shining in the darkness. "Me, too!"

♠

NOW

"Look up," I say. "You're on a date with me."

He searches in the wrong direction, then turns, spotting me. I run to the road—a car streaks by, and in a blink, there stands Alex right on the other side, arms spread. I jump into them, grinning as he spins. "Hi."

My "Hi" echoes from the phone in his palm. He's got me listed as *Sweetheart* in his contacts.

Something inside of me that snapped in half long ago burns bright as it heals itself, stronger than ever before, like a bone after a break. I wonder if he notices. If he can see all of my emotions pouring out of me, painting the air.

He loads my groceries into his truck. "You headed home?"

I stare at him as he waits patiently for an answer, like he has all the time in the world to stand here and listen to whatever I'm about to say. I notice that his shirt features a flower wearing a cowboy hat, which says WHAT IN CARNATION, and it makes me weak in the knees.

"What if you took me home with you instead?"

Then, because it's an important distinction to make: "Inside your house, I mean. I just grabbed dinner for us, if you want to eat together."

He does a double take, fishing through one of my bags for the Mountain Dew he knows is for him. "Yes." His voice deepens so instantly that I'd laugh if I weren't nervous. But good nervous. Spectacularly good. "Yes," he repeats. "I'd *love* that."

In light of a smile like that, anything is easy. I would do anything to see that smile.

I gulp a deep breath. "I'm all-in. I want you to know that I'm all-in, that I'm obsessed with you, that I want you more than I've ever wanted anything. You still wanna take that next step with me?"

He hugs me tight, the pressure of his arms supplying the words he can't sweep together just yet. Then he kind of forgets what he's doing, moving toward his truck, then me, then revolving again. He jerks a thumb toward the gas station. "You got dinner, I'll get dessert. You still love Milky Ways?"

The weight of a hundred tangled feelings, sparkling, effervescent, are working their way around that fracture, tightening, golden threads that glow in my chest. "They're my favorite."

He nods, then turns to sprint inside. "Be right back."

I watch him go, blinking the dreamy clouds from my vision. The ripped vinyl seats are warm, engine puttering a comforting tune. Caramel has been an acquired taste for me, but the memories are always delicious.

Chapter Thirty-Five

MISTLETOE:
I send you my kisses,
as many as the stars.

Alex's living room is painted sea-glass green. It contains a dorm-style floor lamp he's probably had for years, a dark gray sofa with the kind of soft, fragile fabric that, if you drag your fingernail across it, leaves a pale stripe. Scarlet pillows. An imitation leather chocolate-brown armchair, gently loved, with crayon markings on the stainless steel built-in cupholder. A round glass-top coffee table littered with AAA batteries, a screwdriver, and a toy race car that's been taken apart. A cream-colored area rug with blue-and-copper patterns that I've seen on Amazon. Between the couch and a dog bed sits a pile of unpacked boxes with all-caps descriptors like MILES BABY STUFF and CHRISTMAS, and shelves he hasn't hung yet.

My eyes sweep the terrain, waiting for a punch to strike when I least suspect—I don't know where it could spring from, maybe a television with Nick Jr. left on, or a photograph of Alex embracing Miles's mom on the mantel, verifying that it was always her, will always be her for him.

The kitchen is narrow, with pine floors, a white refrigerator, a clock shaped like a teapot on the wall. Simple yellow curtains above a small, empty double-bowl sink, clean dishes stacked neatly in the drainer beside it. He has a bouquet of spatulas and ladles in a flower vase, same as I do, and Miles's artwork sticks to the fridge with alphabet magnets, a yellow sun in the corner of every picture. The Polaroid of me has made a return to the fridge, as well, spotted with water damage, corners curled. Dog bowls rest on a mat next to the back door, the other side of which I investigated when my sisters, niece, and I went on our snooping expedition.

It's neat and homey and smells like hazelnut coffee. Like that tropical fabric softener he uses, too. If I face the hallway where three doors split off, I get a faint whiff of orchids from the door on the right. What a revelation, to be standing exactly in this spot, with the person I thought was forever lost to me. And his expression is serene, as if this is all quite normal rather than the phenomenon that it is.

This is what his house looks like on an average day. He didn't know I'd end up here when he cleaned it earlier, which means he's genuinely tidy. Responsible. If we lived together one day, I wouldn't be the only one contributing to upkeep. I pin this piece of information to the top of his file.

Standing in this space, visually collecting all of the odds and ends of Alex's everyday life, I become aware that I've been unconsciously expecting the layout of Spencer's house, his colors and decorations, Adalyn's toy bins. Now that I'm here, it's so different in size, shape, color, smell, texture that Adalyn herself could appear and I would be able to handle it. There's an air-conditioning unit in the living room window that rattles with a clatter like ice cubes are inside it, blowing frigid air—I'd forgotten how cold he likes it—and dog toys half jammed under the couch. A red plastic tub overloaded with toys. This is a new place where only new memories are permitted.

"I'm waiting on a mountain of tenters and hooks," Alex remarks, setting plates on the kitchen table next to containers of lunchmeat sandwiches, macaroni salad, potato salad, and pink salad—wobbly pink strawberry Jell-O with Cool Whip—all of your basic salads. A Sunoco bag is half concealed behind a sugar canister.

I turn. "Hmm?"

"Your verdict on the house." He hands me silverware. "What do you think?"

"It feels so much like you." I can't stop taking it all in. "It's perfect."

He smiles, gratified. "Are you a kitchen-table-eater or a couch-eater?" I ask, shifting awkwardly with my plate and glass of iced tea.

"Romina, what kind of host do you take me for? We eat *food* here."

"Har har. You've got the dad jokes down pat."

He grins. "C'mon, we eat on the couch."

I hardly taste my food, I'm still so topsy-turvy from entering his fortress at last, finding it nothing like I expected, everything like I *should* have expected. I'm awash with a curious, impossible concoction of jumping-out-of-my-skin-antsy and bone-deep comfortable, like I've been here before. My heart peers around and says, *I know this place.*

Before I take a bite, I notice a shelf stocked with puzzles and have to jump up to inspect them. "Hey, I've got this one!" I tap the side of a cardboard box. "You have more puzzles than I do. Impressive."

"I like the thousand-piece ones that are mostly sky and grass, for the challenge."

"I have a Lisa Frank collection. Got them with Luna at Caesar Creek Flea Market."

"I like flea markets. We'll have to go sometime."

I can't force myself to sit back down. I'm taking inventory of Miles's toys, what interests him—dogs, LEGO playsets, monster trucks, a toy shopping cart with its basket full of dented plastic food. I think of a Fisher-Price child-size kitchen set in the thrift store window, and mentally insert it in the empty space along one kitchen wall, below a calendar scribbled with upcoming activities. With all that toy food, I bet Miles would like a place to cook it. My magic senses a strong, steady thrum: This is where love lives.

"You're a wonderful father," I say, pensive.

He's surprised by this comment but pleased. "Thank you. I'm definitely not perfect, but I do my best."

If Alex were any other man, I would save this line of questioning until we'd been together for six months or longer. But I need answers now. I'm not getting any deeper until I know. I try to adopt a casual tone. "We've talked a little about family life, what we envision. But I think we need to speak clearly so that there's no room for confusion. Do you want more kids?"

He doesn't hesitate. "Yeah. I'd like to have about two more."

"Or three?"

He laughs. "Maybe. Depends on where I'm living someday, the size of the house."

I wander to a window, chewing the inside of my cheek. "Where might this imaginary someday house be? In Moonville?"

Arms wrap around my waist, a chin settling on top of my head. "Do you know the place out past the old tobacco barn where all the yellow trees grow, and the road is shaped like an S?" He traces the letter into my back.

"Yes." I shiver. He presses against me, lips to my neck, stubble a light scrape. My eyelids drift shut.

"There."

I almost stop breathing. "Are there any houses over there?"

"One that I know of. It's a little small, but I could build on. Give it dormers, French doors, lots of natural light."

I can picture myself out there where the road twists into an S, weaving between yellow trees with my bucket of chicken feed, silkies at my heels. I can visualize a garden that stretches on and on, rosebushes twined around apple trees, honeysuckle climbing birdhouses, bird feeders and witch bells dangling from ancient sugar maples. Alex and I biking through the woods, taking our kids camping, kayaking on Raccoon Creek. Winding down at night with a cup of tea, murmuring softly about our day over a puzzle. Losing at Scrabble. Winning at Monopoly, then indulging him when he insists on a rematch. Hanging a charm bag from his rearview mirror so that my protection follows Alex wherever the road goes. Celebrating many more Beltanes to come, around a bonfire, with Luna, Ash, and Zelda. Kristin, Daniel, Trevor. Miles. And other faces I haven't met, their identities scattered among the stars.

Someday, when I am a mother again, I want to have a partner who instills in our children that they can do anything, be whoever they want to be. So that they can go out into the world and make it their own, and whenever they come home to us, they will know—*I can open up this door and walk right into love. I will walk into acceptance, unconditional support. I know my parents love me for me, whoever I am.* Our home will be the place you go to be wrapped up in a radiant love that never ends. We'll watch them grow up together, becoming whoever they're meant to be. Guiding them along the way but not trying to force them in any particular direction. Kind, silly, empathetic humans who I hope will light candles in every window on the Snow Moon, carrying on the traditions I learned from my grandmother.

His mouth travels to my ear. He whispers, "What do you think?"

"I think it sounds like you reached into my head and looked at my dreams." I turn toward him. "What do *you* think?"

"I think . . . come here." He walks backward, dropping into a chair. I move to sit beside him, but he grabs me around the middle and seats me on his lap instead.

"Well, I never," I say.

He plays with my hair, smoothing it back, spiraling it around his hand. I wonder what it's like for him to watch me walk through his house, touching his belongings. "Well, you should." He skims a thumb along the corner of my mouth. "Right here? One of my favorite places on Earth. Your smile just tears me apart, you know."

I smile again and tear him apart some more.

He sifts his hands through my hair. "I like how, whatever the color, your hair twists out at the ends, and you've got this cute rumple up here." He touches a dent in the hair at my crown, then the wayward ends flipped out and inward. "How your eyes sparkle when I touch you."

"Yours turn black," I observe. "There's always been this magnetic energy about you that drives me wild. It's like you know everybody's secrets, like you're going places, on a journey we all want to be part of."

The corners around his eyes crinkle. His voice cracks just a bit when he says, "Really?"

"And this dimple?" I kiss it, the curve deepening. "When you hit me with that smile?" Hand over my heart. "Makes me die. You showed up after all these years, and I can't handle it, how you've only gotten more attractive. You're so *direct*, too."

"And you like it?"

"It's my kryptonite."

"You're shyer," he remarks. "Quieter. But you have that lightning, I've still never seen anything like it in anybody else. All I want is for you to zap me and let me in, so that I can be your goner."

I lay a hand against his chest. *"Zap."*

I know that emotion in his eyes when he slowly tugs me forward, hands linking in mine, to kiss him. It makes my body turn to liquid.

Our faces are a hair's breadth away. "I want you," I murmur, my lips ghosting across his. "Here. Tonight."

His eyelids, heavy with lust, spring back open. Alert.

I kiss his neck, delight in how he arches against me. I tug his earlobe between my teeth, then work my way to his mouth, where he's waiting, kissing me hot and deep. "I saw what else you bought at the gas station, Alex King," I whisper raggedly, "and it wasn't just Milky Ways." His breath hitches; I feel him go hard beneath me. "Take me to your bed."

🍃

"It's fine, honestly. I don't mind."

"I do." He yanks his shirt over his head on his way into the hall. "I only get one first time with you. I'm not bringing the hot, sweaty, gross day I've had along with us." He pats his cheeks. "Oughta shave, too."

"Don't you dare."

He raises an eyebrow. "You like the five-o'clock shadow?"

I spread my arms along the back of his couch, chin lowered to my chest. I better appear as seductive externally as this looks inside my head. "Yes."

"I'll be five minutes. Make yourself, ah . . ." He thumbs open the button of his jeans, tossing a glance around as though trying to take the measure of his place through my eyes. "At home. And Romina?"

I pop up from the sofa. "Yes?"

He almost smiles. Fights it back. "Please don't disappear."

I stare after him as he enters the bathroom, closing the door behind himself.

I'm stuck on a high, jittery frequency. I bounce like a rubber ball, because holy shit, he just gets better every day, for some reason he wants to be with *me*, and I have to do something to make this more special. I need ambiance.

Candles!

I scrounge up a few that he apparently ordered online from The Magick Happens and scurry into the bedroom. As suspected, his bedroom lies behind the orchid door. It's simple; most of his decoration efforts have concentrated on higher-traffic areas like the kitchen and living room.

Everywhere is airy and inviting except for the bedroom, which he's fashioned into a cave with the darkest textiles invented. Heavy blackout curtains. A thick midnight comforter and charcoal sheets. Soft-as-clouds, cool pillows, and dark gray walls. The temperature in here is colder than anywhere else in the house, with a large metal floor fan left running. This room is all business, designed for deep sleep rather than aesthetic. Even his bedside light is the softest of shimmers, throwing a halo over a voluptuous navy headboard.

He's already got a candle on the dresser, pillar lopsided and half melted. *Make Her Yours*, the tag reads. I am feeling like an awfully powerful witch, to have braided up this die-hard skeptic into so many knots that he's resorted to using candle magic.

"Silly Alex," I murmur under my breath. "She already is, you goose."

I light that one first, then spread the others across every available surface. Is there time to run to my garden for rose petals? I check the clock. Four minutes down, one to go. Wildflowers and pretty weeds, it is.

I bolt outside, screen door banging behind me, and whoop at my luck—Alex hasn't mowed in a few days. I pluck every wild violet in his front yard and dash back to the bedroom, strewing them over the bed in the shape of a heart. Speaking of hearts, mine is a rocket ticking down to launch, sweat beading on my collarbones, my upper lip. I wipe it on my shirt, checking my reflection in a hallway mirror. I wish I'd worn my lacy red bralette, but at least my underwear's cute.

I gnaw on my lip. This shirt has too many buttons.

I'd envisioned slowly lifting my shirt over my head, shaking out my hair, while Alex watches. To make it easier, I begin the laborious process of unbuttoning. But that makes me look too desperate, maybe? And he might want to undress me instead. I hop around, rebuttoning. Then I seize the small box from the Moonville Market bag on the kitchen counter so that condoms won't be far away when we need them, and while I'm in the kitchen, I grab the Alexa, too. I'm plugging it into the outlet next to Alex's bed when he slinks into the room in a billowing steam of Irish Spring.

"That was seven minutes," I reproach. "And what's this business?" I gesture to his T-shirt and basketball shorts. "You're fully dressed. I was hoping you'd walk out here naked."

"We're starting from the beginning. We have all night." He stops, dread lacing his tone. "Don't we? Or were you wanting to leave . . . after?" He tries to sound casual about it, like whatever I want is cool with him, but I know better.

"You got a spare toothbrush?"

"I have a super pack you can choose from."

"Then we're good." I swallow, trying not to fidget. I forget how to use my arms—keep them pinned to my side? Maybe that's too severe. I cross them over my chest, but that looks defensive, like I don't want to be ravished. And I definitely want to be ravished. I settle for clasping my hands behind my back, which has the added bonus of pushing my chest out. Perfect.

I'm beginning to wish we'd kept our fire going in the kitchen. Pressing pause has led to me overthinking, which isn't an issue we ran into that night in the field.

I wait for him to approach, but now *he* seems nervous, gaze roving over my body, probably daunted that I'm wearing a garment with so many buttons. He sits down on the bed without glancing at it and smears purple petals all over.

I try to brush the petals away, but end up tearing them, so they roll into tiny pellets. "Ugh, it's making a mess. Sorry."

"Are you kidding? This is adorable. I'm all about it."

I smack my forehead. "And you have pollen allergies! I completely forgot."

"Nah, I take meds, it's fine."

We face each other.

"Okay." He smiles slowly. "I'm going to kiss you now."

"Good." I shake out my hands. "Let's do this."

He has to stop so that he can laugh at my solemnity, trying to regain seriousness. But the second before his mouth descends on mine, I inexplicably burst into giggles. He leans back. "What?"

"I'm fine, I promise. Kiss me." I sit up on my knees, moving to slide across his lap, but accidentally knee him in the groin.

He hisses through his teeth.

"No! Oh, no! I'm so sorry!"

"I think I'm going to throw up." He closes his eyes.

"What can I do? I'm sorry. I'm *so* sorry. Do you want an ice pack? Heating pad? I don't know which one helps!"

"I'm okay, just give me a minute. Why are we so bad at this?" He moans. "It's like the first time we kissed, when you—"

"Don't remind me. I forbid you."

"—kept your lips fused shut and your eyes wide open."

"*Sto-o-o-op.*"

"It was hilarious."

I slug his arm gently. "Let me show you that I'm much better at kissing now. How's your dick? Still wanna throw up? Wow, the effect I have on men is poetry."

"I can play through the pain, maybe."

"Is that how it works?"

"No." But he cages my face in his hands and presses his lips to mine, anyway. I inch closer, positioned awkwardly, and make very certain I do not stick my knee anywhere sensitive as I hover over his lap. I run my palms over his stubble, down his chest. While I don't feel a reaction in his shorts, he's undeniably into this. His hands vanish under my shirt, gliding up. Oh, yes. This is happening.

"Alexa," I call out. "Turn on Marvin Gaye."

The black circle lights up with a ring of brilliant blue. "Heard It Through the Grapevine" swells from the speaker.

Alex stops kissing my shoulder, shadow of a beard abrading me when he turns his face toward the Alexa. I can tell he's trying not to laugh.

Obviously, I'd meant for a more carnal song to serenade us. Technology requires too much hand-holding. "Alexa, play 'Let's Get It On,'" I revise.

Okay, it responds in robotic monotone. *Turning on "Let's Get It On" Radio on Pandora.* A second later, Otis Redding is crooning "Sittin' on the Dock of the Bay."

"Goddamn it!" I yell. "That's not what I said."

Alex's chest is shaking. I push two fingers into his stomach. "Don't laugh! You're still turned on."

He begins to sing along with Otis. "I'll have to add this to the playlist now. You give me no choice."

"Alexa, *next*," I say firmly.

The next song is also not what I asked for. "*Ain't too proud to plea-ead, baby, baby*!" Alex belts out. "*Please don't leave me*—Hey! I was listening to that." I'd lowered the volume. "How you gonna turn down The Temptations? Have you no taste?"

I blow out a breath. "This is a disaster."

Alex rolls on top of me in one quick motion.

"Whoa." My eyes fly wide open, arms splayed above me on the blanket. "Hello."

"Just like that," he says teasingly, trailing a finger down my bottom lip, the arch of my throat, between my breasts. He flicks open a button on my shirt. "That's what your face looked like when I first tried to kiss you."

I paw his hand away. "You're so mean."

"Still the most amazing kiss I'd ever had, at that point." It was his first.

I try to tickle him, but he seizes my arm.

He raises my shirt at a leisurely pace, exposing my stomach. His lips whisper soft kisses below my ribs, around my navel, fingers playing with the waistband of my shorts. Lowering them centimeter by centimeter. *Yes*, I think ardently, heat pooling between my thighs. Then my stomach growls, directly against his mouth.

He lays his cheek against my stomach and the blaze between us dies at once, plumes of smoke curling up into the ceiling. "Romina."

"Keep going or I'll combust."

"But you're hungry."

"Hungry for *sex*."

"You didn't eat much, did you? I noticed you didn't touch your sandwich. I was going to ask if I could have it, but then you distracted me with all your seductive puzzle talk." He stands up, an impenetrable wall against my (loud, colorful) protests. "All night, remember? We have all night, and once we get started I want to continue for *a good while*. C'mon, flower girl, let's get some food in you."

"I want something else in me," I mutter, but reluctantly allow myself to be wrenched off the bed. He wraps around me from behind and sways us to whatever song he's still listening to in his head.

"What if we spend all night laughing and getting your dick stepped on and we never do it?"

"I promise you'll come before the sun does." He kisses the nape of my neck. *"Promise."*

Chapter Thirty-Six

MAIDENHAIR:
I am utterly yours.

He pops another of my buttons with one hand—the other is spread flat against my stomach—rocking us side to side down the hallway. Hums in my ear.

"What's that song?"

"Shhh." Kisses the skin between my neck and shoulder.

"Is it Disney again?"

"Miles is obsessed with Disney movies, I can't help it. I'll be texting you while one of them's playing and before I know it, one of the songs becomes a you and me song. Beyond my control." His fingers are making quick work of my buttons, shirt gaping open at the front. We wander into the kitchen, where he breaks out the strawberry salad and scoops some into a bowl. Slips a bite into my mouth.

He dabs a speck onto my upper lip just to watch my tongue dart out, lick it off. Slides my shirt down until the sleeves are at my elbows. Presses a kiss to my left shoulder, across my collarbones, to my right. Feeds me another spoonful. I can't move my eyes from his face as he goes about his ministrations, touching and kissing, savoring. There will be times we don't savor, when we don't go slow. But I'm glad tonight is feeling like forever, winding me up with anticipation.

He tips another bite past my lips, our eyes locking. His mouth kicks upward, and I think, *I love him*.

Loving Alex is innate language. I don't remember how I learned it because by the time it dawned on me to consider the concept, I was already fluent. I didn't stop loving him, I didn't forget that I loved him, either. All I did was put the words behind a door to prevent them from escaping into conscious thought. They've been waiting there all this time, alive, just as loud, just as strong, as they ever were.

He licks the back of my spoon. *Stronger*, I think, mouth dry as I watch his tongue twist. He slants me a hungry look.

Leaving the bedroom, with that big, intimidating bed, has busted a levee and we're flooded with want. I grip his shoulders, dragging him closer. He kicks my knees apart, standing between them. He cups the back of my head and kisses me, kisses me. How did I survive living without him? How am I going to unpeel myself from his side ever again? I suck his lip between my teeth, drag my nails down his arms. Divest him of his shirt.

I'm in a bra and shorts, then only my shorts, his hands scalding, the weight of my breasts in his work-roughened hands incredible, calluses smoothing over flushed, sensitive skin. His eyes blaze, and I'll die if I don't watch him come looking exactly like this. Hot liquid pumps to every pressure point, a fluttering in my breastbone where an emotion flowers bigger and bigger, uncontainable. I can't get close enough, body rubbing against his, a brush of mouths; first a feathering, then a bruising. Closer, closer. "I want to wrap you all around me," he says, timbre rough and low, uneven as each word slides a different way through the blood that pounds in my ears.

I feel a hand splaying across my back and I instinctively recline, legs hooking around his hips. He drags me off the counter like a meal to be devoured, bringing my mouth back to his.

A belt of wind slaps the windowpanes, reverberating. It howls beneath the cracks in the doors, but I only feel Alex, carrying me back into the bedroom, bulbs in the living room ceiling fan sputtering erratically. This can't possibly be the same room that we sat in only minutes ago—this one is darker, delicious, impossible not to lose ourselves in. He tosses me onto the bed, chest rising, falling deeply, watching me as I lie naked from the waist up in the space where he tosses and turns at night, stroking himself to thoughts of me. Which I know because he's admitted it, in the dead of night while we talked on the phone about all the things we weren't yet brave enough to say to each other in person.

I hold out my arms and he falls into them, hips pressing me down, down. I hum with pleasure, eyelids lowered to half-mast. My fingertips slip into his shorts, easing them down his thighs. He's hard and ready, listing slightly to the left with each thudding pulse. "Yes," I whisper.

He yanks down my shorts. Looks long at me, spreading my thighs. Runs a tongue up the seam of my underwear, right where it's wet, and I spasm, back bowed. And then I'm fully naked, his hands brands on my calves, touching me reverently right up until his teeth find my hip and sink in. I half yell, half moan. Curl my hands around either side of his throat.

His pupils blow wide like windows showing me the deep, dark bottom of him, his heartbeat swift, jumping against my palms. I squeeze, only a little, not enough to hurt. His cock twitches. He swallows. Manages hoarsely, "Please . . . please keep doing that." I grasp his throat in one hand, and do the same to his cock, gliding my hand up and down, grip tight, pumping until he's breathless, perspiration breaking out on his forehead. The muscles in his legs tremble.

He rolls us without warning, grasp secure on my arms, reaching onto the nightstand for the box of condoms. While still thrusting into my hand, he tears a condom wrapper with his teeth, rolls it quickly over his length. Tree branches tap the windows persistently, and I'm seized by the inexplicable thought that he and I are responsible for this weather, ebbing and flowing with our emotions.

My hands on his shoulders, he bucks beneath me, helpless not to roll his hips, cheekbones glistening. I kiss his chest, traveling my way up, tilting forward until my breasts are close enough for him to taste. He closes his mouth around a hard nipple and tongues it, sucks, eyes shut, forehead furrowed in ecstasy that he wrestles under control—*Not yet.* I sink down onto him, inch by inch, muscles clenching. *"Ohhh,"* I sigh, taking a beat to accustom myself. "You feel so good."

"You moan like that and this won't last long," he warns, guttural. Then I move, he moves, a slow, euphoric drag that makes all the blood rush from my head. I hold on to his throat as we rock, careful not to apply too much pressure. The skin beneath my hand is ruddy, a spreading blush in his swollen lips. Stars appear one by one in his glassy eyes.

I'm searing hot everywhere—eyelids, the backs of my knees, shells of my ears. My hair sticks to my neck, damp. Alex grips my hips, moving me, holding me down harder, harder as I rub against him, friction wicked, and it's watching where our bodies meet that tightens every sensation until I think I might snap. I hear him panting and look down, watch him throw his head back.

"Are you close?" he grits out.

My response is a breathy moan.

His hands are clamps; he spreads his knees, digging his heels into the mattress, and tilts me upward so that we fuck each other, hard, while he dips his head forward and runs a tongue up my breast, twisting around a nipple. Teeth lightly biting, then sucking. "You like this?"

I can't speak, can only nod.

Biting. Sucking. His stomach clenches, body shuddering, thrusting and then grinding, tight, tight, tight against my clit, and when I come it wipes all the sound from the earth. My vision is a black-purple field. There's no noise, hearing collapsed.

It's forty seconds to a minute before sounds return: the rattle of the air conditioner, wind chimes clanging, gales upon glass. Alex is staring up at me, lips parted on a silent groan, still coming, still clenching. My release is on its journey back down but there is such a fierce pressure building up inside me in tandem, so staggering that I'm going to fly apart and become the walls around him, fragments of Romina embedded in his dresser, his mirror, the roof, the floor. Irreversibly ingrained. No matter what, I'll never be able to leave him, I'll be his home wherever he goes.

His undulating hips are slowing down, calming, until he falls still against the sheets. I have the strange, manic desire to lick him everywhere he gleams. This is new. This is beyond me. I don't know myself, at all, in this moment.

"Alex," I rasp. "I . . ."

Over in the corner, the small Amazon robot winks back to life and replies, *Hm. I don't know that one.*

I forget what I was going to say, if I even had the words to thread my thoughts together. It's a good thing we both already came, because we're laughing again, and I think—

I love this man. I'll never love any other.

Chapter Thirty-Seven

ASH TREE:
My love is lionhearted, high as mountains, deep as the ocean.

Hours later, I watch ceiling-fan blades rotate, mentally trace grooves in white paint swirls on the ceiling until my eyes grow heavy. We've finally exhausted ourselves; he truly meant it when he said he intended to enjoy each other *for a good while*. Alex switches off his bedside light, the soothing pattern of his breathing lulling me to sleep, facing me with his cheek on the sloped edge of his pillow so that we can stay close through the night.

I'm startled awake after what feels like a handful of minutes have elapsed, but the numbers on my phone glare 4:17 a.m. I sit up, groping in the darkness. Alex groans softly in his sleep.

I slouch against the headboard, hand over my racing heart. Real. Still real.

I'm too keyed up, and I can't play on my phone without waking him. He's told me that he needs absolute darkness when he sleeps, or else he's susceptible to headaches. I creep out of bed on tiptoe and into the hall. Before I know it, I find myself in his shower, hot water sluicing over my head, locks of my hair hanging over my face. My hair appears grayish when wet, over-processed, with a rubbery, synthetic texture. I watch the suds of

Alex's shampoo trickle down. A bottle I recognize sits next to his shaving cream: Twilit Dreaming's Lady of the Night Orchid Bodywash, the exact one I use. He never smells like that body-wash, which means he's had it here waiting around just in case I might ever use it.

This breaks me. Alex is my *one*. I've wasted so much time finding him again, years that I'll never get back. I wasted time getting to right here, right *now*. Every minute of the past two months that I've spent hemming and hawing, letting fear run my life, is a tragedy. Look at my bottle of bodywash. How long has it been sitting here? I want to throw it at my past self, right in the kneecaps, and shout, *What are you waiting for! Go on! Go get your life!*

I towel off while rooting through the dryer for something to wear, opting for a Cincinnati Bengals shirt and black boxer briefs. Then I pad barefoot to the back door. Wind batters the trees, leaves swaying violently as a diagonal rain cascades. It's storm season.

I wander back to Alex's room, hallway night-light spilling across his form as the door fans open. He's lying facedown, one arm curled under my pillow. A sparkle in the gloom catches my eye: his magpie stash of jewelry—my rings, earrings, necklaces. I perch on the edge of his mattress, depressing it slightly, and slide my rings back on. I've been naked without them.

A hand reaches out, catching my left in a quick shot. He sits up fast, switches his lamp on. "Where'd you get that?" His voice is sleep-roughened and alarmed, not entirely awake.

I stare at him. "It was sitting right there."

He reaches past me to smack the nightstand drawer, checking if it's open or closed. Turns my hand over to inspect my rings, then lets go. Relaxes.

"What'd you think I was doing?" I ask suspiciously, eyes straying to the drawer. I watch his reaction as I try to tug it open, and he blocks me. His expression is a wall.

"What's in that drawer, Alex?"

He doesn't respond.

"What's in the drawer, Alex."

He scrutinizes me closely, then his arm goes limp, hand withdrawing. "Open it."

Now I'm not sure if I want to. I don't move.

He opens it instead, and I dare a peek at its contents—

There's a ring inside. Not in a box. Just a ring resting on the IKEA faux wood grain. "What is . . . ?" I turn it beneath the lamp to chase away shadows. The band is tarnished. A tiny diamond flanked by an oval sapphire and empty prongs, the third stone missing.

"My mother gave it to me on her wedding day."

This doesn't resemble any of Kristin's rings that I've seen. "Why?"

"Because it's yours," he returns blankly. "She found it while gardening seven years ago."

I wait for further explanation, but he doesn't continue. "I don't understand."

"This is your ring, Romina. From when we were engaged."

I shake my head. "I didn't have a ring." That's one of the reasons why I was able to convince myself that calling off the engagement was no harm, no foul—nothing was official. No solid plans, just two kids and their desperation to stay together after peering into their future toward a path that diverged in opposite directions.

He merely stares at me, not saying a word.

"No."

He holds out an expectant palm, which I drop the ring into. Alex's gaze travels to a place and time I can't see, a shape in the fog of his memories. "After Dad died, Mom put a little money from the settlement into a trust I got access to when I turned eighteen. I was going to use it for school, but when we decided to get married, I wanted to get you a ring right away. The band was my grandmother's. It had this sapphire in it already but was missing the two other stones, which fell out ages ago."

He appraises it thoughtfully. "Your grandma gave me an emerald from a ring of hers, which I took to a jeweler to have added. Gone now." He taps the empty prongs. "I couldn't afford much, for the diamond, but it was a beautiful ring."

"You got a ring," I repeat hollowly.

"Well, yes. I wanted to marry you. I mean, I knew we were underprepared financially, and the concept was a lot to get my head around initially, but I got . . . attached to the idea. I pictured you walking down an aisle toward me, all in white, with flowers—" He clears his throat, voice a little scratchy. "Flowers in your hair. Funnily enough, because this was long before you ever wore flowers in your hair." He winds one of my locks around his finger, then lets it slowly unspool. "A couple days after you ended the engagement, the jeweler called to tell me the ring was ready. Put it in a velvet box, big smile on his face. 'Good luck, kid.'"

Alex isn't smiling. White noise creeps between his words, slurring in my ear.

"But your mom—you said she *found* it? Gardening?"

"I threw it."

It takes me a second to comprehend. My face falls into my hands. "Oh."

"I couldn't have it around me. I needed to get rid of it; couldn't stand having it in the house."

Even though I remain rooted to the spot, I'm simultaneously falling through the bed, through the floor, lost. "You seriously wanted to marry me."

"Yeah, but it's okay." He rubs my arm. "Really. I was crushed, but I got over it—"

"Did you?"

A few beats pass. "No. But you were gone, and the world kept turning, and I had to figure out how to walk around without feeling like a piano was sitting on my chest."

I squeeze my eyes shut, a tear rolling down the bridge of my nose. He leans toward me, gaze curious. His forehead creases. "You didn't want it, sweetheart."

I have nothing sensible to say.

Did I want it? At the time? Or did I want an unbreakable promise, a certainty? Would it have drastically altered our futures, if I'd known?

He wipes away my tear. "At first I held on to it because I thought you might come back. When . . . after that voicemail you left, I tried giving the ring back to my grandpa, but he was stubborn, kept insisting that we were meant to be."

The mention of Joshua King is another cut.

"My mom told me to keep the ring. Use it whenever I proposed to another woman someday, but one of the stones was your grandmother's. I couldn't give some other girl a combination of our two families' heirlooms."

My throat closes. *I am the luckiest person,* I think, *and all the others have missed out.* He's been walking around in broad daylight like a priceless treasure, and nobody's tried to snap him up? What were they all thinking? What was *I* thinking, when I let him go? Too bad, rest of the world! Your loss! I'll stitch my shadow to this man's shoes like Peter Pan.

"So, one day I was sitting on Mom's back porch, miserable. Angry and missing you. Then without thinking, I just." He reels his arm back, demonstrating. "Threw it as far as I could." A shadow crosses his face.

"I thought it was gone. Then, I'm talking to Mom right before we're about to pose for the wedding photographer, and she puts this in my hand. Tells me she found it while gardening. Mom said she'd been watching us all week, the way we looked at each other, thought maybe I'd want this back. It's been in her jewelry box for years. Your grandma's emerald must have fallen out in the dirt . . . I'm so sorry about that."

He's watching me silently lose it. "You didn't want the engagement anymore. You didn't want a ring," he repeats, less sure this time. "I thought you didn't want it."

I turn away, the tears falling faster. He's got his arms around me in an instant.

"I would have kept it if I'd known you wanted it," he tells me, voice thick with tears he's trying to hold back. "I was bitter and angry and so goddamn sad. I wish we'd talked it out. I was so in my head about you changing your mind, thinking you changed your mind about *me*, not just a wedding. But you said so yourself, you didn't actually break up with me. In retrospect, I see all the places where I should have said this, should have done that, but I didn't."

"Neither did I. We were both stupid." I heave a ragged exhale.

He got me a ring. He got me a ring. He wanted me.

The tangible truth that Alex had wanted me forever carves a tiny scratch in the turning of the world, making time skip in disjointed bursts. I wonder what my life might have looked like if Alex had slipped this ring on my finger long ago, before I got the chance to bolt—a ring that was a little bit his family, a little bit my family, and with the new stone, a little bit us.

"But," he says, interrupting my thoughts. "Maybe we can make it work now. Maybe that's all that matters."

I shake my head slowly, smearing the pad of my hand across my eyes so hard that slivers of color zip along like tiny fish. "I think I'm going to have a panic attack."

His mouth is against my jaw. "Breathe. In and out. Nice and slow. It's okay. It's just a ring."

"Not just a ring," I mumbled. "It was *my* ring."

"I didn't know it was still your ring, sweetheart," he murmurs. "Or I would've kept it in my pocket every day since."

"I'd thought . . ." I struggle to verbalize it, because maybe saying the words out loud will make him realize they're true. "That I didn't deserve you. That you were too good for me. I still think that sometimes." I'm downplaying this. "Okay, I think that a lot, actually."

Alex stares.

And stares and stares. Finally: "I'm sorry, can you repeat that?"

I dig the heel of my hand between my eyes. "I always thought you were too good for me. Everyone did," I mutter, uncomfortable.

"I sure as shit did *not*, and neither did your parents, your grandma, your sisters, your friends, half this damn town. And even if they did?" He throws an arm. "Fuck 'em. You have no idea how excited I am, how much I can't believe it, that I get *all* of Romina Tempest. And that idea still troubles you?" He wipes a hand over his face, sitting up higher. "If that's what you think, then I've failed you. Miserably."

"You haven't—"

"You are so much more important, more indispensable to

my happiness, my survival, than you can know, than you've given yourself credit for. You thought that by minimizing your presence in my life, I would flourish. You thought you were giving me more choices, but you were also taking one of my choices away."

I watch him for a few moments. "An option you would have chosen."

"Yes."

I try to hide my face in my hands as I digest this.

"You're incredible," he tells me, voice hard as he endeavors to keep his emotions under control. "I'm the luckiest man alive, and I *know* it. I am desperate to keep you."

His serious tone, coupled with the half-crazed wilderness in his eyes tells me he's vowing here and now to make sure I never forget it. I nod, my world still adjusting.

"I will never let you go again," I tell him through tears. "I'll always choose you, Alex. I'm not as good at verbalizing my feelings as you are, but you have to know—I need you to know— how much I need you. You make everything better simply by being." I kiss his forehead, his cheek, his mouth, desperate for someone who's already mine. "You just make it all better."

He slides a hand against my wet cheek. "Someday the ring'll be here, if we need it, and I'll replace the missing stone. Okay? It isn't going anywhere. I'm certainly not going anywhere. You *own* me."

I curl up into him, ring cast back into its drawer until someday, maybe. I kiss my way down his chest, feeling him react to me, and soon he forgets it all; feverish color, lips dark and swollen, fingers curling the blanket. I'm not going to forget what he told me, but I'm not going to spend any time pressing the bruise on purpose, missing him when he's right here.

Right here with me.

Chapter Thirty-Eight

ORCHID:
I shall make your life a sweet one.

My greenhouse is a mirror for a thousand fairy lights, glass flashing garnet and gold in the setting sun. Moonvillians are snacking on Bushra's shortbread, some clustered together in conversation while others thread from booth to booth, magic pulsing through the ground to amplify everyone's energy. Morgan is peering into Grandma's crystal ball, pretending he can read futures, conjuring a fair amount of traffic. I suspect this has more to do with his thick black hair and disarming smile than any aptitude for clairvoyance.

Above, starlight begins to freckle the sky; and around, chattering voices ebb and flow with Gilda's mixed tape of atmospheric music. Next to her sits a horror from my childhood, pulled from its exile in a closet in the back of her costume shop for years. It's an eyesore. It's the eighth wonder of the world. Grandma Dottie once petitioned for it to be killed by fire.

It's a coin-operated automaton of a psychic woman in a fortune-telling booth. *Gilda the Majestic* flourishes across its glass front in a silver arc. Toward the bottom, in smaller script: *Her wandering eye sees all.*

The automaton does look like Gilda. If her head were made of dented papier-mâché and she had haunting glazed eyes with lashes that were falling off. The lower part of automaton-Gilda's head is slightly melted, so even when her mouth is supposed to be closed it gapes open, which makes for a ghastly experience when she "speaks." But the lobster-red hair in barrel curls and filmy disco shimmer shawls are dead-on.

I feed automaton-Gilda a quarter. The machine clicks loudly to life, its slot dispensing a small slip of paper exactly like the kind you'd find inside a fortune cookie.

"What does it say?" Zelda wants to know, joining me.

"*Avoid burritos.*"

I wave it in Trevor's face as he passes by. "Look, it's a sign. Not even the fates want your burrito bar."

"Those fortunes are all ass, man." Trevor flicks the booth. "I got one earlier and it said: *You will fall into a swamp while trying to feed a raccoon.*"

"Sounds about right," Luna inserts, slinging an arm around my shoulders. "Remember when we took Ash to the zoo for her birthday and Trevor ate a sardine that was supposed to be for the penguins?"

"I was *dared*. I had no choice."

Luna and Trevor glare at me. I throw up my arms. "I didn't think he would actually do it!"

"You should *always* assume he'll actually do it," Luna scolds. "Puked all over my van on the drive home."

"I think some of it's still inside me," Trevor says, face green.

Zelda slips a quarter into the machine. Then she stares in disbelief at the unrolled paper. "*You're next.*"

I burst out laughing. "What's that supposed to mean?"

"Is it a threat? Am I being threatened?"

"Maybe you're supposed to be the *next* one to cook dinner," Luna replies in her sage voice, which has the uncanny ability to convince her sisters.

"Sardines, maybe?" Zelda suggests with a playful glance toward Trevor, who dry-heaves.

For a spell, we all find ourselves admiring the labyrinth of lights and magical trinkets. Tarot, teas, and tapestries. Crystals, diaries, stickers, tote bags. A cauldron bubbling with purple punch. "Can you believe we actually did this?" I murmur.

"Of course I can," Trevor says. "We're amazing. Speaking of how amazing I am, I came up with a new way to get rich."

We all groan.

"I'm for real this time! I'm working on developing an Oregon Trail–style game. It's called *The Oregon Entrails*. Or maybe *The Organ Trails*, I haven't finalized it. All the pioneers who drop dead on their journey become zombies. So, you're the player, and you're a zombie, but other pioneers are trying to shoot you, and your guts fall out. You have to keep running around collecting your guts to stay alive in the game. Might find a spleen over here, a kidney over there, hidden in a cave you can't access until you've fought a group of gunslingers. Hearts and brains are the rarest. The more hearts and brains you collect, the more powers you get. Just wait till I sell this thing, then we'll be *rolling* in money."

I smile. We've heard many, many similar spiels before.

Teyonna runs over and launches onto Trevor's back. "Hey, you. I found a fireworks sale and have a great big stash of them in my trunk if you wanna drive out to Coe's Park and—"

Trevor takes off at a run, carrying a laughing Teyonna along.

"I need to start brainstorming our next project," Luna says.

Zelda looks at her, bemused. "Maybe relax and enjoy the success of *this* project for a while?"

Luna purses her lips. "Mm. No, probably not."

She and Zelda wander off in different directions, leaving me with only my nerves for company. There's a frenzied charge in the air—new beginnings, magic, community. My dreams are coming true, and I should be mingling with vendors and browsers. Instead, I can't focus. What tonight represents is more nerve-wracking than a first date. Than meeting the parents.

But beneath the nerves, there is excitement.

I picture the calendar on my fridge with its barrage of sticky notes. Some are inspirational quotes I found on the Internet. *You are worthy.* Most of the words, though, are Grandma Dottie's. I mentally coast over the note that reads: *Moving forward is how this whole Being Alive Thing works. The people you loved in your past loved you back, and they would want you to be happy. So bring their love with you, and keep it moving.*

I'm ordinarily a mellow creature, with an easy, soft little life. And I prefer it that way—or at least, I thought I did. What I didn't know I needed was for Alex to sweep in and light a fire beneath me. All it takes is one sideways glance from that man, and my nerves twitch like crossed wires. I didn't like it, at first. Struggling as he invaded my home and place of work, witnessing my life, forming opinions I wanted to be impervious to. I didn't want Alex to be capable of making me feel anything. I didn't want to *feel*, if it wasn't easy, and especially not if it was scary. The unknown holds no guarantee of safety.

But I'm eating up the unknown now, and every layer that I peel back is a brand-new favorite flavor. I'm rapidly wanting more.

I swallow, checking the time on my phone. Alex will be here to pick me up any minute, and this isn't just any ordinary date.

As if thinking about Alex summons him to me, a black truck appears on the curb. He exits, then helps Miles out of the back seat.

My foot taps the pavement uncontrollably, schooling my smile so that it's more subdued, polite. I want to come across as friendly, fun, not too eager.

Oh, I hope he likes me.

They're in new, matching Cincinnati Reds hats, so adorable that my heart twinges, heels rising up off the pavement on tip-toe as my hands press together. Alex gives me a huge grin and a hug hello, smelling of sweat and popcorn.

"Hi," I say tentatively to Miles, who's jumping around pointing his giant foam finger at passersby. I tuck a strand of hair behind my ear. "Did you have fun at the baseball game?"

"Can we have macaroni and cheese when we get home?"

Alex sweeps him off his feet, upside down. Tickles him while Miles laughs and wriggles. "Sure, we can have macaroni and cheese. Romina? You vote yes for macaroni and cheese?" He sets Miles back on his feet, then stage-whispers, "Romina's a big-time cheese fan. I think we've got this in the bag."

Miles jumps up and down. "Say yes, say yes!"

I pretend to deliberate. "Hmmm. *Yes.*"

"Hooray!" Miles punches the air with both fists. "Romina, do you want to watch *Moana* with us? Daddy said you're coming over to watch a movie."

"I would love to, Moana's one of my favorite Disney princesses. It has great songs, too." My eyes flick up to Alex, who smiles.

"Are you and my daddy friends?"

"She's my girlfriend," Alex answers for me. "She'll hang out with us sometimes. I promise she's cool."

"Maybe you and I can be friends," I tell Miles, hope creeping up inch by inch. "Would you like to have another friend?"

His response is rapid-fire. "Do you play Roblox?"

My mouth opens. Is this the deciding factor?

Alex grins. "*Do* you?"

"I can learn!" I insist. Here's the Romina who read stories to kids at daycare, putting on accents and sound effects, who helped them craft Popsicle stick picture frames and sing silly songs while pulling silly expressions.

"Yeah, I like new friends." Miles pokes me with the foam finger, then laughs and jumps away, his grin so much like his father's that I can't help but melt. And all in a moment, I know the answer to a question that's plagued me for years.

If I had the power to go back in time and change it all with a snap of my fingers, I wouldn't do it. I still would have called off the engagement, would have watched us break up, go our separate ways. In an alternate reality where we didn't, there would be no Miles.

And who wants that reality?

Not me.

"This place looks SO COOL," Miles says, spinning around. "Can I buy something?"

"Yeah, sure." Alex hands him five bucks. "Make it quick, though. We've gotta get home and get started on that mac and cheese."

"Yeah, okay!" Miles bolts off.

I look back at Alex, amazed. "Didn't he used to be shy?"

"Not when he's fueled with junk food and spent the day cheering in a stadium. This is slap-happy Miles."

He sifts his fingers through my hair. "I am so happy," he tells me, voice low. Alex's smile is warm as August.

I bury my face in his chest, breathing him in. "Me, too."

A contented humming reverberates against my cheek. "Romina?"

My eyes are closed. "Yes?"

"You know I'm in love with you, right?"

My eyes fly open. I try to speak, but we're interrupted by Miles, rushing back at us with something metal in his hand, held high. It's one of Gilda's suncatchers, a butterfly ornament with prisms on chains dangling below.

"Daddy, look!"

"That was quick," Alex remarks. "Did you buy the first thing you saw?"

"Yeah!"

We both laugh. As Alex holds the suncatcher aloft, I'm gripped by a peculiar sensation, as if we're being watched by a rapt, unseen audience. Goosebumps prickle down my spine.

"It's for you," Miles tells his father.

"Aww, really? That's so sweet, little man. Thank you."

Miles spins proudly. "You're welcome! Do you love it so much?"

"I love it *big* time. All right, you ready to go?" He tousles Miles's curls, and we all pile into the truck. I wave goodbye to Luna, who's watching us leave. Her returning wave is absent, her expression strangely hollow. As if she just saw a ghost.

Windows down, a warm wind blows as we make a left turn toward the future and my mind runs through all the things we could do together—camping! Fishing! Horseback riding! Pie baking! Not that long ago, even *hoping* for these relationships was scary. Now I can't wait to see what happens next.

By the time we pull into the driveway, Miles is asleep.

I laugh into my hands, trying to muffle the noise. "You think he'll wake up for *Moana*?"

"Yeah. We'll just let him rest for a minute first." Alex turns off the engine and releases his seatbelt, but stays in the truck. Fiddles with the CD player.

"Teach me everything you know about Roblox," I command in a low, urgent tone.

"You're cute. I do know that."

"But did you know . . ." My gaze drifts to the suncatcher that he affixed to the rearview mirror, prisms spinning the weak light of a streetlamp as they slowly revolve. I look closer at the butterfly, which isn't a butterfly at all—

But a moth.

A luna moth. The prisms refract light upon its silver body, upon a disc sliding into the CD player, and Miles's sleeping face. Upon Alex, watching me with stars in his eyes. The magic feels like *Here we go!* as it travels at the speed of light from all points of the world to converge in my chest, glowing so fiercely that it's a wonder I'm the only one who knows it's here with us.

"That I love you?" I say at last, laying a hand to his cheek as we lean close until my mouth grazes his. Kissing Alex, touching him, feels like a door unlocked, like all the right magical ingredients combined. Loving Alex makes the magic sing. His eyes close, lashes a dark sweep. His gaze is luminous when I pull away, and I trace the shallow groove of his dimple with my thumb.

Mine.

"I do," he tells me.

I knew he would say this, that he must know already, because he's been carrying my love around with him all this time.

It's why I could never give it to any other man. All along, he's the one who's been keeping it safe.

"Are you ready to listen to my top-secret playlist?" he asks, fingertip hovering over the CD player buttons.

Time to climb inside Alex's head and feel what he feels when he listens to music with intention, dreaming about us and our future.

"I'm ready for everything."

ACKNOWLEDGMENTS

I've been waiting about six years to write these acknowledgments, and whenever I remember (about three times per day) that this book is, in fact, going to be published, I am overcome with the wildest joy. I still can't believe that Romina and Alex will soon be out of my computer and in the hands of readers. To my amazing agent, Taylor Haggerty, who helped me polish the manuscript and who loves (this fictionalized version of) Moonville as much as I do—thank you, thank you, thank you. And thank you also to Jasmine Brown, Taylor's assistant, for everything you do.

Putnam! You're my heroes for making this dream come true. Kate Dresser, it was such a pleasure to work together on this book; because of you, *Old Flames and New Fortunes* is ten times more magical. Thank you, Tarini Sipahimalani, for all of your hard work. Eternal gratitude to everyone at Putnam who's had, or will have, a hand in making this book the best it can be and bringing it to the world: Nicole Biton, Lara Robbins, Emily Leopold, Ashley McClay, Alexis Welby, Emily Mileham, Maija Baldauf,

Marie Finamore, Ashley Tucker, Vikki Chu, Hope Breeman, Dorian Hastings, and Sally Kim.

One of the best parts of being an author is finding other authors who are My Kind Of People. Martha Waters, Sarah Grunder Ruiz, Chloe Liese, Zoulfa Katouh, Mazey Eddings, Sarah Adler, and everyone else I have had the incredible luck of celebrating romance with—you are diamonds. Please keep writing books that make us all laugh and swoon forever.

Shout-out to Nida, Bushra, Suhi Samannaz, Iqra, and Michelle Anwar for your kind help with my queries regarding Wafting Crescent.

A million hugs and kisses as always to my family, for making my life such a sweet one, and to my readers, who make it feel surreal. I am so grateful for each and every one of you.

RT and Me Playlist

"Past Lives" by BØRNS

"Sometimes" by Goth Babe

"Running Back To You" by For the Foxes

"4Runner" by Rostam

"Now & Then" by Sjowgren

"big fat mouth" by Arlie

"From The Back of a Cab" by Rostam

"Peach" by Future Islands

"Edge of Town" by Middle Kids

"You're So Vain" by Carly Simon

"Can You Feel the Love Tonight" performed by Joseph Williams, Sally Dworsky, Nathan Lane, Ernie Sabella, and Kristle Edwards, from *The Lion King* soundtrack

"Forever" by Walter Meego

"Before We Knew" by Day Wave

"New Slang" by The Shins

"Go Away" by Omar Apollo

"Midnight City" by M83

"My Girl" by The Temptations

"Dissolve" by Absofacto and NITESHIFT

"Cold Cold Man" by Saint Motel

"Tear in My Heart" by Twenty One Pilots

"Iron Lung" by Black Marble

"Sweet Talk" by Saint Motel

"Young Folks" by Peter Bjorn and John

"Where Do You Go" by Day Wave

"Sunblind" by Fleet Foxes

"Sweet Disposition" by The Temper Trap

"Si Bheag, Si Mhor" by Glenn Morgan/Southwind

Praise for
Just Like Magic

'A hilarious holiday romp with a splash of magic' *Paste*

'Pair the unhinged Christmas spirit of *Elf* with the redemption narrative of *A Christmas Carol* and you'd get something like *Just Like Magic* . . . Hogle has the unique ability to take an absolutely bonkers premise and spin it into an instant classic—this will be a keeper on our holiday shelf for a long time'

Entertainment Weekly

'[An] outrageous, hilarious adventure . . . Exactly what I needed to kick off the season!' *First for Women*

'[A] whimsical yuletide twist on fantasy' *The Week*

'The book has layers of emotions, mystery, lots of characters that you somehow grow to love, a sunshine and grump trope . . . comical lies and their even more comical consequences and most importantly: humor and love' *The Nerd Daily*

'The perfect comfort read: emotionally healing and so much fun' *Book Riot*

'Whatever Sarah Hogle writes, I'll be reading it' *BuzzFeed*

'With over-the-top antics, lovable characters, and a romance sure to melt even the coldest of hearts, *Just Like Magic* cast a spell that kept me turning pages all night just to see what would happen next'

Sarah Grunder Ruiz, author of *Love, Lists, and Fancy Ships*

'Brilliant and totally bonkers . . . It's sheer joy and true heart and utterly glorious pandemonium, and I adored it'

India Holton, author of *The Wisteria Society of Lady Scoundrels*

'I cannot remember the last time a book made me literally laugh out loud this much'

Martha Waters, author of *To Marry and to Meddle*

'This gloriously zany holiday rom-com completely stole my heart'   Chloe Liese, author of *Two Wrongs Make a Right*

'Mischief and mayhem and pure, unfiltered joy!'

Timothy Janovsky, author of
You're a Mean One, Matthew Prince

Praise for
Twice Shy

'The perfect springtime romance'   *PopSugar*

'Excellent . . . Readers are sure to be enchanted by this couple and their deeply felt struggle to open their hearts'

Publishers Weekly (starred review)

'Funny, engaging, and enchanting'   NPR

'A lighthearted story full of surprises, redemption, and love'

USA Today

'Hogle's story takes a gentle, knowing look at anxiety, its debilitating effects, and the importance of stepping outside our comfort zones in this slow-burn romance with plenty of charm and witty banter'   *Country Living*

'The softest, sweetest book releasing this year'   *Frolic*

Praise for
You Deserve Each Other

'Achingly sweet and laugh-out-loud funny . . . Packed with emotion, humor, and sexy tension, this book is a welcome punch straight in the feels'
Lyssa Kay Adams, author of *The Bromance Book Club*

'I could not get enough of this fresh, insightful, and totally hilarious book! Sarah Hogle is a master of comedic dialogue and sexual tension'
Kristin Rockaway, author of *How to Hack a Heartbreak*

'A sharp and witty look at how relationships take work to succeed, and how being true to yourself and each other is at the very core of a romantic connection. Earthy, authentic, and laugh-out-loud funny'   Samantha Young, author of *Fight or Flight*

'One of my favorite books of the year'
Jennifer L. Armentrout, author of *Wait for You*

'Laugh-out-loud funny and a love story with incredible heart'
Katie McGarry, author of *Pushing the Limits*

Don't miss out on Sarah Hogle's hilarious debut.
The perfect, escapist feel-good romance!

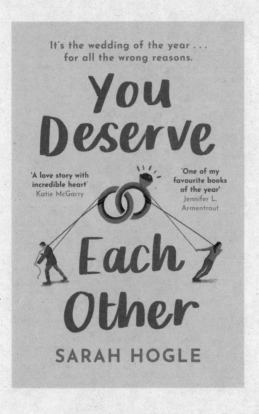

Don't miss out on the hilarious
grumpy x sunshine rom-com!

Available now from

PIATKUS

A charming, festive rom-com, perfect
for fans of Christina Lauren!

Available now from